Michael Moorcock's
Legends of the Multiverse

Michael Moorcock's Legends of the Multiverse

stories by
Michael Moorcock
and
**Matthew Baugh, Pierre Bordage, Richard Canal,
Fabrice Colin, John Davey, Paul Di Filippo,
Johan Heliot, Travis Hiltz, Jean-Marc
& Randy Lofficier, Xavier Mauméjean,
Christian Vilà, Daniel Walther Ehrich Weiss**
and **Tony White**

edited by
Jean-Marc Lofficier

translations by
Michael Shreve

A Black Coat Press Book

Acknowledgements: Thanks to Michael Moorcock, Linda Moorcock, Michael Shreve, Richard Comballot and Michel Borderie.

Visit our website at www.blackcoatpress.com

TABLE OF CONTENTS

MICHAEL MOORCOCK

ELRIC
LE
NECROMANCIEN

A Multitude of Moorcocks

The origins of this book are to be found in the obsession-al interest, at times verging on mad love, that the French have always felt for Michael Moorcock, the man and his *oeuvre*. As Mike reminisces in his introduction, it started in 1969 with the first French publication of *Stealer of Souls* and *Stormbringer* under the portmanteau title of *Elric le Nécromancien*, in a handsome clothbound edition by Editions OPTA in their *Club du Livre d'Anticipation* imprint, that included lavish illustra-tions by Philippe Druillet and a foreword by Jacques Bergier.

The two end-papers, as well two of the b&w illustrations, some of which were later collected in an eponymous portfolio, are reproduced below:

Les dieux
soufflaient
des images, les
hommes dres-
saient des ido-
les.
Chacun des blocs
arrachés aux car-
rières, aux gouffres,
aux volcans et au
ciel aurait pu écra-
ser une des cités
aux noms oubliés.
La nuit en venant
de l'Orient
semblait lutter
avec l'ombre des
temples.

The portfolio was eventually meant to be turned into a full-blown comics adaptation of *The Dreaming City* by Druillet, with text by French SF author Michel Demuth, but for a variety of reasons, that didn't happen.

Instead, Demuth and Druillet reused the art for a graphic novel entitled *Yragael*, which was serialized in the magazine *Pilote*, then collected in book form in 1974. After some spectacular chapters on the creation of the universe, the book roughly follows the plot of *The Dreaming City* with Melniboné replaced by Céméroon, and the trio Elric, Yyrkoon and Cymoril by Yragael, Saber and Néréïs.

The story then quickly diverges, and the second volume, *Urm le Fou* (1975), owes little or nothing to Mike's universe.[1]

---

[1] Elric is also mentioned in one of Druillet's *Lone Sloane* adventures, "Terre," in which Old Earth is said to be the refuge of the gods who fled the destruction of Elric's universe.

Then came Moebius and his sprawling, stream-of-consciousness graphic novel *Le Garage Hermétique de Jerry Cornelius*, first serialized in *Métal Hurlant* in 1976-79, then collected in book form as *Major Fatal* and, later, *Le Garage Hermétique*. The story first appeared in English in *Heavy Metal* starting in 1977, and was reprinted by Marvel/Epic in 1987 as *The Airtight Garage*, the third volume of a Moebius imprint, in a new translation by Randy and the undersigned.

Moebius' Jerry Cornelius bears no resemblance to Mike's original. What can be inferred from the rather discombobulated (but, in the end, surprisingly coherent) back story, is that Jerry and the book's protagonist, Major Grubert, were once friends, agents or servants of a mysterious god-like entity called the Nagual. Together, they fought evil creatures from outside time and space dubbed the Bakalites.

At some point, the Major left the service of the Nagual and used whatever secrets he stole or borrowed to create his own multi-leveled world, a planetoid called the "Airtight Garage." When the graphic novel opens, the Nagual has sent Jerry to infiltrate the Major's world and bring his errant ex-partner to justice.

In *The Airtight Garage*, Jerry eventually turns out to be a superhero (see image above) and he is obliged to again team up with the Major in order to save his world from the Bakalites.

One question frequently asked was: why was Jerry Cornelius renamed Lewis Carnelian in the 1987 translation? The truth is quite prosaic. At the time, various parties had expressed an interest in turning the graphic novel into an animated feature, an ultimately doomed quest that took Moebius to Moscow and Tokyo, amongst other places. It would have been, of course, both unethical and unlawful to, in the process, sell the rights to a character that rightfully belonged to Mike to some film studio. Therefore, Jerry's name was changed—not altogether cleverly, since there is also a Carnelian (Jherek, from *The Dancers at the End of Time* series) in Mike's multiverse!

And then, we come to this book, which sprang from French editor Richard Comballot's notion of assembling a collection of new Elric stories, written by French authors.

The book was published in 2006 by Editions Fleuve Noir under the title *Elric et La Porte des Mondes* (Elric and the Gate of Worlds), with a magnificent cover by Guillaume Sorel reproduced on the right-hand page. Its contents were:[2]

- *Introduction, by Michael Moorcock*
- Le Rêve en la cité, by Léa Silhol
- La Montagne Dormante, by Jonas Lenn
- Les Douleurs fécondes, by Pierre Pevel
- La Cavalière, by Christian Léourier
- Kane, by Laurent Kloetzer
- *Éloge des Poissons-Gouffres, by Fabrice Colin*
- *Frère des Hyènes, by Christian Vilà*
- *Cœur de glace, by Daniel Walther*
- *Qayin, by Xavier Mauméjean*
- Le Cœur et l'épée, by Jean-Pierre Vernay
- *Elric et l'enfant du Futur, by Richard Canal*
- Le Cirque des épées, by Patrick Eris et Nemo Sandman
- La Forteresse de l'Obscur, by Darek Erthal
- Les Seigneurs de la Firme, by Ayerdahl et Eric Cervos
- La Dernière conquête du Loup Blanc, by Pierre Stolze
- *La Musique des âmes, by Johan Heliot*
- Bloodsword, by Yves Ramonet
- *L'Archiviste, by Pierre Bordage*
- La Porte des Mondes, by Jacques Barbéri

The talented Michael Shreve, who has already translated many French SF classics for Black Coat Press, including the *Madame Atomos* saga, industriously adapted most of these stories into English.

---

[2] Stories in *italics* have been translated and are included in this volume.

Some authors chose to not be included in this English-language collection, but we have also sought to widen its scope by including other characters from the rich and varied Moorcock Multiverse, as well as relying on writers from other shores.

One aspect we wished to emphasize was the natural sense of cohabitation between Mike's works and French works in the same vein, or that drew inspiration from the same sources. After all, Rocambole and The Black Coats are not so different from The Scarlet Pimpernel; Sherlock Holmes and Sexton Blake cohabit easily next to Arsène Lupin and Rouletabille. In the movies, Fantômas, Judex and the Vampires may share the silver screen with Tarzan, The Shadow and The Perils of Pauline.

Despite the language barrier, this anthology hopefully is not simply a collection of stories; it is the description of a metareality that first sprang from Mike's fertile imagination, but is now shared between our collective minds: Elric, Corum, Bastable, Jerry Cornelius, etc., belong to all of us. They are the stuff of which myths are made. They *are* the myths.

Jean-Marc Lofficier

Michael Moorcock: *Foreword to* Elric and The Gate of Worlds

Thanks to Philippe Druillet and Maxim Jakubowski, who began a comic of Elric in a short-lived magazine called *Moi Aussi* in the early sixties, and introduced Elric to a French audience, Elric has been appearing in France almost as long as he has in the UK, giving me a special affection for my French readers. Indeed, I have always been extremely well-served by French publishers, editors, translators, designers and illustrators. They have understood the peculiar atmosphere and ambiguities surrounding a romantic character whose adventures represent for me a kind of psychic autobiography.

I began publishing Elric's adventures in 1961. The first story was commissioned by E.J.Carnell, editor of *Science Fantasy* magazine during a conversation in a pub. At the time I thought I was writing one story which would be a kind of homage to the fantasy I had enjoyed as a teenager. I had no plans to write more. That story was *The Dreaming City.* It was surprisingly popular and established the fundamentals of the rest of the series. Thanks to the enthusiasm of Carnell's readers, four more novelettes and a novel were all published in *Science Fantasy*.

After Elric appeared, readers began to demand other heroic fantasy stories from me. *The Eternal Champion,* which established the idea of the recurring hero, was also written for *Science Fantasy* magazine, although I had published an early version in a short-lived fanzine in the 1950s. *The Sundered Worlds*, which established the idea of the multiverse and predicted, among other things, black holes and macro-computers, was another story commissioned by Carnell and published in the same two-year period, in the companion magazine *Science Fiction Adventures*, which published Ballard's *The Drowned*

World around the same time and specialized in stories rather more literary than the title suggested. By the age of 23, I had already laid the ground for almost every other fantastic story I was to write in the next forty years. I must say, however, that I never planned to write so many.

The third Carnell magazine to publish myself and Ballard regularly was *New Worlds*. Ballard and I met as a result of our mutual ambitions, expressed in guest editorials in *New Worlds*. In 1964, when Carnell named me as his successor, I was 24 and ready with the editorial policy which would eventually be christened, not by us, the "New Wave."

Because I was supporting a magazine whose budget was not sufficient to permit my ambitions, I agreed to write more and more fantasy stories. Most literary movements have a way of rejecting and embracing the past at the same time and the SF New Wave did exactly that. We wrote and published experimental stories for *New Worlds*, breaking fresh ground almost with every issue, but heroic fantasies, with their roots in Peninsula Romance and the 19th century Gothic, sustained those experiments. Demanded by publishers in an increasing number of countries, Hawkmoon, Corum, Erekosë, von Bek and others all followed. The stories began to connect naturally, without any grand initial plan, just as, I suspect, the stories of Balzac or Zola began to connect, until a pattern became visible to the writer. Characters who had relatively minor roles in one book would become central to another book. I was 21 when they began to appear, though I had conceived the character and some of the story rather earlier, during my teens.

For all their fantastic nature, it is my characters rather than their worlds or stories which remain strongest in my own memory. I began writing consciously in the romantic tradition of Shelley, Byron and Maturin. Frankenstein, Don Juan and Melmoth the Wanderer were my models. I was convinced that these writers and others were essentially describing what was known as the "haunted palace of the mind." Mervyn Peake, therefore, with his grand conception of Gormenghast, was my hero and remains so to this day. Indeed, as I wrote a series of articles for *Science Fantasy* on the roots of modern fantasy, I also described the nature of my own characters. Unlike those of Tolkien and his followers, my landscapes are not examples of what today is called "world building." Just as it does in *Wuthering Heights*, my scenery reflects the mental states of my characters. I did not develop elaborate maps, because my landscapes were the maps of the characters' interior worlds. I had no interest in concocting complicated glossaries and languages for my various worlds, because the lexicon I was using was one of images, which in turn reflected internal conflict, what we used to call "The Alphabets of Unreason." My grand palaces and cities had no limitations because the architecture of the unconscious has no limitations. My invented languages are more familiar to psychologists than they are to etymologists. Like Poe and others, I was interested in words and names whose resonances echoed states of mind rather than the grammars of ancient races.

That could be why I am flattered, but always a little mystified, by the way in which my work has been co-opted into the world of *Dungeons and Dragons* and other games. I have no answer to a reader or gamer wanting to discuss the chief national product of Oin or Yu, or how many miles lie between Shazaar and Jharkor across the Marshes of the Mist. The Marshes of the Mist certainly contain undiscovered aspects of Young Kingdoms geography, but they are primarily undiscovered aspects of my own and my protagonists' psyches. They are, therefore, infinite. Perhaps they will only become finite when I die. My fantasy fiction is, in this respect, no different to my "realistic" fiction, such as *Mother London* or *Byzantium Endures*. I use it to explore my own memory, my own character, as well as to make a moral examination of the objective world and its workings. That is why so much of it is set on the borderlands between reality and nightmare. If the 20th century, which gave us amongst so many examples, Flanders, Auschwitz and Rwanda, taught us nothing else, it taught us how little distinction there is between the two.

I am, of course, flattered that Elric's character and adventures have entered the common gaming lexicon, just as I am pleased at his frequent appearance in other guises, in comics and in *anime*. I must admit that I prefer to be *asked* if people wish to write about the character, and these days Elric is not quite as free as he began, since a major studio bought the rights to his adventures and have a characteristically corporate attitude to what they regard as their "intellectual property." For many years, I resisted the inducements of corporate entertainment to co-opt Elric. Now, as I write, there is a possibility that a major producer plans a film faithful to my original intentions. I am lucky in having readers in the film business who understand Elric's nature very well, and I am assured they will not take too literal an approach, which was what I had feared in other directors and producers who, in the past, attempted to purchase the rights.

I have already expressed the hope that, if they do not choose to direct the movie themselves, they will give the job to a French director, not merely because of my admiration for so many French films from the classic silents to the present, but because I believe a French director will bring the appropriate sensibility to my character, just as so many French writers have understood him, often, perhaps, better than the majority of those English and American writers who have already recorded his apocryphal adventures. Indeed, I still harbor a strong desire that one or more of my stories will be filmed entirely in France. Meanwhile, with Fabrice Colin,[3] I am now writing Elric stories which *originate* in France! The first of these novels is *Les buveurs d'âmes*.[4]

I hope this helps go towards explaining why I have, for instance, been happy to see Jerry Cornelius appear in so many forms, by so many hands, from Mal Dean to Mike Harrison, from Moebius to Norman Spinrad, and have never sought to control those interpretations, just as I have never laid down the

---

[3] See his *Eulogy for the Abyss-Fish* in this volume.
[4] Published in 2011 by Editions Fleuve Noir.

law as to his appearance nor controlled the manifestations of Elric (though personally I have clear ideas of what he looks like). New authors offer fresh revelations, new aspects of a character which can often surprise me. What's more, who could not be fascinated by seeing their reflection in so many different mirrors? My self-image as a writer is that of someone in constant public dialogue with his readers around the world.[5]

That vision is exemplified and amplified by this kind of experiment. All my working life I have enjoyed that dialogue, frequently responding to reader requests to write about certain characters or events, ideas suggested by those who have seen an aspect of my stories which I might have missed. Of course, I have all the usual egocentric traits of a self-obsessed creative person and have insisted, sometimes against considerable resistance, in making my own path. I am obsessive, arrogant in molding other peoples' tools and ideas to my own uses, sometimes disappointed by the way my own tools are used to crude or unoriginal effect. I refuse the dictates of publishers and will not write more stories merely because I am offered large sums of money or because the majority of readers demand them. I will only write what I believe furthers my own literary ambitions and offers the reader some-

---

[5] See my website *www.multiverse.org.*

thing fresh. There is always a temptation to write the same story over and over again, and indeed this is probably the best way to become a very rich writer, but precisely because I hate the thought of becoming repetitive and creatively infertile, I love to open my creations to fresh interpretation.

With the completion of my most recent Elric trilogy, which began with *The Dreamthief's Daughter* and continued through *The Skrayling Tree* and *The White Wolf's Son*, I have retired from writing heroic fantasy novels in English, at least in the conventional form of the romance. I have done some work in describing Elric's youth and education in a comic done in collaboration with Walter Simonson, called *Elric: The Making of a Sorcerer*, and a new series of comics by other hands are already appearing in English,[6] one in French whose title I don't yet know. I am taking an active interest in a film, which will probably combine the novel *Elric of Melnibone* with the short story *The Dreaming City*, and can hope that if this film finds favor with the public, there will be two more, bringing Elric's story to the conclusion described in *Stormbringer.*

It is possible that I will continue writing novellas detailing the "missing" years of Elric's life; but I have decided to stop writing heroic fantasy novels for a number of reasons. I am more interested in the experimental narratives of such books as *Blood* and *The War Amongst the Angels* or *The Whispering Swarm*—which offer readers a less familiar fantasy. They work, as my original stories did, against established literary and generic conventions. The irony of writing for as long as I have been writing is that the experiments of one's youth become the conventions of one's old age and involve me in subverting these new conventions as I subverted the earlier ones! Moreover, I honestly believe I can add little more to a form which I helped create. There are also many good, newer writers, as this anthology proves, who can expand the

---

[6] *The Balance Lost* by Chris Roberson, Boom Comics 2011/12.

form and make it do fresh things, attack different problems, offer more spectacular dreams. When I began writing Elric it was in very much the same spirit that I began performing rock and roll—precisely because it was a new, fresh, unmapped territory, where you could learn by selling your mistakes, where you could begin something never quite knowing how it was going to turn out and be pleasantly surprised by the result. This characterized the age we call the Sixties. Today, it is impossible to write or perform what we started then without a sense of repetition. There is now a vast canon, a context within which you are creating. It does not mean that the creations are any better or worse, but they are conceived and brought to completion in a very different atmosphere. People like Ballard, Spinrad, Disch, Aldiss, Zelazny and others were attracted to fantasy and science fiction precisely because there was no established body of criticism, no magazines devoted to its discussion, no academic theses. Nowadays, comics and games and other literary and musical expressions offer that same sense of venturing into uncharted territory. This is not to say that there is no uncharted territory left, but when I began it was almost entirely *terra incognita*. *New Worlds* first manifestation as a fanzine before World War Two was actually *Novae Terrae*. You set off on those unknown seas, much as the Vikings set off, hoping that your ship was sturdy enough and your compass not too crude for the job. Certainly in rock and roll there was a very good chance you might not come back alive and to some of us around *New Worlds*, experimenting with drugs and lifestyles, there was a very similar risk.

As the frontiers shrink, of course, you become dangerously close to turning into one of those old farts who wag their fingers at the young and say how much more glamorous life was in their day. Clearly, it is in the nature of glamour to take on different forms, find different voyages, different kinds of ship, different destinations and navigational aids. It is in that spirit, I hope, that I offer Elric to younger writers, just as I gave Jerry Cornelius to others so many years ago, in the hope they will take him on new explorations. I am delighted by their novelty, intrigued by the aspects of Elric's character and world they reveal, applaud their courage and remain, as always, flattered by their interest. And, as hardly needs to be said, I am delighted if this Francophone experiment strengthens my already strong and affectionate bonds with France (where I now spend much of my life), French literature, French writers and, above all, my French readers to whom I express, as always, my best wishes and thanks.

Michael Moorcock,
The Old Circle Squared,
Lost Pines, TX,
2006

This story was originally published in 2007 in our annual an-thology devoted to crossovers between French and Anglo-Saxon literature, Tales of the Shadowmen, Volume 3, Danse Macabre. *It is a rather unusual story, even by Mike's stand-ards. Yes, we encounter his signature character, Una Persson, as well as Sexton Blake's nemesis, Monsieur Zenith the albino (created by Anthony Skene), a character who, by Moorcock's own admission, was one of Elric's models. But at our behest, Mike also delved into the pool of French lit and returned with Detective Lapointe from Simenon's Maigret books, Vera Pym/Irma Vep from Louis Feuillade's silent serial* Les Vam-pires *(1915-16), and Vautrin (Jacques Collin) and Esther Gobseck (misidentified as Sarah in the first publication of this story) from Balzac's* Comédie Humaine *novels.*

Michael Moorcock: *The Affair of the Bassin des Hivers*

I. Le Bassin des Hivers

Until the late part of the last century, the area known as *Le Quartier des Hivers*, was notorious for its poverty, its nar-row, filthy streets and the extraordinary number of crimes of passion recorded there. This district lay directly behind the famous *Cirque d'Hiver*, the winter circus, home to performing troupes who generally toured through the spring and summer months. Residents complained of the roaring of lions and ti-gers or the trumpeting of elephants at night, but the authorities were slow to act, given the nature of this part of the 11th ar-rondissement, whose inhabitants were not exactly influential.

The great canal, which brought produce to most of Paris, branched off from the Canal Saint-Martin just below the Cir-cus itself, to begin its journey underground. For many bargees, what they termed *Le Bassin des Hivers* was the end of their voyage, and here they would rest before returning to their home ports with whatever goods they had purchased or traded. Surrounding the great basin leaned a number of wooden quays and jetties, together with warehouses and high-ceilinged halls where business had always been done in gaslight or the semi-darkness created by huge arches and locks dividing the upper and the lower canal systems. The banks rose 30 meters or more, made of ancient stone, much of it re-used from Roman times, backing onto tall, windowless depositories built of tottering brick and timber. The sun could gain no access here and, at night, the quays and markets were lit by gas or naphtha and only occasionally by electricity. Beside the cobbled canal paths flourished the cafés, brothels and cheap rooming houses, as well as the famous Bargees' Mission and Church of Our Lady of the Waterways, operated since the 9th century by the pious and incorruptible White Friars. Like Alsatia, that area of London also administered by the Carmelites, it formed a secure sanctuary for all but habitual murderers.

The bargees not continuing under the city to the coast, and even to Britain, concluded their voyages here, having brought their cargoes from Nantes, Lyon or Marseille. Others came from the Low Countries, Scandinavia and Prussia, while those barge-folk regarded as the cream of their race had sailed waterways connecting the French capital with Moscow, Istanbul or the Italian Republics. The English bargees, with their heavy, red-sailed, ocean-going boats, came to sell their own goods, mostly Sheffield steel and pottery, and buy French wine and cheese for which there was always a healthy market in their chilly nation, chronically starved of food and drink fit for human consumption. It was common for altercations and fights to break out between the various nationalities and more than one would end with a mortal knife wound.

And so, for centuries, few respectable Parisians ever ventured into *Les Hivers* and those who did so rarely returned in their original condition. Even the Police patrolled the serpentine streets by wagon or, armed with carbines, in threes and fours. They dared not venture far into the system of under-

26

ground waterways known collectively as the Styx. Taxi drivers, unless offered a substantial commission, would not go into *Les Hivers* at all, but would drop passengers off in the Boulevard du Temple, close to the permanent hippodrome, always covered in vivid posters, in summer or winter. The drivers claimed that their automobile's batteries could not be recharged in that primitive place.

Only as the barge trade slowly gave way to more rapid commercial traffic, such as the electric railways and mighty aerial freighters, which began to cross the whole of Europe and even as far as America, Africa and the Orient, did the area become settled by the sons and daughters of the middle classes, by writers and artists, by well-to-do North Africans, Vietnamese, homosexuals and others who found the rest of Paris either too expensive or too unwelcoming. And, as these things will go, the friends of the pioneering bohemians came quickly to realize that the district was no longer as dangerous as its reputation suggested. They could sell their apartments in more expensive districts and buy something much cheaper in *Les Hivers*. Warehouses were converted into homes and shops and the quays and jetties began to house quaint restaurants and coffee houses. Some of the least stable buildings were torn down to admit a certain amount of sunlight.

By the 1990s, the transformation was complete and few of the original inhabitants could afford to live there any longer. The district became positively fashionable until it is the place we know today, full of bookshops, little cinemas, art-suppliers, expensive bistros, cafes and exclusive hotels. The animals are now housed where they will not disturb the residents and customers.

By the time Michel Houellebecq moved there in 1996, the transformation was complete. He declared the area "a meeting place of deep realities and metaphysical resonances." Though a few barge people still brought their goods to *Les Hivers*, these were unloaded onto trucks or supplied a *marché biologique* to rival that of Boulevard Raspail and only the very desperate still plied the dark, subterranean waterways for

27

which no adequate maps had ever existed. The barge folk continued to be as clannish as always. Their secrets were passed down from one family member to another.

When he had been a lowly police inspector, Commissaire Lapointe had lived on the Avenue Parmentier and had come to know the alleys and twitterns of the neighborhood well. He had developed relationships with many of the settled bargees and their kin and had done more than one favor to a waterman accused unjustly of a crime. They had respected Lapointe, even if they had not loved him.

A heavy-set man in a dark Raglan overcoat and an English cap, Lapointe was at once saturnine and avuncular. Lighting a Cuban cheroot, he descended from the footplate of his heavy police car, its motors humming at rest. Turning up his collar against the morning chill, he looked with some melancholy at the boutiques and restaurants now crowding the old wharfs. "Paris changes too rapidly," he announced to his long-suffering young assistant, the aquiline LeBec, who had only recently joined special department. "She has all the grace and stateliness of an aristocratic whore, yet these stones, as our friend de Certau has pointed out, are full of dark stories, an unsavory past."

Lapointe had become fascinated by psychogeography, the brainchild of Guy Debord, who had developed the philosophy of "flaneurism" or the art of *dérive*. Debord and his followers had it that all great cities were the sum of their past and that the past was never far away, no matter what clever cosmetics were used to hide it. They had nothing but contempt for the electric trams, trains and cars which bore the busy Parisians about the city. Only by walking, by "drifting," could one appreciate and absorb the history which one inhaled with every breath, mixing living flesh with the dust of one's ancestors. Commissaire Lapointe, of course, had a tendency to support these ideas, as did many of the older members of the *Sûreté du Temps Perdu* and their colleagues abroad. This was especially true in London, where Lapointe's famous opposite number, Sir Seaton Begg, chief metatemporal investigator for the

Home Office, headed the legendary Whitehall Time Center, whose very existence was denied by Parliament, just as the Republic refused to admit any knowledge of the Quai d'Orsay's STP.

LeBec accepted these musings as he always did, keeping his own counsel. He had too much respect to dismiss his chief's words, but was also too much of a modern to make such opinions his own.

Reluctantly, Lapointe began to move along the freshly-paved quay until he had reached the entrance to a narrow canyon between two of the former warehouses. Rue Mendoza was no different from scores of similar alleys, save that a pale blue STP van stood outside one of its entrances, the red light on its roof turning with slow, almost voluptuous arcs while uniformed officers questioned the inhabitants of the great warren which had once housed grain and now was the residence of publicity directors, television producers and miscellaneous media people, all of whom were demanding to know why they could not go about their business.

Behind him on the canal, Lapointe could see a faint mist rising from the water and he heard a dozen radios and TVs, all tuned to the morning news programs. So far, at least, the press had not yet got hold of this story. He stubbed out his cigar against a masonry-clad wall and put it back in his case, following the uniformed man into the house. He told Le Bec to remain outside and question the angry residents as to their whereabouts and so on. There were no elevators in this particular building and Lapointe was forced to climb several stories until at last he came to a landing where a pale-faced young man, still in his pajamas covered by a blue check dressing gown, stood with his back to the green and cream wall smoking a long, thin Nat Sherman cigarette, one of the white Virginia variety. He transferred the cigarette from right to left and shook hands with Lapointe as he introduced himself.

"Bonjour, M'sieur. I am Sébastien Gris."

"Commissaire Lapointe of the Sûreté. What's all this about a fancy dress party and a dead girl?"

Gris opened his mouth, but there was no air in his lungs. His thin features trembled helplessly and his pale blue eyes filled with helpless fury. He could not speak. He drew a deep breath. "Monsieur, I telephoned the moment I found her. I have touched nothing, I promise."

Lapointe grunted. He looked down at a pretty blonde girl, her fair skin faintly pockmarked, who lay sprawled in the man's hallway, a meter or so from the entrance to his tiny kitchen filling with steam from a forgotten kettle. Lapointe stepped over the body and went to turn off the gas. Slowly, the steam dissipated. He took a large paisley handkerchief from his pocket and mopped at his head and neck. He sighed. "No name? No identity? No papers of any kind?"

The uniformed man confirmed this. "Just what you see, Monsieur le Commissaire."

Lapointe leaned and touched her face. He took something on his finger and inspected it carefully. "Arsenic powder," he said. "And almost certainly cochineal for rouge." He was growing depressed. "I've only seen this once before." He recognized the work on her dress. It was authentic. Though unusually beautiful for the period and with an unblemished skin, she was as certainly an inhabitant of the early 19th century as he was of the 21st and, as sure as he was alive, she was dead, murdered by a neat cut across her throat. "A true beauty and no doubt famous in her age. Murdered and disposed of by an expert."

"You have my absolute assurances, Monsieur, that her body was here when I got up this morning. Someone has done this, surely, to implicate me. It cannot be a joke."

Lapointe nodded gravely. "I fear, Monsieur Gris, that your presence in this building had little or nothing to do with the appearance of a corpse outside your kitchen." The young man became instantly relieved and began to babble a sequence of theories, forcing Lapointe to raise his hand as he dropped to one knee to inspect something clutched in the corpse's right fist. He frowned and checked the fingernails of the left fingers in which some coarse brown fibers had caught. The young

30

man continued to talk and Lapointe became thoughtful and impatient at the same time, rising to his feet. "If you please, Monsieur. It is our job to determine how she came to die here and, if possible, identify her murderer. You, I regret, will have to remain nearby while I question the others. Have you the means to telephone your place of work?"

The young man nodded and crossed over to a wall bearing a fashionably modeled telephone. He gave the operator a number. As he was speaking, LeBec came in to join his chief. He shuddered when he saw the corpse. He knew at once why their department had been called in. "1820 or perhaps '25," he murmured. "What's that in her hand? A rosary? An expensive gold crucifix, too? Poor child. Was she killed here or there?"

"By the look of the blood it was there," responded his chief. "But whoever brought her body here is still amongst us, I am almost certain." He turned the crucifix over to look at the back. All he read there were the initials *J.C.* "Perhaps also her murderer." With an inclination of his massive head, he indicated where the bloodstains told a story of the girl being dragged and searched. "Did they assume her to be a witch of some sort? A familiar story. Her clothes suggest wealth. Yet she wears too much makeup for a girl of her age from a good family. Was she some sort of adept or the daughter of an adept, maybe? What if she made her murderers a gateway into wherever they thought they were going and they killed her, either to be certain she told no others or as some sort of bizarre sacrifice? Yet why would she be clutching such an expensive rosary. And what about those fibers? Were they disguised? You know how they think, Le Bec, as well as I do." He watched as his assistant took an instrument from an inside pocket and ran it over the girl's head and neck. Straightening himself, Le Bec studied his readings, nodding occasionally as his instincts were confirmed.

The commissioner was giving close attention to the series of bloody marks leading away from the corpse to the front door of the apartment. Again he noted those initials on the back of the crucifix. "My God!" he murmured. "But why...?"

II. Monsieur Zenith: A Brief History

"I suspect our murderer had good reason to dispose of the corpse in this way," declared Lapointe. "My guess is that her face and body were both too well known for her to be simply dropped in the Seine, while the murderer did not wish to be observed moving her through the streets of Paris, either because he himself was also highly recognizable or because he had no easy way of doing what he needed to do. And no alibi. So, if not one himself, he called in an expert, no doubt a person already known to him."

"An expert? You mean such people understood about metatemporal transcience in the 1820s?"

"Generally speaking, of course, very few of our ancestors understood such things. Even fewer than today. We are not talking of time-travel, which as we all know, is impossible, but movement from one universe to another where one era has developed at a slower rate in relation to ours. Needless to say, we are not discussing our own past, but a period approximating our own present. That's why most of our cases take us to periods equivalent to our own 20th or early 21st century. So we are dealing here with a remote scale, far removed from our own. Another reason for our murderer to put as alternative planes scales between our own and theirs."

Lapointe was discussing the worlds of the multiverse, separated one from another by mass rather than time. Each world was of enormously larger or smaller scale to the next, enabling all the alternate universes which made up the great multiverse to coexist, one invisible to the other for reasons of size. Not until the great French scientist Benoit Mandelbrot had developed these theories had it become possible for certain adepts to increase or decrease their own mass and cross from one of these worlds to the other. Mandelbrot had effectively provided us with maps of our own brains, plans of the multiverse. This in turn had led to the setting up of secret government agencies designed to create policies and departments whose function was to deal with the new realities.

Now almost every major nation had some equivalent to the STP in some version of its own 21st century, apart from the United States, which had largely succeeded in refusing to enter that century in any significant sense and was forced to rely on foreign agents to cope with the problems arising from situations with their roots in the 21st century.

"But you are convinced, chief, that the murderer is French?"

"If not French, then they have lived in France for many years."

Used not to questioning his superior's instinctive judgments, Le Bec accepted this.

As their electromobile sped them back to the Quai d'Orsay, Lapointe mused on the problem. "I need to find someone who has an idea of all the metatemporals who come and go in Paris. Only one springs to mind and that is Monsieur Zenith, the albino. You'll recall we have worked together once or twice before. As soon as I get back to the office, I will put through a call to Whitehall. If anyone knows where Zenith is, then it will be Sexton Blake."

Sexton Blake was the real name of the detective famously fictionalized as Sir Seaton Begg and Lapointe's opposite number in London.

"I did not know Monsieur Zenith was any longer amongst us," declared LeBec.

"There is no guarantee that he is. I can only hope. I understood that he had made his home in Paris. Blake will confirm where I can find him."

"I understand, chief, that he was in earlier days wanted by the police of several countries."

"Quite so. His last encounter with Blake, as a criminal, was during the London Blitz. He and his old antagonist fought it out on a cliff house whose foundations were weak. The fictional version of the case was been recorded as *The Affair of the Bronze Basilisk*. Zenith's body was lost in the ruins of the

33

house and never recovered, but we now know that he returned to Jugo-Slavia where he fought with Tito's guerillas against the Nazis, was captured by the Gestapo before he could smoke the famous cyanide cigarette he always kept in his case and was found half-dead by the British when they liberated the infamous Milosevic Fortress in Belgrade, HQ of the Gestapo in the region. For his various efforts on behalf of the allied war-effort, Zenith was given a full pardon by the authorities and in his final meeting with his old adversary Sexton Blake, both men made a bargain—Blake would allow no more stories of Zenith to be published as part of his own memoirs and Zenith would not publish his memoirs until 50 years after that meeting which was in August 26, 1946. Both men have been exposed to the same effects which conferred longevity upon them, almost by accident. That 50 years has now, of course, passed."

"And Monsieur Zenith?" asked Le Bec as the car hummed smoothly under the arches into the square leading to their offices. "What has happened to him?"

"He has become a kind of gentleman adventurer, working as often with the authorities as against them and spending much of his time in tracking down ex-Nazis, especially those with stolen wealth, which he either returns in whole to their owners or, if it so pleases him, pays himself a ten percent 'commission.' He will now sometimes work with my old friend Blake. His adventures will take him across parallel universes where he assumes the name of 'Zodiac.' But he still keeps up with his old acquaintances from the criminal underworld, mostly through a famous London thieves' warren known as 'Smith's Kitchen' which now has concessions in Paris, Rome and New York. If anyone has heard a hint of the business here, it will be Zenith."

"How will you contact him, chief?"

Lapointe smiled almost to himself. "Oh, I think Blake will confirm I know where he will be later this morning."

III. Familiar names

A broken rosary, a silver crucifix bearing the initials
J.C., a few coarse, brown fibers, some photographs of the
corpse seen earlier at *Les Hivers*... One by one, Commissaire
Lapointe laid the things before him on the bright, white table-
cloth. He was sitting in a fashionable café, *L'Albertine*, situat-
ed in the Arcades de l'Opéra whose windows looked into a
square in which a beautiful fountain played. Outside, Paris's
haut-monde strolled back and forth, conversing, inspecting the
windows of the expensive shops, occasionally entering to
make purchases. Across from him, sipping alternately from a
small coffee cup or a glass of yellow-green absinthe, sat a
most extraordinary individual. His skin was pale as alabaster.
His hair, including his eyebrows, was the color of milk, and
whose gleaming, sardonic eyes resembled the finest rubies.
Dressed unusually for the age, the albino wore perfectly cut
morning dress. A grey silk hat, evidently his, shared a shelf
near the cash-register with Lapointe's wide-brimmed straw.

"I am grateful, Monsieur, that you found time to see me,"
murmured Lapointe, understanding the value the albino placed
on good manners. "I was hoping these objects would mean
more to you than they do to me. Evidently belonging to a
priest or a nun..."

"Of high rank," agreed Zenith continuing to look at the
photographs of the victim.

"We also found several long black hairs, traces of heavy
red lipstick of fairly recent manufacture."

"No nun wore that," mused Zenith. "Which suggests her
murderess was disguised as a nun. In which case, of course,
she is still unlikely to have worn lip-rouge. It was not the
young woman's?"

"Hers was from an earlier age altogether." Lapointe had
already explained the circumstances in which the corpse had
been discovered, as well as his guess at the time and date
when she was murdered.

35

"So we can assume there were at least two people involved in killing her, one of whom at least had knowledge of the multiverse and how to gain access to other worlds."

"And at least one of them can be assumed still to be here. Those footprints told us that part of the story. And some effort had been made to wrest the rosary from her fingers after she had arrived in *Les Hivers*."

"The man—shall we assume him to be a priest?" Monsieur Zenith raised the rosary as if to kiss it, but then sniffed it instead. "*J.C.*? Some reference perhaps to the Society of Jesus?"

"Possibly. Which could lead us to assume that the Inquisition could have been at work?"

"I will see what I can discover for you, Monsieur Lapointe. As for the poor victim..." Zenith offered his old acquaintance a slight shrug.

"I believe I have a way of discovering her identity also, assuming she was not what we used to call a 'virtuous' girl," said Lapointe. "I have already checked the police records for that period and no mention is made of a society disappearance that was not subsequently solved. Therefore, by the quality of her clothes, the fairness of her skin, condition of her hair, not to mention her extraordinary beauty, we must assume her to be either of foreign birth or some kind of courtesan. The cut of her clothes suggests the latter to me. There is, in that case, only one place to look for her. I must inspect our copy of De Buzet."

Zenith raised an alabaster eyebrow. "You have a copy of the legendary *Carte Bleue*?"

"One of the two known to exist. The property of the Quai d'Orsay for almost 200 years. Of little value, of course, in the general way. But now—it might just lead us to our victim, if not to her murderers."

Monsieur Zenith extinguished his Turkish cigarette and rose to leave. "I will do what I can to trace this assumed cleric and if you can discover a reasonable likeness in *La Carte Bleue*, we shall perhaps meet here again tomorrow morning?"

"Until then," declared Lapointe, standing to shake hands. He watched with mixed feelings as the albino collected his hat and stick at the door and strolled into the sunlit square, for all the world a *flaneur* from a previous century.

Later that same day, wearing impeccable evening dress as was his unvarying habit, Monsieur Zenith made his way to a certain unprepossessing address in the Marais where he admitted himself with a key, entering through a door of peeling green paint into a foyer whose interior window slid open and a pair of yellow, bloodshot eyes regarded him suspiciously. Zenith gave a name and a number and, as he passed through the second door, pulled on a black domino which, of course, did nothing to disguise his appearance but was a convention of the establishment. Once within, he gave his hat and cloak to a bowing receptionist and found himself in those parts of the catacombs made into a great dining room known to the aristocrats of the criminal underworld as *La Cuisine de Smith*. Here, that fraternity could exist unhindered and, while eating a passable dinner, could listen to an orchestra consisting of a violinist, a guitarist, double-bassist, an accordionist and a pianist. If they so wished, they could also dance the exotic tango of Argentina or the Apache of Paris herself.

Zenith took a table in an alcove under a low stone ceiling that was centuries old and blew out the large votive candle which was his only light. He ordered his usual absinthe and from his cigarette case removed a slender oval, which he placed between his lips and lit. The rich sweetness of Kashmiri opium poured from his nostrils as he exhaled the smoke and his eyes became heavily lidded. Watching the dancers, all at once he became aware of a presence at his table and a slender woman, whose domino only enhanced her dark beauty, an oval face framed by a perfectly cut "page-boy" style. She laid a hand lightly on his shoulder and smiled.

"Will you dance, old friend?" she asked.

Although she was known to the world as Una Persson, Countess von Beck, Zenith thought of her by another name.

He rejoiced inwardly at his good fortune. She was exactly whom he had hoped to meet here. He rose and bowed, then gracefully escorted her to the door where they joined in the rhythms of *The Entropy Tango*, that strange composition actually written for one of Countess Una's closest friends. In England, she had enjoyed a successful career on the music hall stage. Here, she was best known as a daring adventuress.

Arranging their wonderful bodies in the figures of the tango, the two carried on a murmured conversation. When the final chords rose to subtle crescendo, Zenith had the knowledge he had sought.

At his invitation, Countess Una joined him, the candle was relit and they ordered from the menu. This was to prove dangerous for, moments after they began to eat, a muffled shot stilled the orchestra and Zenith noted with some interest that a large caliber bullet had penetrated the plaster just behind his left shoulder. The bullet had flattened oddly, enough to tell him that it was made of an unusual alloy. Countess Una had recognized it, too. It was she who blew out the candle so that they no longer made an easy target.

They spoke almost in chorus.

"Vera Pym!"

Who else but that ruthless mistress of Paris's most notorious gang would ignore Smith's rules of sanctuary, respected even by the police?

But why had she suddenly determined to destroy the albino?

Zenith frowned. Could he know more than he realized?

IV. Fitting the Pieces

Commissaire Lapointe was unsurprised by Zenith's information when they met at *L'Albertine* the next morning. Vera Pym (believed to be her real name) was the acknowledged leader of a gang which had in its time had several apparent leaders. Only Pym, however, had remained in control of the *Vampyres* throughout their long career. She was one of a small group capable (to one degree or another) of moving between the worlds and living for centuries. The rank and file of her gang, for all their sinister name, had no such qualities. Some did not even realize she was their leader, for she generally put her man of the moment in that position. Occasionally, she changed her name, though generally it remained a simple anagram of her gang's. And she had many disguises. Few were absolutely sure what she looked like or, indeed, if she was always the same person. Several times she had been captured, yet she had always been able to escape.

"She has been a thorn in the side of the authorities for well over a century," agreed Lapointe. "And, of course, she is one of the few we can suspect in this case."

"What's more," added Zenith, "she has recently been seen in the company of a man of the cloth. An Abbé by all accounts."

"My God!" Lapointe passed a photocopied picture across the table. "Tell me what you make of that!"

Frowning, the albino examined the picture. "Not much, I'm afraid. Is she?..."

"The likeness is remarkably similar to our victim. Her name was Esther Gobseck, a Jewess better known in her day as *La Torpille*."

"A surprisingly unfeminine sobriquet."

"I agree. But at that time a torpedo was something which lay in the water, half-hidden by the waves, until hit by a ship. Whereupon it would explode and as likely as not sink the ship. She is most famous from Balzac's *Splendeurs et Misères des Courtisanes*."

"Ah!" Zenith sat back, drawing on his cigarette. "So that's our Abbé! Carlos Herrera!"

"Exactly. Vautrin himself. Which would explain the initials on the rosary. So he is here now with Madame Pym. Which also explains anomalies in his career as reported by Balzac. Vautrin is Jacques Collin, the master criminal, who vanished from the historical records at about the time our 'Torpedo' became an inconvenient embarrassment to more than one gentleman. Suicide was suspected, I know. But now we have the truth."

"No doubt Collin also vanished into the 21st century, since Balzac becomes increasingly vague concerning his identity or his exploits, and appears to have resorted to unlikely fictions to explain him. He knew nothing of La Pym, of course!"

"But this does nothing to tell us of their whereabouts," mused Zenith.

"Nor," added Lapointe, "how they can be brought to justice."

For some moments, Zenith was lost in thought, then he glanced at his watch and frowned. "Perhaps you will permit me, Monsieur le Commissaire, to solve that particular problem."

Lapointe became instantly uncomfortable. "I assure you, Monsieur Zenith, that while I appreciate all your help, this is ultimately a Police matter. I would remind you that you are already risking your life. La Pym has marked you as her next victim."

"A fact, Monsieur Lapointe, that I greatly resent. Because of a promise I made to a certain great Englishman, I regret to say I have been forced to live the life of a bourgeois professional, almost a tradesman, and no longer pursue the life I once relished. However, in this case a certain personal element has entered the equation. I feel obliged to satisfy my honor and perhaps avenge the death of that beautiful young creature who, through no fault of her own, was forced into a profession for which she had only abhorrence and which resulted, at least according to de Balzac's history, in an unholy, early and wholly undeserved death."

"My dear Monsieur Zenith, if I may make so bold, this remains a matter for the justice system."

"But you are helpless, I think you will agree, certainly in the matter of Collin. He will evade you, as no doubt also will La Pym."

"If so, then we will continue to hunt for them until we can arrest them and prove their guilt or innocence in a court of law."

The albino bowed from where he sat. "So be it." And with that he got to his feet and, making a polite gesture, bade the Policeman *au revoir*.

Commissaire Lapointe immediately made his way back to the Quay d'Orsay where LeBec awaited him. He read at once the concern in his superior's face.

"What's up, chief?"

Lapointe was in poor humor and in no mood to explain, but he knew he owed it to LeBec to say something. "I'm pretty sure that Zenith has an idea of our murderers' whereabouts and intends to take the law into his own hands. He is convinced that he knows who they are and how to punish them. We must find him and follow him and do all we can to thwart him!"

"But, chief, if he can deliver justice where we cannot...?"

"Then all our civilization stands for nothing, LeBec. Already the Americans and the English have adopted the language of the blood feud in their foreign affairs, demanding eyes for eyes and teeth for teeth—but that is nothing more or less than a reversion to the most primitive form of law available to our ancestors. France cannot follow the Anglo-Saxons down that road and I will do all in my power to make sure we do not!"

"And yet..."

"LeBec, for 20 centuries, we have steadily improved our civilization until our complex system of justice, allowing for subtle interpretation, for context, for motive and so on, has become paramount. It is the law I live to serve. Zenith, for all he behaves with courage and honor, would defy that justice, just as he used to, and I will have no part in it. Though I lack his resources and knowledge—even, perhaps, his courage—I must stop him. In the name of the Law."

Understanding at last, LeBec nodded gravely. "Very well, chief, but what are we to do?"

"Our best," declared Lapointe gravely. "I suspect that Countess von Beck, your own distant cousin, is still helping him in this. For that reason, I put a man to follow her. If we are lucky, she will lead us to Zenith. And Zenith, I sincerely hope, will lead us to the murderers—to Vautrin and Vera Pym—while there is still a chance of our apprehending them."

"Where are they going, chief? Do you know?"

"My guess is that, since they failed to kill Zenith last night, they will attempt to return from whence they came. But how they will make that attempt remains a mystery to me."

V. Zenith's Resolution

Una Persson's car had been seen heading up the Boulevard Voltaire towards the Boulevard du Temple, carrying at least two passengers, so it was for the Marais that the Policemen headed in their own Citroen ECXVI, perhaps the fastest car in France, powered by three enormous super-charged batteries. The sleek, black machine had them outside the *Cirque d'Hiver* within minutes, but from there they had to run towards the canal and down the steps to the great basin by now, at twilight, alive with dancing neon and neurotic music. There at last Lapointe caught a glimpse of his quarry and pointed.

Zenith, as was appropriate, wore white tie and tails, carrying a slender silver-tipped ebony cane, an astonishing sight to LeBec who had never seen him thus. "My God, we are pursuing Fred Astaire and Ginger Rogers!" joked Lapointe's assistant.

The Commissaire found no humor in this. "This could be a dangerous business, lad. There was never any profit in making that man one's enemy. He was once the most dangerous thief in Europe and Europe is lucky that he gave his word to an old friend to forsake his life of crime or he would still be causing us considerable grief!"

Suitably chastened, LeBec panted, "What is he? Some kind of vampire?"

"Only in legends. And not in any way associated with Vera Pym and her gang." Lapointe continued to push his way through the crowd as the evening grew darker. "At least, I have some idea now where he is heading. There must have been a gateway created by the murderers..."

Crossing the old wooden bridge over the basin, they saw what had brought the crowd here. It was a huge black barge of the kind once used in the canal folk's funerals, two decks high. "It came up out of there—not ten minutes ago!" said an underdressed young woman wearing garish face-paint. "It just—just appeared!"

Lapointe stared into the still-mysterious maw of the underground canal. "So that's where they've been hiding. A veritable water-maze," he muttered. "Hurry, LeBec, for the love of God!"

At last, they had forced a passage through the crowds, back to the tall looming house in rue Mendoza where the corpse of Esther Gobseck had been discovered. As Lapointe had guessed, the two ahead of them had abandoned their own car and were hurrying towards the entrance of No. 15 into which they swiftly disappeared.

By the time Lapointe and his assistant had reached the door, it was locked and bolted. Much time was wasted as they attempted to rouse the residents and gain access.

Now, at the very top of the building, they could hear a strange, single note, as of an organ, which began to drown almost all other sound and made communication difficult. As they neared the fifth floor, they became aware of a violent, pulsing light filling the stairwell below. It seemed to pour through the skylight and have its origins on the roof. The air itself had an unnatural quality, a strong smell of vanilla and ozone which reminded Lapointe irrationally of the corniche at Bourdeaux where as a boy he had holidayed with his family.

Next, an unnatural pressure began to exert itself on the men, as if gravity had somehow tripled in intensity and they moved sluggishly with enormous effort up to the final landing where Monsieur Gris, an expression of terror on his features, was attempting to descend the stairs. Behind him, a ladder had been pulled down from the ceiling and now gave access to an open door in the roof.

They were at last straggling the ladder to the roof. There, amongst the old chimneys and sloping leads, stood four people–a vicious-looking woman whose beauty was marred by a rodent snarl and a tonsured priest whom Lapointe immediately identified as Vautrin—otherwise known as Jacques Collin, but here disguised as the Abbé Carlos Herrera!

Confronting Vautrin and his co-conspirator Vera Pym were Zenith the albino and the Countess Una von Beck. All were armed—Vautrin with a rapier and Pym with a modern automatic pistol. Zenith carried his ebony sword-stick while Countess von Beck had raised a Smith and Wesson .45 revolver which she pointed at the snarling leader of the Vampires.

And, if this scene were not dramatic enough, there yawned behind Pym and Vautrin a strange, swirling gap in the very fabric of time and space which mumbled and cried and moved with a nervous bubbling intensity.

"Sacred Heaven!" murmured Lapointe. "That is how they got here and that is how they intend to leave. They have ripped a rent through the multiverse. This is not a gateway in the usual sense. It is as if someone had taken a sledgehammer to the supporting walls of Saint Peter's! Who knows what appalling damage they have created!"

Then, suddenly, Vautrin had moved, his long, slender blade driving for Zenith's heart. But the albino's instincts were as sharp as always. Dodging the thrust, he drew his own rapier of black, vibrating steel which seemed to sing a song of its own. Mysterious scarlet runes ran up and down its length as if alive. He replied to Vautrin's thrust with one of his own.

Parrying, Vautrin began to laugh—a hideous obscenity of sound which somehow seemed to blend with that awful light pouring through the rift in multiversal space their crude

44

methods had created. "Your powers of deduction remain superb, Zenith, even if your taste in friends is not. She was indeed 'La Torpille.' I thought I had driven her to self-destruction, but she failed me in the end. I struck her down, as you and the others have guessed, and then, to make sure the body was never discovered, and seen to be murdered, I employed the services of Madame Vera Pym here. She is an old colleague."

Now Lapointe had drawn his revolver and was leveling it. "Stop, Monsieur Vautrin. In the name of France! In the name of the Law! Stop and put down your weapon. On your own admission, I arrest you for the murder of Mademoiselle Esther Gobseck!"

Again, Vautrin voiced that terrible laugh. "Prince Zoran, Commissaire Lapointe, your powers of deduction are impressive and I know I face two wonderful opponents, but you will not, I assure you, stop my escape. The multiverse herself will not permit it. And put up your weapons. You cannot kill me any more than I can kill you!" He used Zenith's given name, Zoran, which went with the title he had long-since renounced, almost challenging the albino to prove his humanity.

Then, perhaps goaded by this, Zenith struck again, not once but twice, that black streak of ruby-colored runes licking first at Vautrin's heart and then, as she raised her pistol to fire, at Vera Pym's.

The woman also began to laugh now. Together, their hideous voices created a kind of resonance with the pulsing light and almost certainly kept the gateway open for them. Vera Pym was triumphant. "You see," she shouted, "we are indestructible. You cannot take our lives in this universe, nor shall you be able to pursue us where we are going now!"

And then, she stepped backwards into that howling vortex and vanished. In a moment, Vautrin, also smiling, followed her.

For a sudden moment there was silence. Then came a noise, like a huge beast breathing. The roof was lit only by the full Moon and the stars. Lapointe felt the weight disappear from him and knew vast relief that circumstances had refused to make Zenith a murderer and Countess Una his accomplice, for then he would have been obliged to arrest them both.

"We will find them," he promised as the snoring vortex dwindled and disappeared. "And if we do not, I expect they will find us. Have no doubt, we shall be waiting for them." He raised exhausted eyes to look upon a bleak, emotionless albino. "And you, Monsieur, are you satisfied you cannot be revenged on the likes of Vautrin?"

"Oh, I fancy I have taken from him something he valued more than life," said the albino, sheathing his black rapier with an air of finality. He shared a thin, secret smile with the Countess von Beck. "Now, if you'll forgive me, Monsieur le Commissaire, I will continue about my business while the night is young. We were planning to go dancing." And, offering his arm to Countess Una, he walked insouciantly down the stairs and out of sight.

"What on Earth did he mean?" LeBec wondered.

Commissaire Lapointe was shaking his head like a man waking from a doze. He had heard about that black and crimson sword cane and believed he might have witnessed an action far more terrible, far more threatening to the civilization he valued than any he had previously imagined.

"God help him," he whispered, half to himself, "and God help those from whom he steals..."

Matthew Baugh lives and works in Albuquerque, NM. He is the pastor of a small church and an editor for Permuted Press. He is also the author of The Vampire Count of Monte-Cristo, *a mash-up of the classic story of adventure and revenge with vampires, ghosts and Faustian bargains, the co-author, with Win Scott Eckert, of* A Girl and Her Cat, *which continues the adventures of classic TV heroes, Honey West and T.H.E. Cat, and a regular contributor to* Tales of the Shadowmen. *This story, featuring Prince Corum Jhaelen Irsei, was written especially for this collection.*

Matthew Baugh: *The Garden of Everything*

Corum Jhaelen Irsei, the Prince in the Red Cloak, reined in his steed and looked out over the rugged plain. Raising his face, he closed his eyes against the intensity of the sun and remained still.

"Enjoying the desolation?" his companion asked.

Corum opened his eyes and regarded Jhary-a-Conel with a touch of amusement. Even in this wild waste, Jhary dressed like a dandy in a suit of his own design.

"There is peace in desolation, my friend," Corum said. He dismounted and walked to the edge of the precipice. Behind them lay thick woods while ahead and below stretched a blasted heath as far as the eye could see. Jhary moved to stand beside him. He tilted to the brim of his hat to better shade his eyes. The small black and white cat that sat on his shoulder yawned and blinked sleepily.

"Breathtaking," Jhary said. "Though I'm afraid Whiskers is not impressed."

The little creature yawned again and burrowed its face beneath one fur-covered wing.

"I did not come here for the view but for the solitude," Corum replied.

"If that is a hint, I must remind you then I am fated to be your companion. I do not choose where I go, nor when."

"Truth be told, I am glad of the company. Though there are things I wish I could leave behind." Corum raised his left hand, an artificial thing of gem-studded silver, and flexed its six fingers.

"Well do I know it," Jhary said. "You champions are a broody lot in all your incarnations."

Corum smiled—a little sadly—at his friend's barb. He took a step closer to the cliff's edge and gestured outward.

"It's quite beautiful in its own way, don't you think?"

"All places have their beauty, though this is not to my particular taste," Jhary replied, in his voice rose in alarm. "Corum! Beware!"

As his friend spoke, Corum felt the ground give way under his feet. He fell then tumbled down the face of the bluff amid a small avalanche of sandstone. His mind tried to process the rush of sensations: pain as a small boulder struck his hip, the sound of Jhary's voice, a glimpse of the ground, scores of feet below. Then something struck his head and all sight and sound and feeling left him.

Corum woke to darkness, which puzzled him. He knew he was not dead, for this resembled no afterlife he was familiar with, nor was it the darkness of oblivion—for he could feel and think. He tried to move his body, which ached, but something held him down. He tried again, with more force, and was rewarded with the sound of shifting stone and the lessening of the weight on his body.

Buried, he thought. *I must have been buried in the landslide.*

His entire body hurt, though a few pains stood out with special clarity. His ribs burned with every breath, his hip felt as if it had been impaled by a flaming javelin, and his right leg would not obey his commands. Despite the pain, Corum pushed again and, this time, enough of the stone that covered him fell away that he could see light. His vision was blurry, but he could tell he was in a cave-like space; a pocket of stone made by the folding boulders. The light came from above, an opening that he assumed led to the surface.

Corum grasped a cleft between two rocks and tried to use it to pull himself free. To his dismay, the metal hand slipped free, his fingers refusing to close. He raised the Hand of Kwll his face and tried it again to close it into a fist. The six fingers twitched and spasmed like the legs of a dying spider, but refused to cooperate. Though it did not appear to be damaged, the hand would not function.

Using his human hand and one good leg, Corum cleared away the rest of the débris that imprisoned him. Then, he closed his eyes and lay there, waiting for the pain to subside.

When Corum opened his eyes, he saw that the light had dimmed and now entered the opening from a different angle. Hours must have passed as he rested. Fear gave him new strengths and helped him overcome the pain as he crawled toward the hole. It was important to get out before night fell. Jhary was certainly looking for him, but would have difficulty finding him under cover of darkness.

It was a short journey in terms of distance—half a dozen yards. Yet, by the time he neared the opening, the light outside had faded to the orange hues of sunset. Focusing his will, he pushed forward and reached for the lip of the cave. Something small sprang from the shadows. A thin-bodied lizard, nearly as long as his arm sank its teeth into his wrist. Corum cried out in anger and surprise. His metal hand slapped at the hilt of his dagger in a futile attempt to draw it. He thrashed his good arm, hoping to dislodge the animal, but its grip only tightened.

The flesh around the lizard's teeth began to burn and Corum realized the bite was venomous. He tried to drag it to his face, thinking perhaps he could kill it with his teeth. To his astonishment, Corum saw his left arm move. The dagger, grasped firmly by the Hand of Kwll, struck the lizard's neck, cleanly removing the head. The creature's body scuttled into the shadows, while the jaws tightened their grip.

Corum raised the knife to cut the grisly head away, but, just as suddenly as it had come to life, the hand went limp again. It dropped the dagger, which clattered into a small crevasse and disappeared. With a frantic burst of energy, Corum managed to scramble out of the cave. He placed his human hand on a flat rock and began to strike it, using the lifeless silver hand like a flail.

After half a dozen blows, he found he could pry the creatures shattered jaws open. His hand freed, he grasped the bloodied head, and threw it as far as his waning strength would allow.

Too weary to call out and too badly injured to rise, Corum closed his eyes and waited for what must come.

This time when Corum awoke, it was to the feel of soft sheets and the sound of a woman singing nearby. He opened his eyes to find himself in a wooden bed in a dimly lit room that he did not recognize. He struggled to rise but was hampered by the fact that his left hand still would not work, and his right was painfully swollen to grotesque size. His actions only served to topple a small bedside table, which hit the floor with a loud thump.

The singing stopped and, a moment later, the door opened. A tiny dark-haired woman entered and moved quickly to the side of the bed. She spoke to Corum in gentle tones, but he could not make sense of her words. After a moment, she crossed the room to another small table which held a basin. She dipped a cloth into the water, then crossed to Corum and wrapped it around his injured hand. Almost immediately, the pain left him and it seemed he could feel the swelling subside. He wanted to speak, to thank the woman and ask her what she had done, but he was still too weak to form the words. She laid a cool hand on his forehead and made comforting noises until he slept again.

The next time he woke, Corum's pain was gone. He sat up and was amazed at how strong he felt. Not only did his hand not pain him, but the swelling was gone, and even the teeth marks had faded to a faint, red puckering of his skin. His ribs, hip, and his crushed leg all felt whole and pain free.

Corum then noticed that he was not alone in the room. The woman he had seen before sat, gently snoring, in a wooden chair not far from the bedside. Had she healed him? He did not sense any great power in her, though he knew that could be deceptive. Her dress was of unadorned, white cotton and she wore no jewelry. Her hands, though small, appeared strong, and her nails were trimmed short—not the hands of a noblewoman. She was Mabden, he guessed, and lacked the unearthly beauty of the Vadhagh. Yet, Corum found her pretty in an unassuming way.

He turned his attention to the Hand of Kwll. The fingers still twitched at random and failed to respond to his attempts to control them. He wondered what could be interfering with it, for it was a powerful artifact. He touched his jeweled eye patch and wondered if the Eye of Rhynn was similarly affected.

Only one way to find out.

He raised the patch, exposing the multi-faceted gemstone that sat where his Mabden eye had once been. Normally, the eye let him peer into other worlds, in particular the shadowed afterlife that held the souls of those he had slain with his hand. This time, though, he saw a uniform brightness all around him; a white light so intense that it caused him great pain. With a cry, he flipped the patch back into place.

The woman woke at that and moved to the bedside wearing a look of concern.

"Are you alright?" she asked, laying her hand on his forehead.

"I… am fine," Corum said. "I was only startled by… a dream."

She nodded and removed her hand. Her mouth curved into a relieved smile, and Corum changed his earlier assessment. "Pretty" was far too feeble a word for the owner of such a smile.

"I think I have a great deal to thank you for, lady," he said. "Did you heal me yourself?"

She dropped her eyes. "I didn't do much. Just dragged you in here and bathed your wounds with water." The smile returned, impish this time. "You weigh a ton, you know?"

"Water? Surely not ordinary water if it has such healing power."

She shrugged. "It's the water from my spring. If there's anything different about it, I don't know it. Of course, I've always lived in this place, so I don't have anything to compare it to."

"What is this place? Does it have a name?"

She shrugged again. "Maybe, but not that I know. I just call it, this place."

"Very practical," Corum said, smiling himself. "I ask because I have a friend who will be looking for me. Is there anyone who might know more than you?"

"No," she said, her smile becoming sad. "I'm the only one in this place."

"Have you seen my friend? He must be close."

She shook her head.

"Perhaps you have seen his cat," Corum said.

"Cat?"

"It is an unusual creature for it has wings. If it was high overhead, you might have mistaken it for a bird."

"Bird…" she said. "I know about birds and cats. I've read about them in my father's books, but I've never seen one."

This puzzled Corum, though he didn't let it show on his face. There was something very strange about this place…or perhaps with the woman. He rose and spotted his clothes folded neatly on a small dresser, simple but well-made. His longsword leaned against the wall next to them.

"I should go and look for my friend," he said.

"Do you feel well enough?"

"I do. Thank you for tending to me."

Corum spent several hours retracing his steps. It was difficult for there seemed to be nothing but sandstone in this place, with a thin layer of dirt that gathered here and there. He spotted the woman's tracks but not his own and wondered how such a tiny person could have brought him to the house if he was unconscious. It also struck him that he had not thought to ask his rescuer's name. An impolite oversight he should correct on returning to her.

He followed the prints, sometimes losing them and having to stop and circle until he found the trail again. As he entered a wash with an inch or so of sand in the bottom, he saw her prints bracketed by two narrow drag marks. On closer inspection, he decided that she must have made a travois from a pair of long branches and used it to drag him. That raised another mystery: where had she found long branches?

Not only had Corum not seen any trees or large brush, he hadn't seen *any* plants. So far, there had been no sign of weeds, wildflowers—anything. And the lack of flora was matched by the absence of fauna. He had not spotted any living creature, whether mammal, bird, lizard, or even insect the whole time he had been walking. It could be that life here was strictly nocturnal, but that seemed a stretch. Surely there must be some animal that would dare the heat of day.

The other thing that puzzled him was the unfamiliarity of this place. He couldn't see anything that resembled the lands he had gazed out on from the cliff. He couldn't even see the cliff. Corum—no stranger to travel between the many planes of reality—decided that he must have somehow crossed into a different world without being aware of it. Which left the questions of what this world was, and how he might leave it and return home.

It occurred to Corum that the Eye of Rhynn might give him a clue. Remembering his earlier experience, he was reluctant to try it. Still, there was no way to be sure without trying. He raised a hand to the jeweled eyepatch and lifted it.

Pain stabbed deep into Corum's eye socket and radiated through his head. The eye registered the same blinding light as before. If anything it was more intense now. Falling to his knees, he clapped his hands over the gemstone that was his eye and teased the eyepatch back into place.

Wherever he was, he decided, it was someplace antithetical to the powerful magics of the eye and the hand—perhaps even a place beyond the eternal struggle of Law and Chaos—if such a thing were possible. Corum pondered this as he waited for the pain to subside.

Rising, he continued to follow the tracks. It was not long before he discovered something that seemed vaguely familiar, a jumble of massive rocks with a warren of gaps and passages running through it. It could easily be the place where he had emerged. As he drew closer, Corum sensed movement on his blind side. He dodged away as a massive reptilian head snapped at him, and then he sprang to the top of a boulder, drawing his long sword in an easy motion.

The monster hesitated and stood there regarding him. It resembled the long-bodied lizard that had bitten him but on a much grander scale. Its body was as thick as his torso and at least three times as long as he was tall. The scales were different also, thicker and spiny, like those of a horned lizard. He wondered if his sword could even pierce them. But, the monster began to scuttle up the rock and he had no choice. Corum slashed at the lizard's head, the blade piercing the skin but not cutting deeply. It drew back for a moment, gathering its long body for a strike, and Corum imagined it was as venomous as its smaller counterpart.

Corum held his blade before him, and when the creature struck, thrust at the inside of its mouth. The point struck deep into the roof of the lizard's maw. The creature recoiled and did not seem eager to attack again. Instead, it watched Corum carefully, hoping to find a way past his long steel fang.

Corum retreated slowly, keeping his weapon between himself and the monster. If followed him, at a distance for a while, but eventually tired of the pursuit and returned to the pile of rocks. Seeing that the sky was darkening, Corum sheathed his sword, and set out on the path back to the woman's home.

He heard her singing as he approached the house. Her voice was low and sweet, and though the language was strange, he thought the song sounded lonely. He drew closer and caught the aroma of something cooking. He paused at the door and knocked. It seemed an odd gesture as they were the only two people in this trackless waste, but he wanted to show courtesy.

"Ah!" she said, offering a brilliant smile. "I'd hoped you would return before dark. I've made enough for two." She ushered him in, and he saw two chairs at the small table. The plates were carved from wood, the cups from hollowed gourds, and there were no utensils. He moved to the cooking fire over which an earthenware vessel sat on an ingenious wooden stand.

"You do well for yourself, lady," he said. "You seem to live comfortably in the midst of this harsh desert."

"It's what I know," she replied. "Do people not live well where you come from?"

"Sometimes they do not."

"I am sorry to hear it. Please, sit. I have not had the chance to serve anyone since my father died."

Dinner was a bland vegetable stew along with cups of cold, pure water. It did not suit Corum's sensitive Vadhagh palate but, not wishing to offend, he ate it with gusto.

"I have questions I would like to ask you, lady," he said when they had finished.

"I have questions also. Shall we trade?"

"Very well. Me first. What is your name?"

"Lualu," she said. "It has been a long time since I spoke it."

"It has a familiar sound," Corum replied.

She nodded. "My father told me it was the name of a beautiful round stone that is white but holds many colors."

55

"A pearl," Corum said. "It is like the name for 'pearl' in several languages I know."

"He told me that it grows in the shell of a creature that lives in a vast expanse of water. Can there be such a thing?"

"There is," Corum said, smiling gently. "It is called an ocean."

"Have you seen it? You must tell me about it."

"Later," Corum said. "For now, can you tell me how you survive in this lifeless place? Where does your food come from?"

"From my garden," Lualu replied.

"I should like to see it."

She rose and, beckoning for him to follow, led the way to the rear door. It opened into a small yard—really nothing more than an empty patch of dirt hemmed in by boulders. At the far end lay a pool of bubbling water, scarcely as broad as the length of his arm.

"Is that your miraculous spring?"

"What else could it be?" she asked, with a pixyish smile.

"What indeed? But where is your garden?"

That brought a puzzled expression to the girl's face. "But, you are standing in it."

"There are no plants."

"Because I have not planted anything yet."

Corum stared at her, trying to discern what she was talking about. She seemed to understand that he was confused for she moved to the back of the house where a number of small sacks stood. She opened one bag, revealing the seeds it held and carefully drew one out with her thumb and forefinger. Moving to the center of the dirt patch, she scooped out a little hole, placed the seed in it, and then smoothed the arid soil over it. A moment later, a tiny, green shoot pushed its way into the sunlight.

The sprig thickened, becoming a vine that grew large, triangular leaves as it spread. Small buds near the leaves began to swell and turn color, becoming some sort of green and orange squash, almost the size of Aquila's head.

She went to the vine and, with deft twists of her hands, broke each of the melons free. That done, she moved to the spot where it was rooted and dug it up.

"Why are you doing that?" Corum asked.

"It would not be good to let it continue to grow," she replied. "It would eventually wreck my home and fill all of this place."

"You grow all your food?"

She nodded as she gathered two of the melons in her arms. Corum moved to help her and picked up the other three, then followed her inside.

"And the wood for your home and furniture?"

She nodded.

"My father planted a tree when I was small. It was a great challenge for him to dig it up after he had cut it down. When he missed even the smallest root, the tree would grow again."

"Unlimited growth." Corum shook his head in wonder.

"It is the nature of this place," she said. "Is it different where you come from?"

"In my worlds—my world—there are limits. There is a balance between Chaos and Law that holds all things in check."

She nodded, but her expression was blank.

"Have you not heard of Chaos and Law?" he asked.

"What are they?"

Corum burst out laughing. Those twin forces had dominated his life for so long—the thought of being somewhere their reach did not extend made him giddy.

"Are you alright? What did I say?"

"I'll explain later. I promise," he said, regaining his composure. "Do you mean that you...your father brought all the seeds you need with you?"

"As far as I know. I was very young."

"But nothing lives here naturally?"

"Only the things I plant."

"And no animals?"

"My father told me about animals, but I have never seen any in this place."

"What about the great lizard I saw today?"

A puzzled frown appeared on Lualu's face.

"Where did you see this?"

"Near the cave where I entered this place, I..." Corum paused as something occurred to him. "Lualu, is it only seeds that grow in this place?"

"No," she said, eyes wide. "The earth will return whatever you plant in it."

Corum cursed, remembering the lizard head he had discarded. He had unwittingly created the guardian that barred his way home.

They talked until late into the night, she answering his questions about her life, he telling her tales of forests and seas and all the places she had never seen. After a time, she took his human hand in both of hers.

"Will you leave, once you've found a way past the monster?"

"I don't know," he replied. "In my world I have been forced into an unending war, and there are...other things that tempt me to stay."

"If you chose to stay, it would make me happy."

Corum reached to brush a strand of hair from her face. The Hand of Kwll was inert until it neared her face, then it lunged forward of its own volition, its six digits locking around Lualu's slender throat. Her eyes bulged and she tried to scream but all sound was choked off.

"No!" Corum shouted. With his free hand he pried at the metal fingers but the hand's inhuman strength was too much for him. He beat his fist against it but only succeeded in bloodying his knuckles. Finally, he grasped his jeweled eyepatch and tore it loose. The intense light stunned him, and he felt the hand lose its strength as he fell. Several torturous moments later, he managed to replace the eyepatch. The pain subsided, and his hand no longer moved on its own.

He was relieved to see Lualu standing at the far side of the room. She looked terrified and held one hand to her throat, which was darkening to a bruised purple.

"Are you alright?"

The girl tried to speak, but the effort brought a grimace. She nodded instead.

"Forgive me," he said. "This cursed hand doesn't want me to stay here, it seems. It has killed before against my will."

In her face pity fought with horror.

"I should sleep outside tonight," Corum said.

The girl did not reply.

Corum brooded for some time then rose with the first dim light. Moving quietly, he gathered several large, hollow gourds Lualu kept outside the door and filled them with water. When he had all he could carry, he set out into the desert.

His steps took him back to the cave and the jumble of boulders. There was no sign of the lizard monster, and he wondered if it had slipped into some warm burrow to escape the chill of the night. No matter, as long as the monster wasn't here to interfere with what he had come to do.

He laid his red cloak on the ground, then placed the gourds around it. Drawing his long sword, he slashed the top off one gourd, making a wider opening. He held his right hand in front of him; the Hand of Kwll twitched, as if knowing what was to come.

With his left hand, Corum raised his sword, then struck. The blow cut through his arm, just above the juncture of flesh and metal. The hand fell to the center of his cloak in a gout of blood. Corum dropped the sword and clutched the bleeding arm. Reeling with shock, he barely managed to shove the stump into the water-filled gourd.

The pain subsided quickly; his mind took longer to clear. He remained there until the sun began to rise then withdrew his arm. The water had worked its healing magic, and the stump had healed as cleanly and well as he could have hoped.

Now came the hard part.

Drawing his dagger, Corum placed the point against the corner of his eye. He drew in a breath, then thrust deep. If the pain of the hand had been bad, this was a dozen times worse. He nearly passed out but managed to push the handle. Using the blade as a lever and the bridge of his nose as the fulcrum, he pried the eye-gem out of its socket. The pain lessened as it came loose and he wondered if he was going numb with shock. While that seemed likely, it actually helped him.

He groped for the Eye of Rhynn on the rocky ground and tossed it onto the cloak. It landed next to the hand of Kwll, whose fingers were twitching like the legs of an overturned crab. Breathing heavily, Corum bundled them up in the heavy cloth then staggered to the cave opening and tossed them in.

Turning, he gathered his dagger and sword and staggered back toward the little house. He was within sight of it when shock and blood loss finally overcame him.

"Corum?"

He groaned and shifted, recognizing the soft voice.

There was something over his face. He reached for it and felt damp cloth.

"Here." The cloth lifted away and the blurry image slowly resolved itself into Lualu's smiling face. He blinked several times and the image grew sharper as his eyes cleared.

"My eyes!"

With a start, Corum realized that he was seeing her with two eyes. Two human eyes. He raised his hands to touch his face and discovered that his stump had been made whole too. It had been so many years since he had lost hand and eye in the Earl Glandyth-a-Krae's dungeons that he had forgotten what it meant to be whole. Lualu held Corum as he wept.

After a time, when he was himself again, he spoke.

"The water...you healed me?"

"You should not have gone by yourself," she said. "You could have died."

"I had to. The hand would have continued trying to kill you until it succeeded."

"That doesn't make doing it alone any less stupid."

"Perhaps. I had to, though, to see if it was possible. I couldn't have stayed otherwise. The hand would never have stopped trying to kill you."

"Stayed?" Her voice held an unspoken hope.

"It's the only place I've found where I am not burdened by an unwanted destiny."

"Is that the only reason?"

He brushed away a few strands of hair and laid his hands—his flesh and blood hands—on the sides of her face.

"No, that is not the only reason."

They made love on Lualu's small bed. She was eager for the consummation, but Corum, feeling her trembling, knew it was her first time and was gentle and deliberate. Afterwards, she nestled close and soon fell asleep. Corum held her close until the heat of her body became uncomfortable then drew away a little to watch her sleep and to trace the curves of her body with a fingertip.

He contented himself with this pleasant activity for some time, until his hand drifted across her belly and felt a contour he hadn't remembered. He explored a little more and found he was not mistaken. Her belly was distended in a smooth curve that he could not have missed had it been there before. Moving his hand up, he discovered her breasts had grown fuller and heavier.

"Stop that," she murmured. "They're sore."

"Lualu, wake up!"

Her eyes fluttered. She looked at his face then followed his gaze to her body. She put her hands to her belly and turned a frightened gaze to Corum.

"What is happening to me?"

His voice was grim. "It's not just the earth here. It seems that any seed planted in this place will grow."

He tended Lualu through the night as it became clear the birth would be a difficult one. As her belly grew, she became feverish and he bathed her with water from the spring. Fever turned into delirium and, when labor came, she bled freely, despite anything he could do. The baby came quickly and let out a loud squalling, which Corum took as an encouraging sign.

"Corum?" Lualu's voice was so weak it frightened him.

"You have a daughter," he said, drawing close so she could see.

Lualu smiled and held out trembling hands. Corum gave her the baby, noticing as he did that his lover was cold as ice. She drew the infant to her breast where she stopped crying and fastened her mouth to a nipple.

Corum found another blanket and placed it over mother and daughter then slipped into the bed, hoping to warm them with his body.

"What...shall we name...her?" Lualu's voice was almost inaudible.

"Hush," Corum said. "There's time for that later."

She sought out his hand with hers.

"No...it must be now."

"Very well. You remember the white stone your father named you for, the pearl?"

"Yes..."

"In my language it is called 'Mhegynn.'"

"I...like that." She closed her eyes for several moments. When she opened them again they held the distant look of one no longer focused on this world.

"Corum...you have brought...so much...to my life..."

"Hush," he said. "Tell me later."

"I'm...so sorry...to leave you both..."

"Then don't go!" he whispered fiercely. "Don't go!"

But when he looked into her eyes, he saw that she had already gone.

The next day, Corum broke up some of the furniture to make a pyre for Lualu. Mhegynn had grown in the hours since her birth and was beginning to walk. She stood by his side, her tiny hand in his, watching the fire. Afterwards, he carefully gathered Lualu's ashes and placed them in a hollowed gourd. The thought of what might grow from any part of a body planted in the impossible fecundity of this place filled him with dread.

The child grew quickly, learning language and concepts with a speed that matched her physical progress. By the end of the first day, Mhegynn was a curious girl of perhaps eight—by the end of the second a slender maid of sixteen, already a hand's breadth taller than her mother had been. Her eyes were her mother's, Corum thought, and her mouth, especially when she smiled. From him, she had gained her height and more than a touch of Vadhagh beauty. She shared her mother's curiosity, and it was all Corum could do to keep up with her questions.

"Can I see your world?" she asked that evening after they had shared dinner.

"There is a great deal of pain in my world," he replied.

"But there is so much else; flowers and animals and rivers and people."

"It's mostly the people, isn't it?"

"I want to see all the other things too," she said, pouting.

"But mostly the people?"

"Yes."

Corum sighed. He was not eager to return to his world but, with Lualu's death, life in this place had lost most of its appeal. Would he be pressed back into the service of Law if he returned? He couldn't say, but he knew his daughter was right. This isolated life was not right for her.

"The way is dangerous," he said.

"The big lizard? *Please!* You told me yourself that he hides under the rocks at night."

"He did the one night I went back. It may not be true every night."

"Then we'll kill him!"

"*If* we go, we will not fight the lizard. You will run and I will follow, is that clear?"

63

She frowned for a moment then brightened.

"Then we're going?"

"We're going," Corum said.

They reached the cave in the dead of a moonless night, though the starlight in this place was so bright that they could walk without stumbling. Mhegynn's prediction about the lizard seemed to be true, for there was no sign of it.

"Stay back," Corum said. He moved toward the cave cautiously, sword drawn, hoping that it had not become the monster's lair.

"Coooruuum!"

The voice that issued from the entrance was unearthly, the sound of a tormented giant with lips of ice and a throat of steel. It was loud and mournful and caused Corum to take a step back.

"Coooruuum!" the second cry was accompanied by the sounds of shifting rocks as something large moved inside the cave. Corum backed up to Mhegynn, who stood with dagger at the ready.

"What is it?" she asked.

Before Corum could respond a large manlike creature emerged from the cave, the thing had three legs, and six arms, each ending in a six-fingered hand. Its body was made of jewel-adorned silver and a single jeweled eye blazed in its forehead.

"Even those?" Corum whispered.

"*What is it?*" Mhegynn cried.

"Run!"

The creature lunged at him and he danced back out of reach and slashed with his sword. The blade glanced off the metal skin without leaving a mark. The thing lashed out with another multi-arm strike that he barely managed to dodge.

"Father!"

The voice distracted him. Fortunately, it also distracted the creature, who turned toward his daughter.

"I told you to run!"

"Coooruuum!"

The monster lunged again, batting away Corum's blade and bearing him to the ground. It pinned him and, holding his head in place with one hand, it pressed the tip of one finger into his eye.

Corum cried out and struggled to twist away. As the pressure became unbearable, he heard something, a metallic thump, and the finger stopped pressing. Another thump and the creature's weight lifted off of him.

Corum rose to his knees and saw the monster lurch toward Mhegynn, who held a fist-sized rock in each hand.

"*Run!*" he shouted again.

This time the girl did as he said, after throwing one of the stones. It bounced off the monster's head but had no effect. The monster lashed out at Mhegynn with a series of brutal strikes. She was able to stay out of its range, but it was clear to Corum that one blow from those metal hands would kill her.

He gathered up his sword and turned to pursue them, only to catch something large moving toward him from the corner of his eye. The giant lizard's jaws snapped shut as he twisted away. Corum struck at the beast but his sword skittered harmlessly off the scaled skin.

Is there anything in this place that isn't impervious to my weapons?

He retreated, cutting and thrusting as he went. His mind worked frantically, trying to find a way to get past the lizard and to his daughter. He took a solid stance. If the creature lunged, he would thrust his sword into its eye, hopefully piercing the brain.

A movement to the side caught his attention. The metal monster was moving in as quickly as its odd, three-legged gait would carry it. The lizard hissed at the intruder, and struck at it. Undeterred, the one-eyed giant waded into the lizard, hands striking and grabbing. The lizard coiled itself around its new foe and the two began to roll on the ground.

Corum didn't stop to wonder about this turn of events. He turned and ran into the darkness in the direction Mhegynn had gone. He found her a short distance away, waiting on him.

"Father!"

"Run!" he snarled, though a part of him was proud that she hadn't.

"What is that thing?"

They had reached the house safely and Mhegynn was tending to Corum's injured eye with water from the spring.

"I think it is what grew from my hand and eye when I cast them away," he replied. "I'd hoped that the cave was beyond the influence of this place, but it seems I was wrong."

"Then…it was trying to gouge your eye out as an act of vengeance?"

"Perhaps."

"Why did it leave you to pursue me? And why did it fight with the lizard?"

"I don't know," Corum said.

"Do you think it wants to kill you itself?"

"I don't know?"

"Or, perhaps, it sought to kill me, knowing that would make you suffer."

"I don't know."

"I'm sorry, father. I'm asking too many foolish questions."

He took her hand.

"Child, you've only been alive a few days and you've learned so much. I don't count your questions as foolish; it's just that there are many of them I cannot answer."

"Coooruuum!"

With an incoherent curse, he rose and moved to the door, Mhegynn following. He could see it, gleaming silver in the starlight, its single eye blazing.

"I guess we know who won the fight," Mhegynn murmured. "How do you suppose it followed you?"

"The hand and the eye were linked to me for many years," he said. "It must have an affinity for me."

"If that is the case, how can we get away?"

Corum didn't respond. He took her hand and they fled.

They ran through the night and into the morning and always the thing dogged them. It was not as quick or agile as they were, but it never seemed to tire. Corum watched his daughter stumble, felt the weariness in his own muscles and knew that it would only be a short time until it caught them.

"I have a plan," he said, "but you must trust me."

"I do," she said, but he saw doubt in her eyes.

"There." He pointed to a maze of ravines that lay ahead. "Go into those and hide yourself there. I don't think the monster will be able to find you and I will lead it away."

"Father—"

"Do as I say!" His voice softened. "Trust me, child. I have no intention of dying."

"She nodded and he could see the tears gathering in her eyes."

"I will lure it through the cave and into my world. Magic is different there and it may be weaker. Even if it is not, I have magic of my own there, and allies who will help me fight it. Go now. If this works, I will return for you as soon as I can."

She set her jaw and he expected an argument. Then the creature bellowed his name again and he saw resignation in her eyes.

"You had better," she said.

"Coooruuum!"

Glancing over his shoulder, he measured the distance. He was still ahead of the creature, though it had cut his lead to a score of yards. The journey back had been even harder than his flight with Mhegynn. He had stopped at the spring, refreshing himself with its waters, but even so, his energy was close to an end.

Rounding an outcrop of sandstone, he saw the cave. Before it lay the body of the huge lizard; evidently, its tough skin had not been a match for the metal monster's flailing hands. He wondered what the magic of this place would do with the body. Would it make more monsters, or perhaps another as much bigger than this one as it had been from the original venomous reptile? How many more iterations would it pass through before it was enough to overpower his silver nemesis?

He could imagine a continued struggle, as inexorable and pointless as the war of Chaos and Law between the monsters. Silently he vowed it would not come to that.

He reached the opening of the cave and paused. Once he entered, he didn't know if there even *was* another exit. Then the creature lurched around the outcropping and Corum knew he had no choice. He ducked through the opening and scrambled down the narrow, dark passage.

"Coooruuum!"

He could hear the grating of metal on stone as the monster followed him. Its bulky form made it slower in the tight space, but still it came. He pushed through the twisted channels between fallen boulders until he came to a large chamber. Here there was enough room to stand, if only barely, and enough light to see the roughly circular hollow a dozen paces across. The light came from several small chinks in the ceiling and revealed what seemed to be three more passages leading out.

Corum moved to the first and hesitated. Did one of these lead back to his world? If so, did the others also, or would they take him to other strange realms? Did the passages lead anywhere at all?

"Coooruuum!"

With a rattle of falling stone, the brute shoved its way into the chamber. It started across but sank to its knees after making it only halfway.

You get weaker the deeper we go, don't you? Corum thought.

"Cooo…ruuum…" The voice was weaker now. The only sign of vitality was the jeweled eye, which blazed with undimmed intensity. The creature pushed itself backward a few feet and struggled to rise.

"Coooruuum!"

"Yes, creature, Corum! And if you want me, you're going to have to follow me!"

The massive head lowered as if in thought. When it rose again, the eye shone with fresh malevolence.

"Mheeegyyyn!"

Corum was speechless for a moment. Then, as the monster turned to go back the way it had come, he charged after it. Drawing his dagger, he leaped onto the thing's back and stabbed repeatedly at its face, trying to dislodge the eye. The monster spun, arms grasping as it tried to shake him off. It smashed into a wall and stones began to fall. Corum stabbed again, lodging his blade at the edge of the cyclopean eye and began to pry. The creature slammed into another wall and the ceiling collapsed, rocks and dirt covering them both.

"It's good to see you finally wake," Jhary-a-Conel said, smiling wryly.

"Jhary… I was in a cave with a monster…the ceiling fell in."

"A monster?"

"Yes, it…Jhary, we have to go through the passages again. My daughter…"

His voice trailed off as he grasped his companion's shoulders. His right hand was an alien thing of silver, with six digits."

"What is it?" Jhary asked.

"My hand…the Hand of Kwll."

"What of it?" Jhary said, glancing at the appendage.

Corum touched his hand to his face, confirming the eyepatch was there again.

"Jhary," he said, "tell me how you found me."

69

The man frowned. Clearly there were many questions he wanted to ask as well, but he relented.

"When you fell, you were covered by the falling rocks," he said. "I couldn't find you so I sent Whiskers off to summon help." He nodded to a group of sturdy peasants a little distance away. "With their assistance, I was able to find you and dig you loose. I'm astonished you weren't more badly hurt."

"I was in another place," Corum said.

"Another world?" Jhary asked. "I am not aware of any magic here that would allow that."

Corum shook his head.

"Nonetheless, I was there, and there is still someone there who I must reach."

"Then you rest and we will resume digging," Jhary said. He turned to his men and barked out orders that set them in motion. Even as he did, Corum felt with sad certainty that the door between worlds was gone forever.

"What was this place?" Jhary asked.

"I cannot say," Corum replied. "Only that it was a place where I wanted to belong, but did not."

Pierre Bordage is one of today's most prolific authors of French SF and fantasy. He has written over forty novels, including Les Guerriers du silence *(1993) and* Wang *(1996), which are both considered modern classics. His works often reflect humanist ideals and a concern for the spiritual aspects of society, dealing with the hijacking of religion and the fight against fanaticism. Pierre has won several major genre awards, including the Grand prix de l'Imaginaire (1993), the Cosmos 2000 Award (1996) and the Paul-Féval Award (2000).*

Pierre Bordage: *The Archivist*

He seemed to have always been excluded from the rest of the world.

His hair and his white eyelashes, his fragile skin, especially his red eyes, his rabbit eyes, sparked the inevitable reactions of rejection from the people he met. Mockery in the best of cases and then pity or really horror in the worst.

The prenatal exams had detected no anomaly however, not even the total lack of pigmentation, so that his parents had decided to keep him even though he had not been programmed—the new form of male contraception, the SOD, the sperm ovule destructor, developed by the Sanotis laboratories, had experienced a few setbacks that were answered with a significant decline in the stock price and a generation of unwanted children called "rambos."

The troubles started when he came out of his mother's belly. After consulting article 2893 of children's rights, mom and dad asked for authorization to euthanize him before he was six months old, the age limit for the AILEPD (authorized interruptions of life for excessive post-natal deformities). Their case was dismissed and they had to keep the child since albinism was not a crippling disability, but a genetic novelty, just plain bad luck. However, the legal obligation to raise a child did not oblige them to love it, so his parents only fed him, clothed him and sent him to public schools until he was of legal age. Their hard looks made him suffer and they treated him differently than his older brother and sister, the objects of all their attention, registered in the best private classes, nauseatingly fussed over. He was careful not to complain, aware that his family would jump on the slightest excuse to get rid of him by exploiting every legal means possible, tipping into the illegal if need be. Silence and discretion were his best—and only—allies. His white hair and skin condemned him to live permanently in the shadows.

He had had only one childhood friend, a little redhead, another escapee from the SOD, another genetic novelty. Wanting to show their strength and courage in front of the girls, the other boys had often waited for the pair of rambos, "Carrot and Rabbit," when school got out so as to humiliate them or on gala afternoons to beat them up, stomp on their school bags and rip their clothes.

One day Carrot's parents moved and he was forever condemned to solitude. He had graduated from school in spite of the sneering disgust and reservations of his teachers. In a world used to perfection, in a world that banished chance, there was no place for the tall, skinny, white-haired, white-eyed ones or for the chubby redheads—he had found out that Carrot was sacrificed by fire in the name of all rambos, of all the unloved on earth.

Rejecting the games of love and every form of human relation, he had learned to survive in his emotional desert. Since he could not put up with the sun, he stayed in his dark little apartment and kept the shutters closed. He had become a pro at surfing the thousands of satellite channels on the synthetic DNA wall screen. Or he listened to adventure books whose reading was animated with images to illustrate the words.

After receiving his diploma, the guidance bureau had strongly urged him to look for a job in the archival field. A highly recommended job for someone who could not support the sunlight: in the archives, at least, he would not have to worry about the bitter sun or mocking colleagues—hideous smiles or that damn compassion. A few companies, mainly in insurance, still filed away documents in hygrometrically controlled rooms. They were wary of the synthetic DNA databases whose reliability the courts sometimes challenged. They also preferred to have every possible guarantee and present indisputable paper documents to the lawyers of the opposing parties.

Therefore, he had become an archivist for a company taking care of insurance, financial products and morticians headquartered in several buildings of the old city. The modest salary paid the exorbitant rent of his tiny studio apartment, kept him from starving and once in a while allowed him a little luxury. At last wanting to feel the great thrill of love, he had on several occasions approached the prostitutes coming from the fringes of Europe who hustled on a few streets around his place, but even when he showed them a fistful of good and solid euros, they refused to go upstairs with him. It was out of the question for these girls already ravaged by mutating AIDS to rub flesh with an albino. Humiliated, he drowned his fires of revolt in the monotony of his existence. He went to work every day before sunrise and did not leave until after nightfall, going home, eating a bland dinner, sitting in bed in front of the wall screen, changing channel after channel until a dull sleep carried him away.

"Go and get this file for me in the condemned room, boy."

The old archivist stared at him mischievously. The end of his bushy, black beard crawled up his bulging belly. The meager light from the old neon reflected off his bald, spotted head. In the corridors they called him the living memory of the firm, more reliable than the synthetic DNA computer. The management came to consult him about everything. He did not like them, these male and female wolves in suits ready to snap at any throat within fang's reach, but he told them everything they wanted to know with kindly enthusiasm and always smiling. Then, when they left his lair with their information, he turned to his new, white-haired assistant and spit out a string of grumbling, threatening words.

"You always told me that this room only held old, forgotten documents from last century."

The old archivist pursed his lips impatiently. "It's not like the other files. It has a symbol on the edge, a kind of circle with eight arrows coming out of it."

"Why don't you get it yourself?"

The goggling eyes of the old archivist turned as red as burning coals. "Because I am your hierarchical superior, I remind you. Because certain things should be done by certain persons and only by them. You believe in chance, don't you?"

He shrugged. He had never thought about it. His existence had been stamped with the seal of fatality and no doubt had very little place for chance.

"You think our destinies are directed by a higher will, right?" the old archivist insisted.

He looked around, surprised at the turn their conversation had taken, suddenly not sure that the words from the person before him were meant for him. But he saw no one else in the endless aisles piled high with millions of forgotten files, multitudes of existences forever buried in their cardboard folders.

A universe of order.

Life stopped in these concrete basements washed with sinister neon lights.

"Life has given me no gifts, that's all I know," he murmured. "If it was decided by a higher will, then the bastard was fucking with me."

The archivist frowned in disapproval. "Come on, what might look like a curse is maybe the greatest blessing. Our friends upstairs are proud of their success, proud of their salaries, proud of their houses in their chic suburbs, proud of their country clubs, proud of their wives and husbands with perfect bodies, proud of their white teeth, proud of their brilliant children, and yet their apparent luck might be the greatest curse. So, go and get this damn file."

His old colleague gave him a ring with code cards mixed up with old keys. Then he turned around and disappeared down the aisle.

The condemned room deserved its name. To get to its metal security door, he had to go through a series of rooms not equipped with hygrometric systems and buried in dark shadows. The suffocating odor of moldy paper was everywhere. The beam from his flashlight exposed the gutted folders with torn, yellow files hanging out. Life here had escaped the trap of order with exasperating slowness and started flowing again. Strangely, in spite of the stench, he felt revived in this decomposing universe, these caves where silent and inevitable metamorphoses were taking place. If the once frozen existences could break out of their material prisons like this, wasn't it, therefore, possible to conquer fatality, to deflect adverse destinies, to defy the higher wills?

He had no problem finding his way in the maze of corridors and low-ceilinged rooms that he was seeing for the first time. It was as if he were following a path that had been marked out inside him for a long time, as if he were going to an appointment set up at the dawn of time.

Likewise, he had no need to think about what key to choose when he punched in the code on the lighted pad on the wall. The fifteen or twenty-inch thick steel door was fitted with a dozen locks, from the oldest, simplest, unsophisticated mechanism, to the latest iris recognition device. Once he had opened the first nine, he remembered that they had taken his iris prints on his first day of work, so he put his eye up to the little hole. After a few seconds of humming examination and a series of clicks, the steel door turned silently on its hinges.

He was expecting to enter a room full of mildew but was surprised to find the aisles perfectly clean and in order. No trace of dust on the black, shiny metal of the door or the shelves or the low ceiling or the walls. He would have sworn that a cleaning company had come through the day before. On the other hand, the flashlight could not penetrate the darkness, which was denser and icier than a winter night.

He started trembling, not out of fear or cold, but out of excitement, knowing now that he would not leave this room unscathed, that his old colleague was not just a simple company man. He put the useless flashlight in his pocket and walked down the aisles trying to spot the large cardboard file marked with a circle and eight arrows. None of them had a name of number. Packed in tightly, they looked absolutely identical and perfectly anonymous. According to the old archivist the condemned room held the firm's oldest files—some of them dating as far back as the 18th century. However, they did not give the same impression of antiquity as the previous rooms. The odor was not of moldy paper but, more oddly, of molten mineral.

His eyes became accustomed to the darkness. Although there was no visible source of light, he saw almost like in daylight. He ran quickly up and down the aisles without being able to find the file that the old archivist had talked about. He examined them more closely, but his second attempt was no more successful, nor the third nor the next two. The silence absorbed his footsteps clopping on the metal floor, his rustling through the files and the far-off noises of things flowing on. He decided to go back, discouraged, convinced that he had failed a test put to him by his colleague, that he had missed the opportunity to change the course of his destiny.

He was dragging himself to the exit when he caught sight of a panel set in the frame of a bookshelf. His colleague's words came back to him: *it's not like the others, it's easy to recognize...* He went up to it and quivered in joy when he saw, engraved in the steel, a kind of wheel with eight arrowheads coming out of it like sunrays. The rectangular panel was around twenty inches high and ten inches wide. Since no way to open it was visible, he unconsciously put his hand in the center of the figure. The steel retracted under his palm. Surprised, he started to step back but the wheel kept sinking and humming softly. A ray of crimson light sprang forth and unlike the beam of the flashlight it shot straight through the darkness of the room and formed a glowing circle on the ceiling. The panel rose up and swung to the side, uncovering a recess padded in scarlet. He saw a slender black shape in the back of the niche. It looked like the padding around it was quivering like naked flesh. His heart was pounding in his chest like a gong. A wild energy was flowing in him, sweeping away frustrations, suffering, hesitations and fear. Sounds passed through him, like the ones the old archivist made after the visit of the company executive. He felt like he was invoking phenomenal powers, that he was being raised up in a whirlwind and thrown into another dimension.

In the middle of the elemental forces a black weapon with a slender blade was resting. His fingers wrapped around the slightly bulging hilt. A blazing torrent of energy jolted him like a shockwave. Clouds of memories that belonged to other men and women flooded him. All of them had breathed their last breath after tasting the kiss of the sword. Drinking in their souls, it fed its evil power. It was waiting for a new bearer so it could continue drinking from the human well, sowing Entropy and breaking the cosmic balance.

With the flesh of his index finger he caressed the runes engraved in the steel blade. The sword purred with pleasure and shined with a black radiance that darkened the shadowy room even more. He had finally found his purchaser. He who had been weakened by his genetic defects, he who had been demeaned and denied by his fellowmen, he who had despaired was being filled with vitality and courage. It was sharing with him the secret of the ancient incantations, it was allowing him access to forgotten secrets, it was teaching him the magic of the elementals, the magic before the first civilizations, before human history. With it the times of chaos, of the generative friction of matter would return.

"From now on you no longer belong to this world."

The cavernous voice snapped him back into the condemned room. He turned around, sword raised, ready to strike at the unwelcome visitor who broke the magic of this moment. He lowered it gently when he recognized the old archivist. Recognition is not the right word: the man walking into the room had little in common with the small, round, bearded, bald man with whom he had spent the last few weeks. His round eyes were gleaming and turning his round face and bushy beard a bright red.

"I am Arioch, Lord of Chaos, Protector of the ancient kings of the Earth. I have been waiting for you for a long time. For a long time I have been waiting for a being weakened by his birth and magnified by his hatred."

From the sword emanated a black fire that burned his hand and scalded his soul. If he accepted it as a companion, it would give him its vigor, but he would never know peace again. "How did you know I was here?"

"I have been standing in the shadows of men for thousands of years," Arioch answered. "I knew it when I saw you arrive."

"What do I have that the others don't?"

"None of them have this potential for anger that I see in you."

"What do you want from me?"

"That you begin a new cycle and become the lord of this world."

He looked at the runes engraved on the blade for a moment. Signs so ancient that no man of his time would be able to decipher the mystery. "A sword to become the lord of the world?" He did not try to hide the irony in his voice. "In this age of nuclear weapons? When it only takes a push of a button to destroy half the planet?"

Arioch's smile heightened the cruelty in his face. "Your thought, your simple thought is far more powerful than all the nuclear weapons on earth. It is men's thoughts that destroy and not their arms. The storms you will sow with your sword will knock down this civilization like a cheap house of cards."

"Why would I do such a thing?"

"Because it is good for the cosmic balance that Chaos sometimes gets the upper hand on Law. Look at it the another way: if you came upon this sword, it is because the time has come for it to awaken."

"Oh right, you don't believe in chance."

The red glow had clearly lowered its intensity. It also seemed like Arioch's figure was losing consistency, that his edges were blurring; the shelves, walls, floor and ceiling were all slowly fading away.

So, this was just a dream vanishing away now and he was about to wake up and plunge headlong back into his quotidian nightmare.

"Chance," Arioch chuckled. "A very practical concept for those who spend their time running away from or denying their responsibility."

"Did I ever have a choice?"

An almost absolute blackness had fallen upon the room. He pictured Arioch pointing at the ceiling when he said, "You think that if the people upstairs really had the choice, they would be rotting in such a sordid existence? Do you think that they would be wasting their days pouring over their bank accounts and impressing their friends? Do you think that they would accept sacrificing their vitality to an idol that dreams of nothing but getting bigger and fatter and stuffing itself on their vital essence? An illusion of freedom has never been a choice."

He raised the sword and had the impression that an endless, dead-end night was burying the room. "What will I get from it?"

"It will bring you strength, strength will offer you torments, torments will teach you lucidity, lucidity will abolish your judgments. That alone is a giant step toward freedom. You will be able to invoke me when the need arises. I will appear wherever you are. That is your privilege. That is our pact."

Arioch's laughter rolled like thunder under the low ceiling and then slowly subsided, giving way to a sepulchral silence. The metallic panel stayed open for a moment on the frame of the bookshelf.

He had the choice, just then, to put the sword back in its hole. He had the choice to return to his solitude and his dreary life. He had the choice to nauseate others with the sight of him. He had the choice to shut himself away within these walls like the lives ended in these files. He had the choice to implant himself in the excess of order and calmly dissolve until he completely vanished…

He woke up with a start.

He looked at the wall screen: 11:35.

He was seized by the onset of panic, which he controlled by breathing deeply. He had slept past the alarm by almost four hours… a disaster! No need to go to work: the firm considered being four hours late like a terrorist attack against liberal society. Professional misconduct; layoff without compensation.

He finally dared to look at the little wool rug lying in the middle of his studio apartment. It was lying there, basking in the glow of its frightening black light, humming softly. He waited a little while before getting out of bed. The fear of experiencing one more disappointment in a life full of deception; the fear of having once more made the wrong choice. He made up his mind around 11:56 and looked at himself in the mirror on the wall as he went by, finding he looked better than usual, self-assured, sparkling red eyes, radiant white skin, messy, full-bodied hair.

He grabbed the sword. Irradiated by its fantastic energy. Played with it for a long time before feeling unusually hungry. Starving. He shoved it into his belt to keep in contact with it while he had breakfast, to keep enjoying the vitality that the black steel gave him. Now that he had it, no prostitute, no woman at all would turn him down. Now nothing and no one would stand in the way of his desires, of his will. Now he felt in the mood to conquer the world.

He left his room at 2:20 p.m. and took the tram to his parents. The sword, slipped under his coat, diffused a sweet, invigorating heat throughout his body. The rays of the sun, shining with all its fires in the sky, for once caused no reaction in him, no dizziness. There was no more scorn in people's eyes. He even detected a smile of complicity in the eyes of some pretty young women. A few promises at last were springing up along his way.

On opening the door, his father could not help taking a step back. "You could have warned… We… Your mother and I are just about to go out."

"You're a bad liar," he retorted, smiling.

"Really … but really, I don't see how you can say such a thing."

"Don't bother to pretend that you're offended. I'm just a Rambo after all, an undesired child, a thorn, an albino."

His father recoiled again without letting go of the door. This parent all bogged down in his dreams of order, in his fanciful visions, unable to understand reality as it was, unable to confront the chaos—he found him pitiful. Muffled conversation drifted into the entranceway. He recognized the voices of his mother, his sister, his brother and their spouses and children.

"What exactly do you want?"

"To introduce you to my new friend."

"Don't bother. Your mother and I…" The sword groaned impatiently. "What's that…"

He brought out the black steel. The sword vibrated, howled as it leapt forward and rushed so voraciously into his father's chest that it almost flew out of his hands. He shuddered with disgust when he felt part of the energy of this man who had never accepted him as a son pass into him. When it was sated with its victim's soul, the sword pulled him into the family house in quest of more prey.

Richard Canal has a PhD in computer sciences and is one of France's leading researchers in artificial intelligence. He began writing SF in the 1980s and soon established himself as a leading author, winning the Solaris Award in 1986, the Grand prix de l'imaginaire in 1989, and the Rosny Award in 1994 and 1995 for his novels Ombres blanches *and* Aube noire. *He is also known for his cyberpunk novels* La Route de Mandalay *(1998) and* Cyberdanse macabre *(1999).*

Richard Canal: *The Child of the Future*

The last Prince of the Royal Line of Melniboné was lying on a bed of straw devoured by vermin and watching the rising sun surge through the planks of the old door. He saw only hazy lines of burning, vertical light, like bars of fire at the window of a magic prison. His sight was weakening every day. His red, albino eyes no longer tolerated the bright sunlight.

A new day was brewing with its torments and its share of misery. More and more often Prince Elric dreamed of the times when the scarlet banners of Melniboné flew over every city of the land. That was the time of the Dragon Masters, the time of magnificent banquets among the coral blue and emerald green towers of the Dreaming City, the time of the Sea Lords, when Chaos and Law had found their balance and shared the Kingdom Below.

Nowadays all these dreams were turned to ashes. Only the Siamese Gods of Entropy had survived the Final Battle and the world was disintegrating in no great haste, carelessly, like all things that know they are dead. There were only humans left, still just as blind, swarming against this rotting backdrop, believing either that they were forging their future with their own ridiculous hands or that a merciful god was guiding them on the path to the golden age. Maybe it was their time, but barely begun it was already rushing to its end. Nothing is eternal, even eternity—such was the lesson that the Prince of Melniboné had learned in his futile wanderings.

So, Elric no longer deluded himself. One night of the full moon, hard by the village where he had sought refuge, he had willfully deserted the paths of glory to let his albino body wither away. If he sometimes surrendered to nostalgia, it was not out of spite or envy, but to rediscover the colors of the past, its bitter scent, the flight of white sails on the Sighing Sea, the dawn over the Isle of the Purple Towns, the sound and fury of battles fought against the mythical creatures of Pan Tang when Stormbringer groaned with pleasure as it stole its enemies' souls.

The weary hero's eyes were closed. He was lost amidst his grandiose memories when a barrage of grunts dragged him out of his lethargy. Someone was moving around outside his hut. He propped himself up on an elbow, wary, his right hand already fumbling on the dirt floor in search of his graven sword only to find some flimsy straw mocking his nervousness. But it was just the pigs from the nearby farm, rooting around at the foot of the moldy planks looking for mushrooms or truffles.

It was not that he was still of interest to any wrathful divinity or some mighty man looking for a challenge, but he had kept, from his past, rolled up in dirty linen, the fillet of black bronze set with gems, peryx, mio and golden otredos, that held his long, white hair, as well as the Ring of Kings, that magnificent Acrtorios stone set in silver that made of him the crown prince of an extinct line. In this time of chaos it was more than enough to stir up the greed of unscrupulous bandits.

But pigs! Pigs! The idea itself was so intolerable that he forced himself to sit up and reach for his velvet jerkin, so moth-eaten that it looked like a starry sky. He threw it on, staggered to his feet and put on his breastplate of black metal. It seemed unbearably heavy, but he braced himself and even found enough strength to pin the heavy blood-red cape to his shoulders. Fireflies of the same color danced before his eyes.

Standing in the doorway of his shack, leaning his right shoulder against the frame, he waited for the dizziness to pass. Keeping his eyes closed, he mustered his strength to keep up appearances. He could feel the blinding spasm of the sun that was going to blast his fragile eyes and assault his defenseless white skin. He could not stay long in this position. As soon as he felt a little strength return, he hastened to grope his way into the shade, kicking away the pigs that kept bumping into him and grunting. Then he felt his way along the row of blueberry bushes and took the path that led up to the Mountain of the Sleeping Giant. The stench of manure was still unbearable, as well as the roar of the waterfall below. But he was getting farther away and this prospect alone urged him on.

By the crackling of dead leaves under his boots, he knew that he had finally reached the grove of ash trees and its ever-present shade. He opened his eyes. The light sifting through the undergrowth was soft and refreshing, but it took some time for him to adjust to the day. He should have faced the facts: he was losing his sight just like he was slowly losing his strength, as if he were growing old in the way of humans.

He sat on a mossy rock lying on the edge of the forest in the shade of the 200-year old beech trees. At his feet was a precipice that looked like it was hacked out of the rock with an axe, on the brink of which nature had reigned in its creative momentum. From this exclusive vantage point, the heir of the throne of Melniboné looked down over the valley. The outer reaches were bathed in bluish mist, layered in subtle hues. There had been a time when his eyes took pleasure in contemplating the singing columns of the Inflexible City, its plumes of smoky crystal over the River of Sighs, the dance of soulless Dragons. Nowadays the fog had overrun the land and the prince could barely see the Headland of Ryorkinn, even though it rises more than 6,500 feet over the alluvial plain.

Where were his companions? Moonglum and Tanglebones? Where were his lovers? Cymoril, Yishana, Zarozinia? Where were his brothers, his images? Corum, Dorian, Kane, Erekosë? The Eternal Champion, what irony! The world was a gigantic cemetery. So many dreams, so many illusions had burst like little soap bubbles! What was left to build when everything was condemned?

Elric was meditating on the doom and gloom when the undergrowth suddenly stirred, dragging him out of his bitter reverie. Someone was running through the tall trees. Strangely distorted shouts rang out from all sides. A hunt, no doubt! The first white boars had been spotted three weeks earlier near the Wolf's Gorge. In the village they had been rushing to sharpen their spears and knives and hooks.

The hunt was coming closer. Elric turned around and brought his hand up to the hilt of his blade, purely by reflex. Curiously, there were no barking dogs, nothing but the sound of rustling bushes and that wheel of odd voices whose accents were hard to make out, like they were speaking in some old, forgotten tongue. The most troubling thing was the silence that came charging through the bushes, hushing the songs of the blackbirds and orioles, the furtive flight of field mice, the snakes and civets.

Elric was expecting anything but this puny form that sprang out of the undergrowth, rushing at him. It was a child, around twelve-years old, with spindly legs scratched by the brambles and dressed in a simple brown tunic that fell to her knees. She sped along barefoot, her panic-stricken eyes looking constantly over her shoulder.

She tripped on a bump in the ground and jumped right back up to start running again toward the imposing stranger in his black armor with his long white hair and eyes of fire. She tried to speak, to call out, her mouth opened, but she had no breath. That was when she realized that her flight had carried her to a dead end. Behind her was the black mass of forest and her pursuers, in front of her the cliff. She came to a stop 15 feet from Elric and planted her hunted, child eyes into those of the albino, begging for unlikely help, before she backed up all the way to the brink of the abyss.

Elric's ancestors were demi-demons, so he used to consider the affairs of men of little interest to him. Men were an accident of the world's History, a whim of the Gods that thought it was immortal, a leprosy that would die away when its time came. Rarely did he intervene in their affairs except to foil the plot of a divinity who was using them like pawns on a chessboard with twisted rules.

This time would be no different. On the one hand because he knew absolutely nothing about what brought this girl up his road, and on the other because he had no more strength to play hero. After a moment of hesitation and hope, the little girl understood that the stranger, despite his stature and royal outfit, would not come to her aide. With a quick glance she calculated the slope of the canyon, the overhanging rocks, the patches of gravel that were lying there waiting for her lamb's weight to slide to the bottom of the precipice in the possibility of finding a way out. Then she turned around to face her enemies, who were still unseen, but with the sound of their voices getting louder, undoubtedly very close.

Although he had resolved to remain still, Elric, before this frightened child's face, could not help feeling something that he had thought was gone forever. It was, indeed, a face of rare innocence, with eyes that were heavenly bright, as blue as the pearls in the Crown of Imrryr, cheeks the color of ancient pearl, a heart-shaped mouth that was, alas, deformed by terror. Her dirty, tangled hair around her head formed a lead halo bristling with thorns. It would have been easy to fall into the pity trap, but the hero had met thousands of angel faces like this in the course of his long life: as many among the little prostitutes in Jharkor as among the killers of the Clan of Straasha Worshippers or in the galleys on the Boiling Sea. The Gods of Chaos had taught him very early on not to trust appearances. Pretty faces often hide black souls.

It was only on seeing the despicable horde come tumbling out of the depths of the forest that Elric knew what he had to do. It had been a very long time since the creatures of Entropy had ventured into the World Below. The unstable nature of their bodies made them flutter above the ground like felucca sails being battered by a strong gale. With their ragged, malformed wings, their topaz eyes bloodshot with liquid gold, their yatagan-blade claws, their mouths hoed out of granite jaws, they looked like canvas dragons drawn by an accursed artist on the eve of the Apocalypse. The misshapen troop exuded the stench of burnt flesh and their flurry of voices evoked the blaze of a pyre, the crackling, the moaning, the shrill wail of an inferno in the twilight.

He knew that it was the worst mistake he could make in his condition, a mistake that could risk the little life he had left in him. Nonetheless, he moved forward, dagger in hand, to get between the horde and the child. Then a kind of jubilation rose up inside him, as if his whole existence finally found meaning in a hopeless battle. He could barely stand up; his armor weighed a ton. Even if he squinted, the monsters remained blurry forms, ragged and storm-colored, advancing on him haphazardly.

"Save yourself, girl!"

"There's no way out, sir!"

"Give it a try, you're light. Let yourself roll all the way to the bottom, grabbing onto roots, it's your only chance. I'll try to hold them back for as long as I can."

The old poignard was so heavy in his hand that his arm was trembling. The first beast was on him. He barely had time to duck the mouth and strike with his blade, but the blow was so weak and so badly aimed that it only grazed a paw. A wing tossed him backward. He thought his bones were crumbling. The shades of Entropy gathered around him, veiling the sky and the armada of clouds behind a wave of darksome lights. He would never manage to save the girl.

He had nothing but his magic left.

"Arioch! Lord of the Seven Darks!"

His cry was inaudible among the barrage of fiery voices. He howled, still on the ground, while clumsily fending off the claws that pounded his breastplate.

"Arioch, come to aid your faithful servant!"

But Chaos refused to hear his plea and no black mist manifested between him and the dragons of Entropy. He had just enough energy to dodge the knifelike wing whistling by his ear.

When he realized that Arioch was not answering, that the era of the Gods of Chaos was over, he mustered the little energy he had left, stood up and began moving back toward the abyss to protect the child. All around him were darting claws, whirling wings and snapping jaws. He avoided them miraculously, trusting in his old reflexes that he had believed were gone forever. But he did not strike; he was too weak to wield a lethal blow.

He felt more than saw the little girl close to him. He could see nothing but the horde assailing him. He would not hold out much longer. His arms were melting in the foundry; he was panting; the atmosphere was saturated with sulfur, clogging his lungs.

The child trembled against his thigh. He raised his voice to drown out the roar of wings and fiery syllables that clashed in his ears, "Go! Now! Or else it will be too late!"

He pushed her away from his leg, forcing her to step toward the precipice. She screamed, a single scream, fragile like a crystal cup. Then she was no longer there.

Seething with rage, Elric launched himself into the fray, trying to hold off the horde of Entropy as long as possible in case the girl survived her long fall. For an instant he found the needed vitality to drive back the charge and slaughter one of the creatures, but the dagger ended up slipping from his fingers, which could no longer grip it.

He wrapped himself in his crimson cape and closed his eyes, thinking that with the death of the last survivor of the Glorious Empire of Melniboné, the rise of the Young Kingdoms was consummated. A hundred centuries of constant struggle for power, a hundred centuries of glory, splendor, grandeur, and then decadence and always the end. The ultimate end. The inevitable end. The triumph of Entropy. What a waste!

A powerful slap sent the prince of Melniboné rolling into the void.

The sun was pulsing, rippled by the tent fabric stretched over the albino. It looked like he was covered with a sheet of gold. He thought for an instant of his funeral, but the pain quickly snapped him out of it and he knew that he was still in this world. He hurt everywhere, as if his bones had been crushed then reconstituted, his muscles torn apart and then recast.

"Sire! Do you hear me? Sire?"

Old Anterich was leaning over him, his eyes full of concern. The twisted beard of the law-breaking sorcerer brushed against Elric's brow. Elric tried to wave him away, but a horrible pain stopped him. He had to suffer both his tickling beard and his breath stinking of grain alcohol and pickled beets.

"How do you feel?"

"As good as any Prince coming back from the Brink of the World."

"I don't know how you survived. I found you among the fallen rocks, more dead than alive."

"Only me?"

"And the body of a creature come straight out of hell! You were all tangled up like you'd smothered it in your arms. Even dead the nasty thing kept shimmering like it wanted to disappear from this life plane. It was the storm glow that caught my attention so I could come help you."

"Tell me, did you find a young girl around me?"

"You're talking about the Child of the Future?"

Elric suddenly felt old and useless. Out of the world. If a fallen sorcerer knew things that even he did not know, what was the point of living? He tried to keep his composure. "Of course! But do you know why all the monsters in Entropy are after her?"

"Now that's too much to ask me, Lord." The sorcerer had a shifty look in his eyes, as though he were lying so as not to offend his touchy patient. "I got here just in time to see the Child escape into the Limestone Maze, hunted by a whirlwind of light and dark wings that were hissing a cruel song. What a pity!"

"Help me, Anterich! I can't let her die like that. I am the last hero. The only one who can help her!" Elric tried to sit up before falling back down, sweat on his brow. He could not take three steps in this condition. "Anterich!"

"No, Lord. Ask me anything you want, but not this. I don't want to be responsible for the death of the last heir of the Ruby Throne. Without *it*, you are nothing! You won't be able to save the little girl." The sorcerer stood up and walked away, repeating his final words as if he had gone too far and was afraid of the albino's wrath. No doubt he did not mean what he said. He just stood there, shoulders hunched under his sea-otter hide coat, his crooked fingers playing with the threads of his ivory beard, waiting for the punishment he deserved.

Elric closed his eyes and sighed. In former times he would have cut the head off the impudent man, but the fact was that the old fool was right. Since he had abandoned his mate, he was nothing anymore. And it was the only solution to save the Child of the Future, to get back enough strength to chase after the howling beasts of Entropy.

"Do you know where it is?"

"Who doesn't?"

"Me, thinking it'd been hidden from the eyes of the world!"

"It was too powerful to remain hidden for long, sire."

"And no one has gone near it?"

"Lord!" The sorcerer was almost offended. It was a stupid question, true.

They had not mentioned it by name, but both of them knew that they were talking about the same entity. An entity that was older than the Kingdom, forged by subhuman creatures in the time of the Dead Gods and destined to send these cruel Gods back into space.

"Bring me there!"

"Are you sure?"

"Right now, Anterich, before I change my mind!"

When he had made the decision to separate from Stormbringer, it was like cutting off an arm, or worse, like accepting death. A strange deliverance that left a black whorl in the depths of his soul. A freedom that he paid for in blood. The albino barely remembered the circumstances, except that a terrible storm was brewing that night. The thunderclaps seemed ready to split the sky asunder. He must have been crazy to venture so close to the Tree of Origins. Crazy or desperate…

"But you're in no condition, Lord!"

"Use your magic, Anterich! Show me what you were made of when you officiated at the court of my cousin Yyrkoon."

"That was before, prince."

"I know. We are old and weary. We have given too much, lived too much and lost all hope. But out of great fires come beautiful ashes. Arouse your memory, friend, and help me. One last time. Afterward, we shall rest."

The sorcerer left the tent and inspected the sky for a long while. Over his furrowed face passed a flood of emotions, expressions: fear, desire, envy, pride, defiance. The words and diagrams of the old grimoires paraded through his memory, more enduring than he had imagined. He felt the power returning to the tips of his arthritis-bent fingers and it was like streams of light flowing under his skin, snakes of lava and ice that were pouring through his arteries. His tired old heart was beating as hard as a war drum, but he kept gathering energy.

The image of the Tree of Origins took shape in his mind. A brisk, green wind-swept time and space away, confounding distance and duration.

"Now!"

Elric felt himself rise up from his bed of moss. The tent was torn from its pegs and soared over him, snapping ominously, as if a titan's hand had suddenly whisked it away. In the next second, he plunged behind the sorcerer into the emerald-dotted maelstrom that had just risen up over the rubble at the bottom of the canyon.

A moment after being sucked in, red-eyed Elric was at the foot of the Tree of Origins. The earth was opened, hollowed out in deep crevasses around the tangle of giant roots, which, one imagined, sunk all the way to the heart of the world that they held tightly in their intricate web, a cocoon of sap. The trunk rose up higher than the eye could see, beyond the cloud shelf toward those spaces where even condors suffocate. It was milky white and covered with countless parasitic plants of the same color, climbing up it, twisting around its surface, so many of them that one wondered whether they themselves did not form the tree. The first branches bent out more than half a mile off the ground, barely visible, like a blurry halo mingling with the lower clouds, as if the vegetal was vaporizing. How could the world support such a mass without collapsing on itself and turning to dust? Only one explanation: the Tree was the world.

As soon as he was transported to the place, Elric felt better and forget about his aches. He stared at one of the roots, hypnotized by the black sword that was stuck there up to midblade. He saw nothing else. And yet it seemed ridiculously small, lost there in this mesh that plunged into the deepest depths of the earth. But it must be said that the magic sword was gleaming and the rune-carved metal emitted a sweet lament that was hard to resist, an indefinable sweetness, but easy to imagine it turning into a shriek.

Elric took a deep breath. Obviously, Stormbringer was expecting him. It knew that he would come back when the time came. The Melnibonéan heir was seized with both joy and bitterness as his energy gradually returned under the influence of the cursed weapon. Now he was thinking of how much he had wished never to have recourse to this soul-devourer again, but rather end his life in an obscure village, in a clay hut, even if it meant listening to the pigs rooting around the walls looking for tubers. But events, once again, had decided otherwise. Elric wondered if his entire life had not been the plaything of this weapon in which the battle-hungry Gods were vented, leaving him no choice but to kill or die.

It had been so hard, so painful to separate from the rune-carved sword that he wondered whether he would be able to start all over again. For a moment he thought of leaving, of fighting off the temptation, letting his body suffer, breaking it like glass. Growing old like humans, losing his memory, forgetting the sunrises over the Pale Sea, the dance of Dragons over the Tower of Monshanjik, forgetting even the sweet body of Cymoril.

But there was that terrified face of the little girl, that puny figure that had run up to him to ask for his help; and he had disappointed her. As long as there were children in this world being chased by the forces of evil, the last hero could not rest, let alone grow old. That was a luxury he could not allow himself.

Resigned now, Elric reached out and the long, black sword flew singing into his hand. Right away a wave of well-being rushed through him and he felt like a new youth had been granted to him. There was no more pain, as if his bones had become diamond hard again, his muscles resilient, his senses keen. As if he had never hurtled down the rubble. As if no beast of Entropy had ever struck him.

He only had to look up at the trunk of the Tree of Origins to realize that his eyes of old had returned. His eyes saw far beyond the level of the lowest branches, through the curtain of clouds, climbing the epiphyte vines up to the pure night of stars and comets behind the blue sky, far beyond the Cosmic Balance.

And yet Elric felt no joy. Only a great weariness that came after the physical fatigue. A profound disgust for himself. He knew that he had just lost a battle, the most important battle, the battle against himself. The vitality that the sword was conferring on him would have to be paid back a hundredfold. Stormbringer was not the type to give gifts.

Anterich watched him with respect. The old sorcerer had knelt on the ground in obedience and his otter-skin coat sprawled in the dust among the roots and psilocybes.

"Bring me back to the cliff, my friend. I have a task there that cannot wait any longer—a child to save from the clutches of Entropy. My sacrifice must not be in vain. I would never forgive myself."

"I can't do it, Lord. My last drop of energy has been spent."

"Can you, at least, find the Limestone Maze? Have you kept a picture of it in your mind?"

"Don't worry about a picture of it. Certainly my memory sometimes plays tricks on me, especially when I drink too much blackberry wine, but Chaos take me if I can't conjure up the Maze."

"In that case, give me your hand and guide me. You will have all the power you need. Stormbringer is shuddering in my hand like a snake full of life."

The bitter, green Wind of Change rose up at the foot of the Tree of Origins as soon as the sorcerer's fingers touched those of the nigromancer. It was if the maelstrom sprang out of the tip of the black blade, so eager was it to rejoin the battlefield.

They entered the emerald flurry with mixed feelings. As they vanished like ridiculous shadows in a shadow play, the Tree of Origins, undisturbed, continued growing; its roots reached down tirelessly for the true heart of the Earth; its branches reached for the stars. They said that when they finally reached them, the Dead Gods would be reborn from the ashes and haunt the alleys of Ameeron in the depths of the Great Cavern, like in the time of the fall of the Universe. But maybe they were just lies.

The Limestone Maze literally swallowed up the sun. It was like a salt mine with its crystals destroyed. It spread out over several square miles, a wild land riddled with bright pits that every form of life had abandoned. No trees or moss or even lichen could have survived on such terrain. Before even entering it, one suffered an unquenchable thirst. Only a few jet-black ravens dared it, flying low over the fossilized twists and turns, more for the pleasure of seeing their dull, gray shadows march over the feminine curves of the nearby foothills than in the hope of finding a corpse.

The Child of the Future had chosen her refuge well.

Elric hesitated before the gaping white mouth in the spotless stone. The storm that had brought him to the entrance of the Maze was dying out behind him but the Wind of Change was still blowing through his crimson cape. Now that Stormbringer was quivering in his hand, the albino was rediscovering the sounds and sensations of old, as if the world was being reborn, as if time had reversed to carry him back to the glorious age of the Dragon Princes when the barbarians were still only words in the mouths of seers, when Melniboné the Magnificent believed itself eternal and pretended to defy the Cosmic Hand.

He heard the snapping of his cape in the dying wind, the beating of his heart at the approach of battle, the black blade bewailing its long years of solitude, shrieking in hunger. He felt the energy of the Spheres returned, youth, force, newfound desire to take the world in his hand and fashion it anew to make it his own.

Just as he was about to enter the Maze, he heard old Anterich calling out in a feeble voice. He turned around, annoyed.

The weary sorcerer was sitting against an ash tree. He was having trouble controlling his trembling hands. "Lord, do you at least know what kind of battle awaits you?"

"If you are holding me back for such a thing, old man! I saw a child being terrorized. The hordes of Entropy wanted her blood! That's enough for me!"

"Don't you want to know the reason for their fury?"

"Do you know? You told me earlier that you knew nothing."

"I know what everyone says. And what you seem not to know, ever since your withdrawal from the world."

"Tell it quickly, Anterich! Every second counts!"

The sorcerer was obviously drained by the magic that he had used to transport them to the Maze and was trying to catch his breath. Elric wondered how much Stormbringer might have fed on his energy. The sword was capable of such treachery.

"Well?" the albino was growing impatient.

"The common people say that the Child carries within her such an idyllic vision of the future that the Siamese Gods of Entropy are jealous."

"And why would they be jealous?" Elric laughed. "Like always, you other humans have understood nothing about the designs of the Lords On High. Just the fact that this child carries the future in her is enough to disturb the Gods. Think about it! If the future is written, Entropy is just another illusion. One more. What will become of the power of the Gods of Entropy in that case? Except to sit on their Porphyry Thrones and witness the decline of the Young Kingdoms, the coming of a new Golden Age, really just Time passing, with their hands tied and as useless as the lowliest of your servants."

"But why go after this Child?"

"Because the Gods want to model the world, they want to play with us, to make us their servile creatures. Well, the Child of the Future is proof of their powerlessness. If they kill her, they will also be destroying the future that this messenger Child carries inside. And this message of a magnificent future that they did not dole out will disappear with the Child, another trail of dust that will remain for a few years in the hearts of men who will never meet her. Another legend that the years will take care of eliminating."

"They say you only have to touch her to see the vision." The sorcerer had closed his eyes. His wrinkle-slashed face looked ecstatic. "If you save her, my Emperor, do me a favor. Take off your glove and touch her for me. When you come back again, you can tell me what you saw. Men need images of happiness to die in peace."

"If these images exist, I will bring them back to you. Trust me."

At these words, which left the old sorcerer in tears, Elric stepped firmly into the Maze. It was cold under the high vault. Cold and wet.

The sound of his footsteps echoed softly, reverberating like balls of cotton rolling down a long gentle slope. There was no smell in the bare corridors except, very faintly, of chalk. But it was more like a smothering than an odor, a kind of bitter, desiccating steam that crept under the black armor and jerkin, all the way to the skin, creeping into his lungs, swelling his tongue and scratching his throat.

While moving forward in the network of tunnels, Elric was learning again how to live with Stormbringer. He was trying to imagine what he would do after he saved the girl. To prepare himself better for the real battle that he would have to wage after accomplishing his final mission, he imagined himself bringing the rune-carved weapon back to the Tree of Origins and with all the energy he could muster plunging it up to its hilt in the thickest root of the Tree. The mere thought of it made him uneasy, as if the sword were reading his thoughts and trying to remind him which of the gods held power.

He also imagined himself going back to his hovel in the village near the forest, his muscles turned flabby again, his sight beclouded in a constant fog, no more illusions, or memories, or maybe, with a little luck, desire to live. And he realized that all the dangers he had faced, at the Shade Gate, on the Isle of the Purple Towns, in the procession of Dharijor, confronting the most powerful Gods in the Universe, were nothing compared with the simple, humble gesture of forsaking, once and for all, the cursed sword.

He had already done it. He would do it again. That is what he kept telling himself as he paved his way through the Limestone Maze. But the difference was that now he knew what it meant to go without it, to feel his fragile skin cracking, his bones turn brittle, his long white hair thin out, his steps become halting, his movements jerky. Growing old was certainly the hardest thing in the world, the bravest, and the most unbearable, too.

The Prince of Melniboné stopped abruptly. He heard voices now. They were calling from one tunnel to another. He listened carefully. They were clicking out the same red-hot consonants as in the forest, as if the language of Entropy had been forged by philosophical dwarves at the bottom of a volcano. The configuration of the maze dampened the crackling tones a little, but it could do nothing against the sulfurous stench from the creatures' mouths. Enough to wrinkle your nose.

The Gods must really have wanted to wipe out the Future of this child to send their winged creatures like this into such a tortuous passage. But what did they have to fear from a child with no power except that of seeing the future?

Elric hurried his pace. As the voices of Entropy became clearer and stronger, Stormbringer started signing its song of death.

At a bend in the corridor, although Elric still thought they were some distance away, he ran into the creatures' rearguard, shining with the dark light of Entropy. The size of the tunnel made it impossible for them to spread their tattered wings, which made them look ridiculous, waddling around on their dewclaws. Only the uncertainty of their presence in reality, their fluttering between the planes of two universes, between light and night, gave them any semblance of dignity.

Before Elric had even brandished it, the rune-carved sword was slicing through the crowd. It vibrated at the same frequency as the dragons, following them in their blurry world, showing no mercy. With every blow dealt, the hero felt the energy flow through him from head to foot. It was a kind drunkenness. His arms swung the sword effortlessly, giving it just enough force to decapitate the beasts and split their blazing throats, as they turned around to face him, clawing at his ankles.

The creatures had no chance in such a tight space. Their freedom of movement was too hampered to pose a threat to the albino, who continued to clear a bloody path toward the front of the demon troop. Stormbringer worked wonders. It whirled before Elric, tracing a black sun that extinguished the gold and topaz eyes of the creatures. The voices of Entropy became hysterical, echoing in the Maze like trumpets sounding the retreat. The smell of sulfur became noxious.

Soon there was nothing but a tight mass of snouts and claws stuck between two realities, flashes of violence, explosions of fury. The last monsters were huddled in front of a tiny opening, too narrow for their misshapen bodies to enter. It was the perfect place for a hunted little girl to hide, the only place where she might hope to survive while waiting for some unimaginable aide.

Elric smiled. Obviously he had not arrived too late. If the nightmarish beasts were still scampering around this crack, it was because the Child of the Future was still alive.

Fending off the repeated blows, the Prince dove into the final battle with growing fervor. He marveled at seeing how easily his arm supported the weight of Stormbringer, how his legs were firmly planted giving him the perfect balance to wield the blade precisely where he aimed it. He was astonished at how smoothly he controlled his breath and energy. The raging sword was drinking the souls of the corpses with cruel greed and the ranks of the creatures mashed against the opening were thinning out by the second.

A claw or a beak might scrape the black armor, but what could they do against a metal forged in the depths of the earth? The voices went out one by one, like a circle of flames before a tidal wave. The razor-sharp wings beat the air hysterically, trying to draw at least one drop of blood from the hero before being wiped out, but they only managed to tear themselves apart a little more. Soon there was just a pile of corpses that shimmered darkly on the white stone.

Elric let his sword drop pointed down. Faced with the pools of blood spreading out over the dusty ground, seeping into the grains of chalk, staining them forever as if to mark the spot of the Prince of Melniboné's final battle for future generations, he felt worse than disgusted. The thrill of battle had gone. There only remained this loathing, this feeling of failure despite the victory, these tremors of shame that ran through his body as he sheathed Stormbringer. The sword was satisfied; it was shrilling its joy.

The silence mounted in the Limestone Maze. Now that the din of battle was gone, the child could be heard crying softly.

"Are you all right, girl? Are you hurt?" No answer. She kept weeping. No doubt her tongue was knotted in terror... "It is I, Elric, the Prince with red eyes and silver hair. There is nothing more to fear. You can come out."

The Child of the Future still made no sign of moving. She crouched in her hiding place as if she feared some dirty trick from the Forces of Entropy. Kicking away the corpses piled up before the crack, Elric cleared a spot and squatted down. The Beasts had left a stench of sulfur that brought tears to his eyes.

"Give me your hand. I'll help you."

The Prince deliberately took off his glove and stuck his arm inside the crevice with his hand open, palm upwards in a gesture of peace. First he had contact, the light touch of tiny, sensitive fingers, something infinitely soft and pure, but it did not last. A flood of raw, sepia images rushed into the albino's mind, breaking through the barriers of his consciousness, sweeping away the deepest layers of his memory and a plethora of information was engraved on it in red blood.

Elric toppled over backward, his eyes rolled up, struck down by the future.

Holed up in the ruins of the boarding school, the terrorized youngster was watching the sky congested with rain clouds. With a little luck they would not come today. The visibility was too low. Rubble cluttered the steps leading up from the basement. At the top of the steps was the bloated sky, the menace.

There was practically no more water in the jerrycan. He had to go out to get more if he wanted to survive. For food he had collected a small supply of canned foods during the first hours of the blitz, which would tide him over for one or two weeks.

The boy slipped out of the basement, disturbing a bunch of rats that were digging into a pile of clothes that had once been the school's bursar, a long-nosed man with a lisp. The south wing of the building had received a direct hit. The smell of corpses buried under the wreckage was becoming unbearable. The rescue teams were useless. The raids on the capital had multiplied lately as if they were not supposed to leave a stone standing. There were not enough able-bodied men to give a decent burial to the dead.

Passing by the empty classrooms where the jumbled desks faced the blackboard like they were involved in some deep discussion, the child wondered where his friends had gone, at least those who had survived. Had their parents come to get them or were they wandering in the streets, their eyes wide open and swollen from crying too much?

He pushed open the gate and found himself in Drury Lane. The sight was even more atrocious. Entire walls of buildings had collapsed onto the road, revealing the guts of apartments: shredded wallpaper, drooping floors, furniture perched on islands of reinforced concrete, abandoned cribs, lopsided grandfather clocks. The fog cast ghostly shadows on the apocalyptic scene and specters drifted by wringing their hands, terribly silent and dignified.

Walking was hard. He had to climb over mounds of cinder blocks trying not to twist his ankle and then make wide detours at the orders of the men in armbands from the civil defense who were keeping people away from the collapsing buildings.

The boy was almost at the water station when the sirens wailed their mournful cry over the city. He stopped, his heart beating fast, the empty jerrycan in his hand. He was too far from the school. He was going to have to find shelter right here.

A little lost, not very familiar with the district, he turned in circles. The jerrycan dropped at his feet. He pressed his hands against his ears. He could not stand this nagging howl that drowned the capital every day, the herald of disasters. It was like a handsaw severing the reality of the world, gashing it in a thousand places. Everything was disintegrating under his feet and he was going to fall into the void.

He started running haphazardly. Thoughts of death were banging around inside his head. The world doomed to the night—there was no more hope. He leapt aside to avoid the helping hands trying to stop him and dodged two men who wanted to hold him back. He stumbled, got back on his feet. His knee was grazed, but he did not feel a thing.

He ended up in Trafalgar Square, which had been miraculously saved. He was alone and tiny. The stone lions watched him with that cynical stare they always had. He scrambled to the middle of the esplanade, raised his arms to the sky in a V for victory and started screaming and whirling around. His screams were so strange, so odd that they sounded like he was laughing at the same time, like he was happy.

He barely had time to see the black cross of the V-1 diving out of the sky at him. A second later a blinding light engulfed him and a geyser of dirt, gravel and pebbles soared up from the place where he had been dancing.

Night. Fog.

The rocks fell slowly back down in a thick cloud of smoke and dust. The flames burned brightly amidst the haze. The image blurred and London faded away like a mirage, or a nightmare.

With a quick, sharp movement, Elric grabbed the Child's hand and yanked her out of the crevice where she had taken refuge.

Night. Fog.

The ashen images continued raining down inside his head. Gray flakes that forever stained the soul, that charred the heart.

Fury. Death.

So, that was the future that the Child bore, the envisioned hereafter of the Young Kingdoms with their masses of humanity full of hope for better times, with the common people in the cities and countryside dreaming of a golden age when there would be no more hunger, no more great plagues, when everyone would have a roof over their heads.

The Child of the Future was smiling at him, confident, a little like the boy in the city of ruins. Her candid eyes sparkled in the white light of the Maze. She was so beautiful with her tousled hair, her crystalline cheeks, her fairy's face, that he almost forgot the horrors she carried inside her.

Almost.

Elric shuddered. Stormbringer had jumped into his hand so naturally that he wondered to his dying day if the rune-carved blade had known his intention or if he had moved his arm.

The Child was backing away now. She understood. The curse had caught up with her. A kind of resignation was painted on her doll's face. Elric was blocking the passage to the crack in the wall. He left her no chance.

She fell to her knees, begging. "Have pity, Lord! It won't do any good!"

Stormbringer flew out and sang as it severed the head of the Child of the Future. Its song was not as merry as usual, but it was a special soul to absorb, a sweet, sad soul, full of frenzied images that should never have existed.

At the same time, this future was broken and the Siamese Gods of Entropy, leaning over the Kingdom Below, could sit back in their double Porphyry Throne, relieved. The Future was still to be written, they believed.

At the same time, on a makeshift raft being tossed about by the Serene Sea off the coast of Scorpion Isle, a baby was born. It cried tears of blood because it carried within it the same vision. Only its mother knew the truth. But like all mothers before her, she said nothing.

Elric sheathed Stormbringer, leaned his forehead against the tunnel wall and vomited. A bitter taste hung on lips, a taste that he had never known before—the taste of defeat.

Without turning around, the Prince of Melniboné went back the way he had come. Despite the sword, his energy was spent and old age was catching up with him, relentlessly. The road was long from the Limestone Maze to the Tree of Origins, surely the longest and most grueling he had ever traveled.

When Elric stumbled out into the light, the world had become blurry again.

Fabrice Colin began his literary career as a writer-editor for gaming magazines. His first novel Neuvième cercle *(1997) launched him on a very successful career as a fantasy writer and YA author. Fabrice is a four-time winner of the Grand prix de l'Imaginaire, including for his novel* Dreamericana *(2003). He has since diversified his production to include crime thrillers, graphic novels, radio plays and mainstream novels. In 2011, his Elric novel,* Les Buveurs d'âmes*, based on an original story by Mike, was released by Editions Fleuve Noir.*

Fabrice Colin: *Eulogy for the Abyss Fish*

This is for Bénédicte

Yr-Mokkk

She came with her husband, her name was Etyhelia, Ethelwee, Ethel of Calmor, Etyhelia of Anthelm, she was young, she came from another world, a sophisticated and cruel metropolis where everything, absolutely everything could be bought. An extravagant place where, by paying your weight in sequins, any high-ranking citizen could take a trip to else-where—and that is exactly what she did.

Her personal physician had approved the decision. "Another plane," he had agreed as she was walking away, rustling her dress, "…um, would be ideal considering the melancholy that's gnawing away at your mind." But in reality he did not believe a word of what he was saying, he knew that the end was near and he knew that he was not mistaken: the desire to travel was a painfully typical sign.

One morning she went to her husband on the balcony of a lava palace, her crimson silk robe open onto her blinding nudity. The three suns stood impassive in the ashen sky, but not her husband, no: he was still having trouble getting used to the sight. She had married him for his naïve fortune, he for her obscene beauty, and he suffered. Suffered knowing how perfect and distant she was, beyond the bounds of his concern.

She had told him that someone had disappeared. This someone was her brother. She had not seen him in sooo long—she had begged—and all at once she had heard dire rumors, oh, please let him understand her, she could not stand it anymore: she had to find him again, she needed him, her beloved husband, she had to find a travel demon, which would cost a fortune, but he had money, didn't he? All the gold and diamonds one could want.

He did not argue.

He never argued with her.

She came from a race that would not last, a race that time was driving mad, a race that was about to disappear and knew it.

The husband summoned his household. He gave instructions to prepare the baggage, he wrote letters, ordered them to buy a demon and when everything was ready he sat on his bed for a long time until, in a gesture of forlorn hope, he tossed on top of his carefully folded shirts the old leather notebook that he had once promised himself he would never fill in—because he wanted to believe this lie now: that writing was a way to quell the suffering and he preferred to be misled than to keep suffering—faced with the inevitable, reason becomes as hard as parchment brought near a flame.

Lord Lanthor of Anthelm

I cannot cope with this world. The sea the color of sick emerald. The pointed galleys sailing off to sea. My pouting, sulking wife, black hair falling over her face. My name is Lanthor Alvekh of Anthelm, merchant of demons and sprites, originally from the world of Olfaer.

It is thanks to the powers of a potent magical artifact that we are lucky enough to be traveling through the Young Kingdoms. I wrote the word "lucky:" a pretty, imaginative fable

106

would be better than the true story of the freefall. We came in sight of the land where my wife's brother is being held and, see, I wrote "brother" too, I know very well that the time has come, her doctor confirmed it. They all end up like this: they all let themselves be *devoured.*

Elric of the Dragons

The days pass, the specter of your adventures fades away in coils of bloody mist, you wander in the hallways and antechambers, waiting for a comfort that will never come. Languishing on your balcony, in the bleak hours you dream of your city, the cacophonous age when your people were at war against the Dharzi Empire, their amazement when a volcano suddenly appeared in the middle of the Pale Sea. You would have loved to be there, in the heart of the melee; destiny decided otherwise.

You drink philters. You swallow potions. Unguents penetrate your skin, their principles creep into your veins, flow up to your mind, caress it, sing venomous lullabies to it. Your life is a zesty wreck, a long, sweet wreck from which only your will can save you. With great swigs of poison, you dedicate yourself to killing this tiresome enemy.

On some secret night the courtesans file into your room: their sweet embraces leave the black taste of metal on your lips.

You watch the bay, the ships passing through, you dream of the next departure, a mirage among so many others. You snap your fingers, they bring you a fancy, brass spyglass and you scan it over the city.

Yr-Mokkk

Etyhelia lying down on the forecastle, naked. Sighs swell her chest. The stunned sailors are fighting over the places at the top of the foremast. At first it is like a game. Lanthor leans over his wife, full of indulgence. "My beloved…" She shoos him away like a fly. She is thinking of that man she saw in her dream. She is thinking of that friend of hers who spoke to her about a man who had come back from this country and who had met Lord Elric: Elric of the Dragons: an albino: a cursed being.

At full sail, the ship glides over the coruscant sea. Etyhelia does not sleep. When twilight sprawls its starry contortions over the immensity of the ocean, she gets up, grabs a sailor, no matter which, throws him against the rail and runs her hand up his thigh. The sailor shudders, his heart races. Two expert fingers: the woman frees his genitals. Centuries of ennui, of endeavors, of speeches to come back to this very simple reality—desire.

The others circle around and watch her. The others do not dare do anything. They will not do anything. This woman is a priestess, a succubus, a lethal empress. She slips her shapely thigh against the man's and without looking at him, slides him deep into her. Fast, she grabs his hips, urges him to move, she wants him to go faster, she wants him to put all his heart into it, to rip her out of her convictions. But the man cannot do it and she remains faced with herself: the void inside her, she senses it, she is sure of it now, the void is impossible to fill.

Lord Lanthor of Anthelm

Visitors are not welcome in Imrryr. When we come in sight of the fortifications—a hundred-foot sheer, smooth wall—and our astonished eyes make out the haughty towers of the Dreaming City, a Melnibonéan frigate comes alongside us. A pilot boards and talks briefly with our captain, who motions for us to go below. We do so, even though we are all first class passengers. Etyhelia darts a radiant glance at the pilot. The man grits his teeth. He takes me aside and asks me what brings me to Imrryr.

I am here on business, I say: my brother-in-law, Leem Keleth is being held somewhere in the city and we have to do what we can to get him out of the hands of his abductors—his ship, or so my wife tells me, was boarded on the Melnibonéan sea under false pretext. Maybe he has joined the ranks of the countless slaves abounding in the city? Then, I add, I also figure on acquiring some valuable relics here: they say that once night falls there are secret shops that open their doors to the most trustworthy foreigners.

He nods. He knows that I am lying. The stories we invent are the walls that protect the world from our own madness.

Before going down to our cabin with the black veils over the portholes, I have time to peek over my shoulder. The pilot is holding out an alabaster mask to our captain, who puts it on his face, grinning with disgust. The precaution seems unnecessary to me, seeing how proud they are of the complexity of the inextricable tangle of rocks that forms the structure—and in which, legends say, many have died having never found the exit. But such is the regulation: no visitor can keep their eyes open as they pass through the channels of the sea maze that separates the ocean gate from the inner harbor.

Elric of the Dragons

They lust after your throne. They want your death. They say that you are weak, unfit, corrupt, they say that this island will sink with you into the fathomless waters, the waters of despair, if no one does anything, that is how it will end.

They are right.

And yet, you have the sword. You are used to its hum, you know its voice by heart. The cry for blood. You dream of becoming deaf to this cry.

Yr-Mokkk

At the time of arrival, and while the ship is gliding through the incomprehensible maze, Etyhelia sleeps once again. She has a dream, sees her first lover, a warrior, a shaven-headed swashbuckler, a thaumaturge—an ichthyologist by obsession. He was crazy, completely: during his nights of crisis the doctors thronged around his bedside, he raved, slobbered, clawed the air with his long, curved nails and then, as soon as the learned assembly had left, he jumped on her, roared over her and she loved it, she loved feeling possessed, she had this power to belong to men, to make them think that she belonged to them—if only she had left before he dropped dead.

Once his desire was sated, her lover breathed deeply and took a book from his baggage, the same one, the only one, a treatise on the fishes of hell. He spoke to her about the abyss fish. The abyss fish lived in the depths of the planes of chaos, the Young Kingdoms—oh, how that name resonated!—they spawned in the silty layers, their mouths were garnished with sharp spikes, they were as big as elephants and when they swallowed you, you went directly into the infernal limbo where, he emphasized with desperate gluttony, he, too, would end up one day, inevitably.

Etyhelia caressed his smooth, oval head, she sang, cradled him, she was fascinated, she let his words flow into the depths of her soul, dull pebbles that time would polish relentlessly and still he ended up foundering, his head on the knees of his lover, a tiger glutted with carnage. A thousand doors opened in his wake.

Lord Lanthor of Anthelm

An agonizing calm, a sickly lethargy hangs over the harbor of Melniboné. Only thirty Melnibonéan frigates are docked here. A few fishing boats and a handful of galleys are rocking on the waves. The low towers crowd around the stone wall surrounding the city. Crenellated cranes, rickety storehouses, barracks and barges stacked with cords are piled up around them.

Desolation.

My wife does not look at me. I grit my teeth. I tried to talk about it, but she walks cruelly away from me, she is already gone—a ghost in the wind.

As is customary, I spent my time memorizing the five rules of the harbor edict that was delivered by our captain this morning. In particular, I know that except for rare exceptions, no foreigner is allowed to enter the city of Imrryr. We will have to use, how to put it—Persuasion. Ah, curse on us. I know that Etyhelia is ready to exploit her charms to force a decision. With a bored pouty look, before caressing my cheek, she confessed to me this treasure, if need be... Curse on us and let us burn.

Here I am in the Hall of Concordance. I want to meet Darin Malvag, the harbor captain. A Melnibonéan, looking unbelievably superior, stares at me. "Captain Malvag doesn't see foreigners." That is the answer.

"I know," I say boldly. "But it's a matter of the utmost importance." My wife looks him up and down. The Melnibonéan smiles.

Elric of the Dragons

You aim your spyglass at the harbor. You see her. Her. Fragile. Detestable, highly desirable. When your eyes linger on her throat, wander down the low neckline of her embroidered tunic, there is a little of the old life coming back to you, a little of your ancestor's energy. Tonight, if she is still alive, you will go out to meet her.

Yr-Mokkk

She stared openly at the men, eye to eye. She was acting like a predator. The men were animals whom she could use at will. What she gave them in return was of little value to her: her body. They thought they were using her. What they did not know and what she was just beginning to see was that by following the downward spiral of her desire, she was heading straight for death

Lord Lanthor of Anselm

After bitter negotiations Captain Darin Malvag agreed to see me—that is a favor that very few foreigners can boast of receiving. My gift had the good fortune to please his Incomparable Magnificence: a higher demon from the world of Olfaer, a rather small creature but of which Malvag had rarely seen the like.

"It comes from another plane, Your Highness. I hope it will satisfy you."

I was thinking that he would at least ask me some details about my own world. He does nothing of the kind. I am of no interest to him. I bow before him. I cannot look him in the eyes. Behind the bars of its silver cage my demon writhes in anger. Its new master invites me to stand up.

"State your request."

The critical moment.

"Your Lordship, my esteemed brother-in-law Leem Keleth was on board the *Golden Wind*, a merchant ship that, if I'm not mistaken, was inspected by your fleet a few days ago and the crew was taken off into slavery. I come, Your Incomparable Magnificence, to beg You for his pardon. Rest assured that my deepest desire in this matter is to submit to the will of the noble lords of the glorious city of Imrryr."

"The *Golden Wind*, you say? On my word, I've never heard of such a ship. Maybe I should ask the harbor captain."

He and Etyhelia do not take their eyes off each other.

After a few moments of quiet reflection, Darin Malvag makes me an offer. Etyhelia will stay with him as a hostage: to be sure that I will return. In thirty days I will bring to the Captain five demons like the one I have just offered. In exchange he will help me in my search. If I break my word, I will be sent into slavery or thrown to the moray eels, we shall see. He will know how to find me, he concluded, I can wholly trust him on this point.

Finding five demons is possible, yes, I will pull some strings. But to leave my wife with these bandits? To leave my lascivious, crazy wife full of pining desires, leave these beasts to fondle her, grab her thighs, spread her open like a flower and empty their despicable juices into her? "Oh, come on, it's an obvious choice," my young wife whispers, smoothing her long, dyed hair. She is probing my soul, tearing out my heart. Then, stepping to the side, she places herself under the authority of Malvag, who looks pleased and puts his arm around her.

I have nothing else to do but leave.

Elric of the Dragons

You could go find Malvag. You could run him through with your blade. You could demand that he deliver this woman unconditionally. He would not dare to confront you. Except, you prefer to stay in the shadows. Possessing her is bound to bring pain. To enjoy your power, the consequence of your singular virtue, you have to seduce this creature, fascinate her, make yourself precious, sparkling with mystery.

Yr-Mokkk

Here now in the Dreaming City. Her husband's ship has left for its world. She watched it for an instant with Malvag's hot breath on her perfumed neck and then she turned to him, ran her hand though his oily hair and pulled him close to her so he could savor the fruit of her mouth.

Afterward she told him why she was here. She told him that she wanted to meet Lord Elric more than anything else. If, in return, he wanted her to teach him the infinite subtleties of her art—he only had to ask.

He asked.

Head down, she goes through the dome of the central gate leading to Procession Avenue that connects the harbor to the sumptuous Imperial Palace. Captain Malvag makes a sign to his secretary, Shinsen, a mute giant whose huge, black braid sweeps over the lapis lazuli paving stones. Shinsen gives Etyhelia some ornamented jewelry and a coppery loincloth. She puts on the loincloth: now he holds her by a harness strapped to her chest. It would be unthinkable for a native Melnibonéan, no matter how far from royal lineage, to debase himself by treating a foreigner as anything but a slave. From time to time, he gratifies her with a "Move, female" that cracks like a whip and for an instant, before continuing, she trembles at the thought of what these two are going to do to her: it is nothing, she knows why she is doing this and let Shinsen have fun pulling on her chain. If there is a price to pay, she will pay it, she will choke back her tears, for what are tears compared to the sea?

Everywhere she looks, there is a new surprise, a new shock, and her heart races. She would like to scoff at it all, at the people's cruelty, at their pretense, but a terrible lethargy floats over the city, a desperation varnished with complex trappings, guilt, desire for death, the sovereignty of ennui, and she cannot ignore the dreadful intensity.

At the crest of the hill they are climbing, in the distant mists, sprawls the great Esplanade of Dominions, surrounded by the Imperial Palace, the Elemental Court and the Cathedral of Chaos, whose legend has crossed multiple planes of existence. On each side of the wide paved road rise towers and multi-colored palaces of sophisticated architecture and highly sought materials: nacre, ivory, obsidian are the most common, but there are also towers of water, citadels of furs or bridges of flesh whose repugnant walls change color and texture according to the angle of the sun's rays.

Lord Lanthor of Anthelm

I picture her.
I watch the sun. I grit my teeth.

Five demons. I do not know if I will return. I remember the day I met her in the tiers of the Imperial Circus. She came in a litter, carried by women and surrounded by courtesans. I was with a friend. Her eyes devoured me. Sized me up. Could this be an acceptable man? A praying mantis. Take it all. And I went crazy, crippled before her beauty, I was ready to believe what she did not tell me, to take what she could not give.

We made love behind her silk curtains. The texture of her skin was perfect. I nibbled her, licked her lovingly. I would have cut off an arm for her, I would have drunk the water from her bath. She laughed uproariously. I thought she was happy. She laughed even more. I understood nothing.

Elric of the Dragons

You will go tonight. You have your information. She is of that race. She needs oblivion, punishment—she does not know what she needs.

She *wants* to meet you. She told Malvag. Very well, you will go down the dark alleys. You will wear a mask. You will touch her skin. You will be faithful to your rank. You will claw her back. You will not say who you are.

Yr-Mokkk

They have stayed seven days in Malvag's palace: libations and debauchery, a mad frenzy, she licks, they bite, she swallows, they bellow, she curls up in their muscles, they get drunk on liquors, she suffers, she cries, she gives thanks.

Other Melnibonéans join the dance. They wear masks, executioner hoods, bracelets jingle on their thin wrists, their breath is burning hot, peppered, they explore her with their genitals, their fingers, their frantic tongues and she is there without being there, and her nails scratch out white furrows.

When they are tired, when night falls they leave and the city is more and more like a dream, an insistently heavy dream, one with the perfume floating over its roofs. Behind the drapes of their sagging divans, she sees the shadows of the languid nobles, wrecked in some narcotic trance that nothing but their slaves crying out in pain or the ingestion of some new, even stronger, rawer drug can pull them out of. The alleys and walkways that interweave every which way vibrate with subtle fondling; groaning seems to seep out of the ground. She knows that thousands of slaves live underground, subject to the cruel will of their masters. She knows that Leem is not among them because Leem does not exist, never existed, Leem is the name of her lover. She never had a brother and when she founders in the fumes of sleep, she dreams of him and the mouths of the giant fish opening and snapping like traps. Then on the night of the seventh day, she drops to her knees before Malvag, takes his penis out of his pants and speaks impious words, things like "I'll swallow you down to your blood." She wants to see Elric, she wants to see him now, she came for that, she will not wait a second longer, let him go get him, since he knows him so well, and tell him that Etyhelia is here, that she wants to meet him and Malvag clutches the woman's hair, a satisfied smile passes across his face because without knowing it, she has already been given to the Dragon Lord ten times and now she is begging. He could almost laugh.

Lord Lanthor of Anthelm

Back home. I was blind. I forgot all those years, waking up startled, my trembling hand feeling the empty bed, my mind working like a machine, frantic pistons and pulleys, speculations, hypotheses, ruminations—when the explanation is clear, the fluid that flowed in the veins of my wife is so hot that she tries constantly to get in touch with skin that burns ever hotter, white hot, no embrace can calm her, she told me one day, it is the curse of our race, we run with our arms outstretched toward the abyss, we thirst for hell, one day or another we will take the plunge.

I pretended to believe her stories. I wanted to follow her.

What does the truth matter.

Elric of the Dragons

You are waiting for her. Let her come, let her ask, let her beg, that is what matters. Your nails on her skin: they do not count. Your cheek against her thigh: it is unimportant. The waiting is consumed in the desire. Desire is a flower that dies when exposed to the azure fires. At the moment of blossoming, already, she withers. An idea comes to you.

Yr-Mokkk

They stride along the Garden of Melancholy Roses. Surrounded by a wall of white marble rising in shaded terraces, the park is strewn with black petals, scattered by the gloomy trees between which meander glittering streams. Alabaster bridges, midnight blue groves. The place exudes an intolerable nostalgia. Etyhelia thinks she sees a statue, a movement. She turns her head: the statue has disappeared. "Something was there," she says.

Shinsen looks at her and shrugs. He pulls hard on her leash. They leave the garden. Shinsen is in charge of bringing the young woman to Lord Elric of the Dragons and even though he is obsessed by the idea of taking her one last time and leaving her for dead on a bed of petals, he will do nothing of the kind: he figures that the master, who came to join them several times disguised as a rich, masked merchant, would not forgive him for breaking such a charm.

Lord Lanthor of Anthelm

I prefer not to think about what she is doing right now, who she has been with, the seas of loneliness that we have crossed, because all these reveries only brighten the glare of an unbearable light, she is too vast for me contain, I am too insignificant to exist in her, I can only get lost, melt in the immensity of her memory, there in the heart of our short history, among the glowing strands of our trajectories, if life is a blind creature diving into always deeper waters, then, maybe, I will find her again, and I will disappear in her.

Elric of the Dragons

You are lying on your bed. Wait. Your breath, little by little, slows down. The most beautiful thing that you can do, the only thing that counts, will be to not let this woman disappear, not offer her up to the tyrannical lust of your blade. Here in this yearned for meeting, the insurmountable space that will open up between you—therein will dwell the infinite, fleeting beauty. It will not last a long time, but this time will save you both.

Yr-Mokkk

They cross into the Elemental Court. The Garden of Lassa, the Hearth of Kakatal, the Dark of Grome and the Aquatic Garden of Straasha pay homage, each in their way, to the Lords for the glory in which they were built. They wait a moment on the flying platform with its slender pillars of ivy-twisted jasper before entering the darkness of Grome's bowels. The Cathedral of Chaos breathes affliction and is occupied now by only a few sick priests who shuffle around in silence. Rays of dusty light caress the pale features of the indifferent statues, gods of chaos whose sinister smiles grow larger as they approach. Their footsteps echo through the granite vaults as they walk along the Gate of the Dead that leads to the Catacombs. Even Shinsen is in a hurry to come to the end. From the Imperial Palace, they can see only the cyclopean towers in pastel shades, the delirious architecture of truncated facades, jagged footbridges, colorful ramparts, crystal and jade domes, arrows and bulbs sprinkling their amber glints over the precious surfaces.

Lord Lanthor of Anselm

Sitting in my brocaded armchair facing the teeming, sublime city of my ancestors, I hold out my hand, open my fingers and my servant girl lets a few drops of the mortal potion fall into my palm. I only have to bring my hand up to my face, daub my lips, my half-closed eyes, open my mouth, put in a finger, finally, a middle finger glistening with semen, I only have to lick, suck, inhale, feed on the cursed juice, before casting one last look at the bottle, a few glyphs in an ancient tongue that others have deciphered for me and paid for it with their lives—demon's sperm.

Elric of the Dragons

A racket in the hallway. Whiplashes.

The door opens. There *she* is, whom you asked for, she who also begged for you; in fact your meeting is the result of converging urges.

She lies down at your side—they lay her down, rather, so weak. You talk briefly with the servants, then the door closes.

Her voice is heard, a broken melody. She says that she came looking for something here. Precisely here. She says that she wants to die. She shakes you by the shoulder, who is she, how dare she? She speaks to you about the abyss fish. Do you know the abyss fish, Lord?

You turn over to face her, on the side.

She wants to be yours.

She wants to stay here, to belong to you. She wants to rejoin her lover, but she cannot bring herself, she explains, to disappear completely.

She wants to go to hell. Her eyes shimmer: stick your blade into my breast, perfect king, and throw my body into the dark bay.

You smile. At your side, the sword is humming. Things do not happen like that, you say.

She cries.

You get up, she gets up with you.

You walk to the window. She moans, exhausted.

She sticks close to you. At your side, Stormbringer quivers with a desire that is hard to contain. You whisper in her ear. Her shoulders tremble. In one movement you open her thighs. She looks at you, forbidden. The moist outline of her lower lip. She is naked under her dress. You slip in a finger. A second. She is barely wet, but it will come, now. It is coming.

After half a minute of in and out, now she is crazy, twisting around, her hand on your wrist for you to go faster, harder.

Are you ready to give everything up?

Yes, she whispers.

Do you deny everything that you have been? Your sweet dreams of a pampered child?

Yes.

Do you deny love? Do you vomit out love, reject everything that makes you what you are?

She nods, throws her head back, offers her throat.

You are bored of affection, bored of empty words, of speeches without destiny.

You go out, you stagger toward the balcony in a syncopated waltz, the wind slaps you, the sky is crimson, the sea is black, deep, bristling with shiny fangs, choppy and turbulent, and the fangs are like flashes of silvery truth and the turbulence just like the contortions of your mixed up soul.

You trap her against the railing. Your fingers slip into her with infinite ease. Do you believe in anything?

No—No, she says, I submit to the power of your desire, I—

You stare into her eyes.

I do not believe you. I believe that you have a soul. And that you want to keep it wherever you go.

Hit me, she says.

You grimace. You do better than that. You show your blade, you slide it down between her breasts, you lift her up, she is so light, you perch her on your balcony, your eyes are widened by the drugs, with a firm hand you cling onto the railing, she whispers obscenities, she writhes, bury your hand in her—you know, you, that the hell of the abyss fish is only a world beyond, she will live, she will be dead but she will live, you owe her this, you desired her, you renounced this desire for the desire to save her, a desire infinitely more arid, she gave you back to yourself—and Stormbringer groans as it glides over her burning skin, all of a sudden you pull back your hand and she looks at you terrified, you grab her mouth, huff and puff into it—you think you are cursed, you say, but you might really be so. Realize what I am offering you now, a simple disappearance, a change, my blade desires you so *strongly*, see what you are escaping…

…and as she staggers, your blade shrills with violent desperation, Etyhelia's arms cling to the void, she struggles with gravity, with what had been her life, she hits the water, now she has no more effort to make, she only has to wait, she sinks, bubbles come to the surface, you stay there watching, but nothing, you sniff your hand, nothing either, nothing will happen for her anymore in this world, the abyss fish do their duty, the abyss fish encircle her whiteness falling endlessly, if this is the hell she wanted to know, then her wish is fulfilled, but hell is everywhere, does she understand that? Hell floats over our inner landscapes and what you give it is like love, Elric, so while you close the window and sit on your bed, while the grumbling twilight races over the bay, your blade lying next to you on your bed, your blade wailing like a be-trayed mistress, a sick man denied a cure, a dog whose bone was thrown too far and under the myriad layers of venom, there like a treasure twinkling faintly, lies, silent, the essence of your compassion.

John Davey is a writer, editor and bookseller (see www.Jaydedesign.com). He lives in London, England, with his wife Maureen, has two daughters, and is the author of three novels to date, Blood and Souls *(Nephyrite Press, 2002),* The Hole: A Teen Fable *(2008) and* Misère: A Ghost Story *(2011). Amongst his Moorcockian editorial works are* The Best of Michael Moorcock *(Tachyon Publications, 2009),* Into the Media Web: Selected Short Non-Fiction, 1956–2006 *(Savoy Books, 2010) and* The Michael Moorcock Collection *(36 volumes, Gollancz, 2013–15).*

John Davey: *An Organ of Bones*

Prologue

Ingleton's attractively ugly, decrepit Time Center was in turmoil. Even more than usual. It was by far the oldest, but also the most solidly built, and had seemed actively to resist the long-overdue upgrade.

Sergeant Alvarez, every bit as reluctant to embrace the changes that were being imposed, was pulling his hair out in handfuls, from head and beard in equal measures. The chemotherapy had been a bastard.

Piled high in one corner of the room was a veritable mountain of débris. Circuit boards, keyboards, switchboards, consoles, and cables galore. There were PVC-sheathed cables, rubber-sheathed cables, even some ancient lead-sheathed cables from goodness knew when. How the old place had never burned itself to the ground was beyond comprehension.

There were times when, out of the corner of his overtired eye, Alvarez could swear that he saw things moving within the Pile. He knew this was merely a symptom of his exhaustion, and best ignored, at least until after this initial boot-up of all the new equipment.

Aside from a little bit of fiber-optics at the point of entry, everything was now wireless. He had never been entirely sure whether this sort of data should be allowed to float unchecked around the aether—*any* aether—but he had been comprehensively overruled.

In place of the series of toggles, pulleys, levers, keys and elastic bands that he was used to, previously needed to set things in motion, there was now a single, plain on/off switch, reassuringly large and bright red.

He flipped it.

The multi-touch wall panels burst into swirling life.

Where once were displayed his trusted arrows of multiversal flux and fluctuation, Alvarez now had before him all of Cawthorn's original key maps. Each had been amended to varying degrees, by Collier; another poor choice, the sergeant felt, but even he had to admit that the old man's constant shakes had assisted ably in redrawing some of the recently Chaos-warped coastlines.

Now on every map, thanks to the latest tracking technologies, there blipped a number of bright dots, signifying most of the principals involved along with their respective whereabouts.

They were all seeming a little haywire, at the moment. Alvarez could not afford, yet, to take his eyes from the screen, even when he heard a comforting, familiar voice at his back.

"How's it going?"

"It's hard to tell, at the moment, Mrs. Persson."

"But everything came online okay?"

"As far as I can tell. I'm still learning the ropes when it comes to these new ideas of radiant time and such."

"You'll get the hang of it, I'm certain." She placed a friendly hand on his shoulder. "I did."

"But you've always tended to have a head start on the rest of us."

"True." Una Persson glanced all around, at the innumerable dots. "There's one sure test of how well things are working. Where's Cornelius?"

"Which one?"

"*All* of them."

"Well, Cathy's been asleep for quite a while—" he pointed—"here. There's nothing unusual in that, of course. This latest pregnancy has been taking its toll. Frank's dead. For the moment, at least."

Una sighed. "And Jerry?"

Blip.

"He seems to be in several places at once. I haven't figured out yet if that's a glitch, or if he's been playing about with versions of himself again."

"Bloody typical." She squinted at various smaller images. "Can you bring up the Young Kingdoms?"

"Sure." Alvarez stood, walked forward towards the wall panel and swiped one map aside, replacing it with another.

Mrs. Persson stared intently now, at a particular stationary dot. "There's our boy."

"What, Cornelius?"

"In the Young Kingdoms? I think not."

The sergeant nodded, looking closely at the zoomed-in map as if for the first time. The dot in question rested over a place name: Karlaak. "By the Weeping Waste," he said, going on to read other marked regions. "The Sighing Desert? It's no wonder he's such a moody bugger."

"Oh, I don't know. Perhaps we shouldn't be so hard on him."

A new voice, gruffly melodious, joined Una's behind Alvarez. "Oh, I quite agree. It's hard not to retain something of a soft spot, always, for one's firstborn."

I

In Karlaak by the Weeping Waste, Elric of Melniboné, proud prince of ruins, stood brooding at a window of the large bedchamber he shared with his new wife, Zarozinia.

She was asleep, soundly and quite beautifully, her innocent young features gracing the deep pillows, her long raven

hair in stark, dramatic contrast to the crisp white of the surrounding silk.

It was raining, as it so often was in this region of the
Young Kingdoms.

Despite the weather, a large full moon hung low in the
sky, visible more often than not between the fast-moving, ragged clouds.

Trees were few and far between, around the City of Jade
Towers, but a strong breeze moved the long, lush grasslands
like an ocean and blew the damp, scented air from the palace's
gardens into Elric's sensitive nostrils.

He breathed in deeply and deliberately, equating his
aroused senses with the feelings of peace, of belonging, that
he had known only since meeting and marrying Zarozinia. He
allowed these thoughts to drive away the darker notions that
had threatened to occupy their customary place in his mind
when first he came to the window.

Elric had so much to forget—so much he had already
forgotten, in all but his dreams—on which it was all too easy
to brood, should he indulge his penchant for introspection.

But now he also had such a great deal to look forward to.
For the first time in his life, he had a wife whom he loved and
who loved him fully in return, whose family, after initial mis-
givings at their union—and who would not have, given the
Melnibonéan's history?—now embraced him as one of their
own.

In time, perhaps, a family for the two of them? Children.
Descendants…

A sudden chill ran though Elric and he shuddered, moving closer to the fire which burned low in an iron grate. It did
little to warm him, and he decided to re-join Zarozinia in bed.
Before turning from the feeble flames, he caught a glimpse of
his own visage in a flat, highly polished shield hung decora-
tively above the mantelpiece. Glowing in the half-light, his
eyes shone a far brighter, deeper red than the guttering embers
at his feet; they were two inextinguishable coals, aflame in the
bleak colorlessness of his features. No earthly fire could bring

even a hint of bloom to Elric's sickly, albino flesh.

The drugs which he used to maintain his strength needed only to be taken occasionally, these days.

Before gloom invaded his thoughts once more, he returned to Zarozinia, lifting the covers and sliding in beside her, moving against her body. But instead of gaining warmth from her, he caused his wife to shiver at the touch of his skin on hers, and she mumbled something in her sleep.

If they were words at all that she uttered, he failed to catch them.

Elric began to slow and regulate his breathing, as he had trained himself to do through many years of long, restively wakeful nights.

Soon, therefore—more from habit than exhaustion—he was asleep.

Elric of Melniboné, proud prince of ruins, was known in certain circles by a different, even more derogatory soubriquet: that of Kinslayer.

It was a tragic, oft-recalled act which had brought him that name, an act which was to haunt his dreams that night, as it had so many others.

He woke with a start and a half-stifled cry aloud.

It was still dark. It was still raining. He had no idea how long he had slept. It might have been no more than a few moments, it might have been for hours, it might even have been for much of the night.

He turned to see if his startled awakening had disturbed Zarozinia. But she was gone. He stroked at the pillow, still dented from where her head had lain. It was warm; the scent lingered. Her absence was very recent.

Believing her to be in the nearby bathroom, its door not quite visible beyond the anteroom separating it from the bedchamber, Elric returned his back to the deep, firm mattress with every intention of resuming slumber.

"Elric."

It was Zarozinia's voice, coming as he had suspected

from just beyond their bedroom.

"Elric?" This time it contained a hint of questioning concern, of need.

"Zarozinia?" He arose, grabbing a long robe quickly, wrapping and tying it around his thin, not unmuscular body. Donning footwear as he went, Elric moved towards the bathroom.

She was not there.

"Elric!"

This from the passageway leading from their suite of rooms.

He followed her voice.

"*Elric!*"

Panic in Zarozinia's tone now. Panic also in her husband's mind as he began to run down the long, darkened corridor.

"*Elric, help!*"

The staircase.

A wide twist of marble steps, leading down to the palace's vast entrance hall, lit brightly by large, well-maintained flambeaux, but still there was no sign of her.

"*Elric, help me, please!*"

The voice—half scream—came from outside now, beyond the palace; into the grounds.

Yet the main doors, when he reached them, were barred and bolted from within. *Then how...?*

Wasting no more time puzzling over this, he wrenched all barriers aside and flung open the heavy doors, stumbling desperately out into...

Imrryr.

The Dreaming City, ruined capital of Melniboné, heart of that ancient island nation's sundered empire. The Bright Empire. As was. Razed by a seaborne horde led and, many said, later betrayed by Elric himself.

This city's last emperor spun quickly around, hoping to see behind him the gaping doors to Karlaak's grand palace.

Nothing but an endless sprawl of shattered, fragmented buildings, charred remains.

I dream...

It was Elric's only thought.

This vision could not be anything else.

But he knew that even dreaming, he and more importantly his wife could still be in great peril.

"Zarozinia!"

His cry died instantly in the brittle, dusty air, stifled as it left his lips, as if someone or something did not want it to carry.

"*Zarozinia!*"

He looked around, trying to get his bearings among the ruins.

Little of the rubble gave any hint of where in Imrryr he stood.

None of the great towers was still standing, which only added to the scene's dreamlike quality, for he knew that several had avoided total collapse following the reavers' sacking of the city.

Elric's enfeebled eyes sought what was left of the Tower of B'aal'nezbett, scene of his greatest crime.

He began to recognize where its remains were supposed to be, but they were missing. At the spot where its partially destroyed stairway, if nothing else, should have been visible fairly close by, the ground was devoid of any débris at all. A hollow seemed all that there was in the tower's place, its sides dropping away sharply so that he could not see what might lay at its bottom.

Now that he had a point of reference, Elric turned again to see if he could discern the Tower of D'a'rputna in relation to the other. Where its charred shell should have been there was nothing but a second vast indent where the earth fell away from his line of sight.

He stood, feeling helpless, all but equidistantly between the two pits.

"Zarozinia!"

"*Elric, please!*"

But the cry which came from behind him, from the first hollow he had discerned, was not that of his wife. It was a voice he recognized, but it was an impossible one. The voice of a ghost.

"*Elric, help me, please!*" This time it was Zarozinia, and came unseen from the other deep, dark indent.

He looked around for a raised area, any vantage point from which he could see the sources of the two desperate pleas. There was a collapsed building to his right; he ran towards it and began to clamber up the rubble.

As he reached the pile's summit, he could see nothing in the pits at first but black, viscous-looking fluid. It writhed as if alive, sentient, deadly.

"*Elric, please!*"

The other voice, the voice from his past, the dead voice. He stared again in the direction from which it came. Struggling to the liquid's surface now, fighting for breath, there she was…

Cymoril.

His cousin. His first beloved. She who was to have been his Melnibonéan bride, had she not died at Elric's own hand in the Tower of B'aal'nezbett, on the point of his cursed runesword Stormbringer, thrust onto it by his other cousin, Cymoril's brother, the evil Yyrkoon even as he, too, died by the same blade.

If Elric had any doubts before now, that he dreamed this entire scene, they dissipated with the sight of long-dead Cymoril imploring him to rescue her from this lake of sorcerously animated slime.

"*Elric!*"

"No! No, Cymoril. This is not real. You are dead. I… I killed you."

"Not so, my love. Not so. I live. I know not how, but I live."

"You cannot."

"But I do. I love you, Elric. Save me, please!"

129

"I…"

From the other submerged hollow: "*Elric!*"

He spun around again, in danger of toppling from the unsteady mound of débris.

Zarozinia, now, was fighting to stay afloat in the other direction, the other pool.

"*Elric, save me, please!*" she cried.

"*Elric!*" called Cymoril from behind him.

He half-staggered, half-fell down the side of the collapsed building's ruins, landing painfully at their base.

Struggling to his feet, Elric placed his hands over his ears but still both women's voices penetrated his brain, each screaming for salvation.

Somehow he knew—*if* he were to believe at all that Cymoril was indeed alive—that he had the chance to save only one of them. The other, in the time that it took, would die horribly beneath that foul, writhing fluid.

Elric knew this. He accepted it wholly, as he took for granted always the warped logic of dreams.

He knew this, and he accepted this, and he realized that he had to decide between them, between the only two women in the world he had ever truly loved.

His arms fell limply to his sides, and he sobbed.

In agonies of both body and mind, Elric took his first faltering steps in the direction of…

II

"Elric!"

The Albino stops and looks around.

It is dark—not just a moonless dark—it is black. He is cold, shivering.

On a featureless horizon, a crack of light begins to show, which soon blossoms and swells to fill and illuminate the place where he now finds himself. It is not sunlight, yet neither does it seem artificial.

He stands on some kind of immeasurable plain, which

is utterly devoid of anything but Elric. The light does not even cast a shadow to share this barren world with him, if world it is. What he stands on does not appear to be rock, nor any other substance he recognizes. It is an unbroken, blemish-free, uniformly pale grey.

As, now, is the sky.

Is it even sky? The fact that it is above him is its only semblance to any earthly firmament. A joint between 'sky' and 'land,' if there is one, is imperceptible.

This lack of features begins to hurt his eyes. He closes them, rubs at them, reopens them and stares... straight into the eyes of a woman.

"Ah, madam," says the Melnibonéan, sighing deeply, "now I am certain that I slumber, somewhere. For you, I know, are most definitely dead."

"Lifeless, yes," smiles the woman. "Powerless? No."

But Elric had seen her slain, like Cymoril, or rather he had found her slain. The treacherous Pan Tangian wizard, Theleb K'aarna, had slit her throat, near-decapitating her.

Now she is standing there before him; no wounds, no scars.

The sorceress Myshella, sometimes called the Dark Lady of Kaneloon, sometimes the Empress of the Dawn. Her long, wavy black hair shines on the shoulders of her red sheer-silk dress. This is no corpse. This is no death shroud.

Elric snarls: "So it was some sick whim of yours, was it, *lady*, creating that terrible dream back there, just to enable you to plague me once more?"

"I know nothing of any previous dream, Elric. Only of this one, which admittedly I did need in order to address you."

"Then I am still asleep." It is not a question.

"Of course you are. Still in bed, still in your new palace, still with your... with your child bride beside you."

"Do not presume to judge me, Myshella."

"I do not. I promise you I do not."

"Then what do you want of me?"

"My powers are much diminished, I admit—being deceased will mean that, even for me—but I still work as best I can to aid the forces of Law against those of Chaos."

"*Hm...*" Elric muses. "My own allegiances in that respect are, if anything, even more ambivalent now than when last we met, my lady."

"Then that can only be to our advantage."

"Ours?"

"Of course."

"There may be little doubting that we have been of assistance to each other in the past. But whether those times have ultimately benefited me or you the most, I know not."

"There is nothing I can say to convince you that we work, you and I, towards the same ends. The greatest ever battle between the Lords of Entropy and of Law is nigh. You know that you have some part in this."

"So I am *told*, madam. I do not *know*."

"You still feel that you would like to?"

"Who would not?"

"Most, Elric, I think. You sought such knowledge once before, I seem to recall, in the fabled Dead Gods' Book."

"I did. Unsuccessfully."

"Well, I can tell you this only because you dream, and I can ensure that you will not remember it upon awakening. One of the Dead Gods has begun stirring, and has designs on our realm. This threatens all."

"Why bother to inform me of this at all? Especially if I'll recall nothing of it. The Book is dust. Its authors, by their very name, are beyond remembering what it said, what they wrote."

"Nothing can thwart this particular Dead God's ambitions. That he will come to this realm is written; it is destiny. What happens once he arrives is still to be decided. It will become the opening gambit in the last great battle."

"In which I shall play a part?"

"A key part. That is all I can tell you."

"Then why, I ask again, are you here? What do you want of me, now?"

"Have you heard, Elric, of the Organ of Bones?"

"Of course. It is no doubt a myth, but it is said to lie within the Forest of Souls, which itself surrounds the final resting place of Melniboné's royal line and greatest nobles. Not a necropolis, as such, that place, but one in which all live on after death, together and in harmony—some say that it is, or perhaps resembles, legendary H'hui'shan, the City of the Island which preceded Imrryr the Beautiful—a place where neither Law, nor Chaos, nor even a Cosmic Balance, holds sway."

"And the Organ of Bones?"

"It is said that one of the first ever rulers of Melniboné—perhaps, questionably, even of long-abandoned R'lin K'ren A'a—arranged sorcerously to be accompanied on his journey to the Forest of Souls, when he died, by his Court's most favored composer and musician. This maestro's work was so peerlessly exquisite that the emperor could not face eternity, even in the idyllic Forest of Souls, without it.

"This musical genius, it is said, then designed and constructed a unique instrument, solely for the purpose of entertaining his master and patron. It was, as you may by now have guessed, or I assume you already know, an organ. For its pipes, the maestro collected the bones of every vertebrate creature known to have existed since the beginning of time. Every fish, amphibian, reptile, bird and mammal, from the tiniest frog to the greatest of the Phoorn, Melniboné's dragons. Where any beast was extinct, a fossilized bone was used. Each one was hollowed out by hand to produce a single, distinct note."

Myshella the sorceress has never known the normally taciturn albino to be so loquacious.

He has surprised even himself, and now sinks as a result into a more typical and moody silence, although he cannot stop himself from thinking: *I have no idea how many creatures' bones make up this great instrument, which is doubtless only a myth anyway. How many different beasts have walked this earth? Thousands, naturally. Millions? Billions? I could not guess. The music of the Organ of Bones, if it exists, would perhaps be like no other sound ever heard, as it accompanies one's journey through the Forest of Souls...*

"Tell me, Elric, do you know at all of the instrument's means of amplification?"

"Amplification?"

"Yes, how it transmits its music beyond those skeletal pipes?"

"No. I did not realize that it needed to."

"*Ah*, there is a little more, it seems, to the legend as you recall it. This may be apocryphal, even if the Organ of Bones itself is not, but I read in a grimoire once that in addition to the bones of every vertebrate, the horns of every creature so adorned, the shells of every crustacean, gastropod and such, were all used to amplify the instrument's sound. Not only that, but there is said to be a horn or shell specifically chosen and placed on each plane of existence, which can be used when called upon to transmit the music of the Organ of Bones anywhere in the multiverse."

"To what end?"

"Who knows? A clarion call, perhaps. Or maybe just the whimsy of a long-dead emperor's long-dead tunesmith."

"At the risk, my lady, of laboring a point, or indeed of further wearying my already overtaxed larynx, what has all this to do with me?"

Myshella smiles. "I need you, Elric, to obtain for me one of these fabled horns."

"If it exists."

"Oh, I assure you, this horn is most definitely real. Regardless of the veracity, or not, of the Organ of Bones, not only does the horn exist but it is a key component in the coming struggle. It is also key to your own part in that conflict."

"How so?"

"This artifact is known, or rather it will come to be known, as Roland's horn, the Horn of Fate."

"These are not names that I recognize."

"Neither should you. Yet. The horn, so I gather, was en route to Roland's realm—wherein it must lie until required—

when it was waylaid, presumably by a party foraging suitable candidates for the Organ of Bones."

Elric, in an attempt to avoid what he has begun to see as the inevitability of involvement once again in schemes and machinations beyond his understanding, all in the name of his oft-hinted-at destiny, begins to look around him.

Nothing has changed. They still stand on the same featureless, sunless plain. Neither he nor Myshella has moved, in however much time he has been enduring this overlong and customarily elliptical conversation.

The sorceress seems content to wait as long as it takes for his attention to return to the matter at hand.

Realizing that they are unlikely ever to feel exhausted, physically, in this timeless place, he asks, "And where is it to be found, this horn?"

"Only one person knows its whereabouts: the maestro who commissioned its capture."

"Am I to travel, then, to the Forest of Souls? That is *if* I choose to take up this challenge at all."

"You are."

"It is not a place from which one is supposed to return."

"I can put you on the right moonbeam road, and tell you how to come back from there once your task is completed. You can return, because you will still be within this dream."

"It is many years, my lady, since I last undertook a dream-quest. Such a state does nothing to protect one from harm."

"True. You do not, I notice, carry your runesword."

"No, and neither shall I again. I have relinquished my dependence on it."

Myshella merely smiles a little wryly, choosing to say nothing.

"Stormbringer hangs," Elric adds, "locked away in the armory of Lord Voashoon, my wife's father."

"It is perhaps of little consequence. You are unlikely to need to resort to violence."

"Why? What is the name of this musician?"

135

"No one knows. Perhaps you could call him, like so many of his kind, nothing more flattering than 'Maestro.' But you will recognize him as the only one who can come and go around the Forest of Souls. He is never drawn, as you might be, towards the lure of its center."

"And he will just give me this horn... simply hand it over?"

"Unlikely. But it is said that he is, for whatever reason, incapable of lying. If you ask him the whereabouts of Roland's horn, he will have to tell you."

"And he will know it by that name?"

"Perhaps not. Although all at the Forest of Souls should be aware of the Horn of Fate and what it signifies."

"And what is that?"

"I cannot say."

Elric grows angry. "Oh, I tire of this, Myshella. I tire of you, and of your kind. Puppeteers bore me every bit as much as the marionettes they dangle. One day I might choose just to cut the strings and be done with it all!"

"Such histrionics, my lord, do not become an emperor of Melniboné."

"A prince of ruins!"

"But a Melnibonéan, nonetheless. I cannot force you to act on my behalf, Elric. On our joint behalf. I can only ask you to trust me, as you have trusted me before, and do as I ask. I cannot promise that success will benefit you. I can only tell you that failure will without doubt bring greater torment to those about whom you care."

"*Greater* torment? So there is strife yet to come."

"I thought I had make that clear."

He sighs. "I suppose you have. So what happens next?"

"Close your eyes, Elric."

He does so...

III

"Open them."

He did.

Wherever Elric was, it was not where he had been. He was no longer in Karlaak. He was no longer in Imrryr. He was no longer on that bleak, featureless plain.

He was alone.

Of course he knew, if what Myshella said was correct, that he was in fact still lying in his palace bedchamber.

But Elric was accustomed to such feelings of disassociation. He had spent enough time in the Dream Realms to know that, asleep or awake, he was to all intents and purposes in a real place, where he could encounter real people and real dangers.

It was more than possible to die within a dream, and thus to perish beyond it.

Something that Myshella said now came back to him: "I can put you on the right moonbeam road," she had told him, "and tell you how to come back from there once your task is completed."

But neither of those things had happened.

He had not been placed by her on a roadway of any kind, and he knew no means of getting home from where he was now.

Elric began to wonder if he had not been subject to an interception of sorts; if some other agency had not dragged him away from his destination for its own ends.

He had long since become weary of being hurled around from realm to realm at the behest of beings—some mortal, others immortal—who all claimed knowledge of the Melnibonéan's greater destiny but seemed singularly disinclined to share any such insight.

Wherever he was now, and for whatever reason, it was time to get his bearings.

This was at least a more pleasing environment than the

one he had shared so recently with Myshella.

A deep blue, near-cloudless sky stretched from horizon to horizon, hung with a bright, natural-looking sun.

The tiniest of warm breezes pushed a handful of clouds—puffs of unthreatening white cotton—lazily from left to right. Even the occasional brisk gust proved hardly able to move the albino's long, fine, equally pale hair from his shoulders.

Elric stood on flawlessly green, well-cropped grass; it rose in front of him, so that he was unable to see very far in that direction. Turning he saw that it fell likewise behind him, in a slight and steady gradient, unbroken lawn for as far as his eyes could see.

From somewhere ahead, he could discern the sound of moving water, perhaps a stream or river, and it was towards this that he began slowly to walk.

He felt no sense of urgency. No sense of danger.

The last lord of Melniboné knew all too well that such seemingly peaceful surroundings could prove in an instant to be anything but. Having spent much of his youth on the dream couches of Imrryr, gaining life experience beyond his years and an unequalled sorcerous knowledge, Elric had learned never to doubt his senses, but always to question them. Things—particularly when they appeared at their most pastoral, and especially within the Dream Realms—were seldom what they seemed.

Rather more out of breath than expected, he reached the brow of the deceptively taxing hill and looked upon a valley, at the bottom of which was indeed a river and what appeared to be a winding path leading away from its far bank.

The way down to the water was shady and steep, and Elric once or twice slipped on the lush grass and came close to tumbling most ungainly.

Reaching the river in the end without mishap, he paused again to take in his situation. The valley was dotted with wild flowers of every hue, and the scent from many of them was heady indeed. The water was wide, but shallow, and noisy as it tumbled over innumerable mossy rocks of all sizes, few of which offered themselves up as stepping stones, leaving Elric no alternative but to get wet if he was to cross to the pathway on the other side.

Removing his indoor footwear—he had not embarked on this adventure expecting so much travel—and lifting the hem of his equally unsuitable robe, he walked to the river's edge and stepped into the bracingly chilly water which stung at his aching feet.

Gaining the far side was accomplished, incident-free, and the albino rested for a while on the sunnier slope of the valley, beside a track which appeared to be more or less naturally formed by the treading of a great many people and perhaps their beasts over countless years. It wove meanderingly upwards and, in time, ready to move on, he stood and began to trek along it.

It did not take long for Elric to realize why the path tended to veer from side to side, randomly at first glance. Its twisting ways avoided patches of ground that, although now well overgrown by grass and flowers, had at one time been molten, had bubbled and erupted and then solidified into bizarre patterns. Chaos had at some point held sway here, or had tried and failed to gain dominance. How long ago? he wondered. Had they been actively thwarted, or had the forces of Chaos merely grown bored and moved on?

He realized suddenly that he was missing his friend and comrade, Moonglum the Outlander, who would have enjoyed debating these questions with Elric and no doubt injected some humor into any possible answers with which they might come up.

The two had shared many past adventures, but Moonglum had soon grown justifiably restive after Elric and Zarozinia settled in Karlaak by the Weeping Waste, and had opted to revisit his homeland, Eshmir of the Unmapped East, and Elwher, the city of his birth.

The Melnibonéan felt uncustomarily lonesome, concluding that he would benefit greatly from Moonglum's robust company now, if that were in any way possible.

Which of course it was not.

Elric was sweating profusely by the time he crested the valley's sun-drenched slope. The pathway he was following wound over the top and onwards along flatter, undisturbed ground, in a more or less straight line now towards what appeared in the far distance to be an impenetrably solid wall of brownish green.

The sun had begun to set by the time this 'wall' revealed itself in the half-light to be a dense swathe of trees, packed so closely as to seem one single, vast botanical organism.

Could this, he wondered, while still afar, be the legendary Forest of Souls? Had he all this time been exactly where Myshella wished him to be, in search of a horn said to be a remote component of the Organ of Bones? Did that mythical instrument really exist?

Elric found himself wishing once again for the comfort of Moonglum's down-to-earth approach to all things natural, and especially for the little Eastlander's healthy distrust of all things supernatural.

What was the best course? To march straight along and into the forest as if it were any normal greenwood, or to skirt its perimeter until the make-up and any possible dangers it might present could be ascertained?

The albino, all too used to losing himself and forgetting his woes in action, would normally proceed uncautiously in such a situation as this, ready to resort to violence or sorcery, if need be, in order to combat any peril. But he had to remind himself that he was wholly unarmed, and had no idea if wizardry would be permitted here.

In the end, that immediate decision was taken from him. The sun had already set by the time Elric arrived at the forest's outer edges, and the moon, whilst full and bright, failed utterly to penetrate the flora. Without any means to light his way, he could not move on until morning.

Another indication of existing within a dream manifested itself in his total lack of exhaustion, despite having walked a great many miles that day without resort to the drugs he had discovered in Troos, potions which these days kept him strong and healthy in lieu of dependence on his half-sentient runesword.

So he rested his back against the bole of a gigantic tree, of a type he failed to recognize. The bark seemed soft, almost fleshy, and therefore remained comfortable when leaned upon for the whole of the night which Elric spent watching the moon's stately passage across the sky. The stars were in no constellations that he could name. Wherever he was, it was not his homeland plane.

Eventually, the sun rose, replacing its lunar sibling in a dawn that was crisply cool and refreshing. Although still not feeling tired from the previous day's activity, Melniboné's last lord now ached considerably as a result of his sedentary night.

He bent. He stretched. He massaged stiff muscles, and took in deep breaths of the chilly morning air before striding purposefully into the woods, disturbing as he went a low mist which shrouded the soft, mossy turf beneath his feet.

Although the path that he had followed on the previous day had come to an end, Elric saw no reason not to head towards what he perceived to be the center of the forest. But after a while, having deviated from his straight route more than once in order to avoid areas where the trees grew impenetrably close together, he became thoroughly lost.

Then came the sound.

It was so quiet, at first, that he put it down to his imagination, but it grew gradually, persistently, until there was no doubting the reality of a music so haunting, so melancholic, so pure and so sweet that Elric wept openly as he walked towards it.

But the closer he felt that he got to its source, the more it seemed to surround him, coming now from behind as well as in front and also to both sides. Still he remained drawn in a single direction; the trees themselves seemed to allow this course more readily than any other.

His ears were filled with the exquisite melody; atonal,

polyphonic, yet formed and structured so perfectly that he could imagine nothing else ever moving him to such bewildering heights of emotion. It rose and it fell. It soared. Voicelessly, it sang to him. The song was one of limitless love and hate, loyalty and betrayal, war and peace, of life and of death.

Then it stopped.

Elric stopped.

Before him now was what looked like an organically shaped picket fence. It stretched for as far as his eyes could see in both directions. Its slender, tubular uprights seemed fractionally gradated, increasing almost imperceptibly in height from left to right. Not so tall, at this point, that Elric could fail to step easily over it, but to what?

The shallow mist which had accompanied his trek through the forest rose up just beyond this undaunting hurdle, and thickened so that he could see for no more than a few feet from where he stood.

The silence was overwhelming.

This fence, this fog, even this deathly hush; everything seemed to be warning the Melnibonéan to stop here, to turn about, to flee; nothing good could come of continuing.

He was typically about to ignore these forebodings when from behind him blew up a mighty breeze, billowing his robe about him and throwing his long hair across his face, into his eyes.

When his vision cleared, so had the mist, although the fence remained.

In the distance now he could see a glade in the forest, but this, too, had an unearthly quality to it. The color of everything—all of the flora—between Elric and this clearing faded by degrees until the open space itself was in monochrome.

Then, as if out of nowhere, figures began to appear there.

Indistinct at first, they solidified whilst remaining equally devoid of coloration; tall, haughty-looking men and women in countless numbers; most had high cheekbones in narrow skulls with tapering jaws. Eyes slanted slightly—seeming to look not straight at Elric but beyond him—and their ears, small and close to their heads, were near-lobeless at the bottom, coming almost to a point at the top. Mouths appeared to be full, sensuous and cruel; hands long-fingered and delicate.

They were Elric's ancestors, without a doubt.

As if to prove this beyond question, to the front of the gathering now strode his father, Sadric.

There was a look on the old man's face that Elric failed completely at first to read. It took many moments to realize that it could only be a smile, something in death that had never been present in life.

Sadric turned, held out his hand, and brought forward from out of the crowd a young, staggeringly beautiful woman. Her bearing was sublime beyond measure, and Elric recognized in awe that he was looking for the very first time upon the mother who had died in agony giving birth to him.

He knew her only from a miniature image found amongst his father's possessions after Sadric's death many years later. Any other, larger portraits had been destroyed on the old man's orders.

Of all those gathered there, only she seemed to be looking directly at Elric. Her proud, candid eyes seemed to beckon him, and there was nothing else he could do but to answer his mother's summons.

He stepped towards and began to clamber over the low barrier separating them.

"I really do not think you want to do that, my liege."

The voice, thin and rasping, yet penetratingly shrill, came from behind him. Elric stopped, turned and confronted the unwelcome speaker, who would have been short even before an age-added stoop, whose face and hands were dark and cracked like ancient, uncared-for leather, and whose eyes shone with an unnatural, knowing brightness beneath a single jutting ridge of hirsute brow.

"I apologize humbly, my liege, for having the temerity to interrupt your progress, but your time is not yet here." Despite the wretch's apparent subservience, its voice barely hid an unmistakable sardonic tone.

143

"Do I know you?" demanded Elric.

"Not to the best of my knowledge, my liege, but I know you. Not by name, perhaps, but it is impossible not to recognize one of the royal line."

"And yours?"

"To be honest, my liege, I have long since forgotten the name I was given at birth. I have been known, for many more years than I care to remember, by all who reside here simply as 'Maestra.'"

This was when Elric realized that he addressed not an impossibly aged man, but an equally decrepit woman. Loosely ragged, shapeless garments offered no indication, either way. But it seemed that Myshella's supposed omniscience might not be quite so flawless after all.

"Maestra, is it?" he said insouciantly. "So be it."

She nodded. "My liege."

"Are you, by any chance, responsible for the Organ of Bones?"

"I am. Its creator and its curator, both."

"Then I was told that I might find you here." He turned suddenly, reminded of the gathering of his ancestors, but they were no longer visible. The glade was hidden from view again, behind the re-arisen fog. "This is, I presume, the Forest of Souls?"

"It is, my liege. And that, at your feet, is but a miniscule part of the Organ."

Elric looked down at the 'fence,' seeing it for the first time for what it truly was, a near-endless row of hollowed-out bones.

"These 'pipes,'" continued the old woman, "circumscribe the Forest—perhaps even moving in and out of several dimensions en route—and they enclose the last resting place."

"Of whom?"

"You know of whom I speak—" she paused, seeming resentful—"my liege. It was why I had to stop you from proceeding. Now is not your time."

"How do you know that?"

"Because I know the traits of those whose time it is. You bear no such demeanor."

The last lord of Melniboné accepted this, albeit with a pang of wistful regret that his way had been halted. "I have been told," he said, "that there are horns and shells which amplify this organ's music, that they are to be found on every plane of existence, and that if I ask you the whereabouts of one of them, you are bound to reveal that information. Is all that so?"

"It is. I would prefer not to make such a revelation, as I presume it would mean that you wish to remove the item in question, and that would require me then finding a replacement. This I am always reluctant to do. There is such a delicate balance to be maintained, which hates to be tampered with and is often detrimental to the instrument's well-being."

"This has happened before, then?"

"Rarely, my liege. But when one has lived as long as I, all infringements are taken somewhat personally." The old woman shuffled closer to Elric, whose senses were assaulted by a stench of decay and corruption he had never before experienced emanating from any *living* being. "Which of my prized possessions do you intend to rob me of?"

"It is called," said Elric, ignoring her insinuation, "Roland's horn. So I am told."

She shook her head. "I know it not."

"Sometimes, I gather, it is called the Horn of Fate."

The wretch laughed full in his face, making him reel and gag. "And you travelled all this way to find it?" she sneered.

Elric was unused to such treatment. "Beware, *madam*, lest you anger me. Tell me now where this horn lies—in which realm, on what plane—and why, before I depart, my quest for it amuses you so?"

"Everybody knows of the Horn of Fate," she chuckled.

Except for me, it seems, thought Elric, beginning to lose his patience. "Where may it be found?"

"Why, it is to be found on your homeland plane. My liege."

"Where, exactly?"

She held up one foul-smelling hand. "I can do better than just tell you where to find this particular horn. I can put you on your way towards it, and rather quicker, I suspect, than whatever circuitous method brought you here."

"How so?"

"Follow me, if you will." With which the old woman staggered around and began to hobble in the other direction, back the way Elric had come.

He took one last look behind him before following, at the clearing in the Forest of Souls, but it remained obscured from sight.

They came, after some considerable time and not a few alterations in their course, to stand before what appeared to be a dried-up fountain carved out of a single, solid piece of lapis lazuli of the darkest, deepest blue, dotted and veined with traceries of white and gold. It stood at Elric's waist height, and the shallow bowl was almost as wide across as the whole thing was tall.

"Have you ever seen one of these before, my liege?" asked the maestra.

"Never."

"Its purpose is to transport objects, and even sometimes people, through the dimensions in the blink of the eye."

"*Sometimes* people?"

"There are risks."

"What are they?"

"I know only that a few of those who tried to use such devices in the past have never been seen again. Others arrive precisely where they wish to be, when they wish to be, wholly unharmed by their experience."

"How does it work?"

"You simply place your hands and face in the water."

"But there is none."

The old woman pointed, and Elric saw that now the bowl was filled to its brim with clear liquid. "It is," she said, "your only means—*the* only means—of return from the Forest of

Souls. Place your hands and face in the water, my liege, while thinking only of the Horn of Fate. Let no other thought enter your mind, or you could materialize anywhere in the multiverse."

"I do not know what it looks like, this horn."

"Then you must concentrate on it by name alone. This is trickier, of course. But there is no other way."

Tired of debate, not a little nauseous from too much time spent in the company of this wretch, unable to decide if she could be trusted, but equally unable, it seemed, to come up with a viable alternative, Melniboné's last lord stepped forwards and plunged his hands and face fully into the icy water. He felt a shudder run through the length of his body, doubtless from the shock of the cold, realized that nothing else had happened and pulled himself resignedly upright. He shook liquid from his hands, keeping his eyes tightly shut as he wrung it also from his long, fine hair.

"*That*," he said, infuriated, "was a waste of time!"

IV

There was no answer.

Elric opened his eyes.

There was no old woman.

There was no forest.

Beside him was a bowl made all of lapis lazuli, virtually identical to the other, but nothing else came close to resembling the place he had obviously just left.

He felt no ill effects from his 'journey'—had no recollection of it at all—but was he where he wanted to be?

Suddenly he knew exactly where he stood. There was a sound. Unmistakable. Instantly recognizable. Not the heavenly music of the Organ of Bones, but the constant, mournful soughing of a wind which tugged gently at his robe and still-damp hair.

The Sighing Desert.

It was aptly named; those who heard it would swear that

the breeze blowing endlessly across the region resembled nothing but the weariest of human sighs, a sound audible throughout the barren desert in which few oases or settlements existed.

Some said that this wind gained its voice as it blew through the Ragged Pillars, distant mountains eroded over the aeons into huge columns of red stone. The Sighing Desert was a desolate, ochre wasteland of dusky, shifting sands marred only by a few outcrops of tawny rock.

One such collection of overlarge boulders stood close by, and Elric's attention was drawn immediately towards it as he heard an uncouth voice shout: "There he is, lads, just where we were told he'd be!"

Another sneered: "Not much to him, is there? Hardly worth the effort."

Five poorly dressed but heavily armed ruffians were approaching unwarily, full of the confidence that five long, sharp sabers gave them over their weaponless prey.

"We do as we're told," said the obvious leader, taller and slightly less seedy than his fellows, "and get well paid for our efforts."

There was nowhere to hide, no escape from confrontation, so the albino watched each man carefully, looking for weaknesses, hesitations, possible frailties, all the time wishing that he had Stormbringer to hand, despite his pledge to be rid of the Black Sword for good.

"Gentlemen," he said, seeking to unnerve them with a show of typically laconic bravado, bowing but not for a second taking his eyes from the advancing men, deciding that one particular, unsavory-looking individual sporting an eyepatch was the weak link. This lumpen thug shuffled along in the wake of the leader. How to disarm the one without engaging with the other? They were almost upon the Melnibonéan, now.

Just then the desert's perpetual wind rose higher and harder for a moment or two, blowing red dust around them all like water. Elric took his chance, feinting barehanded at the

148

leader, making the man raise his weapon first in defense and then attack. As it swished down towards him Elric ducked under the blow and charged at the eyepatched ruffian, knocking him onto his back and wresting the saber from his grasp. The turning chief was more of a threat than the fallen man, and Elric slashed his new-found weapon across the leading one's throat, stepping fastidiously aside as blood sprayed from the gaping wound and the body fell forwards onto its supine comrade. This unexpected turn startled the other three assailants into temporary inactivity, allowing Elric to open the stomach of one and sever a leg clean off of another just above the knee. The last man turned and began to run back towards the rocks. A low thrusting sweep of Elric's curved sword skewered the man between the legs and continued up into the abdomen, exiting somewhere near his navel. By the time Elric spun around to deal with the ruffian on the floor, he was already crawling too far away through the sighing sands to bother pursuing.

The last lord of Melniboné stood panting, leaning on the saber, unused to fighting without recourse to the energy provided by Stormbringer, stolen from its victims along with their souls. In his exhaustion, Elric no longer cared about the whereabouts of any horn. He wished only to leave this series of deadly dreams and return to Karlaak.

In this shattered state, he was completely unprepared for the next words he heard.

"*Ah*, Elric, sweetest of my slaves, even at your puniest it seems that you are more than a match for these upstart Men. Doubtless I should have taken more care in choosing from those who would do my bidding rather more willingly than do you in these troubled times."

The voice was disembodied. Then there was a faint aerial buzzing, as of a fly, before a dark, amorphous mass rose swirling out of the sand—formed partly of that substance, partly of writhing smoke—and finally there stood where the mass had been a golden, naked youth of terrifying beauty, exuding an aura of near-limitless power.

"My lord Arioch," said Elric coolly, refusing to avert his eyes from the Duke of Chaos, his patron demon. It was long since he had felt any need or urge to abase himself before this imposing but all too fickle godling.

Arioch, presumably expecting more humility from the Melnibonéan, seemed displeased. His radiant face flared with anger; his skin appeared to writhe like quicksilver, molten flesh, sparking and coruscating through myriad dazzling colors. In the next instant he stood there fully robed in liquid gold, a circlet of scarlet fire around his head, and he smiled, in control of his temper once more, his voice silvery, sympathetic and cajoling as ever: "Mortal morsel, you know that you are my dear one and my darling, my luscious little sweetmeat. My most obedient soul. I love you, as you love me and honor always our ancient compact."

It took all of Elric's resolve not to react as he should to this flattery, throwing himself down upon his knees and begging Arioch's mercy for all time, desperate for even the smallest hint of approval.

"My lord Arioch," he said, aware suddenly that they were not—as they might normally be—conversing in the High Speech of Old Melniboné. "It seems to me that, of late, I have been rather more sedulous in adhering to that compact than have you." This was, he knew, deliberately provocative.

Arioch's red lips pursed, and his voice now rang out like a thousand bells, bouncing from one part of the desert to another and back again, yet always intimate as if those very lips were pressed hard against Elric's ear: "Such a brave little weasel, most courageous of my slaves. Do not anger me, pretty pale one. I may choose to allow more impertinence from you than from any other mortal, but even my benevolent patience has its limits."

Yet Elric was determined to have his say. "I have never been sparing in the blood and souls that I have dedicated to you, Lord Arioch. I have seldom begrudged that aspect of our arrangement, except when it has cost the lives of ones dear to me. In return, I have always expected to be able to call on your aid in times of great peril. But that assistance has been less and less forthcoming, in recent times."

"Events are afoot, my tiny treasure, on this plane as on so many others, and I admit that I cannot always aid you as you might wish. But I remain ever concerned for the interests and activities of my little mortals, and you serve Chaos. You *must* serve Chaos, always. The time is nearing, Elric of Melniboné, when both Law and Chaos will do battle for dominance of the Earth. Your allegiance must be unswerving. Yet in my omniscience I know why you are here, what you seek and for whom you seek it. Do not be tempted by the deceptions of degenerate Law, succulent heart, or I shall love you no longer. Obey me or I shall…"

"I do not serve Law, my lord Arioch, but neither am I over-inclined these days to serve any cause but my own."

The Duke of Hell's laughter was terrible in its facile cruelty. Elric felt a chill to the depths of his own soul. Arioch's eyes widened; they were wise, ancient, insane and evil.

"This horn means nothing to you, my sickly slave. You know that I cannot involve myself directly in the affairs of mortals, but I can offer you *so* much more than some glorified seashell."

Elric's fearfulness was transforming, now, into a hard determination no longer to be a plaything of the gods, but to become a player; not the controlled but the controller. If Arioch was attempting to barter for the Horn of Fate, then it must indeed be an important prop in the coming conflict. Why should he, Elric, care which side possessed this thing? Would either bring surcease to his misery?

It was time to bargain.

"My lord Arioch, what would you give me, that I might be persuaded not to seek this Roland's horn?"

"What would you most desire?"

"Answers."

"Do you even know the questions, little one?"

"I seek answers to the purpose of existence. To know if there *is* any purpose to it. Can an *ultimate* god exist? A Cosmic Balance? Does my life have any direction at all? Is there something greater than the Lords of Chaos and Law? Is there order in the chaotic tumult of the multiverse? *If* our brief existence is in fact meaningless and damned, I can accept that. But I need to know, either way."

"These are questions all mortals ask themselves at times, my Melnibonéan marionette. There are no answers. To have answers to these questions is to become one with the gods, and the gods have no need to question anything."

"Then I think I shall, on a whim, find the Horn of Fate, Lord Arioch, and perhaps see what Law can make of it. You offer me no reasons not to."

Elric could tell that this outcome was one his patron was keen to avoid.

"I can offer you the Dead Gods' Book," said the Lord of the Seven Darks suddenly. "What few answers there might be, they can be found therein."

"That book no longer exists."

"But I know its contents…"

"And you would simply reveal them to me?"

"No. You are all too aware that I cannot answer you directly. You remain my most recalcitrant of servants, and whilst I am unable to punish you directly, either, I can hamper you in your ambitions. I know enough to be able to reconstitute the Dead Gods' Book. The horn you seek is here in the Sighing Desert. It has resided here, unstumbled upon, for many centuries. But it is only a matter of time before you find it. Look. It is there—" Arioch waved a slender, golden hand— "and the Dead Gods' Book is there." Another motion.

Elric saw that the Chaos Lord now stood equidistantly between two pools of foul, black and slimy liquid. On the slithering surface of one there lay a large, plain horn, simple and unadorned but for its attachment to a long silver chain. On the other was an enormous, gem-encrusted book, alive with scintillating color. As he watched, each began slowly to sink into the viscous fluid.

"You have time," said Arioch, "to reach only one of

them, before the other disappears without a trace for ever. Have your questions answered, Elric of Melniboné, or aid petrified Law against your beloved Chaos. The choice is yours."

For all of his adult life, the albino had believed himself seeking answers that might now be at his fingertips, should he choose to follow his patron demon's wishes. The search for those answers had cost him dearly; it had lost him his first love, his city, his empire, and left him outcast and despised by both his old world and the new. Chaos had seldom served him well. He doubted that Law would benefit him any more readily, nor be any more willing to resolve his lifelong uncertainties, the huge conflicts warring constantly within him. But if this new-found determination to take control of his destiny was to have any meaning at all, he must surely begin by breaking the ties that bound him so thoroughly to the past. *I am my own man*, Elric said to himself, *and even if I am not, I can allow myself that illusion.* He looked up at Arioch's infinitely beautiful, expectant, greedy face. Unfalteringly, he took his first steps in the direction of the Horn of Fate.

"*No...*" hissed the stunned Duke of Chaos. "What is the meaning of this?" It was as if this supernatural being, in its unearned pride, had never believed—was incapable even of conceiving—the idea of Elric's treachery. "No, Elric. *No.* Stop. I insist, slave. I command you to stop. Now. *Stop!*"

But Melniboné's last lord stepped gingerly into the black pool, feeling the clinging liquid suck at his legs. The horn was now half-submerged. He would have to hurry, if he was to reach it in time.

Arioch continued to shout and rave. "Oh, you will rue this day, Melnibonéan. Call on me as often as you choose. From this point forth, I shall never again come to your aid. I shall instead offer my patronage to one more deserving, one more loyal, one more..." But the human form this Lord of the Higher Worlds adopted had begun to split and burst apart, becoming unrecognizable and unstable. "*No...*" it whispered once more, before dissipating altogether, leaving nothing behind but the sound of the Sighing Desert.

Elric was up to his chest in cloying slime, but was now able to reach for Roland's horn. He lifted it clear of the pool, slipped it into his robe and, as he did so, total silence descended. He thought for an instant, as he pushed on, that perhaps the region got its name not from the breeze that blew through the Ragged Pillars but from the sound made as it passed through this horn. Was the sighing of the desert in fact a by-product of the Organ of Bones?

But then the winds picked up again, and they soughed as eerily as ever they had before.

Reaching the far edge of the pool, Elric shook this fanciful notion from his mind as he began likewise to dislodge, as best he could, the clinging fluid from his body. It dawned on him that Myshella had failed to inform him of what was to be done with the horn, should he obtain it. Was she due to come to him, he wondered, in order to collect it?

He waited for a while, but nothing else occurred. The slime of the two pools was absorbed back into the sand as if it had never existed. The Melnibonéan began to consider the Horn of Fate. What would happen if he were to blow it, here and now? What was its role in either helping or hindering the complex series of events that seemed about to unfold across the world? It seemed that there was some plane on which the horn must reside at a certain moment, a certain movement of the spheres.

There was still no sign of what was to happen next, and so Elric made up his mind to ensure that neither side should benefit from possession of Roland's horn. The great blue fountain still sat, dark and stark against the shifting sands, and he marched up to it, lifted the horn aloft and threw the thing with all his might into the shallow bowl. *Let it end up where it may!* he thought. But as it hit the water and disappeared, the albino was thrown back by a terrific blast of some sort; all of his breath was torn from him as he flew through the air like a rag doll, hit the ground hard and felt darkness engulf him as he passed blissfully from consciousness…

Elric awakes.

Turning he sees beside him in the bed his wife, Zarozinia, her eyes open, alert and startled.

"You cried out, my love," she says. "Is everything all right?"

He smiles as best he can, wishing to reassure both her and himself.

"Of course. All is fine. Just a bad dream. Vivid dreams. Nothing more. Go back to sleep."

Returning his smile, she places her worried head back on the pillows, closes her eyes, turns towards her husband and lays one small, warm hand upon his chest.

"Goodnight," she whispers sleepily.

Next morning, Elric and Zarozinia, arm in arm, walk and talk leisurely through the beautiful terraced gardens of Karlaak by the Weeping Waste.

They are content.

A light drizzle falls, doing nothing to dampen their mood.

But there comes a sudden commotion from below, as in the street someone is shouting and banging at the palace gates.

A servant hurries up to the couple above, who peer down in the direction of the unseen disturbance. "Lord Elric. There is a man at the gates with a message. He pretends friendship with you."

"His name?"

"An alien one. Moonglum, he says."

"Moonglum! His stay in Elwher has been short. Let him in!"

Epilogue

"That'll do for now, sergeant," said Una Persson. "We know more or less what happens next."

Alvarez zoomed out, and all that remained visible on the

screen was Cawthorn's overall map of the Young Kingdoms.

Mrs. Persson turned towards the newcomer at her side. "Walk with me," she said.

As they left the room she glanced up at a couple of newly installed, cryptic-looking clocks hung high on one wall. "*Hm...* It's nearly 1964," she murmured. "Time is short."

Una and her fellow temporal adventurer strolled under bright, cold moonlight through Ingleton's frosted gardens. They came after a while to stand at a disused fountain carved from one piece of lapis lazuli. Lying half-submerged in the icy water of its bowl was an old, rather battered horn.

She reached to pick it up by its silver chain, and handed it to her colleague. "You have only a few weeks left," she reminded him, "in which to make sure that this is in Roland's realm at the precise moment it needs to be. You understand how important this is… what depends on it?"

"Of course, Mrs. Persson. You can rely on me. I've a brand-new ribbon in the Imperial, and am ready to go."

"Good man. Oh, look. It's snowing." Una held out one hand, letting a few flakes fall onto her palm; the warmth melted them instantly.

"Well, it *is* Christmas Eve," he said. "Very nearly midnight, in fact."

"So it is. Shall we go back inside?"

"I think we should."

After stamping their feet on the coir of the Time Center's doormat, the pair re-entered the control room. Sergeant Alvarez glanced up questioningly.

"All done," said Una, the man at her side lifting in confirmation a bulky brown-paper bag from under his arm.

The sergeant nodded approvingly. "I think this new equipment is going to work out okay, Mrs. Persson. Don't you?"

"I've no doubt about it. Well done—" she glanced again at the wall clocks—"and Merry Christmas."

Alvarez sighed, as contentedly as he was able.

"God help us, one and all."

Paul DiFilippo's career began either in 1977, when his first story appeared in Unearth *magazine; or in 1982, when he quit his job as a COBOL programmer to devote himself fulltime to writing; or in 1985, when his second and third stories appeared in* The Magazine of Fantasy & Science Fiction *and* The Twilight Zone Magazine; *or in 1995, when his first book,* The Steampunk Trilogy, *debuted. Whichever date one chooses, 2006 saw the publication of his 25th book,* Top 10: Beyond the Farthest Precinct, *a milestone of which he was understandably proud. Despite the fact that Paul fully intends to retire in stages over the next 40 years, he has managed to collaborate on* Tales of the Shadowmen *in the past.*

Paul DiFilippo: *The Stealer of Marketshare*

Elric of Melniboné, last Emperor of a once-mighty people, dropped on one knee to the cold stones before Arioch, his patron Lord of Chaos and a most puissant Duke of Hell. Using his scabbarded sentient soul-taking sword Stormbringer in one hand as a prop to uphold himself, the albino said, "But my Lord, I fail to understand why the mechanism of distribution across the empire for these new ethereal 'ghost tomes' concerns you so."

Arioch's ghastly and intimidating appearance today took the form of a multi-tentacled abomination, slightly levitating above the floor, whose manifold appendages brandished all manner of consumer goods, as tokens of the wealth and comforts he could bestow upon his followers. Incongruously, the pullulating deity's voice resembled the smooth and seductive tones of a rich uncle seeking to insinuate himself into the good graces of a beautiful young niece.

"It is not part of your allegiance to me to comprehend my motives or goals, and I certainly do not owe you any explanations. But I am in a generous mood today, and shall indulge your curiosity to some small degree. Suffice it to say that these nebulous scrolls, addictive vessels of disembodied information, so different from the leather and parchment codices of yore, are a new thing upon this old world, and contain the potential for much disruption as well as many riches. As master of all disruptive forces, I must be in control of them! I cannot let the White Lords of Law take the reins from my hands. Especially not that accursed Donblas, my hated rival.

"Donblas has leagued with Myshella, the Dark Lady of Kaneloon, Empress of the Dawn, to hatch and etch these ghost scrolls in many alluring forms. Literate citizens are clamoring for these new productions. But Myshella and her minions have chosen to distribute these potent products willy-nilly, in defiance of my former monopoly on codices, and they greedily charge whatever the marketplace will bear. Consequently, their sales are limited in scope to those who possess sufficient wealth to meet their demands. What short-sighted fools, to forsake a slice of a larger pie for short-term extortion! I, on the other hand, would charge only a nominal fee for each ghost tome, insuring that they penetrate to the multitudes, ensnaring even the hoi polloi in my web of servitude. Now, is that sufficient rationale for you, so that you will undertake my orders without further quibbles or cavilling?"

Elric rose to both feet, his innate royal pride combining with his impatience and the weariness of his unnatural physiology to assert a token independence before this patron from Hell. "Yes, I can understand now why we must act. The forces of Order are not capable of maximizing their own influence and profits from these ghost scrolls, and so it is incumbent on Chaos to show them the way. The old Order, regnant without challenge for so long, must fall."

"Quite so. Now, raise up your armies and be prepared to take the Castle of Kaneloon. By the way, just to make certain you do not have a change of heart and betray me, I am sending my representative to act as your second-in-command. She should arrive at any hour now."

With that cryptic promise, Arioch vanished.

158

Before day's end, unto the dreaming city Imrryr came a blonde, armor-clad woman of immense proportions, a true Amazon. Brought into Elric's chambers, she announced herself as Prïmella, leader of the Amazon tribe known as the "Free Shippers" for their omnipresent fleet of cargo vessels that ranged from the Boiling Sea to the Eastern Ocean.

Prïmella's booming voice hurt Elric's sensitive ears. "Ho, white weakling! It is good that Arioch dispatched me to aid you! I doubt you could master a mouse with a puny physique such as yours. Let us now indulge in some healthy carnal gymnastics to cement our alliance. Perhaps you will derive some strength from my lusty embrace!"

Elric fingered the hilt of Stormbringer as he briefly contemplated sucking out the soul of this annoying woman, the antithesis of his beloved dead Cymoril. But then, with a sigh, he gave in to her blandishments, finding them not quite as unsavory as he had foreseen.

Elric sat upon his halted steed on the dreary dun-turfed plain outside Castle Kaneloon, which reared like a series of cliffs to the sky, at the very edge of the roiling pits of Chaos itself, as if guarding the material world from that inchoate dimension. At his side Prïmella the Amazon bulked, upon the massive drayhorse needed to support her. Their mighty forces stretched away behind them as far as the eye could see.

"Let us try a parley first," suggested Elric. "Fighting should be avoided whenever possible."

"For once I agree with you," Prïmella replied. "We Amazons tend to buy out our rivals with gold rather than assault them."

And so a lone messenger was dispatched, bearing a flag of truce. Some hours later the messenger returned, trailed by none other than Myshella herself, with a small retinue surprisingly constituted: no warriors or diplomats or mages, but rather scribes, proofreaders, compilers, and other members of the inky tribe.

The dark-eyed, majestic and beautiful Empress of the Dawn brought her steed up nose-to-nose with Elric's. Prïmella glared daggers at her opponent, but to no effect.

"Emperor of Melniboné, why do you besiege Kaneloon, a sovereignty which has never done you harm?"

"My Lady, know you this: I do not threaten you out of any personal hostility. It is only at the behest of my patron, Arioch, the genius of disruption. He bids me to deconstruct your empire of ghost tomes, which he feels you have overvalued, to the detriment of a wider dissemination of knowledge."

"Bah! This is mere sophistry! Arioch cares naught for the improvement of the minds of any citizen! He only wishes to amass all power and wealth to himself, rendering the forces of Order feeble and subservient."

"Be that as it may, I can only carry out his bidding, upon pain of tortures indescribable."

The Empress indicated with a wave of her arm the assembled inky tribesmen behind her. "Look upon these humble servants of art and wisdom, Lord Elric. All they ask is a pittance to keep body and soul together, while they pursue their craft. Would you deny them and their brotherhood their deserved remuneration?"

"Now who indulges in sophistry, Dark Lady? I know precisely in what ratio the profits from the ghost tomes are apportioned, and these wretches get but the barest ten percentum, while your coffers receive the rest. Arioch offers them a full seventy percentum. Even at the reduced price he would charge per unit, your scholars would earn much more."

A discontented murmuring rose up among the scribes, proofreaders, compilers, and others, till they were silenced by a loud command from the Empress.

"Do not listen to this agent provocateur! He merely seeks new chattels for Arioch. Once you are under the thumb of Chaos, he will arbitrarily change the terms of your servitude whenever he wishes, for his own benefit. With the House of Kaneloon and Order, you have a legacy of gentlemanly conduct that goes back centuries. Your forefathers sealed all dealings with my ancestors with but a handshake, and their back-list was kept ever in print."

Still reluctant to order his troops to battle, Elric was about to try another line of persuasion when matters were taken out of his hands.

Above the armies of Melniboné, the hideous form of Arioch materialized, writhing like a bucket of worms. Spying this manifestation from afar, the inhabitants of Castle Kaneloon opened their gates and the armies of the Empress poured forth in a rush. They halted not more than a spear's throw from Elric, and above their ranks leaped into being their patron Lord of Law, Donblas the Justice-Maker, a tall, handsome man clad in the finests of silks and metals, with a slender sword at his side.

"Arioch!" bellowed Donblas. "This time you have gone too far! These ghost tomes are my intellectual property, and you may not arrogate to yourself edicts about the manner in which I sell them, nor their worth!"

"Fool!" riposted Arioch. "You are like a man with an infinite well of sweet water, who turns away the thirsty peasants in hope of selling one dipperful to a rich man for a hundred ducats!"

Not lightly receiving that insult, Donblas launched himself through the air at Arioch. The gods met with an enormous explosion of sound and light, sending waves of pressure across the field that knocked heavily weighted horsemen entirely over. The intensity of their battle was such that it utterly unnerved the mortal soldiers. The doughty warriors forgot all enmity and fled in many directions. Nonetheless, thousands on both sides were crushed to a red paste as the deities grappled and struggled.

Panting in an unseemly fashion and disheveled, Elric found himself somehow safely immured in Castle Kaneloon with the Empress and Prïmella. On the plains, the forces of Chaos and Order continued noisily to contend.

"Truly," observed the albino in a sardonic tone, "when dragons fight, the ants are trampled."

Myshella eyed Elric and Primella with a dignified lust stoked by their narrow escape. "Let us retire to my private chambers and discuss such matters, on cushions and with wine. There is naught we mortals can do to affect the outcome."

Primella licked her lips, and Elric nodded agreement. "If worse comes to worst, I can always impale the three of us on Stormbringer, and escape all controversies in death. Sometimes I think that would be preferable to serving either Law or Chaos."

Johan Heliot (not his real name) teaches French, History and Geography in the Haute-Saône region of France. He broke into the field in 2000 with a preference for steampunk and uchronia with La Lune seule le sait, *a novel which won the Rosny Award and gave rise to two sequels. He is also known for his magic realism thrillers* Faërie Hacker *(2003) and* Faerie Thriller *(2005). Johan has also become a major YA writer with* Les Vagabonds de l'Entremonde *and* Ados sous contrôle *(both 2007).*

Johan Heliot: *The Music of Souls*

I had just celebrated my eleventh birthday when the Fender factory produced the first mass-produced, solid body electric guitar in history. But I did not see what a Telecaster looked like until years later when I got interested in that new sound coming from America along with the huge wave of sex appeal that hit me at that magic moment in a man's life when, with a little help from blooming hormones, he does not look at girls in the same way. At the end of the 1950s, believe me, the world was suddenly balled over and I think that it was at that moment that the word "modernity" found its full expression.

Eddie and Buddy were still alive. Elvis was still rocking. And me, I was already aspiring to become a writer, at least one of those guys who lived by their pen for want of doing work. I figured on writing about this phenomenon that was digging an unbreachable generational gap day after day; I wanted to be the first—and the greatest, of course—rock critic of the country. So, I started running around from club to club, living only at night, and wearing out the needles of my record player on the vinyl skin of the thousands of records that filled my furnished apartment.

Therefore, it was inevitable that sooner or later I would meet the Albino and his marvelous guitar. His reputation was spreading from club to club. A handful of recordings to his credit, backing short-lived stars. Plus, like the other professionals who scoured the studios at the time, he was rarely credited on the liner notes. But his sound did not lie, that barrage of electric rage coming out in the rare solos authorized by the brevity of the songs; that unique sound bore the footprint of the Albino.

Nobody knew any other name but that. As for me, in spite of the information patiently gathered in my files—the basis of my future articles, as if I was aware of the magnitude that the phenomenon was going to take, and maybe that was the case, but how could I have seen it when most of the time I was floating through clouds of gin and the weed brought into the city by the Latino musicians?—for me, then, I knew nothing about him. When I got wind that he was going to be there at the end of the year in the basement of the Cavern for a gig with the umpteenth band in the vein of Bill Haley and his Comets, I figured it was the perfect opportunity to be the first one to get a confession out of him for an article I was planning to write for one of those poorly printed and even more poorly circulated rags that were passed around in the clubs' coatrooms—our music did not deserve the honor of newsstands, even less of being called journals.

I was living in London, but I started going to Liverpool in January 1957, the date of the opening of the club and the first shows of the Quarrymen in what was really just a dank, squalid cellar. I showed up at the Cavern when the employees were heading back to their happy homes, my pen and notepad in one pocket and a bag of weed in the other. I elbowed my way to the tiny platform that served as a stage in the back of that crudely converted basement where dozens of slick youngsters were gathered, their eyes burning with fever in those still daunting days for anyone with less than twenty springs on their counter. I had been in plenty of brawls in this kind of place; danger was an integral part of the attraction; letting off steam was not reserved only for the musicians.

A basic drum set—a snare and a hi-hat that had seen better days—took up half the platform. A portable amp faced the audience on the left side. A mic stand was planted in front, an upright bass leaned against the stone wall, right side. Cigarette smoke drifted under the low ceiling, the only special effect allowed by the club's management. I dove into a corner, next to a pillar, notepad in hand, and waited, giving the coded nods to a few little punks I knew who were used to seeing me where things were happening and who considered me almost "one of the gang."

Then the musicians showed up to whistles and hoots. They wore fitted, bright purple jackets and had bowl cuts down to their eyebrows. The drummer squeezed onto his stool, his back against the damp wall. The bassist caressed the strings of his instrument while the singer adjusted the mic and checked the connection to the amp. You could see they were scared stiff for their first show, even if they were forcing themselves to look surly. But I had already lost all interest in them because the Albino had just made his appearance, coming through the curtain that separated the stage from the room reserved for the artists—barely a closet set up next to the platform.

He was wearing the most incredible costume I had ever seen, everything tailored in white leather, hugging his skinny limbs like a second skin. His presence alone was enough to quiet the audience. Everyone was watching him, an unimaginable specter come out of the underground night. Me, I stared at him unabashedly, hypnotized by his charisma.

Until my gaze slid down to the instrument he was carrying on the shoulder strap, clinging to his bony side, its neck along his thigh, its curved body perfectly molded to the shape of his torso.

I had never seen a guitar like it. I knew all the models on the market, which were not many at the time. Gretsch, Gibson, Fender and a few others shared the new clientele, a long way from the refined, acoustic demands of jazz musicians. Blues guitarists, as well as rock, the bawling little brother, preferred solid instruments, easy to take apart when they needed to replace something, and practical for traveling. That's how the Telecaster got popular, then the Strat a little later, among most of the musicians—at least those who did not go the way of Chuck Berry! Moreover, in those years no one was out there personalizing their bread-and-butter, not to mention destroying it on stage. One glance was enough for any seasoned guy in my business to recognize the make and model of a guitar that was—or not—about to set his ears on fire.

But here I was stumped. The Albino had a one-of-a-kind guitar, even if it looked pretty much like the work of Leo Fender, no doubt about it. Certain details could not lie: like the black Bakelite pickguard, which Fender gave up in 1954 in favor of the more ordinary white plastic; the "butterscotch" varnish on the body made of a single block of wood (usually birch); and above all, visible on the bridge, a series of lead pickups form the early days that are worth their price in gold today among the stars of the rock business… If you stopped at that you would have thought you were dealing with one of the first Telecasters made at the beginning of the decade. Except that a bunch of things were all wrong. First of all, the neck was too long and thinned out at the end, like it was sharpened to a point; it must have been a good foot and a half longer than normal. And then there was the narrow body, shaped like one of those pin-up girls painted on the hoods of some hot rods on the other side of the Atlantic. Lastly, there was far too much metal on the surface of the strange beauty.

I did not have time to wonder about the mystery of this marvel's fabrication. With no warning they started in on a muddled but sincere cover of "Peggy Sue." I quickly forgot about the singer's unconvincing performance—apparently he had not reached maturity and his voice broke on the high notes—and the rhythm section too, respectable at most. Like most of the other young groups put together in those days, this one would hardly survive the pop wave rising out of the port of Hamburg thanks to the four from Liverpool.

No, these three kids could fall into oblivion the next day without the history of rock feeling a bit shaken. But their guitarist was another story altogether! From the first notes, the first chords struck on the varnished wood by his long, white fingers, I felt it clear as a bell that this sound, this style would not be surpassed for a long time—imitated, plagiarized, yes, in the best cases equaled by a chosen few... I am thinking of Jimi on the one hand and Jimmy on the other, the Black and the White, who were going to set fire, in their turn, to the 1960s and 1970s, each paying homage to the Albino in their way, without ever even knowing that he existed!

But let's not get ahead of ourselves. That night the concert lasted an hour, time for a dozen cover songs and a few less original pieces but without any originality, to say the least. The most intense time of my life. And I was not the only one to think so, as the fervor (I don't see another word for it) of the young punks in leather jackets proved, stamping at the front of the stage, pounding on the platform with their fists, hassling the musicians with ecstatic energy, sweat pouring down their faces, which were deformed by a kind of pagan grace... No, I am not exaggerating. As a great admirer of the Beat Generation, I had knocked around outside of Albion, taken part in certain ancestral pilgrimages in Southern Europe, witnessed the procession of some fanatical sects in the Far East. Now, what I was seeing under the ceiling of the Cavern was absolutely no different from all the mystery worship. The Albino and his guitar were causing this effect. Even Jerry Lee standing up and playing his burning piano had not got a reaction like this...

As soon as the last note escaped, the Albino slipped away. What had to happen happened. The excited audience rushed the stage, shoved aside the poor band members and knocked over the microphone and the instruments. In such a cramped space the struggle turned into a free-for-all brawl. While the club's muscle was busy calming down the overheated crowd, I made my way to the exit. Outside I took a few deep breaths of fresh air. I did not realize what condition I was in: I, too, was in a sweat.

Then I went around the block and down the alley to the "artists entrance", which was, in fact, the door of a squalid corridor that was used to take out the garbage—sometimes a deadbeat customer. I knocked three times fast and the door cracked open. I slipped through my bag of weed, which was snatched up right away by greedy fingers. Two seconds later I squeezed inside.

"Go quick, man… I'm taking a big risk," a voice from the shadows behind me warned.

I answered without turning around, "Don't worry, Hank, I just want to talk to him a little. No one'll know anything."

I headed for the only source of light, a grimy bulb that was shining above another door stuck in the brick. I hesitated for a moment, not knowing exactly how to proceed. Finally I decided to risk it all. I burst in and introduced myself at the same time.

"Hello, I'm Mike Moore, I write articles for music magazines, I just saw the craziest show of my life and I've seen plenty of them, believe me."

The Albino did not even notice my presence. The chick kneeling between his thighs neither. What I saw of her, a butt and a neck pumping with the same up-and-down motion, told me enough about her skills for me not to wonder about her. I let her finish her blowjob by waiting patiently on the side, sitting on a case of beer. It was quick. Not for an instant did the Albino show any emotion, even at the moment of climax. This guy, I was thinking, was colder than a block of ice, and almost as transparent.

He opened his mouth only when the door had closed behind the girl. "I don't give interviews."

I lit a cigarette to give my hands something to do besides tremble slightly. That voice! Today the goth groups have popularized that voice from beyond the grave to the point of mockery, but at that time, it really froze the blood in my veins, especially as it echoed through the darkness of a cellar that had been hurriedly rechristened a "dressing room".

"I just wanted to talk with you for a bit. I won't write anything, I promise." Compared to his, my voice seemed as frail and fragile as the singer I had heard a little earlier. This thought kick-started me with a question I was dying to ask, "Why are you playing with this kind of group? I mean, they're not at the level, at your level…"

"I earn a living, that's all. That's how it works here."

"Here? You're not from around here? That's news to me."

The Albino did not respond. I decided to change the subject.

"Tell me about your crazy guitar. I've never seen anything like it!"

"It's late and I'm tired. Thanks for your visit, Mike."

The right and polite thing to do was expected of me, but I did not take my leave. Before going I put one of my business cards on the case of beer that I was using as a chair. "Call me in London if you want to talk some more," I said. "And again, bravo for tonight."

He said nothing. I left to catch the train for the capital.

I was not expecting to hear anything from the Albino. I was pretty grouchy when the telephone rang in the lobby, at dawn, waking up the whole building. My landlady's sour voice ordered me to answer the phone.

Ignoring the dirty look she gave me, I grabbed the receiver from her hands, "Hello?"

"Mr. Moore? Do you want to continue our conversation?"

At first I did not get it. Then I emerged from the limbo of sleep. I remembered the electrifying concert given by the Albino at the Cavern almost a month earlier. The voice from beyond the grave, even if its echo was muffled by the poor quality of the phone line, brought back to mind our first, too brief encounter.

"Gladly."

"Well, meet me in an hour. And read the papers before-hand."

He gave me the address of a café down on Ashbury and hung up. I bounded up the stairs, put on the first presentable clothes I could dig up in the shambles of my room, and went back down to the street just as quickly. I hustled to the news rack on the corner and snapped up a paper—my hand was shaking when I put the coin in the slot. I did not know why. A premonition, maybe.

Standing in the middle of the street, I skimmed through the newspaper feverishly. After scanning the headlines a few times I finally saw the article, barely a paragraph really. It reported the discovery of three corpses in Liverpool, in an apartment rented by the week. I would have gone right by it if a detail, fortunately standing out in the subheading, had not caught my attention: the victims formed the main part of a "rock music group" that was getting ready to record on vinyl after a noteworthy show at the Cavern—noteworthy because "causing trouble" the author of the article pointed out mali- ciously. The journalist added that the "pathetic" state of the bodies led them to suspect drug abuse. He concluded by say- ing that the police were searching for the supposed fourth member of group who had gone missing: the guitarist.

Needless to say I was in a funny mood when I got to Ashbury on time for our meeting. The Albino was sitting in a corner of the café, facing the entrance, easily spotted, even if he had left his white leather costume behind in favor of a tra- ditional suit, impeccably tailored, vermillion and ochre.

"Do you have an explanation?" I asked as a greeting, lay- ing the newspaper open to the appropriate page on the table next to his cup of tea.

"The question is… are you ready to hear it?"

I saw the guitar case, almost as tall as its owner, stuck upright between the table and bench. I sat across from him, ordered a coffee and eggs and said, "I'm all ears."

"I asked about you, Mike. They told me that you were unbeatable in everything about rock 'n' roll. That you know every recording, every group, etc. What do you know about the bands I was part of?"

Caught short, I had to get my thoughts together before answering. "Well, the least I can say is that none of them have seen any glory yet. You took part in a dozen recordings for as many groups. Now that I think about it, none of them ever put out any others."

"What's your conclusion?"

I shrugged my shoulders. They brought me my eggs and coffee. "Every week there's a new imitator of the King. And another disappears in failure. Despite the incredible quality of your playing, something doesn't click. And since most musicians are young married men or anyway not independently wealthy, they resign themselves to going back to work to pay the rent. I see it everyday!"

The Albino pointed his long index finger at the newspaper article. "Do you see that everyday, too?"

"I don't understand."

"Your activities leave you little time to follow the local news, right?"

And before I could ask him what he meant, he started telling me his story. I listened to him, so fascinated that I let my coffee go cold and my eggs get hard on my plate— anyway, what I heard made me lose my appetite.

Silence followed, broken by the echoes of a few conversations from the other customers in the café. For a long minute I could not stop looking at the guitar case, from which an evil glow seemed to be emanating—certainly the fruit of my imagination, at least that is what I tried to tell myself! I did not know if I was dealing with the nicest, nutty pathological liar that one could imagine, or, from a particularly frightening perspective, with the worst modern imitator of Jack the Ripper that the City could produce from its black brick bowels...

I decided to meet him on his own turf. "If all this true," I instinctively lowered my voice, "if everything you just confessed to me (and I emphasized that word) is the truth, then you should realize that it's my duty to inform Scotland Yard."

The Albino just smiled. "Come on, Mike, you know very well that you won't do anything." He did not even consider being offended that I might not believe him.

"Why make such a confession to me? What do you want from me?"

Again that smile—an open wound in the bloodless pallor of a corpse. "I need a faithful companion who knows my story and can report it."

I played along with him, even if he did seem to be a lunatic, the victim of too much drug use. "Why not just tell it yourself, if that's what you're asking me to do?"

"I don't have the necessary talent. My talent lies elsewhere, as you've seen. And then again, I won't be here much longer."

I started to react like a journalist, not knowing if it was a good or bad thing, but he had piqued my curiosity. "You're going abroad? A tour outside England?"

He nodded. "Quite far, yes. And I won't be back."

"Because your mission here is fulfilled, is that it?"

This time he shook his head. "You're not taking me seriously, Mike. It has nothing to do with a mission! Didn't you understand what I told you?"

He seemed upset. I could have sworn that I saw the guitar case glow more brightly. I straightened things out. "I believe you, yes. Soon you'll complete your harvest. The curse that's on you will be lifted and you can go back home."

I could not believe my own ears. However, I must have spoken with sincerity because the Albino seemed to relax. And it was almost with good cheer that he ended our interview. "Great, Mike. We'll meet again soon for a little demonstration."

He got up, grabbed the case, which was reflecting nothing now but the dull light from the ceiling bulbs, painted red and blue, and he left.

I realized then that even if I wanted to turn in a dangerous, criminal madman to the police, I would have been unable to give his name or address. Not to mention the fact that the weird description of him would surely bring the suspicion of every inspector in the Yard onto me as being a little unbalanced…

Over the next few days I had a hard time concentrating on my work. The records I listened sounded uninteresting to me—in truth, most of them were, except for the rare imports from the United States that cost me an arm and a leg, among which one surprising concentration of adrenaline and black nitroglycerine just over five feet tall and appropriately called Little Richard—the articles that I got out of them had lost all their "pep."

The Albino's confession was taking over my thoughts, consuming my energy. I could not take it anymore, so after a useless period of voluntary confinement, I gave up the record player and the typewriter and went out in search of information. I just had to find someone who could tell me more about the Albino, otherwise I was going to start thinking I was crazy.

I jumped on the first train to Liverpool and bit my fingernails the whole trip, which took almost all afternoon. I got to the coast of the Irish Sea around five o'clock. It was too early for the Cavern to be open, but Hank, the bouncer whose palms I greased to get in the "artists entrance", lived in a dump that was crappier than mine, a few hundred yards from the club. I had been over to his place a few times to supply him with weed. I should have told him I was coming, but I was too excited. Too bad if my unannounced arrival cramped the bastard's style.

I knocked on the door in vain. However, the sound of a BBC announcer was coming through the wood. Hank must have been high and listening to the radio, a constructive activity that took up most of his time on his nights off.

I yelled, "Hank, it's me, Mike. Open up, damn it!"

173

Hopeless. I decided to let him come back down to earth and try again in an hour. In the meantime, I would sit my ass on a stool in one of the many dives that were open before the legal time, that were all over the back alleys of the neighborhood. I had barely taken ten steps down the hallway when I heard a terrifying scream behind me, immediately followed by a sound that was both horrible and harmonious at the same time, easily recognizable to a practiced ear—but which, at the time, must have bordered on monstrous cacophony for everyone else: the electric shrill of an amplified guitar riff, warped by a distortion effect that seemed to stretch it out to infinity, like a string of sonic chewing gum being pulled out of the devil's mouth.

An inimitable sound at the time, imitated a million times since.

I did not think. I charged, shoulder first, and busted the lock, crashing through the door. I froze inside the dump. The spectacle was worth its weight in gold. Hank was curled up, half naked, on the linoleum, next to the gas stove, in the fetal position. He was stretching his arm out in supplication, an arm so emaciated that the bones were clearly visible under the fabric of skin, which had turned dirty gray. The rest of his body was in such pathetic condition that it is not worth talking about—I've seen corpses in better shape!

Hovering over the dying bouncer, the Albino in his magnificent white leather suit was brandishing his guitar, the end of its neck aimed at the victim's throat. Flabbergasted by what I was seeing, I could not figure out if the electric cry of death was coming from the vocal chords of poor Hank or from the strummed chords of the guitar. But it was not possible because it was not plugged in. And I saw no amplification system in the room!

Then the Albino realized that I was there. He struck another chord and casually swung his instrument to the side, where it poised like I had seen it at the start of the show given at the Cavern: clinging to his groin like a strange musical sword hanging from a strap.

Obviously I thought right away about the incredible story that he had told me. I asked, even if I knew the answer, "What's going on?"

"Stormbringer drank the poor thing's soul," the Albino admitted. "What could I do? I warned you. I'm not the master of my weapon. It demanded its due."

I assimilated the information. I had to force myself not to scream. Of the millions of questions that rose to my lips, the only one that came out was, "Why Hank?"

"It's your fault, Mike. You shouldn't have got him involved the other night. You piqued his curiosity about me. He wanted to question me, too."

I let a few seconds tick off before asking another question. "Is that the fate that your damned Stormbringer is also planning for me?"

The Albino looked surprised. "No, Mike. I already told you what it expects of you."

"Yeah," I snickered. "Play the faithful companion who has to report the exploits of the hero… Shit, go fuck yourself, sick bastard! This is murder!"

"You're right. That's why I suggest we don't stay here. The neighbors have already called the authorities."

That was common sense. The Albino put his guitar away in the case, which was lying on the ground away from the corpse, and then, without a last look at Hank's carcass stripped of his soul, we left the building. The doors of the other rooms stayed closed as we went by, but I easily imagined the tenant's ears glued fast to them. In this kind of neighborhood, no one gets mixed up in the life of his neighbor, at least not directly.

We walked side by side down the crowded streets, in silence, him majestic in his immaculate suit, his guitar safe in the case he was carrying; me haggard, disoriented, my brain about to explode.

I do not know how, but we finally landed in a pub that had just opened, somewhere near the port.

I could not even touch my pint. The Albino, on the other hand, drank calmly. I managed to gather the thoughts that were jostling around in my head.

"How did you know that I was going to turn up at Hank's?"

"I didn't have the slightest idea. But you showing up there at the moment when his soul was leaving him was not by chance... any more than you being attracted to the music of souls in general."

There I gave in. "The music of souls? Now what the bloody hell is that?"

He sighed wearily, just like, I supposed, anyone who was about to repeat for the thousandth time their version of a story to an incredulous public.

"It's the same thing everywhere, Mike. Everywhere I go, a traveling companion shows up, a chosen one, call it what you want. Sometimes it's a warrior, sometimes his role is more modest, like with you."

I was astonished. "Because it's not the first time you've been a victim of this kind of curse?"

This time he did not sigh, but I saw an infinite sadness in his eyes, despite the blood-red glints of his glare. "It has happened so often that I can't really remember how many times."

"But," I objected, "since you... since Stormbringer (I lowered my voice and nodded toward the guitar case) swallows its fill of souls in each world, why do you keep traveling like this?"

The Albino shrugged his lean shoulders. "Don't try to make sense out of the will of Chaos," he said.

And this, far from clearing things up for me, made me more lost. I preferred to get back on familiar territory and get him into the music trip. "OK, I'll give you that. So, in this world here (with a sweep of my hand I indicated the pub and beyond, Liverpool and the rest of the universe) I have been appointed to be your travel companion. You admit that's it's not by chance, that my taste for rock compelled me."

"You're sensitive to the music of souls," he repeated, as if this was supposed to clear things up for me.

I understood that I would not get anything more out of him. Before he left I asked him, "What's going to happen now?"

"I'm going back to the studio. I need to earn a living. And Hank's soul shouldn't stay a prisoner for too long."

He paid and left.

I decided to stay and get drunk before going back to London.

The following week I received a package from Camden, from number 3 Abbey Road to be exact. Inside was a record with four songs, the first recording of an unknown group: The Blue Foxes. Don't go looking them up, I have made sure to destroy all the copies that had escaped the scrapper. These little guys had adopted the look raging at the time, black leather get-up and silver chains around their necks, popularized by Gene Vincent after moving to England recently. Musically they cloned their idol, not too badly either, but the brilliant creator of "Be-bop-a-lula" was far enough ahead of his time to hold out for a few years to come before the decline…

Of course, the Albino was again not credited on the sleeve. He did not even appear on the cover photo. But I doubted whether the pouty runt who was posing with the huge, black and fire-red 1956 Byrdland in his mitts was the origin of the sonic wave that almost drown me when the needle reached the solo that was squeezed in between two dull verses.

My eyes teared up. An icy hand closed around my heart. Those few notes strummed with a kind of confused, almost casual savagery were exactly the thing that I could imagine coming out of the poor soul of a misfit like Hank.

So that is what the Albino meant when he talked about not keeping it a prisoner. The musician from another world, or maybe the demon in the form of a guitar that was imposing itself on his will, set fire to man's most precious possession. It was translated by a never before heard electric scream, the music of souls, which I and a few other amateurs called the spirit of rock. I was no longer surprised at the fervor of the fans during the show at the Cavern. The guys in leather jackets were soaking up, in their instinctive way, a little of that primal energy contained in the metallic flights of their guitar hero, enough to put them in a trance.

The image of Hank's corpse, emptied of its vital substance, came to mind. As well as the article about the death of the band members whom the Albino had played with.

"Oh no… Bloody hell!"

I just got the meaning of the message he had sent me. A signpost for the "travel companion", an item for future papers that would be my responsibility to write as a witness of his passage among us.

The Blue Foxes were the next on Stormbringer's list.

I ran down the stairs to the telephone on the first floor. I asked for the studio on Abbey Road in Camden. With no problem I go in touch with the secretary of George Martin who, since the beginning of the decade, had held the reins of the business. George was particularly well-known for his recordings of the two Peters, Sellers and Ustinov, but he remained open to new sounds and had understood that the young people born with the war wanted to listen to something other than the soup being spooned out by the BBC—so he had just signed Cliff Richard who was not really what the rockers were waiting for, but the 1960s promised riches to come…

"I need the address of those guys, the Blue Foxes… Yeah, it's really neat, I figure on doing a great write-up, I'd love to interview them…"

A minute later I had the address of each of the band member's parents—none of them were old enough to live on their own.

"Thanks, babe! You're an angel."

I hung up and went to catch a cab. The boys lived in a suburb, which did not surprise me, most of the novice rockers were working class boys. The intellectuals were still getting off on jazz, they would not bow down to pop until a decade later, with the disastrous results that we all know.

In short, I got to the first address a half hour later. A little, red brick house like hundreds of others that are obediently lined up along the street that is like the thousands of other streets around it. Always the same thing, in fact: how can we be surprised that the rage to shake up the world enters the minds of kids raised in such an environment?

Mr. and Mrs. Farrell welcomed me with a balanced mix of politeness and suspicion. I was not shown into the living room, but they told me that Johnny, the boy, was with his "bandmates".

"Oh really? And where might I find the boys, please?" When need be, I knew how to act like the worthy offspring of a nation who could still stand up straight, with the help of a few well-placed broomsticks.

"There's an abandoned warehouse near the docks… I don't know the address, but I can explain how to get there."

Mr. Farrell gave me directions. I wrote everything in my notepad, very professional. That must have made a good impression on Mrs. Farrell who looked at me in a better light.

"Honestly," she said, "they're going to talk about Johnny in the papers?"

I nodded, all the while hoping that it would not be in the obituaries. I thanked the guitarist's parents—I had ended up at the home of the little guy with the Byrdland, but I no longer thought it was by chance—and got back in the taxi. I had to convince the driver to get him to go to the dodgy area of the docks, which cost me my last quid.

After another half-hour lost driving around in circles on the wharves of the Thames, I finally found the warehouse described by Mr. Farrell—he had worked there in his younger days, he told me, apparently not just a little proud of the upward social mobility that had propelled him into the brick paradise promised to working class heroes after a life spent in sweat and labor just so as not to die of hunger.

I sent the taxi away. I did not want any possible witnesses. The place was deserted. Rust-colored grass was growing out of the broken pavement. The front of the warehouse was dank and sweaty. The seagull turds had repainted the walls Pollock-style. I heard the vague, distant sound of port activity, but it might just as well have been coming from another planet.

The ideal setting for a one-night, private show—on the program this evening: music of the souls.

I walked around the building looking for an entrance. I stopped at the corner when I heard the first faint voices coming from inside. I was arriving in the middle of an argument; it sounded like things were heating up between the Blue Foxes. I found the service entrance unlocked around the corner and entered on tiptoes, slipping in behind a pile of dented barrels. The rest of the space looked empty as far as I could tell in the shadowy light. The three musicians were standing in a corner under a metal overhang that must have housed the erstwhile office and that was accessed by a flight of spiral stairs.

I was right; sparks were flying between the boys. Johnny was facing off against his singer while the drummer was calling both of them names—I recognized them from the cover photo.

"It's crazy! You're whacked, mates!"

"Shut up, Jeff… You agreed, too, didn't you?"

"Yeah, but this fucking… vampire is pissing me off!'

I was starting to get it. Until now I had not thought too much about why the Albino sacrificed the groups he played with. If Stormbringer needed his lot of human souls, why not go shopping on the streets or among the down-and-outs whose disappearance would not even raise an eyebrow at Scotland Yard? Three words provided the answer: Music of Souls. The demon in the shape of a guitar fed on the vital energy of rock. Well, that shined in only a chosen few at the time and hell, outside of Nashville where else except for the working class slums of England could you find such a bumper crop of authentic rockers?

I could very well imagine the deal struck by the Albino. A few chords strummed on his guitar must have easily convinced the boys to hire the magician, who seemed to have dropped out of the sky. Once he had them in his clutches a highly charged show or a first recording would be enough to galvanize the kids so that their souls would be to the demon's taste. And then…

"I hope I'm not the source of your disagreement."

The Albino's voice echoed through the metal hangar. You would have thought it fell from the sky! The boys immediately stopped wrangling. I could not help jumping out of my skin. He had been there from the start, hiding out over their heads in the disused office that looked out over the inside of the warehouse.

Disregarding the winding stairs, he jumped to the ground and landed nimbly in spite of the instrument slung over his shoulder.

"No, it's not that," Johnny defended, "it's just that…"

"Well, it's time to settle accounts," the Albino stated.

I knew exactly what was going to happen since I had been allowed a demonstration at Hank's. But I stood petrified with fear. That was not the case for the drummer, Jeff, the most belligerent of the Blue Foxes. I saw him search his coat pockets and pull out something thin and sharp. The dry click of the switchblade made a hell of a racket in that huge, empty space.

"Okay, man, come a little closer…"

He did not have to show off. He did not even look especially worried. His friends either. Strength is in numbers, it seemed—there were four of them.

Johnny tried to smooth everything out. "Listen, mate, it's just that we don't think what you're asking is right. I don't know what you are, maybe really a vampire, maybe nothing but a lunatic, in any case I know that you've got a gift as far as strumming… But we're moving on. We made a record and we want to continue. We could go places together if you weren't so cracked. But I believe we'll have to travel the rest of the road without you."

"You met me on the road. I was standing there at the crossroads," the Albino hummed, parodying an old blues tune. "You always have to pay your dues."

Jeff attacked without warning. I saw the blade sink into the white chest and come back out. The Albino barely flinched. He grabbed the body of his guitar and used it like a double-edged sword, wielding it in a circular motion that severed the drummer at the throat. The head soared up and disappeared in the shadows before flopping onto the floor in the back of the warehouse.

Strombringer's strings vibrated as it cut through the air and flesh.

Johnny and the other Blue Fox bolted for the exit. But the show had started. The Albino's fingers ran up and down the neck at an insane speed. The boys froze, as if their limbs were too weak to keep moving. I saw them collapse like puppets suddenly cut from their strings.

Then I heard the cry of souls, distorted in a crescendo of metal turned to sound… The electric howl of the damned, sent back into endless feedback rolling under the roof, bouncing from wall to wall, like in a monstrous amplification chamber.

I could not stand it anymore. I closed my eyes and listened, fascinated.

The Albino played for a long time, until his fingers dripped blood, shorn by Strombringer's strings. I had never heard anything like it and that still holds true—even though I was at the foot of the stage for Jimi at Woodstock, and at Altamont before the long-barreled gun would murder the spirit of rock; I saw the first shows of MC5 and the Stooges; I was there at the take off of Zeppelin, but it was nothing in comparison. It couldn't be, thank God!

I did not realize that it was silent again until the Albino spoke to me, "Come on out, Mike, it's over. I know you're there."

I left my hiding place trembling, still suffering the emotion. The Albino had a red spot, no bigger than a penny, where Jeff's blade had stuck him. It did not seem to bother him.

"Did you like it? Be honest."

I cursed him for forcing me to admit, "It was… extraordinary. I didn't think such sounds were possible from a guitar. Even if that is not really one."

"Don't kid yourself. Stormbringer is an instrument like any other, except that it has a little extra soul."

The vision of the stiff corpses kept me from appreciating the humor of his remark. "How many does it still need?"

"Don't worry, they're the last as far as I'm concerned. The demon's thirst is quenched. I'm going, leaving this world for another."

"And me?"

He misunderstood the question. "You'll stay, of course."

"Alive?"

"Absolutely. To bear witness."

"Why is that so important?"

He shrugged, headed for the winding stairs, climbed up and came back down with his guitar case. He carefully laid Stormbringer on the red velvet lining and closed the cover. Before leaving the hangar, he said, "The will of Chaos, remember, Mike? Who knows if it makes any sense… not me, anyway. Goodbye, friend."

He disappeared. I stayed there a moment with the three soulless bodies, one of them decapitated, thinking about everything. I put my soul in the cosmic balance—I had heard this expression from the Albino during his first confession—and found that it did not weigh very much.

I spent the next few years trying to wipe out every trace of the Albino's existence. In truth, it was not very hard. The records he had played on did not list him and the articles written about the disappearance of the bands rarely mentioned the extra member; and they never dwelled on him. Nevertheless, I scoured the record stores until I got all the copies of the in-

183

criminating vinyl, which I dutifully destroyed. Soon the Beatles fad swept away all memories of the pioneers of English rock and I did not have to knock myself out. The collective memory of the new generation crossed out the 1950s.

But it did not keep the music of souls from being played again. Not often and not for long because there was always the same price to pay in the end. Nevertheless, I heard it again and I felt the exact same shivers as I did that first night in the Cavern and then later in the warehouse on the docks.

At one time I thought of telling the Albino's story like he had asked me to. But I abandoned the idea because who would take me seriously? I could have dressed it up, put it in a fictional universe where this kind of thing, a magic, soul-drinking sword, makes sense. The idea preyed on me, particularly during my desert crossing at the beginning of the 1980s—a hell of a time for all the old-timers who, like me, had drank the acid juice of the 1960s like it was milk. Believe me, still today, just the name Maggie Thatcher makes me shiver! In the end I gave up the idea of breaking into heroic fantasy after discovering the incredible amount of crap that had been written since a certain Conan drew his sword from the scabbard… Who would be interested in my story of a cursed Albino traveling in parallel worlds, with a demon at his side, thirsty for souls, taking on all kinds of shapes and sizes? Even if he had, in my universe as well as yours, readers, helped invent the inimitable sound of rock 'n' roll, it would not add a thing to the lack of credibility of the story, quite the contrary!

And then one fine morning, they turned the page on the synthesizer years and I woke up as a veteran of the psychic wars: the spirit of rock 'n' roll was back and with it the inimitable sound of savage guitars—I understood then that the souls had not finished howling and moreover they were paying me handsomely for the articles that I was ashamed of forty years earlier…

What could I do? I had become a cult figure, as they say, without realizing it. So, I took up the pen again, as the Albino had taken to the road that day to continue his eternal wandering.

I hope now for only one thing, as I lie on this hospital bed with my guts being eaten away by cancer and I write my confession as a kind of testament: to hear, one last time, the music of souls—and let the angels with divine voices go fuck themselves!

Travis Hiltz started making up stories at a young age. Years later, he began writing them down. In high school, he discovered that some writers actually got paid and decided to give it a try. He has since gathered a modest collection of rejection letters and had a one-act play produced. Travis lives in the wilds of New Hampshire with his very loving and tolerant wife, two above average children and a staggering amount of comic books and Doctor Who *novels. He is also a regular contributor to* Tales of the Shadowmen. *This story, written especially for this collection, features Oswald Bastable, Von Bek and Antoine Gerpré, the protagonist of Alfred Drious's* The Adventures of a Parisian Aeronaut in the Unknown Worlds *(1856), a social satire in which our satellite is reached via hot air balloon. Drious's novel stands out as a markedly anomalous literary item, not merely for its imaginative extravagance, but also for its keen interest in technological progress, and predates Jules Verne's* Five Weeks in a Balloon *by seven years.*

Travis Hiltz: *War on the Moon*

(*Or, The Adventure of the Three Aeronauts*)

On a particular night in January of 1863, any insomniac citizen of Paris would have been astonished when the clouds parted and they caught a glimpse of two full moons hanging in the sky, one larger than the other.

The larger one only appeared so, as it was in fact a hot air balloon, painted silver, with a large basket gondola. Its sole occupant bustled about. He occupied a small oasis amongst several wicker hampers, two carpetbags, a toolbox and a device that looked like a squat roll top desk decorated with levers, valves and gauges.

Antoine Gerpré, a slim man approaching middle age, his trim beard, mustache and collar-length black hair flecked with grey. His clothes, a few years behind in fashion, threadbare but tidy. Over his suit he wore a heavy overcoat, gloves and bulky goggles pushed up to his forehead.

Gerpré was hunched over the control device, occasionally peering up to study the night sky. He reached into his overcoat and took out a monocle, attached to his jacket lapel by a black ribbon, set it into his right eye and studied the gauges. He then straightened up, turned a dial and eased down a wooden lever.

Nodding to himself in satisfaction, Gerpré then retrieved a flask from his inner coat pocket and, after holding it up to the moon in a brief toast, took a healthy sip.

Gerpré, an amateur scientist as well as a balloonist, had discovered there was "more to his philosophy than on Heaven and Earth," quite literally. His experiments in traveling the heavens had lead him to encounter individuals and artifacts from beyond this earthly sphere, including beings claiming to be angels, and an enigmatic Doctor from the future.

He had since thrown himself into an intensive study of aeronautics, until he felt he had perfected a device to control his flight in hope of ascending and catching a further glimpse of what lay beyond.

He soon lost sight of the rooftops of Paris as he rode up into the clouds. He buttoned up his coat, pulled his goggles over his eyes and added a jaunty red scarf to his ensemble, in order to fight off the rapidly encroaching cold.

He steered by various gauges and dials, as his balloon having fully entered the cloudbank, lost sight of Paris and even the full moon.

The gondola rocked, and even with the strange muffling effect of the clouds, Gerpré could detect a rumble of thunder. He adjusted a tiny lever on his goggles and peered intently into the enveloping cloudbank, catching a glimpse of flickering lights that looked to be distant lightening. His forehead crinkling in concern, he adjusted the controls. His glance alternated between keeping an eye on the encroaching storm and the ceiling of cloud over his balloon.

His plan to rise above the clouds stumbled when, instead of breaking through into the starry night sky, Gerpré found the clouds becoming darker, denser and seemingly endless. The cloudbank crowded in around him, until he felt like he had been packed in cotton. It was only the swaying of the basket that let him know he was still moving at all.

The lightening flicked and arced all around him, going from sparks to long threads. Gerpré gripped one of the support ropes tightly with one hand, while frantically adjusting controls with the other. Despite the cold, his brow was soon damp with perspiration.

After several tense minutes, the balloon finally broke through the clouds and immediately found itself on a collision course with two other airships.

One was a plain grey balloon with a crude, unadorned basket: its design all frugality and functionality.

The other airship had a sausage-shaped balloon colored in red, green and gold, supporting a boat-shaped gondola.

The grey balloon was bland practicality while the multicolored was its complete opposite, obviously designed as a festive, showy plaything for some wealthy, amateur adventurer.

Gerpré managed to steer his balloon between the two other airships, scrapping against the rough woven basket of the grey balloon.

The pilot, clad in a threadbare grey military uniform, sported a large, American-style mustache. In one gloved hand he held a service revolver pointed directly at the French aeronaut.

The two men locked gazes: Gerpré surprise mingling with fear, the other with the grim resignation of a long serving military man.

"Helloooo…?" A voice broke into the deadly scene, startling both men. The soldier raised his gun. The Frenchman ducked down behind his bank of controls, anxiously attempting to put some distance between the grey soldier and himself.

His balloon shifted perhaps a few inches and then jerked to a halt and would move no further, either away or up or down. Gerpré peered around and could find no evidence that the ropes had become entangled.

He glanced over his shoulder; saw the pilot of the more decorative balloon had also produced a firearm. The tri-colored balloon pilot's attire matched the almost whimsical theme of his mode of transportation.

If Gerpré's suit was a few years behind fashion, the other pilots' was at least fifty years behind.

He wore a heavy traveling cloak over a blousy white tunic, green breeches and a stylish green tri-corner hat perched on his head. He sported a thin, well-waxed mustache and goatee. Unlike the soldier in grey, this pilot's gun, a heavy flintlock was held in a casual grip and he sported a smile that showed he was currently more bemused than anxious about this strange and unexpected collision.

"Good evening!" he called across the distance. "Traffic is a bit heavier above the city than I had expected. Though, I do believe I had the right of way!"

Despite circumstances, Gerpré found himself smiling faintly at the other aeronaut's jaunty attitude.

"Quite thoughtless of me," Gerpré replied, with a mock bow. He straightened and looked admiringly up at the others' colorful balloon. "Cannot imagine how I didn't spot your transport…?"

"If you two are done acting the clown!" the soldier in grey barked his gun out and moving between the two men. "Unless you can show me your papers, I must inform you that the penalty for spying is execution."

"Spying…?" Gerpré breathed. "On whom? What are you talking about?"

"Yes, you will have to be more specific if you are accusing me of espionage," the fashionable balloonist shrugged, nonplussed.

"You are both in violation of the Virginia Accords," the grey soldier snapped, impatiently. "No unauthorized air travel over Ashanti territory or trade routes."

"Ashanti? Is that south of Prague?"

"I don't understand any of this!" Gerpré shouted, to be heard. "I was over Paris! Would it be too much to ask you both to lower your firearms and perhaps we could speak like civilized gentlemen?"

The more fashionable pilot, acting as though he'd forgotten the pistol was still in his hand, shrugged and tucked it into his wide belt.

The soldier in grey was more reluctant, but eventually lowered his arm. His gaze suspicious and calculating.

Gerpré exhaled in relief, and brushed at his lapels, as he worked to gather his thoughts.

"I hardly know where to begin…"he said, toying with his monocle.

"Introductions would seem to be in order," the other man said, doffing his tri-corner hat. "Hauptman Manfred Von Bek, currently of no fixed abode."

"Antoine Gerpré."

"Humph," the man in grey muttered, frowning. "Lt. Oswald Bastable of the Ashanti Confederacy air corps."

"Ashanti Confederacy…?"Gerpré muttered, puzzled. "Not familiar with…?"

"Africa, isn't it?" Von Bek suggested.

"Its capital is Virginia," Bastable replied. "After the war between the states…"

"I hate to intrude on what's sure to be an interesting history lesson," Von Bek interrupted, "but, what is wrong with the moon…?"

All three moved to the edge of their respective baskets, to peer past their respective balloons and gazed upon the lunar sphere.

"At this higher atmosphere," Gerpré began, "the moon can appear…dear lord…!"

"That's no moon," Bastable muttered.

The sphere above their balloons shone in the night sky. Gone was its grey barrenness, replaced by a warmer blue-green that looked worryingly familiar.

Von Bek's eyes grew wide and he moved to the far side of his gondola and leaned over, peering downwards.

"It is the earth…!" Gerpré breathed. "But…how…?"

Below them, growing ever larger was the moon, shining bright in the black expanse of space.

"How is this happening?" Von Bek shouted.

"Would you two shut up!" Bastable snapped. "Look! Just look!"

All three balloonists stood in silence, first seeing the moon coming slowly, inexplicitly closer and then feeling the movement of their conveyances and the realization that the moon was staying where it belonged and that they were the ones moving, traveling ever closer to the earth's satellite.

"We've left the earth…!" Von Bek exclaimed, his suave, nonchalant mask slipping for a second. "That's not possible…!"

"You'd be surprised," Gerpré muttered, studying the controls of his balloon. He adjusted several dials and switches to no effect. The trio of balloons continued their slow journey across space, clustered together like some surreal bouquet.

Bastable seemed to accept the situation with a strange resignation. He holstered his gun and moved to the edge of his basket.

"What's happening?" he asked Gerpré in a matter of fact way that told the Parisian that there was more to the ragged soldier than he'd originally surmised.

"I have suspicions," the French balloonist replied. " We are being drawn to the moon, for what purpose I do not know."

"Perhaps we should gather in one balloon, rather than shouting at each other?" Von Bek suggested. "My own is built for comfort and company, if you'd care to join me…?"

Both men agreed to this suggestion and made the awkward climb from their balloons to Von Bek's. The space in-between was mere inches, but the drop below could be measured in thousands of miles and made for a nerve wracking few seconds.

The prow of the boat-shaped gondola contained not only the steering mechanism, but also several lounge chairs and a small drinks cart as well.

Gerpré found himself drawn to examine the other's primitive control system. It was a short podium, paneled in polished oak with a small brass ship's wheel and hung above it were two polished metal pull chains, apparently to adjust the fire.

Bastable made his way to one of the wingback chairs and with an audible sigh sank into it, legs outstretched and for the first time since their meeting, Gerpré sensed he had just been gifted a brief glance at the true man beneath the battle-hardened shell in a rare moment of relaxation.

Von Bek helped himself to the wine and sat across from Bastable. He took a deep drink and both men allowed the Frenchman his brief inspection before beginning their conference. Gerpré became aware, after several minutes that his natural curiosity needed to be dampened while they dealt with their current dilemma.

"So," he said, standing by the rail, his hands clasped behind his back, "it would appear we are being deliberately drawn to the moon, but I can see little other common ground between the three of us."

"Monsieur Bastable and I are both soldiers," Von Bek suggested. "Of a sort."

"I am merely a student of ballooning and science," Gerpré shrugged. "I have, due to unusual circumstances, traveled a bit around the world, but am content to spend my time in Paris…"

"I would think circumstances would not make Paris conducive for quiet, learned contemplation," Von Bek said. "I found it expedient to leave."

"How so?" Gerpré asked, pushing his goggles up to his forehead.

"The people rising up," Von Bek prompted. "The revolution?"

"The French revolution…?" Gerpré muttered, bewildered.

"Since it is occurring in France, that would be an appropriate description… What revolution did you think I was referring to?" Von Bek asked.

Gerpré shook his head, mystified by the turn the conversation had taken. He turned his attention to his other traveling companion.

"What of you, Lt Bastable?" he asked. "You are serving in…?"

"Virginia." Bastable said. "The uprising of the black slave population in the midst of the civil war…"

"Virginia…?" Von Bek asked, puzzled. "In the colonies…? They just had a war with the English…? Now they are fighting each other?"

"We did not just travel from the Earth to the moon," Bastable mused, grimly. "But rather through time as well."

He did not sound stunned by the statement, but rather spoke with an indifference that puzzled his companions almost as much as what he had said.

"But who would or even could do such a thing…?" Von Bek exclaimed, his exasperated gesture resulting in his sloshing the remainder of his drink down one arm of Gerpré's overcoat.

"I think we are about to discover that," Gerpré said, looking away while he dabbed at his damp sleeve with his scarf.

All three men moved to the rail.

The cluster of balloons had entered the atmosphere of the moon. As they drew closer, the landscape became more distinct, and they became aware of details beyond craters and long stretches of dusty wasteland.

There were valleys and mountain peaks, as well as vast fields of strange, enormous mushroom-like plants and several crude, blocky structures that were obviously man made.

"Buildings!" Von Bek breathed.

They drifted along, staying a consistent hundred feet above the ground. A steady, dry breeze flowed past the trio.

Flying over a squat mountain range, the balloons came upon a valley in which was nestled a city, a wondrous city. An artists' vision brought to life, appearing as though it had been carved from one enormous block of polished ivory, rather than planned and built piecemeal.

It gave off a faint ethereal glow and while none of the three travelers would say it aloud, they were all convinced that while looking at the city they could hear faint music, a phantom chorus of heavenly maidens.

The balloons began to descend, touching ground several hundred yards from the outskirts of the exquisite city. It was surrounded by a wall every bit as pleasing to the eye as it was imposing and functional.

The balloons touched down with a puff of lunar dust and the three men climbed out.

They stood, entranced by the celestial city and the awareness that they were standing on the surface of another world.

"Amazing!" Von Bek breathed, being the first to break the silence.

Gerpré kneeled down, pulled off his gloves, took up a pinch of moon dirt and rubbed it between his fingers, peering at it as though it were gold dust.

Bastable, huddled into his coat merely stood looking around.

After several moments a section of the ivory wall opened like a drawbridge.

A vehicle, a horseless chariot that looked like an enormous seashell, containing three figures, made its way across the dusty plain towards the balloonists.

The chariot came to a halt several yards from the men from the Earth. One figure exited the chariot and strode towards them.

He was tall, his figure and features resembled a Grecian statue come to life, well formed and near breathtaking in his beauty. Like his city, the man seemed to give off a glow. He was clad in a white toga that reached the ground, yet no dirt would cling to it.

His companions, equally exquisite in face and form, one with a perfectly trimmed beard, remained in the chariot.

He swept toward the three balloonists, his robe long enough that he appeared to be gliding across the ground rather than walking. He stood before them, his hands clasped in front of him, a thin, serene smile on his face.

"Mikael!" Gerpré exclaimed, moving forward, his arm outstretched. He's stride became a leap, due to the moon's lesser gravity.

The man in white robes held a hand up and Gerpré stumbled to a halt.

"We meet again," Mikael said, making no attempt to accept the earthman's offered hand. He nodded with an expression that seemed equal parts amusement and barely contained tolerance. "Who are these others, my dear Gerpré?"

"What?" The French balloonist asked, lowering his hand and wrinkling his forehead in confusion. "You brought us…didn't you?"

"You, yes, but these other two…gentlemen, no," the man in white mused. "We required a thinker, at least by Earthly standards, and a soldier, but these two…?"

"They are both soldiers, I'm told," Gerpré said, looking over his shoulder at his two new traveling companions. "They were caught up in the storm. I assume that was your doing as well?"

The ethereal-looking being, tucked his hands into his sleeves, and strode over to Von Bek and Bastable, surveying them like a skeptical purchaser inspecting questionable wares.

"No," Mikael murmured, thoughtfully, to himself, shaking his head slightly. He looked up briefly at the trio of balloons. "We did not seek out these two. Where is the soldier with the rug…?"

195

The man in white rummaged in his robes, coming out with odd device: an eyepiece, resembling a slightly over-sized monocle on a long ivory stem. Peering through it, Mikael intently studied the adventurer for several moments. Von Bek returned his gaze with faint, puzzled amusement.

The taller man took the eyeglass away and sniffed the air around Von Bek.

"You reek of temporal energy," he said, narrowing his eyes. "Are you here on your patron's bidding, I wonder?"

"My patron?"

"No need to be coy. Not that I expect shining truth from the devil's hound."

He then abruptly turned to give Bastable similar study, raising an eyebrow in surprise.

"And you…?" he muttered. "Pulled sideways through the multiverse… Someone is playing games…?"

He straightened up and strode back to Gerpré.

"Nothing to be done," Mikael said, matter-of-factly, tucking away his looking glass. "We have more important things to deal with."

"Do we?" Gerpré asked. "I confess I don't understand anything you've said or why you brought me here?"

"Yes," Mikael said, straightening up. "After a millennium, war has come to the city of the angels."

He paused and seeing the trio's puzzled incomprehension, sighed.

"We have spent the millennium since the Lord God placed us here," he explained, sounding like a teacher lecturing class of particularly ungifted children. "Focusing all our energies, our immortal lives, towards the arts, the ways of peace, science and philosophy. No blood has been spilt in the celestial city since the very dawn of creation and…"

"And so, you need someone to fight your war for you," Von Bek interrupted, arms crossed. "Lest you are forced to sully your pristine hands."

He gave Bastable a sardonic, knowing look.

Both the ragged soldier and the lunar angel frowned at him.

"You are at war?" Gerpré asked. "With who? There are other cities on the moon? Why would you think I could help you?"

"Having no experience of war ourselves, having only ever observed it, we sought out the only beings we had encountered who were adapt at violence and bloodshed: human beings." Mikael said. " We believed that a scientist, as well as a soldier, would be best in helping us devise a resolution to this coming conflict."

Gerpré glanced back at his new companions and then back at the tall man in white with an air of skeptical concern.

"Perhaps if you showed us the...um... enemy fortifications, rather than just discussing the topic...?"

Mikael nodded, and then turned back towards his chariot.

"Return to your contraptions," the angel instructed, as he walked away. " I will guide you to the enemy."

Gerpré turned to the other two men and gestured towards his balloon.

"My balloon is not built for comfort, but I believe it will suit our needs." he said, with an "after you" gesture.

The trio was soon settled in the French balloonist's gondola, Gerpré at the controls, Von Bek perched upon a large hamper and Bastable standing stiffly at the rail. They ascended a dozen yards up and waited for their celestial guide.

To their amazement, slots opened in the sides of the alabaster chariot and a balloon emerged. It was more akin to watching an enormous flower blossom than a practical device being assembled.

Within minutes, the lunar angels were airborne and drifting away from the white city. Gerpré adjusted the controls and the earthmen followed.

"I do not like this situation," Von Bek muttered as they flew. "My family crest bares the motto 'Do the devil's work,' but I feel with these the angels we need to tread cautiously."

"I will admit, they can be arrogant in their speech and thinking," Gerpré said, not looking away from the balloon's controls. "But, it comes from a millennium of study and learning. They are immortal and seem to sincerely believe they are God's chosen, his first creations…"

"Then I agree with Von Bek," Bastable said, in a low tone, not taking his gaze from the white balloon. "There is no one more dangerous than those who believe their cause is sanctioned by god. There is no end to the horror and atrocity they will perpetuate with a smile and a clear conscience."

All three settled into a grim, anxious silence as they drifted along.

The air on the moon was thin and dry, the silence almost oppressive. So, they heard the army long before they caught sight of them.

It was a rasping sound, like fingernails against sandpaper.

All three men, disconcerted, moved to different sides of the basket, straining to catch a glimpse of the army that generated such an odd noise.

They passed over a ridge of low, dusty hills and found themselves floating above their quarry.

"My god…!" Von Bek breathed, leaning over the edge of the basket. "They are…are…beetles…enormous beetles!"

"Not precisely," Gerpré muttered. "They seem to only have two sets of legs, rather than…"

"Truly?" Von Bek interrupted. "Being charged with stopping a war between angels and insects on the moon, you wish to be pedantic over classification…?"

"I was just…" Gerpré muttered.

"Could the two of you shut up for just a moment!" Bastable barked. "It's of more importance, at this moment, that you make use of your eyes, rather than your mouths."

With an obvious air of chastisement, the other two peered, quietly over the rail at the advancing army.

Perhaps they were not beetles, but were definitely man-sized insects. Like the angels, they were also white, with heavy, dingy shells. They stood on stubby hind legs and held in their front arms what appeared to be spears formed from stone or crystal.

"It truly is an army," Bastable said, after several moments of study. "They're not swarming, but marching in organized formation…!"

"They have weapons!" Von Bek added. "Beetles with spears!"

"Are they marching for the angel's city?" Gerpré mused, consulting the compass on his console. "They have no vehicles…I wonder…if we could calculate their rate of travel…"

He opened some drawers coming out with some pages of crumpled paper and a protractor and began looking for a flat surface to do calculations on.

The others stood at the railing, entranced by the parade of marching insects, the faint light glimmering off their dull white shells.

"It's like being in a strange dream," Von Bek muttered. "Or some particularly bizarre children's story…I don't know what to think…."

"We need to think like soldiers," Bastable replied, absently, glancing at his traveling companion and then back to the insect army. "And think of them as soldiers. War is war. No matter how fantastic the place or the people, that will never change."

"I feel you have stories to tell," Von Bek said, with a grim smile.

"Don't we all?"

After several minutes of thoughtful silence, Von Bek turned toward Gerpré.

"Can you take us lower?" he asked. "Something I'd like to see."

Gerpré nodded and pulled a lever and the balloon descended to within a dozen yards of the insect army. Seen closer, the mass of moving bodies was no less intimidating and surreal.

Von Bek slid a heavy flintlock from his belt and fired. The ball pinged off the shell of an insect foot soldier.

"What is wrong with you?" Bastable snapped, grabbing at Von Bek's shoulder. "Are you mad?"

"Look!" Von Bek snapped, pointing downwards.

All three leaned cautiously over the rail, and much to their surprise not only was there no reprisal, no counter attack, but no evidence that any member of the multitude seemed to even look their way.

"The proportionate size and thickness renders them bulletproof," Gerpré said, scratching his beard in thought. "Interesting."

"So, on top of being grossly outnumbered, our adversaries are immune to our weapons," Bastable grumbled, stepping back and slumping onto the hamper Von Bek had abandoned. "Going ahead with this enterprise is the definition of 'fatalistic.'"

"They didn't pause," Von Bek said, turning back towards his companions. "Not a one even looked up in surprise."

"They are not a multitude of individuals," Gerpré said, with growing enthusiasm. "They operate as a hive mind…we cannot look at them as just large insects that act like men, but rather a swarm. They are merely insects, enormous insects obviously, but insects nevertheless."

He clasped his hands behind his back and began to pace. Realizing how crowded his surroundings were, he turned around once and then returned to the controls.

"We must alter how we approach this," he continued, nodding to himself, as he adjusted controls and the balloon ascended to join their guides in the upper reaches.

Both of the other men nodded in agreement, but kept their own thoughts and theories to themselves. They floated upwards, joining the angels.

"So, you see what we face," Mikael said, not raising his voice, yet somehow his voice projected perfectly to the other balloon. "Even with our advanced science, we doubt we stand a chance against such a foe. We lack the capacity for the battle that must come to drive the Selenites away."

The three balloonists, stayed where they sat or stood, each puzzling over the information.

"Where did they come from?" Gerpré asked.

"And why are they 'declaring' war on an oasis of peace and higher learning?" Bastable added.

"We have shared the moon with the Selenites," Mikael stated. "There have been several colonies on this world. We first suspected that the Radar-men had instigated this attack, but can find no hint that they have budged from their bunkers."

"How many cities are there upon the moon?" Von Bek exclaimed.

"The only ones you need concern yourself with," Mikael told him, "are the celestial city and the hives of the Selenites."

"They appear to be just mindless drones," Gerpré added. "What is controlling…leading or provoking them? Not sure which is the appropriate term."

"There is a guiding mind that oversees the Selenite workers and soldiers," Mikael explained.

"And it just suddenly, after millennium of peace, rose up and decided to attack?" Von Bek puzzled. "Something must have occurred…?"

"Are you accusing us?" the younger angel asked, his voice no less clear, despite that he spoke in a low, dangerous tone.

Mikael held up hand to forestall his companion, but his gaze at Von Bek seemed every bit as offended.

"How did it start?" Bastable asked, his own tone as sharp and weighted as the angels'.

"When it started, we know," Mikael replied. "How, we are in the disconcerting place of having to admit it, we do not."

The three balloonists shared a brief, uneasy silence, unsure how to proceed.

"There were incidents where angels would go outside the city, and were set upon by Selenite scouts. We thought it strange happenstance, the act of rogue drones: it has been known to happen. Then it continued with increasing frequency, and we could no longer deny that it was a deliberate campaign. We were being targeted. The Selenites were actively scouting the landscape, moving ever closer."

"This is a great deal to take in," Gerpré said, tapping at the railing of the basket in thought.

"We need to think about this," Von Bek said, his tone thoughtful and humbled. "Allow us to scout further and then rendezvous at your city and decide the best way to precede."

The three angels turned to each other and spoke quietly for several moments, before turning to face the earthmen.

"Yes, that would suit us," he nodded. "We too, have much to consider."

With no sign that he'd touched a control, the white sea-shell drifted silently away.

"I don't see what there is to consider," Gerpré muttered, once the angels' airship was a perfect white dot on the horizon. "We cannot possibly be of any help to them…"

"Are you so naïve to believe we have a choice?" Bastable said, crossing his arms.

"What?"

"Your angels aren't just going to send us home if we decline to win their war for them," Von Bek added.

"But, we are here merely to advise them…!" Gerpré protested.

"Do you truly believe that?" Bastable asked, curious. "You've encountered these…angels before. Do you see them taking our advice and marching off to war?"

"I must agree." Von Bek nodded. "We are not here to teach them how to fight a war, but to fight for them."

"The three of us?" Gerpré exclaimed, the monocle dropping out of his eye. "We cannot…!"

"And what will your angels do then, I wonder?" Von Bek said, moving to perch on one of the wicker hampers. He shifted about, absently, rummaging through the Frenchman's supplies as he spoke.

"They'll decide Gerpré is right," Bastable said, grimly. "There's no way three men can hold off that army and will set out to obtain an army of their own."

"The angels are incapable of violence," Gerpré said, chewing his lip in anxious contemplation.

"But they know where they can find a multitude, quite capable of the violence required." Von Bek said, reaching down and coming up with a jar of preserved peaches.

He pried the lid loose, sniffed at the contents and then took a deep sip.

"The dandy is talking sense," Bastable frowned. "If we convince the angels we have no chance of stopping the Selenites, then they will use the same…magic, to bring more soldiers to the moon. They won't dirty their own hands, but will be quite content to pile up bodies until their enemy is buried beneath them."

Gerpré sighed and hung his head, knowing in his heart, his companions were right and was weighed down by the grim impossibility of their task.

"Then you realize," Von Bek said, while attempting to fish a slice of peach out of the jar with his fingers. "We only have one course of action available to us."

"We do?" Gerpré asked, baffled.

"We have to stop the war ourselves," Von Bek explained through a mouthful of fruit.

"Are you quite mad?" the Frenchman exclaimed. "How…?"

He turned to Bastable for support.

"He's right," the soldier in grey nodded. "If we can stop it, no one else needs to suffer. I honestly don't see us surviving, but the attempt must be made."

Gerpré looked from one of his traveling companions to the other in stunned horror before sinking onto a small chest and resting his head in his hands.

"Madness…!" he breathed.

The balloon drifted along, its occupants deep in their respective cocoons of thought.

"So," Bastable said, not raising his eyes, "where do we start?"

Von Bek raised an eyebrow, whether in admiration for his companions' bravado or concern about his mental satiability was unclear.

"I think Gerpré is the man to ask," he replied.

"What?" Gerpré said looking up. "I'm no soldier, no fighter…!"

"No, you are a savant," Von Bek agreed, nodding. "Your mind has been formed from books, not battlefields."

"You two are soldiers though; you have more idea about what to expect!" Gerpré protested, waving his hands, as though to shoo away the very idea.

"No," Von Bek said, shaking his head. "I don't think that will do in this instance. Yes, I am a clever tactician, but it is geared to keeping myself alive and, let us be honest, Bastable may be a capable soldier, but he gives one the impression that any plan he concocts will end with the three of us in a bloody, yet valiant pile."

Bastable frowned, but did not contradict.

"You are a scientist," Von Bek continued. "The angels choose you, so they believed a thinker, as well as a fighter, would be needed. If this absurd campaign is to prevail, I think it will be through our minds, not just our sword arms."

"They are not a human army," Bastable muttered. "So, we cannot look to Robert E. Lee or Cicero Hood to bring us victory."

"Neither of those names mean a thing to me," Von Bek shrugged. "But, you are right about the beetles…we need understanding before we can plan strategy."

"I see," Gerpré nodded absently. "They are insects, a hive more than an army. There is a guiding force, a mind a…um…a queen, of some sort, so to speak…that is where we would be best suited to focus our attention."

"Cut off the head," Bastable said. "Rather than face the army head on…I would still like to retrieve my guns."

"I would not be adverse to doing my thinking with a sword in my hand," Von Bek agreed.

Gerpré got to his feet, using his budding curiosity to push back the fear and dread he felt towards this endeavor and his chances of surviving to return home.

Taking his position at the controls, he bowed his head, and made a brief, silent prayer for not just himself, but to give his aged mother strength in the advent he did not return.

He then steered them back towards the city of the angels.

The journey was a quiet one, the only sound being Von Bek's chewing and the creak of the rigging in the thin, lunar wind. They returned to the other balloons, gathered their weapons and resumed their journey, all without any further contact with the angels.

Von Bek saw a trio of white specks on one of the outer walls' towers and gave them a jaunty salute as they passed.

Gerpré stayed focused upon navigating, while the other two men used loading their firearms to cover their concerns.

With no other plan in mind, Gerpré steered the balloon back towards the Selenite army. Once they had passed over it, they then drifted, following the trail left by their march upon the celestial city. It was wide as the main boulevard in Paris and was as clear a trail for them to follow as could be hoped for.

They flew across the lunar landscape, backtracking, Bastable, his rifle loaded and cleaned, kept watch. Von Bek kept a more casual eye on things, while with the other eye he inventoried Gerpré's provisions.

They spent an hour this way, until Von Bek, who had moved to the edge of the basket, holding a support rope with one hand, a wedge of cheese in the other spoke up.

"There!" he shouted, pointing with the hand that held the cheese. "That hill…!"

The others moved to look past him and understood why it had caught Von Bek's attention. It looked like an enormous candle that had been left unattended and allowed to melt or an artist's interpretation of an anthill sculpted from white clay.

Gerpré landed the balloon a short distance from the Selenites' hive and the three disembarked.

Bastable carried his rifle, as well as wearing his gun belt. Von Bek had a sword and his flintlocks. Both men offered Gerpré a gun, but he declined, feeling he was more a hindrance than help if armed, but as a concession, brought along a heavy walking stick.

The three men bounced along in the light gravity, besides the Selenites' trail. It was pitted with thousands of alien footprints.

As they came closer, they spotted numerous cave-like openings and the occasional glimpses of movement.

"Not everyone went off to the wars," Von Bek muttered. "Shall we?"

With the lower gravity the climb was not as arduous as if they'd been on earth. A dozen hops got the trio to the nearest opening. A narrow cave that lead deep into shadow.

The trio crept along, gazing about in wonder, as it grew lighter the deeper they went, due to veins of bio-luminance that glinted off the metal that was sprinkled all along the walls.

"It's gold…?" Von Bek breathed, using a dagger to dig out a piece of the precious metal the size of his thumb.

"Astounding!" Gerpré said, running his hand across the surface of the tunnel wall. "Using polished gold to augment their lighting!"

Bastable merely frowned and continued trudging along.

The tunnel snaked deep into the hive, branching off every couple of yards. They would peek down each branch, but none of the offshoot tunnels seemed to offer any better path then where they were. After what felt like several miles, a crude balcony, widened out on the right side of the tunnel wall.

They looked over what resembled a surreal factory floor. All the workers were Selenites, a diverse multitude of white insects. There were the soldier beetles, but also taller, mantis-looking ones that seemed to be supervising and smaller pill bug like messengers, trundling along.

The floor below them seemed to be in constant motion.

"My god…!" Von Bek breathed.

Bastable nudged Gerpré and pointed to a large cave-like opening at the far end of the gallery.

The Frenchman nodded in reply and all three began seeking a path. They followed the balcony until it rejoined the tunnel wall and then Von Bek spotted a series of holes in the wall below the crude railing, hand and foot holes that would give a determined or foolhardy soul a way down.

All three men looked dubiously at the makeshift ladder, no one eager to go first.

With a shrug, Von Bek tucked his pistol into his belt, climbed over and began his descent. Gerpré gritted his teeth, kept his eyes focused on the dirt wall and tried to ignore his itching nose as he followed.

They reached the floor, coming down behind a large pile of dirt. Their decent seemed to have been completely ignored by the army laborers.

Whether they were dedicated workers or their primitive hive mind simply would not allow them to contemplate occurrences outside their assigned tasks was unclear.

The aeronauts huddled behind the pile, entranced by the swarm of constantly on the move Selenites. They stayed close to the wall, thinking if they did not outright bump into one of the lunar insects they could move about unmolested.

There was a tense moment when one of the taller supervisors walked towards Von Bek. His sword was halfway out of its scabbard before it veered off to investigate a scaffold and chitterling at the nearby crew of pill bugs.

They reached the cave, dodged several of the beetles and made their way down the tunnel.

It seemed darker, there were less flecks of gold in the walls and whatever it was that caused the bioluminescence seemed sickly and dim. The tunnel was wide enough that all three men could have walked side by side, but caution kept them single file and close to the wall.

The tunnel widened out into another large chamber, low ceilinged and practically empty after the mind-numbing business of the other.

All three stopped, their respective weapons hanging limply in their hands.

The back wall consisted of a massive, crude bench of hard-packed dirt and stone. Seated upon it was a grotesque figure, its head enormous and made to seem even more out of proportion, by its shrunken body and stick-like limbs. They were vaguely reminiscent of the mantis-supervisors from the factory floor, but its head had an almost human structure to it, the pale skin loose and rubbery, as though the skull beneath was not yet done expanding.

The creature lay on its side, as though toppled over by the sheer weight of its distorted cranium. Its body was folded up in a fetal position, panting in short, quick breathes. The eyes were closed but the white eyelids twitched, as though the creature was in the thrall of disturbing dreams.

Seated next to the creature, in fact, one arm draped over the massive head as if it was no more than an armrest was a figure, more familiar, yet no less disquieting.

The man was dressed in the tweeds of a scholar that had taken a walking holiday before being transported to the moon. His suit, at one time, modest and respectable, now hung on his body in dingy scraps and tatters. His balding head lulled to one side and a string of drool oozed from the corner of his mouth, dampening his lapel. Across his lap lay a massive sword, its grey steel blade etched with runes in a language unknown to any of the three. Strangely enough, the sword was the only thing on the bench that gave any sign of life.

It seemed to visibly tremble, like a hunting dog desperate to be free of the leash, emitting a moan barely within the range of human hearing.

"On any other day," Von Bek muttered. "This would seem strange beyond words.

"What of…is…?" Gerpré stammered.

"About time you showed up!" a new voice interrupted.

"Una Persson!" both Bastable and Von Bek exclaimed, spotting the young woman at the far wall.

Both men halted and glanced at the other, even more confused that with a century between their lifetimes they could both be acquainted with the dark-haired damsel.

"Dear Lord!" Gerpré murmured pressing a fist to his temple, as he tried to take all this new strangeness in.

Leaving him in the tunnel, the two soldiers ran to the young woman, sparing a glance as they passed, at the strange, slumped figures on the bench.

"What did…?"

"How…?"

"If you would get me loose, we can discuss events to your hearts' content," she chided.

Una Persson was slim, with a pale, cool attractiveness that was slightly obscured by the costume she wore. It resembled, to Bastable, the kind of bulky suit worn by deep-sea divers.

She was held to the wall by what looked like stalactites and stalagmites that had grown and then solidified over her hands and feet.

Using sword and rifle butt the two were able to break her free. She staggered, wincing at the pins and needles in her limbs.

"I had hoped they'd send someone after me," she said, hobbling about and rubbing her wrists. "Didn't think they'd need to resort to… 'freelancers.' I'd at least hoped for Lord Erekosë or Jerry…don't touch that!"

Bastable and Von Bek spun, weapons drawn.

Gerpré froze like a deer caught in headlights, his hand reaching towards the grey sword. Eyes wide, he took a step back and raised his hands in a gesture of surrender.

"I only wished to read the runes…!" he stammered.

"So did he," she said, pointing at the catatonic earthman on the bench. "I came with an archeological expedition. Things didn't go as expected."

"How much of this did you expect?" Von Bek asked, perplexed.

Una Persson glanced about the chamber, despite her circumstances, appearing more perturbed, than frightened.

"We thought the Selenites would be a bit more docile," she shrugged. "Had no idea they had already excavated the sword or that Professor Cavor had gotten a hold of it... that they become agitated so quickly..."

"The angel claimed the Selenites attack is unprovoked," Bastable said. "He said..."

"When you say 'angel,' are you referring to a very tall, bald being in a blue toga who will tell you he can only observe?" she prompted, showing a trace of concern.

"No," Von Bek explained. "They claim to be actual angels."

"The Lunar angels...?" Una mused, annoyed. "That's not right at all. The Angels and the Selenites sharing the moon... somebody is up to something."

Gerpré slumped down on the empty stretch of the bench, while his two companions attempted to get information from this odd new arrival.

"So, which is leading the Selenite army?' Bastable asked, gesturing with his gun. "The Englishman or that... malformed creature?"

"The culprit is the sword actually," she said, matter-of-factly. "I was asked by the coalition of metatemporal scholars to join the expedition searching for the sword. The minute we stepped foot on the moon, things went awry. The Selenites had already found it and recognized it as a human weapon, so they freed Professor Cavor, who came in a previous expedition to the moon, thinking he could advise them. Once the sword had a host, it could easily overthrow the Selenites...king really seems like an inadequate word...main organizer...supreme intelligence perhaps...and then geared them up for war."

"The sword…?" Von Bek muttered. "I'd heard legends… stories…but, I thought it was black…?"

"The sword you are thinking of is a 'cousin' to this one. This grey sword was believed forged by a Lord of Order," Una shrugged, slid off her rucksack and rummaged through it. "It's a troublemaker, but not nearly as bloodthirsty. Once the sword is taken out of the equation, the Selenites will lose focus and… well, whatever happens after that really isn't my concern."

She came out with a pair of gloves, heavy gauntlets of a stiff, leathery substance, studded along the backs with three blood-red gems.

The temporal adventuress slid them on; pushed past the two bewildered soldiers and walked up to the blank-eyed Englishman.

All three aeronauts started as she reached down and took the sword out of his hands. She held it up, peering into the faintly pulsing runes and allowed herself a small, self-satisfied smile, before glancing over at the nearby Gerpré.

"Be so kind as to press the green button on my belt," she asked, angling a hip towards him.

Woodenly, he reached over and preformed the requested action.

"Oh, I suppose I should thank you for your assistance," she said, looking over at Von Bek and Bastable, seconds before a faint, lavender glow enveloped her and the sword and she were gone.

Professor Cavor toppled forward off the bench, lying in a ragged heap on the dirt floor.

"Is he dead?" Bastable asked.

Gerpré leaned over to study him and then sat up, shaking his head.

"Does anyone understand what just happened?" Von Bek sighed.

Again, Gerpré shook his head.

"Politics and war," Bastable said, simply. "The only two constants in the universe."

"Did we win?" Von Bek asked, before frowning at Bastable. "And if you say 'are there any winners in war?' I may be inclined to stab you."

Bastable merely shrugged.

"We can hardly determine who won," Gerpré added. "If we have no idea what game was being played."

The creature with the enormous cranium groaned, blinked its eyes and struggled, feebly, to sit upright.

"I think this is not the place to have this debate," Von Bek said.

The race to flee the Selenite hive before the main intelligence reasserted its control and the multitudes returned to their pre-war mindfulness was frantic and a close thing. In fact, it was only afterwards that they realized they'd left poor Professor Cavor behind.

The trio reached Gerpré's balloon seconds before the Selenites poured out of the cave mouth. Hundreds of alien eyes peered upwards, watching their ascent and escape.

All three were too weary and overwhelmed to do more than hold on and watch the landscape drift beneath them.

The insectoid army had scattered, gone was the precise line in full parade march, replaced by a vast mob that wandered along, like a million drunkards returning home with little notion of how they'd spent the night before.

The balloon was soon setting down near the perfect, white city, the trio of liaison angels patiently awaiting them.

Unlike, the adventuresome vigor they'd arrived with, the trio disembarked with the weariness of travelers too long from home that had reached saturation point when it came to excitement and new horizons.

"Well," Mikael smiled, "you have most pleasantly surprised us, my dear Gerpré! We watched, quite concerned, as the Selenites approached our walls and were on the verge of taking matters into our own hands, when with great relief, we watched them turn and depart. You have our thanks."

"Yes, well, I…um…think sending us home would be its own reward," the French balloonist nodded, in a subdued tone. Unsure what exactly they had accomplished and how much credit they deserved. "I have had enough of discovery and new worlds and long to return to my chair by the fire in my mother's house."

"Of course, of course," Mikael nodded. "Events have been much beyond your mortal scope. It must be quite disconcerting."

Bastable frowned, while Von Bek muttered something uncomplimentary under his breath.

Mikael smiled patiently upon them, as a tolerant adult would an obviously over-tired child and brought a short wand, with the appearance of polished ivory from the folds in his robes.

"Ascend once more and we will see that you are returned to when and where you came from," he instructed. "And go knowing you are most favored in the eyes of those that dwell in the celestial city."

None of the three earthmen's expressions showed any sign of joy or satisfaction at these tidings.

Gerpré turned and offered his hand to his new acquaintances.

"I…do not really know what to say," he said. "Perhaps, under different circumstances…"

"For all the strangeness that has occurred," Bastable said, shaking his hand, "I have no complaint about the company."

Von Bek chuckled and patted the man in grey's shoulder.

"I, for one, cannot wait to regal my friends back on Earth with how I won a war and only fired a single shot."

They finished their farewells, and climbed aboard their respective balloons.

Von Bek sank into the chair closest to the drinks cart, Bastable took up his sentry position and Gerpré stood by his controls wondering why he and the lunar angels' destinies seemed linked and how many more encounters he could have with them and still retain his sanity.

The three balloons were soon lost to sight in the vast tapestry of the night sky.

"You have seen to it, Uriel, that they will awake on Earth, in their proper times, with no memory of these events?" Mikael asked the youthful angel at his right shoulder.

"It has been seen to."

"I do not like how this has played out," Mikael continued, thoughtfully, to the angel on his left. "We only sought to summon the Frenchman, not those other two. Someone reached across the barriers of the multiverse to bring them here, someone who knew of the sword's existence. They have sought to use us in a game of their own. See if you can discover who that could be, Arioch."

"But of course," the bearded angel said, with a smile.

Jean-Marc & Randy Lofficier have collaborated on five screenplays, a dozen books and numerous translations. Their latest novels include Edgar Allan Poe on Mars *(2007),* The Katrina Protocol *(2008) and* Return of the Nyctalope *(2013). They have written a number of animation teleplays, including episodes of* Duck Tales *and* The Real Ghostbusters*, and comics featuring* Superman *and* Doctor Strange*. Randy is a member of the Writers Guild of America, West. As Mike was a proponent of the SF New Wave, French filmmakers Alain Resnais and Jean-Luc Godard were of the New Wave cinema. This story, originally published in* Tales of the Shadowmen 6: Grand Guignol *(2009), uses the character of Jerry Cornelius in the context of the classic New Wave films* Alphaville *(1965) and* Last Year in Marienbad *(1961)...*

Jean-Marc & Randy Lofficier: *J.C. in Alphaville*

Jerry: "I promised them nothing less than the Millennium."
Beesley: "I'm afraid we'll have to put back the Millennium
for a while."
Michael Moorcock. *A Cure for Cancer*.

Berlin, 1944: The Men Who Would Be Gods

They were four. Four brilliant men. Four evil men. They already had more wealth and power than most men on Earth, but they wanted more. They wanted their own world to shape and rule to their heart's desire.

They wanted to be gods.

They secretly shepherded Adolf Hitler's meteoritic rise to power, because they recognized in him a bit of themselves, and they thought he might make it possible for them to achieve their dreams.

They were wrong

Misshapen Rotwang was the architect whose visionary madness inspired Albert Speer and Leni Riefenstahl; he was the necromancer who had sent Heinrich Himmler's *Ahnenerbe* looking for the Spear of Destiny and the Holy Grail in Montserrat and Rennes-le-Château.

Leonard Orlok, last scion of an ancient and dark dynasty, was a mathematician who worked with Leonard Zuse on the design of the Z series of binary electrically driven mechanical calculators, before creating the world's first thinking machine, the Alpha-10.

"M," a tall, gaunt, sinister physicist, was the younger brother of the notorious crime-lord Mabuse; like him, he ruled over an invisible empire of gamblers and whores at the heart of Berlin, playing bizarre variations of the Game of Nim with satanic abandon for the souls of his victims.

The last of the four was dwarfish Ohisver Müller, an apikoric Jew and an alchemist, who was privy to the secrets of Rabbi Loew and Ramon de Tarrega. Some claimed he could animate clay and make gold, and had masterminded the Wall Street *krach* of 1929 which, ultimately, had secured power for the Nazis.

The Four had put their trust in Hitler, but their madness eventually infected the Fuehrer, and his dream of a Thousand-Year Reich died a miserable death in the Russian winter of 1943.

The Four easily managed to avoid the *Götterdämmerung* of 1945. Not for them the shameful benches of Nuremberg, or the hangman's noose! Rotwang went to Pasadena, California, changed his name to Blicero, but still worked on his crazy dreams. Orlok relocated to France, changed his name to Von Braun, and continued designing thinking machines. M escaped to Argentina, changed his name to Morel, and became a writer of some repute. And Ohisver Müller fled to Turkey, didn't have to change his name and continued to despoil life much as he had before.

216

But, at night, when the mundane duties of their days had been discharged, the Four still dreamed of being gods.

Rennes-le-Château, September 1954

Natasha Von Braun had just turned 14. She smiled because she was happy. To celebrate her birthday, her father had invited three friends from his days in Berlin that she wasn't supposed to talk about.

They had brought their own children, including little Maria, who was the same age as she was.

The four of them played in the *pinède* behind the property. The white-walled house, which was now known to the locals as "*la maison de l'Allemand*," had been built on the hillside of the picturesque village of Rennes-le-Château, in Southern France, in the shadow of the Tour Magdalène, the folly built by Father Béranger Saunière in the 19th century.

While the children played hide and seek in the woods, the Four, having enjoyed the delicious lunch cooked by an elderly local woman, went out on the stone terrace and, sitting under multi-colored parasols, began to discuss what had brought them all together again.

"I take it that you've finally succeeded, Orlok?" said the beefy, ruddy-skinned man with piercing black eyes and long slick hair pulled back in a pony tail.

"Please, don't call me Orlok, Rotwang," said Natasha's father. "My name is now Von Braun. Leonard Von Braun. But, yes, I believe that success is within our grasp."

"And my name is now Dominus Blicero, don't you forget it, but we remain who we are. In this company, I shall continue to call you Orlok, and you can continue to call me Rotwang. Now, you will forgive my skepticism, because you have made such claims before."

Ohisver Müller, a small, wizened man—almost a homunculus—whose features were strangely ageless and whose almost colorless eyes sparkled with infinite cunning, jumped in:

"Rotwang is right. It is hard to erase the memories of our failure at Germelshausen."

"It was not Orlok's fault if we failed at Germelshausen," said the fourth member of the cabal, a tall, gaunt, saturnine man, usually known only by his initial, M. "We weren't ready yet."

"I have sunk a huge amount of money into this operation…" began Müller.

"We have all contributed equally," interrupted Rotwang. "Don't forget it was I who killed Otto Rahn after he found the Spear of Destiny, and lied to Himmler about it."

"And I who delivered a true copy of the *Legamaton*," added Müller.

Orlok-Von Braun made a pacifying gesture with his hands.

"Gentlemen, gentlemen! The reason we failed at Germelshausen is that we didn't have the raw computing power necessary to create order out of chaos. Now, with my new Alpha-60 machine, and M's equations, we can fabricate our own pocket realities in the Outlands, those dregs of creation existing on the edge of the multiverse. With the Spear of Destiny, the primordial energy that remains there can be shaped according to our own desires to bring about the very worlds we wish to bring into existence.

"For a long time, we have each wished for our own perfect world, what Hitler promised us, but failed to deliver. But now, the time is right, my friends. The Conjunction of a Million Spheres is almost upon us. The Pattern of Amber has been desecrated. The Infinite Earths are in Crisis. The Gunslingers of Gilead are no more, and Wampus has fought his last battle on Labyrinth. The world is turning. We have the dreams, and now, we have the power to will them into existence…"

"Metropolis," whispered Rotwang.

"Müllertown," said Müller.

"Marienbad," muttered M.

"…And my own Alphaville," finished Von Braun.

The Castle, 1964

"You come highly recommended, Herr Cornelius," said the tall, cadaverous, white-haired old German dressed in an old-fashioned grey suit, of the type worn by bankers before the Great War.

The interview room was painted in drab yellow and brown. The paint had flaked off in a few places, leading Jerry to reflect that the Castle had seen better days. It was lit by two single 40 watt bulbs, barely bright enough to cast shadows. A simple oak table separated the two men. In the Castle, it was late winter afternoon all the time.

"We aim to please, Mr. Klamm," replied Jerry Cornelius, a tall, androgynous, dark-haired young Englishman dressed in the latest and brightest Carnaby Street fashion.

The English Assassin lit up an *Acapulco Gold* cigarette and looked for an ashtray. From somewhere behind him, Herr Erlanger, Klamm's non-descript secretary, brought him one.

"Our common friend, Fräulein Persson, advised us that you were the best man for the job, and I'm now inclined to agree with her," said Klamm, perusing a brittle sheet of yellowed onion-skin paper which Jerry presumed was a letter of recommendation from Mrs. P.

"What is the job exactly? Your secretary here was disappointingly vague when he approached me," asked Jerry, indicating Erlanger, who had returned to stand silently near the door.

"Yes, I gave strict instructions to Herr Erlanger to be the soul of discretion," answered Klamm. "It is not good when too many people know of our business, as I am sure you will agree. Now, what do you know of the Outlands, Herr Cornelius?"

"What I've picked up here and there, mostly. They're bits of 'what was' mixed up with 'what might bes' located on the edge of creation, right?"

"We at the Castle prefer our definitions to be more scientifically exact, but I commend you for your excellent grasp of our problem."

"What problem?" inquired Jerry, who still didn't understand what the officious German wanted from him.

"The problem is, as you've accurately stated, the 'what-might-bes,' Herr Cornelius. Too many of them can disrupt the structure of the multiverse…"

"I thought Chaos was taking care of that?" interrupted Jerry.

"A common misconception, I'm afraid. Both Chaos and Law are in accord with each other. There is always a Balance, as you well know. But the Outlands are outside the multiverse. The Balance exerts no power there. However, as long as they remain, shall we say, on the periphery of things, no one bothers about them. But when they start encroaching onto reality and disturb the equilibrium, then we have to…"

" 'We?' "

This time, Klamm ignored the interruption and continued:

"… prune the excrescent or superfluous manifestations."

"I see. So that's why you need me—to, er, 'prune' a bit of excrescent creation which threatens you. I can do the job all right, Mr. Klamm, but I'm going to need more details. A lot more details."

"Have no fear, Herr Cornelius, you will be adequately briefed… The excrescence we're talking about was formed just about ten years ago… His creator, Leonard Von Orlok, *alias* Leonard Von Braun, brought it into existence—and others just like it—right out of the stuff of creation itself. He called it Alphaville. It now threatens to expand and invade the rest of the multiverse. We have already dispatched several agents through the Outlands. One of them is waiting for you there."

"For me?"

"Didn't you understand? That is what we want you to do, Herr Cornelius," said Klamm. "Find Alphaville—and destroy it.

Alphaville

"*I'm very well, thank you, not at all*," responded the parking attendant in an emotionless, mechanical tone when Jerry handed him the key to his Lotus Seven.

The English Assassin had parked near the Grand Omega Minus Square. He was now dressed in a leather bomber jacket and wore a long, white silk scarf.

Stepping outside the parking garage, Jerry reflected that Alphaville looked like Paris reimagined by Albert Speer, and inhabited by extras from a Leni Riefenstahl movie. It was a glamorous, but depressing sight.

"Mr. Cornelius?"

A beefy man with dark hair and the look of a beaten dog, dressed in a rumpled dark suit under a trenchcoat, had appeared as if out of nowhere.

"My name is Henry Dickson. I work for the Castle."

"Henry Dickson? I knew your father."

"Everyone does," sighed the detective.

"I'm eager to hear your report," said Jerry. "Shall we find a place to have a drink?"

"There are no cafés in Alphaville," replied Dickson, glumly.

"No bars? No pubs? What do people here do for fun?"

"They don't."

"Don't?"

"Have fun," explained Dickson. "Come to my hotel room. I think I still have a bottle of Loch Lomond left from my last trip to the Outlands."

Dickson's hotel room at the Bunker Palace Hotel was as sad and rumpled as the detective. It consisted of a bed, a nightstand, a dresser, a small desk and a chair, all white. It was lit by a fluorescent tube that managed to be both too bright, and yet not bright enough, depending on where one was sitting.

Once inside, Dickson found the bottle of scotch in the drawer of the night stand. Its label wasn't Loch Lomond but ZAT 77. Jerry made a face.

"It's that or tap water," said Dickson, getting two glasses.

"To your health then," said Jerry, grabbing one of the glasses.

Jerry settled on the formica and vinyl chair, while Dickson sat on the edge of the bed.

"I think I've managed to get what we need," finally said the detective.

"I'm listening," said the English assassin.

"Von Braun—Orlok—lied to his partners. Well, not lied, maybe oversold them… He didn't tell them the whole truth..."

"Which was?"

"To create a place like this…" Dickson made a circle with his hand to encompass all that was around them. "…you need more than a super-computer, no matter how advanced it is. Alpha-60 might have laid out the plans for Alphaville, and the other cities, it might even sustain them, but it didn't create them."

"Who did then?"

"A Prince of Chaos, Lord Arioch, with whom the Four entered into a compact. In exchange for a prize, Arioch did what Chaos does best: create this mockery of life, this soulless travesty of all that's holy."

"Have you identified what that prize was?"

"Yes, I have."

"So, what is it?"

"It is not a what, but a who."

"I don't understand."

"Are you familiar with Dostoyevsky's *Brother Karamazov*, Mr. Cornelius?"

"I read it a long time ago."

"In it, Ivan Karamazov asserts that neither truth nor harmony—meaning utopia—is worth the suffering of a *child*."

"I still don't follow you."

"Karamazov was wrong. Utopia is precisely worth the suffering of a child. Like his vampire ancestors, Orlok has taken the life of a child—his child—to create his personal utopia."

"Natasha?"

Natasha Von Braun had turned 24. The fact didn't matter to her, because she was dead inside. To everyone, she appeared to be a stunningly beautiful dark-haired woman, but her empty eyes told another story, for they revealed the absence of her soul.

The inhabitants of Alphaville had been made, or conditioned, by Alpha-60 to be automatons, productive social units. Natasha's life, however, had winked out of existence ten years earlier, when Lord Arioch of Chaos had snatched her soul. If she remembered at all what had happened that day in Rennes-le-Château, it was like the experience of a librarian pulling out an index card from a book and looking at the information printed on it. The memory of her spiritual death was just one more bit of information that had been catalogued in her mind, but remained unfelt.

Using the *Legamaton*, or *Key of Solomon*, the Four had summoned Lords Arioch and traded the souls of their own children for their precious utopias. As Dostoyevsky had sensed, it was with the tears of a child that worlds were created.

Outwardly, Natasha Von Braun seemed alive, but inside, she was dead. She moved about Alphaville like a diligent ant through an anthill, with a purpose, but without a soul. She went shopping, she dined out, she attended functions organized by Alpha-60, and did everything required of her without the least emotion.

Sometimes, she even went to the movies.

Jerry Cornelius had been surprised to discover they had movies in Alphaville. He thought the medium too fanciful to be allowed to even exist in Leonard Orlok's model city. He was wrong.

"Sometimes reality is too complex for oral communication," had declared Alpha-60. "But film embodies it in a form which enables it to be spread all over the world."

So he and Henry Dickson had gone to see *Tarzan vs. IBM* at the Grand Rex. To tell the truth, it was a bit different from what Jerry had expected. Tarzan—the villain of the piece—was a slobbering, raging, barely articulate man-ape spreading anarchy in excremental fashion—quite literally, throwing poop at the world, while IBM—Integrated Basic Man—was the perfectly well-adjusted and socially productive superhero who managed to stop the beast, thanks to the application of General Semantics.

The audience was polite, laughing and applauding in a controlled fashion at all the appropriate moments.

All in all, it was a terrible way to spend an evening, thought Jerry. He wouldn't have agreed to go if Dickson hadn't been able to secure two seats next to Natasha Von Braun's.

Jerry pulled out his needle gun.

I walk down these corridors, through these halls, these galleries, in this structure of another century, this enormous, luxurious, baroque, lugubrious hotel, where corridors succeed endless corridors, thought Jerry Cornelius, as he carried Natasha's inert body to his room in the Bunker Palace Hotel.

After the kidnapping, he and Dickson had split up. The detective had gone to prepare the next step of their mission, while Jerry had taken the girl to his car and driven to a safe place, a room that Dickson had booked in advance at the Bunker Palace Hotel.

Soon, Natasha began to regain consciousness. She half sat up on the couch and gazed at her kidnapper with profound amazement, as if she understood nothing of what she saw.

With a slow, gentle gesture, she brushed her hair back from her forehead and blinked her eyes, dazzled by the room's bright lights. She was trying to get her thoughts together and was looking for words to express them.

"Didn't we meet at that hotel in Marienbad last year?" she asked.

"I don't think so," said Jerry. "I've never been to the Outlands before."

In Alphaville, if you watched a movie, the movie also watched you. The kidnapping of Natasha Von Braun had been monitored and analyzed by Alpha-60.

The image of Jerry Cornelius, however, did not compute. Each frame of the film showed a different man: an albino, a negative man, a dark-skinned warrior, a golden boy... Alpha-60 could not make sense of it and filed it for further evaluation. But the image of Henry Dickson was crystal clear. He could be seen. Tracked. Captured.

And so he was.

The problem with the new breed of humanity that Alpha-60 had brought up, thought Leonard Orlok, was that they didn't make for good interrogators.

To question Henry Dickson, he had had to ask Rotwang to send one of his own assistants: a congenial man with an endearing smile called Jack Lint. A torturer's torturer, as it were.

"I don't expect you to die, Mr. Dickson, I expect you to talk," said Jack Lint.

"But I've already told you everything I know," begged Henry Dickson, strapped into a mechanical chair that might have been designed by Gaudi. There were electrodes poking in and out of his skull, cups attached to various parts of his chest, and even soft tendrils squeezing his eyeballs. He didn't like to think about what was happening below the belt. "Jerry Cornelius has gone back into the Outlands with the girl," he added. "I don't know where."

"You're lying. But it doesn't matter. Say your lie again and again. Alpha-60 is very patient. He will be recording it and checking every minute variation in your narrative. If there is anything more, he'll detect it."

"But there's nothing more!"

"Tut-tut—if there is even a slight tremolo in your voice, it might prove a clue to some nugget of deeper truth that you don't wish to keep hidden from us. My machines will keep your larynx properly humidified and pump anti-sleeping drugs into your body. It is only if you stop talking that that horrible pain will return. We don't want that, do we?"

"…"

"Do we, Mr. Dickson?"

"No…"

"Then let's start talking."

By an amazing coincidence, "Then let's start talking," were precisely the words Jerry had just said to Natasha. The English assassin had uncovered the sign of Arioch, Prince of Chaos, Knight of Swords, in charge of thirty legions, on Natasha's right breast. He was not an exorcist, generally preferring to reason with demons rather than expel them forcibly. Besides, in a case like this one, he didn't think force would prevail. He had an idea, but talking was required.

"What do you want?" replied Natasha Von Braun in a voice that was a couple of octaves lower than normal, and seemed to resonate strangely around the room. *It was Arioch's voice, not hers*, thought Jerry

"Just talk, nothing more," said Jerry.

"What about?"

Jerry pretended to consider their options.

"Let's put our cards on the table: you know who I am, and what my mission is…"

"A mission doomed to fail."

"Possibly. But what if I convinced you to leave this woman of your own free will?"

"That is absurd," said the Chaos Lord.

"I could make you a better offer…"

"What do you mean?"

"How does the exorcism ritual go, '*Strike terror, Lord, into the Beast now laying waste your vineyard*?' Well, this Alphaville is not a terribly exciting vineyard now, is it?"

"…"

"Hardly worth a Duke of Chaos's time, if you ask me," continued Jerry. "You must be rather bored here. I know I would be. Come on, admit it, Your Lordship, you *are* bored."

"Perhaps," said Arioch, with some reluctance. "A little. What do you offer?"

"You made a bad deal, but you don't have to be bound to it for eternity. Let's be frank: when it comes to creating pocket dystopias, Orlok and his friends are pikers. Metropolis is basically about crushing the workers and building taller buildings. Müllertown is capitalism gone amok, runaway speculation and insane Ponzi schemes. M's dream of Marienbad has created a society of apathetic super-rich stuck on the same groove for how long? And this Alphaville here is the worst of all: imperial dreams with mindless drones and an unlimited supply of microchips. Not bad, but what if you could get all of the above in a single package—better and bigger?"

"I'm listening."

"You know that I belong to the Guild of Temporal Adventurers," continued Jerry. "I've got just the place for you and your reprobate friends: America. Fifty years from now. Turn left at the Millennium and when you see the Towers come down, you've arrived. Trust me; you'll be like a bug in a rug!"

"Hmm… I know the time period of which you speak… You make a compelling case."

"Don't I?"

"I would like to seal our pact," said Arioch.

"What do you have in mind?" said Jerry, with a slight frown. Bargaining with demons—especially Princes of Chaos—always contained a small margin of uncertainty, sometimes too close for comfort.

Natasha grabbed his white silk scarf, pulled his face down to hers and sensuously kissed him on the lips.

Jerry relaxed and smiled.

"I see. Love is what makes the worlds go round, eh?"

"Not love. This mortal doesn't know the meaning of the word anymore than I. Just sex."

"Sex is good enough for me," said Jerry, taking off his leather jacket.

The Castle, a week later

"Our next agent has already been assigned, Mrs. Personn," said Herr Klamm. "A Mr. Lemmy Caution. One lump or two?"

Mrs. Persson reflected that she had never tasted tea that was so dishwaterish, except once in Moscow under Gorbachev, but she refrained from saying so.

"Two, please. Mr. Caution is an excellent choice, Herr Klamm."

"I believe so. When Natasha Von Braun discovers love, Alphaville will be destroyed. It's only a matter of time now."

"It is always a matter of time. How is the rest of your, er, pruning campaign going?"

"Very well, I'm happy to report. In Metropolis, Rotwang has relocated Xiombarg, the Chaos Queen who inhabited Maria, into a mechanical creature of his invention, but I'm confident things will fall apart soon. Our agent Pierre Brok has just brought about the fall of Müllertown, and X is presently doing the same to Marienbad."

"What about Mr. Cornelius? I understand he was gone when Alpha-60's men arrived at the hotel."

"Truthfully, we don't know what happened to him. But it's highly likely that Lord Arioch just dropped him off somewhere else in the Outlands."

"Well, in that case, he'll find his way back. I doubt there is anyone or anything that can truly faze our Mr. Cornelius."

Elsewhere in the Outlands

Jerry woke up. Arioch was gone, but strangely enough, the Chaos Lord's seal which had been on Natasha's breast, had been transferred to him during their lovemaking.

He didn't know what it meant. He would worry about it later.

A fat little man with a pointed hat was looking at him with deep suspicion in his piggish eyes.

"*Merdre!*" said Père Ubu! "Come and see what the cat just dragged in, Mère Ubu!"

Xavier Mauméjean won the Gerardmer Award in 2000 for his psychological thriller The Memoirs of the Elephant Man. *His other works include* Gotham *(2001), another thriller,* The League of Heroes, *which won the 2003 Imaginaire Award of the City of Brussels and was translated by Black Coat Press in 2005,* La Vénus Anatomique, *which won the 2005 Rosny Award, and* Lilliputia, *which won the 2009 Rosny Award . Xavier has a diploma in philosophy and the science of religions and works as a teacher in the North of France, where he resides, with his wife and his daughter, Zelda.*

Xavier Mauméjean: *Qayin*

Am I my brother's keeper?
Genesis 4:9

Though we are all assigned a guardian angel,
the unlucky ones have careless angels.
Michael Moorcock

The stars never lie. Seeing that they were out of place, Elric was no longer in his world. The Prince of Melniboné had been riding for three days along with Moonglum. They crossed a red steppe beaten by the winds without encountering a living soul. At most a pack of hungry wolves watching the albino only to turn away immediately. He, too, was scrawny. Maybe they saw in the stranger a pale brother, certainly not prey to be shared. His red eyes would have deterred the bravest and crushed the fervor of a lion. At nightfall Elric decided to halt. The spot was as good as any other to camp. Leaving Moonglum to take care of the horses he prepared a meager fire. With difficulty because his hands trembled. The pain devouring his soul made every movement unbearable. Elric held in a scream. Moonglum finally came up to him. The poet grabbed his bag and took out a wineskin, a few biscuits and some dried meat. He did not share his food. His prince had no need to feed himself. Elric required something else. Blood, gushed forth by Stormbringer, his sword.

"Help me, my friend."

Elric untied the leather bag around his chest. He handed it to Moonglum who took out a pinch of magic herbs to steep in water. The Prince of Ruins drank the boiling hot concoction. Moonglum watched his sullen, milky white face. He seemed calmer under the effect of the drug. For the moment, at least, because the rune-carved sword would not stayed satisfied for long by this ploy.

"Your health is declining, my prince."

"It's the fault of this world."

Moonglum glanced around. "This land looks young."

"It's not yet found its place in the conflict that sets Order against Chaos. My sorcery is weak here."

"How is the sword reacting?"

"Stormbringer is confused. It's howling deep down inside me."

"Maybe we have a role to play here. A mission ordered by the Lord of Chaos. His plans are sometimes obscure."

Elric forced a smile. "You speak the truth, my friend. While waiting to find out Arioch's will, take your lute and force yourself to distract me."

The poet started in on a sweet song that recalled the splendors of the Young Kingdoms. Elric wrapped himself in his coat and fell asleep to Moonglum's harmony. He had no prophetic dreams about what awaited them.

The attack surprised them in the light of dawn. Moonglum was gathering their things when the rock hit him in the head. As his hand came up to his forehead he collapsed at Elric's feet. The albino reacted quickly. He drew the runic sword and prepared to fight. Stormbringer did not react. Usually the black blade would have shrilled in pleasure, hungry for the souls it would be drinking.

The attackers approached, armed with slingshots and knives, closing in their circle. The sword remained silent. The albino prince watched his adversaries. They looked like nomads, covered in furs and metal jewelry. There were both men and women. All of them were redheaded and bore a mark on their forehead. The Melnibonéan could have routed them without the help of Stormbringer but seeing Moonglum get up, furious and cursing, he decided to wait.

One of the nomads, the tallest, stepped forward. He said to Elric, "Our prophecies mention a dark man who is supposed to help us. You are that man."

The man with fire-red hair spoke in an archaic language with harsh inflexions, which nonetheless Elric and Moonglum could understand.

The poet intervened, "Poor fool, can't you see his snow-white hair and pale face?"

The giant looked Moonglum up and down before turning his attention to Elric. "Yes, but darkness fills his soul. It's something we share. Will you follow us?"

The albino stared at the mark on the warrior's forehead. A circle, carved with a knife, like a serpent eating its tail. A symbol of eternity, the interchange of opposites that reminded Elric of the opposition between Law and Chaos. Moonglum's words came back to him: maybe he was here to accomplish a mission on the orders of Arioch.

Elric sheathed Stormbringer and said to the poet, "Ready the horses."

Then, without a word of explanation to his companion, he followed the nomads.

They headed for their city. It was, therefore, a settled tribe. But these people looked like wanderers who would have found their place by default. As they got closer to the city the plains of hard clay gave way to fields of barley, rye and wheat, standing tall and waving in the breeze. Even the wind seemed milder as if trying to guide them. They went along the vast, grassy expanses with flocks of grazing sheep and pastures where magnificent bulls looked free to do as they pleased. In answer to Moonglum's questions the redheaded giant explained the irrigation systems that watered the crops, the vast network of canals that constantly fed the land and transformed it into fertile soil. Elric listened without interrupting. He had inherited his father's reserve, a tendency not to speak when it was unnecessary. He was satisfied with watching the countryside and thinking about what Arioch had in store for him.

The procession finally reached the city. It was surrounded by a 100-foot tall double wall. The outer fortifications had eight gates with riveted doors, were wide enough to let in the three war chariots side by side. The Prince of Ruins and Moonglum passed under a stone arch braced with bronze. They followed a wide roadway to the market.

Male and female merchants selling their goods turned silent when they passed. Feeling uncomfortable Moonglum leaned out of his saddle to whisper in Elric's ear. "Have you noticed, my prince? They all have red hair."

"Yes, and everyone has that serpent mark. Even the children."

The head of the expedition ordered a halt. Leaving his guests to the care of the warriors he entered a whitewashed brick house but soon came back out with an old man. The giant came up to them leading the elder by the arm. At first sight he looked fragile but Elric changed his mind. The patriarch was strong, not with physical strength, which dulls with age, but with a fierce, unbending will. This could be seen in his eyes.

The albino took note of the mark on the old man's forehead. It looked just like the others but had not been carved with a knife. It was stamped on the flesh. Fascinated, Elric watched the pale serpent that looked like scarred tissue. It seemed animated with a life of its own, like a wheel turning endlessly on the old brow. Elric thought that such a face must have troubled many a hardened killer.

The patriarch caught his eyes. Far from being offended he smiled and said, "Welcome. My people call me Qayin. But I'm also known as the First Murderer."

Qayin invited them to his table. They were given choice dishes served by two beautiful young women with tawny hair. Ada and Cilla, the old man's granddaughters. The giant who had led them to the city was named Yabal. They were all descendants of Qayin. Moonglum relished the food, gulped down the fig wine and gobbled up the braised mutton. Elric only drank his potion. When the guests were refreshed the patriarch questioned Elric.

"Who are you?"

"Elric, legitimate heir to the throne of Melniboné."

"I've never heard of the place."

"You're not missing much." Then the Prince of Ruins became serious. His eyes flashed red and putting aside his dark memories he asked the old man, "What is the name of this place?"

"You are in the land of Nod, a region located to the east of Eden."

"Eden?"

Qayin let out a bitter laugh. "Paradise, or so they say, if you like the freedom of a slave."

The guests said nothing for a long time before Moonglum broke the silence.

"Why did you bring us here?"

The old man raised his head. The mark on his forehead looked like it was burning his flesh.

"To face the army of God."

On the following day the travelers appeared at the gates of the city. They were on foot and seemed to come out of nowhere. All three were dressed in long, dark coats. Hoods hid their faces. The gatekeeper led them to Qayin. Before entering they took off their sandals. The patriarch was surrounded by his family. Yabal, Tubal the blacksmith, and Henoch the architect who had built the city. The women were also present. Elric and Moonglum stood in the back. Qayin offered drinks and cakes, as custom demanded. The travelers disregarded the attention.

All together they removed their hoods, revealing three identical faces of perfect beauty. Looking upon such perfection was painful. Everyone looked away.

Qayin was the first to talk. "You haven't changed."

"We can't say the same for you."

They talked in unison, in a captivating and yet monotone voice, devoid of emotion.

"That's the fate of mortals. I've aged."

"Yes, but without learning anything. And worse, Qayin, you disobeyed."

The patriarch pretended to straightened up. "I was banished."

"That's not enough. Have you forgotten the terms of the agreement?"

"Solitude was my lot for years on end."

One of the travelers stretched out his arms. "But here you are today, the head of a mighty lineage. And of a prosperous city. You who were forced to wander."

"Haven't I paid enough?"

"No, and we are here to notify you of the sentence. In six days from today we will come back to your city. To knock down the walls and annihilate your people from the first to the last."

One of Qayin's daughters stepped out of the group. Paying no attention to the men, she held up a baby and spoke to the strangers. "Who among my sisters has not honored her duty as a woman? More than once I have lied down on the bed as a lover and woken up a mother. All of us here have done so. Isn't it our duty to propagate?"

"That commandment did not concern your father's tribe."

"Can you tell this to my child?"

Voices encouraged her to continue. The disheveled woman held out her baby in tears. "He's barely come out of my belly. Would you dare to say that my son is guilty?"

One traveler watched the group, giving each of them the impression that he was staring at them, that he was testing them personally.

"Guilty he is, because of his ancestor. You all belong to a lineage that should not exist, that of the First Murderer. The child, therefore, will be wiped out. Prepare to die."

The strangers turned around at the same time. As they were about to leave one of them spoke to Elric in the ancient language of Melniboné. "We know you, servant of Chaos. Take our advice. For once, do not oppose the Law. This is not your fight."

"They're Angels."

Elric was standing next to Qayin in the dark of the night. They were on the top of a tower, watching the crowd below. Their conversation was sometimes drowned out by shouting. Baffled by the announcement the inhabitants of the city wandered around aimlessly or gathered outside their houses so that they would not be alone. The crowd was waiting, dazed. Some were crying or trying to comfort one another. Everyone looked empty of hope.

"Angels, you say?"

"Archangel is their real title. Princes, Elric, who sit on the throne at the top of the celestial hierarchy. They are commanders of legions. One of them is named Gabriel, the other Raphael. As for the third, he's called Makatiel, *the plague of God.*"

"You seem to know them well."

Qayin looked off into the distance. "Since always. As a child I watched them when they played with my brother in the east of the Garden. They guarded the entrance."

"What did you do to make them angry with you?"

Qayin leaned against the stone and for a moment looked worn out. "I killed Hebel. I murdered my only brother."

The albino thought of his own family. Specifically of Yyrkoon, his cousin who had stolen the throne of Melniboné from him. But this was not the worst of it. Using black magic Yyrkoon had plunged Cymoril, his sister and Elric's lover, into an eternal sleep.

"Sometimes it's necessary to confront your relatives. I can understand."

Qayin shot back up to his full height. "No, you can't! I loved my young brother more than my own life. Do you know what Hebel means? *Short-lived*, he who doesn't stay. By calling him this my parents destined him to die quickly."

"Why murder him?"

"God demanded sacrifices. I offered him the most perfect among us, the best of the flock."

"Your god could have killed you."

"Yes but he didn't. Maybe he realized that he had forgotten something."

"What?"

"Nobody told me that I shouldn't kill my brother. How could I break a law that nobody knew about? No decree against this crime, nothing."

"And he exiled you."

Qayin slapped his forehead. "Yes, after marking my face."

The serpent coiled under his skin. No one could look upon the First Murderer without being struck with horror. The mark of Qayin attracted every man's attention, only to turn it away immediately."

"But you found a wife."

"After years of wandering. And what had been a symbol of infamy became the emblem of our tribe. We are the sons of the Serpent. Havah, my mother, can't deny it!"

The patriarch smiled bitterly. He looked like he was holding back tears. No friendly word could lighten his burden. Moreover, Elric was incapable of charity. But the servant of Chaos could come to his aide.

"We have five days to prepare for the attack."

"You heard the Angel, this battle is not yours."

"Your people saw a savior in me, foretold by the oracles. I am opposed to Law, whatever world I'm in."

"Are you sure? It will be a hard fight."

"Arioch leaves me no choice."

Qayin grabbed his arm. His grip was firm. "In that case, Lord of Ruins, I accept your offer."

The patriarch called his sons together. Elric told them about his decision and they listened in silence. No one would have dared to challenge his word with Qayin vouching for him.

Tubal the blacksmith, however, voiced his doubts. "Father, I don't question the white prince's valor, but we'll be facing Angels, legions of Angels."

The old man stood in the middle of the gathering. "Yes, and that's why there's hope, my son."

"I don't understand."

Qayin spoke to all of them. "One single word, an Angel's whisper, is enough to topple the city. Now, they won't do it. On the contrary, the army of God wants a battle. Iron against iron to inflict punishment on us through thousands of wounds. And to fight they'll need bodies."

"But aren't the Angels pure spirits?"

The old man turned to Yabal, "You remember my teaching well. It's true, they have immortal forms. But to incarnate they need matter. And we can destroy matter."

All of them stood frozen.

Suddenly Tubal the blacksmith brandished his hammer. "Father, if I understand you, we can defeat the legions?"

"At the very least hurt them badly. So that they'll finally understand what pain is."

Qayin's sons roared freely. Jubal the musician picked up a drum, quickly followed by his brothers. A rumbling rose out of their throats, accompanied by their drumming. Like the promise of slaughter, directed to the heavens.

Moonglum turned to Elric. "Didn't the old man say that the Angels are immortal?"

"Yes, my friend, everyone here knows it. I think they're all ready to die, but not without putting up a fight. For the moment, let's not spoil their joy."

At the break of day Elric and Moonglum joined Tubal on the ramparts. The blacksmith was overseeing the work on the fortifications. Masons and laborers were working hard to strengthen the wall. The men and women labored in silence, measuring every action and producing efficient results.

The albino said to the blacksmith, "We'll need archers in this spot."

Tubal uncrossed his powerful arms covered in red stubble. "Our children can do it."

He snapped his fingers. Straightaway a boy no higher than his hip stood next to him. Spotting a vulture flying over the steppe he drew his bow and released the arrow, which hit the bird of prey.

Impressed, Moonglum tilted back his hat. "Well, no need to worry about the defense! If you don't mind, my prince, I'm going to take a tour of the city."

Elric nodded. The poet scrambled down the stone stairs and headed for the center. When he arrived in the big, crowded square he elbowed his way through to the front row. The crowd was watching a fight.

The battle pitted Cilla against Yabal. The young woman was lying at the feet of the giant.

"Stop wallowing on the ground like a bitch in heat. Get up and face me!"

Cilla was having a hard time breathing. On wobbly legs she struggled to her feet while Yabal paced around her, holding his quarterstaff along his side. Cilla leaned on her spear. She tried to attack but Yabal stepped aside and kicked her in the ribs. The young woman coughed and spit blood. Red like her hair. This was an execution. Moonglum was about to jump in when they grabbed him and held him back. Qayin motioned for him to stay put.

The staff sliced through the air. Cilla dodged the blow, blocked a series of attacks and struck back, hitting her opponent on the shoulder. Moonglum was mesmerized by the sparring. The girl had some strength left. Yabal threw down his staff and pulled out a club.

"You want to fight? Let's go."

Cilla limped to the center of the arena. Her adversary was juggling his weapon. The young woman did not take her eyes off it. With a wide, spinning swing she sent the club flying. The giant bounded forward but Cilla threw herself at his legs. Yabal soared through the air and crashed to the ground. He tried to get up but the hardened end of the spear was pressed against his throat.

Cilla threw up her weapon and held out her hand. Yabal stood up, laughing jovially. "I'm proud of you, cousin. The Angels are in for a challenge. And your future husband as well!"

The end of the fight was met with loud applause. Qayin offered to introduce Moonglum to the young woman. The poet improvised a few lines in his head when Cilla spoke to him.

"Maybe I won't have time to find a husband. But some unions don't need to be official."

These people were certainly full of surprises! Moonglum followed the fighter to her home. She lit a lamp before lying down on her bed.

"What are you waiting for?"

The poet stared at the sizzling wick. "What's burning?"

"A kind of fatty oil that we find outside the city. My uncles call it tar. But come over here!"

Moonglum obeyed. Even putting his whole spirit into it, he would not do much justice to his reputation as a lover.

"A wall of flame that they'll light up on the ramparts."

Henoch the architect and Tubal the blacksmith were listening carefully to Moonglum. Elric's companion did not have a hard time convincing them. The women were already getting together to sew the wineskins.

"But we can do better."

Henoch was thinking out loud as he drew a schematic on a clay tablet. He put away his reed and handed the slab to his brother. "Tubal, can you build these tubes in time?"

The blacksmith looked at the drawing, then broke out laughing. "Yes, and I think I can do it using bronze. But the workshops have to operate day and night."

"Well, get going! Our father's already sent off to Yabal to get the pitch."

Qayin's sons left to join their teams. Elric and Moonglum remained alone.

"Something's bothering me, my friend."

"No surprise there, prince. It's understandable."

"I'm not talking about the battle. What must be will be."

"So, what are you thinking about?"

"Stormbringer, my sword. The black blade is absolutely calm. It isn't making me suffer."

"Which is good news!"

The albino's face became taut. "I don't know. Stormbringer seems to be holding its thirst for the attack. As if it were the final combat."

By means of lifting machines they had set up the tubes on the walls. To shoot the tar they just had to squeeze the leather skins. A torch at the opening would light up the pitch. But the first trials did not prove convincing. The jet was too short or shot back at them with the slightest gust of wind. Henoch the architect worked to correct the faults.

The mood was dark the closer the deadline came. Elric, sunk in gloomy thoughts, stayed in Qayin's house.

"Your loneliness is great, white prince. This is something I am familiar with."

The old man sat next to him and offered a cup. Qayin let no one else prepare the drug. Elric drank the brew. Then he turned to the old man.

"It takes courage to oppose the Law."

The patriarch stretched out his legs. Despite his age they were still strong. Qayin would stand firm in combat.

"You mean to start a family? It's not a matter of courage. I just didn't want to die alone. Besides, every man has the right to live in peace. At least for a little while."

Elric thought of Zarozinia, his wife, who was waiting for him in Kaarlak. Would Arioch, Lord of Chaos, allow him to go back to her someday?

"You, too, Prince of Ruins, should build something and have children."

For that the Cosmic Balance would need to come to a point of equilibrium, which would never happen. Stasis and Entropy were engaged in an eternal battle.

Elric clutched Stormbringer's jewel-incrusted hilt until the runes were stamped in his flesh.

And it was the sixth day. At dawn the defenders gathered on the ramparts, on the lookout for the arrival of the legions. Everyone was watching the skies, but the emissary came from below. One single Angel wearing a hooded cloak. He revealed himself and spoke to Qayin:

"So, you are incorrigible. Don't you see that your weapons are ridiculous? Stop this show of pride and accept the sentence."

The patriarch leaned over the bronze tubes, balancing on the parapet. "The faces of Angels are all the same. Sublime but without character and yet I recognize you. You are Gabriel, the herald of God. Go tell your master that men are imperfect, erratic and never predictable. We call this Freedom. Which is the most precious of gifts. And I have made this offering to my people. We're proud of owing nothing to a master. Tell him this and don't leave anything out."

"There's no need for me to tell him. God has heard your final word. And his answer is: Prepare to die!"

The Angel's cloak went up in flames, revealing his ruby armor. Gabriel unfolded his immaculate white wings and rose into the heavens. Straightaway the sun disappeared behind the cloud. A low groan passed through the ranks of defenders. There were thousands of celestial warriors. Against the Angels in their radiant array the people of the Serpent wore only old cuirasses over their rough tunics.

"Don't fire until I give the order."

Qayin was standing at the head of his people. The legions wheeled around above the city forming a vortex. A whirlwind capable of sucking up life.

"No poet could describe this vision. It would make him go blind."

Moonglum was fascinated. The Prince of Ruins drew his black blade. Stormbringer chanted its dirge. The albino could barely contain it. Elric understood why on seeing Makatiel. The Plague of God was brandishing a sword of light that was the opposite of his own.

The army of Seraphim swooped down on the city.

"Now!"

The fiery launches vomited their blazing liquid. An Angel, turned into a torch, smashed straight into the wall. Others fell on the steppe, their wings burned. But they were numerous. The front line stepped onto the ramparts striking with their swords. Tubal the blacksmith roared and swung his axe, ripping through a cuirass. Elric drove his black blade through a shining baldric. He recoiled at the shock. The energy absorbed by Stormbringer, sunk to the very heart of the Angel, was absolutely pure. The runic sword was drinking from the sources of the Law.

But the Seraphim were hardened warriors, veterans of eternal battles. All of them remembered fighting their own renegade legions and casting Lucifer into the depths of the abyss. They had no fear of humans. In fact, the Angels were incapable of feelings, good or bad; they just carried out the will of the Most High.

There were thousands of them, wing to wing, forming a field of enemies that was impossible to cut down. Qayin and his people, however, did not give up an inch of ground. Cilla fired her slingshot, targeting a Seraph and bringing him down with a stone. Four Angels filled his gap right away. They trampled the body of their companion, marching fearlessly, indifferent to the arrows flying through their ranks.

Qayin and his people held a thin line of defense that would eventually fall. They had to fight, however, to keep the swarm from overwhelming their front line. Everyone knew that they were the last defense before reaching the heart of the city. They managed to hold back the waves of attack, but it cost them heavy losses and they started to show signs of weakness. On the other side the heavenly legion replenished its ranks ceaselessly. Tubal and his brothers had already been forced to leave their forward posts and abandon the bodies of sons or spouses. Their souls, snuffed out by the Angels, could not rise to heaven.

"Behind you!"

Moonglum's warning came too late. The Angel gripped Elric by the shoulders. The albino could not get free. Pushing against the low wall he threw himself backward. The Seraphim was impaled on the point of his shield. The fell at Moonglum's feet, his eyes bulging out. The poet turned away. He did not want to look into the eyes because they were empty. A liquid void staring at the sky.

Farther away, in a corner hanging over empty space, Cilla and her sisters were pushing back a furious assault. The Angels were rushing forward without weapons, grabbing the women and throwing them 200 feet below.

In the middle of the day the defense of the main rampart finally gave way. Qayin and his sons broke the line and formed staggered rows, almost slipping on the puddles of blood. They had no more spears or javelins and the bows were useless. They fought hand to hand, swinging axes and swords or stabbing arrows into the throats of the attackers. The red-haired people howled out their courage and screamed out their pain.

A frontal defense was dong no good. Elric yelled orders: "Fall back and get to the stairs!"

Obeying the Melnibonéan they hunkered down on the steps, squeezing their shields together on the landing.

Henoch wiped the sweat off his beard. "Their tactic is simple. They'll wear us down." The architect was speaking true. "We have to use the skins."

Moonglum grabbed a skin filled with bitumen and popped off the wicker stopper. Yabal the giant held up his shield arm, offered the tip of his torch and turned his head away.

Moonglum squeezed the skin. The bitumen lit up on contact with the flame. A jet of liquid fire ravaged the enemy ranks, transforming every warrior of light into a black, sticky mass. Their limbs melted under the heat. Their wings stuck together under their chainmail tunics to end up welded by the tar. Some of them tried to escape the blaze by taking flight.

"They're getting away. We have to clear out before reinforcements come."

On Elric's orders the defenders abandoned the wall, stepping around the burning bodies. Moonglum tripped and almost got stuck to one of the sizzling corpses. Halfway to their goal they stopped. The guards of God were rushing back to intercept them, in spearhead formation to break up the group. The skins were empty. Qayin and his people readied themselves for the clash. But at the last second their enemies veered to the left and swooped down on Yabal. The giant did not have time to react. Backed against the wall, surrounded on all sides, he perished under the blows.

Drunk on rage his brothers leaped into the fray, headed by Qayin. The patriarch fought like in a trance, throwing all caution to the wind. Blade in hand, he sliced his way through to the corpse of his son, nailed to the wall. When he pulled out the spear, the giant slid to the ground.

Tubal the blacksmith stepped forward. He was holding his belly. "Father, I think we've beat them back."

His legs gave way and he fell forward. Cilla ran to him and pushed his hands away. The sword was stuck up to the hilt. Cilla, feeling powerless, held back her tears and turned to Elric.

The Prince of Ruins grabbed an empty cloth bag and plastered it to the wound. "There's nothing we can do for you. But you can hold them off with your machines for long enough for us to get back into the center of town. You think you can do that?"

Tubal managed a bloodstained grin. "Give me that torch and you'll see for yourself."

Qayin did not move. "I'm staying with my son."

Moonglum grabbed the old man's tunic. "You have a duty to your people, otherwise all this will have been for nothing!"

The patriarch finally gave in. He led his people while Elric and the poet tried to create a diversion. They ran into a maze of alleys. The legions were destroying the city around them. Striking at hazard, not caring what they were targeting, as children and adults all fell victim. Elric and Moonglum lost count of the corpses being profaned in this despicable way by the very servants of Law. Suddenly, some Angels dropped out of the sky and formed a semi-circle. In a single movement Elric and Moonglum skewered the Seraphim facing them. Using the bodies as shields the albino and his companion charged through the group.

They had to separate, to split up the hunt. Two different prey, one slight chance for each to survive.

"We'll meet up later!"

Elric saw his companion hurtle down the stairs. The Prince of Ruins decided to cut across the gardens. He ran with no regard for the branches whipping his face, his pursuers at his heels. The omniscient Angels knew the terrain. Elric skirted around a red-haired corpse and came to the top of a terrace. The city had many platforms like this. Henoch the architect had built his city high up, like a provocation to the heavens. Elric considered the various levels stacked up on columns. He had to climb up a huge pillar to get to the upper level.

The Melnibonéan reached the edge of the corbel that hung over empty air but he did not manage to get up the column. The water cascading over the top made the surface slippery and the stone was partly crumbling away. Elric was about to try again when something grabbed his leg. He tried to kick it away but the Angel had a firm grip. He was directly beneath him. The albino prince swung down Stormbringer, severing the Seraph's hand. Then he went back to the central staircase. This seemed too easy but he had no choice. Elric took the stairs two by two leading to the upper platforms. He was on the fifth level when the archangel Raphael stood in his way, holding a net of golden chains.

For the moment Elric preferred to delay the confrontation. The Prince of Ruins held his breath and jumped into the void. His body crashed hard onto the lower ledge. The pain almost made him loose his grip. However, he was able to keep hold and swing his legs over the balustrade. He dropped onto the moist earth covering the masonry. Standing up right away, he swung around just when one of the Angels flew up and straight at him. An arrow shot the warrior down in mid-air. He crashed 20 yards below, his body bouncing down the steps like a rag doll. Elric looked up. The archer with the fire-red hair, who could not have been more than ten years old, gave him a big smile.

The albino got out of the exposed space. The killer with the net made no effort to hide as he followed him. Elric decided to face him. Raphael took up the challenge. The Archangel took a moment to unfurl his net. The albino clutched his rune-carved sword and planted himself in front of the Angel.

Raphael held the end of his weapon. "Since you came here, it means you are resolved. I like a man to be sure of himself. It lets me kill him without remorse."

He spoke in a gentle voice, free of cruelty. With his long hand he invited Elric to come closer. The Prince of Ruins stepped forward. The Archangel swung his net and threw it at Elric. The chains struck his leather shoulder strap, shredding it to pieces. The champion of Chaos gripped Stormbringer with both hands. He swung the blade but the Archangel dodged it easily. The adversaries stood apart and paused.

Raphael pulled in his net like a fisher of men. "You react quickly, servant of Arioch. Let's see how long you can hold out against the Law."

The Angel with translucent skin slid to the left and reached back. Elric tried a frontal attack but Raphael squatted down and swept the ground with his net. The albino felt a searing pain when the chains lashed his ankles. He fell backward and kicked hard to free his legs. The Archangel tried nothing more and gave him time to get back on his feet. Then he blew a kiss at Elric and positioned himself for another round. The Prince of Ruins walked around his motionless enemy and lunged with his sword. The blade sunk into the chainmail.

Raphael yanked the net and Stormbringer went flying through the air. "Pick up your sword. Or give up because you can't do anything to me."

The Melnibonéan picked up his obsidian blade. Raphael tossed away the golden net and marched up to the albino. "Know this, servant of Chaos, I have no need of weapons to defeat you."

The punch went right through Elric's leather armor and struck his ribs. The Archangel stepped back to see the results. A monotone melody escaped his lips. He leaped forward and kicked.

The albino barely had time to step aside. When he missed, the warrior from the clouds lost his balance. With great effort Elric lifted his heavy sword and struck the Angel's thigh. God's beloved doubled over. Elric punched his face. His fist smashed the perfect features. Raphael wrapped around his enemy, covering him completely with his wings, crushing his ribcage. His hands clutched the albino's throat, squeezing like a mighty vise.

"Let me catch your breath, servant of Arioch, you'll be better off."

The Archangel had empty eyes. His attention was distracted, as if bewitched by a perfect eternity. It was Elric's only chance. He gripped Stormbringer and plunged the runic blade into the Seraph's throat. Raphael collapsed like a tower.

A dark veil clouded the eyes of the albino prince. When he regained consciousness, Makatiel was smiling at him.

The Plague of God was pointing his sword of light at Moonglum's throat. "We warned you, Elric of Melniboné. This is not your battle. You killed Raphael. Know now that I'll do the same to your friend."

The albino straightened up. "Wait! If you want to bathe your sword in blood, forget the poet and face me."

Makatiel pushed Moonglum away. "Equal against equal. Law against Chaos. I accept the duel."

Makatiel took off his armor and kept only his sword. He raised the blade up to his chin. Elric took an offensive position. All of a sudden the Archangel lunged. The albino parried the blow and struck back. Stormbringer whipped through the air but the Plague of God blocked it easily. The adversaries took a break while circling around each other, coming in closer and closer. Elric stood up straight, holding his sword out horizontally, awaiting the attack. The Archangel looked like he was hesitating. He measured the distance separating him from the albino and then rushed forward. At the last second Makatiel lunged to the side and swung his sword.

The blade crushed Elric's ribs. The Prince of Ruins lost his breath. The sword of light was a formidable weapon being wielded by an expert. But its twin was no less daunting. Elric swiped backhand, hitting the Archangel's legs. Makatiel tottered forward. The albino stood behind him and brought his sword down hard on his back, cracking the wing bones. The Seraph tried to turn around but Elric kicked him and he fell down.

Lifting Stormbringer over his head Elric struck with all his strength. The Plague of God caught the black sword in his hands and tore it away. Elric was unarmed. Makatiel grabbed his shining blade. He smiled wickedly, as if all perfection had abandoned him.

"Enough!"

Gabriel appeared out of nowhere, his wings covered in soot.

"The battle has to stop."

"Why? He's at my mercy!"

"That's enough, Makatiel. Lower your weapon and look at the sky."

Elric and his adversary looked up into the starry night.

"The sixth day is over. On the seventh God rested and his legions along with him. Anyway, Qayin is dying."

The Melnibonéan and Moonglum found the patriarch in his house surrounded by his family. He was bedridden. Qayin panted for Elric to come closer. Cilla moved aside. The young woman was not even trying to hold back her tears.

"I'm dying, Elric, struck in the heart. Proof, at least, that I have one."

The mark on his forehead was still, perhaps a sign that the old man was leaving in peace. His body was shaken by a violent cough. Then he spit out some oily phlegm veined with blood.

"With you gone, Qayin, so too goes the curse of the serpent. The Angels must be satisfied."

"You surprise me, Elric. Could the champion of Chaos trust in Law?"

"After what I saw today, I'd have a hard time telling the difference between the two. Yes, the difference is beyond me."

"In that case, try to find your point of balance, Elric of Melniboné."

Leaving the old man to the care of his family, the Prince of Ruins shook Qayin's hand and left.

Elric wandered through the alleys of the big market. Children were escaping from the mothers and running among the posts. Life was getting back to normal; the time of disorder seemed far away. However, every house in the city had at least one victim and the patriarch was living his final moments. But the absolution for all pronounced by the Archangels numbed the grief and sorrow.

Gabriel was waiting for him at the foot of the ramparts. He had removed his armor and was wearing a coat.

"From now on, the Eternal One, our sovereign, doesn't want to hear about men anymore. A world has just toppled into Entropy. And you're pleased with yourself, albino prince?"

"What I feel doesn't count for anything."

Contemplating the response the herald of God stood thoughtful for a moment.

"Basically, we're not so different. Even the pallor of our skin is similar. Like two halves of a lost original."

"And each serves his master."

Opening his coat the Archangel drew out the sword of light. Elric put his hand on the hilt of Stormbringer.

"Nothing to fear, the time of fighting is over. From now on I'm the one who has to be on guard. Just like you have to take care of your dark sister."

"Make sure you use it well."

Gabriel was aware of the distant future, Elric's and poor Moonglum's, both of them victims of Stormbringer.

"The same for you, White Wolf, the same for you."

Christian Vilà has been a professional writer since 1973, authoring SF, crime and horror novels as well as graphic novels and teleplays. His novel Sang Futur *(1977) became a cult book for the French punk movement. Christian has also been the president of the French Writers' Union (SELF) since 2011.*

Christian Vilà: *Brother of the Hyenas*

The sky and earth were one and the world was just a dizzying white nothingness. The sea of fog was thinning here and there only to reveal a driving snowstorm where the landscape just became more and more lost. Elric took a wary breath of the icy air and panted it out in little in little puffs. It was so cold that the steam coming out of his mouth froze right away and blew back to sting his face with tiny ice crystals. Over the course of the night, the freeze had been so intense that Elric almost could not breathe. He would have died of the cold if he had been wearing only his usual clothes. Luckily, ten days earlier he had happened upon a great aurochs. The solitary old male was very touchy and charged as soon as he saw him. After dodging the attack, Elric pierced its heart with his sword. When he had rendered the beast harmless, he drank its blood and ate as much as possible of its raw flesh before it turned as hard as stone. Thus sated, he had demoted Stormbringer to the inglorious rank of a skinning knife and made a fur coat out of the animal's thick hide. Then he had loaded as much of the aurochs meat as possible onto his shoulders and resumed his wandering in the land of white death. His feet crunched the snow dully as they sunk up to his knees.

As stringy and tough as it was, the old aurochs' flesh had kept him from starving during the five days when the blizzard had forced him to take refuge under a tall larch tree. Elric had dug a hole in the snow and constantly fed a campfire that the icy blasts threatened to extinguish every minute. When the reserve of meat had ran out, he was forced to put the prey's femur on the fire, grill the bone and then break it between two rocks in order to scrape out the burning marrow, which he gobbled up ravenously. Retracing his steps to replenish his store of frozen flesh from the aurochs' carcass, the albino was sorely surprised to find that the ribcage had been scraped down to the bone and was unable to provide him with any food at all, just empty vertebrae with spinal marrow. For three days now, he had been forced to lick the thin film of fat that lined his improvised coat and tirelessly nibble the leather to suck out some remnant of juice, as insipid as might be, but that at least had the merit of staving off hunger. If Elric did not find some more game very soon, he would be forced to chew the bark of the larch and birch trees in the area. And he certainly could not hope to hold out for long on such a diet. The bitter sap in the bark would intoxicate him in no time, if not kill him.

Located on the borders of the inhabited world, to north of the steppes of Lormyr, the region where the warrior was roaming suffered the full force of the immemorial confrontation between the lords of Chaos and those of Law. In the summer, vast fires ravaged it. In the winter, an inhuman cold froze it. Whatever the season, the vegetation protected itself against the aggression by secreting poisons. Thus it was with the *m'scaris* mushroom that contained a substance that allowed an oracle to raise the veil that hid both the past and the future. Dame ¥ris, the sibyl living in a grotto around the Purple Towns, had asked Elric to pick a few specimens and bring them back from his journey to the north. This purpose, however, was far from explaining his presence in a region located on the borders of the inhabited world... The picking he had come to do here was of a different kind—so dangerous that the albino had refused to let his faithful companion Moonglum travel with him. He had left him in the good care of ¥ris whose tenderness would help overcome his boredom.

The snow was falling heavily in delicate, frosty snow-flakes that deepened the spotless layer that carpeted the undergrowth. Elric stood still after shaking his hair, which was as white as the snow. A mournful cry prolonged into a kind of dreadful laugh attracted his attention. Another, but coming from the opposite direction, answered it. The snow hyenas... Had they smelled his presence or was there another prey? It did not matter. One thing was sure: they had to be at least as hungry as he was.

His red eyes narrowed. He listened more carefully to the sounds around him. Two more calls echoed, much closer. Now there was no doubt: the large pack had spotted him and chosen him as their target. A persistent legend described the hyenas as revolting, cowardly scavengers, but the reality was completely different. Gnawed by hunger, these animals did not hesitate to attack a buffalo or an armed human. One evening, in a tent on the outskirts of the Sighing Desert, near the Wargla Oasis, Husseyn the Nomad had related to Elric a belief of his country. The elders said that in a time beyond memory when the ancestors of men were still only half erect on their legs, they hunted in groups, attacking the most dangerous prey if found alone or weak. Well, with their short rump and their sloping back, the hyenas looked a lot like these human ancestors. Their solidarity was no different than that which united the distant relatives of humanity. Their cunning and ferocity were just as strong. Therefore, it is written that in future ages, when the human race is nothing but a memory, the descendants of the hyenas will take their turn to stand up straight and proclaim themselves the "dominant species", since every upright animal considers itself a demigod.

Worried about not being in full possession of his physical capacity when the time came to confront the pack, the warrior started rubbing his sides to warm up and then jumping up and down to get the blood flowing in his veins. The memory of his fight with the aurochs haunted his mind. Elric hated the way that Stormbringer had reacted when he wielded it to confront the beast. Giving off a frightening shriek and then hissing like a mad snake, the rune-carved sword had tried to turn against him. At first the albino had blamed his own weakness for Stormbringer's reaction, but later he understood what had happened. Its thirst for a human soul was so strong that the sword had tried to sacrifice its wielder. Obviously it judged Elric's prey as insufficient. He had to be cunning, grab it with both hands and use all his strength to bring its fury under control and then plunge it into the heart of the animal. Now he was wondering how it would react to the approaching pack. Would it judge the hyenas' souls more appetizing than the aurochs'? He had to hope so. If the black sword even just pretended to turn against him again, he would have no chance of escaping the predators' jaws. His weapon had never behaved like this before, but its reaction was easily explained. It had been too long since its master had fed it, more than two months since Elric's path had crossed an enemy worthy of the name. The singing sword was lamenting its undernourishment. It had barely groaned when its blade sunk into the aurochs' chest. And Elric had even heard it hiss in anger when it took the soul that must have seemed barely enough to satisfy the appetite of a butcher knife. The formidable aurochs enemy, however, incarnated strength in a pure state—so much so that more than a week after the duel, Elric of Melniboné still felt genuinely proud of having conquered it. The albino had almost made a trophy of its huge head; he had abandoned the idea reluctantly only because such a trophy would quickly become a useless burden, too much trouble to carry around. And of course being dead the animal no longer had that red blaze in its eyes that made it a peerless killer, empty of hate and the embodiment of pure rage. The similarity between the animal's eyes and his own had troubled him a great deal.

Breaking through the cottony blue that obscured the great forest, a scarlet sun crawled over the horizon and cast pools of molten copper on the snowy expanse. Elric moved through the three or four species of trees: black firs, brown

255

larches, pale birches and scraggy willows whose branches were weighed down to the ground in their sheaths of snow. Here and there the albino's path crossed a hare or a fox and he heard the little animal scamper into the shadows, but he was never able to see it. The only animals he could see were the crows. Their sinister bands flew around in relentless circles in the pale sky.

All day long, while Elric was walking east, the snow hyenas followed his trail but never once showed themselves. They could only be heard, closer and closer, more and more menacing, their insidious laughter trying to imprison him in a cage of terror.

The pack attacked at nightfall, just as the shadows started flooding the forest. Almost invisible in the half-light of the undergrowth, they attacked from every side after carefully encircling him, leaving him no way out. Still burning with the memory of the battle against the aurochs, Elric drew the sword only at the very last second, at the moment when one of the beasts was pouncing on him. The howl of fury that the black blade let out did not reassure him in the least. It easily gutted the attacker, but it moaned in frustration when it had absorbed the soul. Stormbringer did not seem to share wise Husseyn's opinions: to it, a hyena's soul was of far lesser value than a human's. As the soul passed from the sword into his own body, Elric understood that its animal's ferocity was nothing compared with a human's. It lacked ulterior motives and was more naïve than a child. For the hyena killing was not a crime. To take another's life was the only way it had to survival.

The rune sword suddenly became very heavy in his hand. Elric had to use both hands and kneel on the ground to raise it into the path of the second attacker. The gutted animal howled in unison with the sword's song as it fell gushing blood that stained the snow in a red runnel. A tremor ran through the sword's hilt. The warrior felt the vital influx stolen from the enemy enter his body. The strange thing was that Stormbringer let the force pass into him without keeping the

256

tiniest scrap. Result: the sword became even heavier and harder to handle.

The death of the two scouts in no way shook the determination of the pack, which tightened the circle. Then Elric went on the offensive. Despite being difficult to wield, his blade slaughtered three animals before a pair of two huge beasts—probably the dominant couple—sprang out of the shadows to attack him with equal savagery. This time Elric had to jump back to avoid being bitten. The smell of his blood had, in fact, already amplified the homicidal rage of the dozen hyenas whose lustrous eyes glowed in the darkness. Nevertheless, he retreated no farther. Stormbringer snarled while he feinted at the larger of the two attackers—a female who was the real leader of the group. But his attack was only a swordsman's ploy to incite the hyena's partner to jump at his throat. The predator never reached him. The sword's edge opened a long, red wound across its neck and dropped it dead in the snow. Elric did not give the female the chance to get out of range. Stormbringer sliced through the air with a shrill scream. Its blade struck the hyena in the middle of its forehead and split its skull open. The sharp tip continued attacking by itself and sunk into the chest up to its hilt. The hyena whined like a baby when the sword stole its soul. Elric lifted up the twitching body on his sword and threw it with all his might at the pack, which was faltering now. The death of the dominant couple discouraged most of the hyenas from pursuing the attack, but there were a few that, no doubt wanting to prove their bravery so they could claim the leadership of the pack, looked ready for another assault. Galvanized by the souls stolen from the predators killed so far, Elric rushed at them. He was possessed by an animal rage. The black sword was silent, but he howled like a wolf as he massacred one, then two and finally three assailants. The rest of the pack quickly lost interest in a prey that looked like too much trouble—and they pounced, fangs flashing, on the corpses of the fallen hyenas. Drunk on bloodshed, Elric overcame the fatigue that was bearing down on him. He slaughtered two more hyenas so that their fellow creatures could have their share of carrion. Afterward the pack paid no attention to him at all, so he picked up a young animal that he had impaled on his sword before stepping back, never taking his eyes off the hyenas, their furtive eyes and rumps lower than ever, settled on eating their dead.

The battle had taken Elric's breath away. The vital energy stolen from the hyenas had done nothing for him. It dissipated in him like a fleeting mist. Stormbringer seemed more lifeless and heavier than ever when he slipped it back into its scabbard. And the blood-soaked blade groaned faintly in frustration; its thirst had not been quenched in the least.

Born the previous spring and just strong enough to follow the pack, the young female hyena provided the warrior with only a small quantity of tough meat, but he had to make do. The carcass fed him for the next three days before a new blizzard forced him to hole up again in the snow.

This time, the wind coming from the pole broke into the forest with such fury that Elric could not even leave his shelter to get the wood needed to build a fire. All he could do was put the young hyena's hide on top of the aurochs' to protect himself from the infernal cold. He was forced to keep his eyes open and not give in to the drowsiness that would certainly prove fatal. Buried in his hole, he sat still, listening to the howling polar winds and letting his mind wander over the frontiers of dream.

During the whole time that he was crouched there, images from his past kept springing up to haunt him—as happens to people about to die. In fact, Elric had the feeling that his time would come very soon... Hardly had he got rid of the hyenas when he a felt another presence dogging him. This presence concealed a danger even more menacing than what he had just faced. Tucked away in the shadows, he had listened hard and kept a close eye on the path. In vain. A heavy silence had fallen over the undergrowth. But it was this silence that put him on his guard, an almost supernatural silence conspiring with the breeze. Summoning all his senses to be on the alert, Elric could hear the faintest cawing crow, the slightest sound of a hare running through the snow, a stoat or one of those tiny rodents that haunt the frozen wastes.

After meditating it, he was able to form an opinion. Only the most ferocious of the forest beasts had the power to create such fright. The Taiga Tiger was prowling nearby.

As quiet as a shadow, stealthier than a snake, the tiger had followed Elric's trail the whole time that he was fighting the hyenas. But the big cat never attacked—not even when the man was trapped by the storm, at the mercy of the predator that was hardly disturbed by the raging elements. Since the tiger was famous for its ferocity and its sadistic instinct, Elric started to think that the one tracking him was delaying the moment of attack in order to terrorize its prey as much as possible to force it into making some fatal mistake. What bothered the warrior the most was Stormbringer's apathy in the face of this imminent danger. He had almost unsheathed it when he felt the wild cat's presence, but the black sword just let out a little squeak that bode ill. As cruel as it was, the tiger's soul was of no more interest than the hyenas'.

The tiger was the favorite animal of the tutelary goddess of the taiga, Protectress of the Hunt. They called her the Red Goddess because her hair was like a lion's mane—and her claws and teeth were scarlet from the blood of her enemies. Like other archaic divinities, this one, also called the Mother of Tigers, still kept herself apart from the conflict that opposed Law and Chaos, but there were rumors that she was rallying her faithful to the dark powers after an agent of Chaos had won her over.

Elric met the clan of hunters five days after his battle against the hyenas. Just beforehand the albino's path had crossed that of an elk—a gigantic male that he would never have had the arrogance to attack if he had not felt new pangs of hunger. Once again the black sword proved uneager to leave its scabbard, so he had to face the animal without it.

Perched on the big larch branch that he had climbed in the hope of surprising the tiger, armed with an improvised club that, along with the animal skins he was wearing, made him look like one of those primitives that his friend Husseyn the Nomad talked about, Elric had jumped onto the elk and clubbed it senseless before snapping its neck. It was strange that the animal did not seem to pay any attention to him until the moment of attack. It seemed to be worried about a wholly other danger.

At the very moment when the warrior, exhausted and out of breath, started to get up after striking the animal down, a voice called out to him, "Excuse me, lord, you're on our hunting grounds here and this catch belongs to us."

Elric of Melniboné looked up and saw fifteen or so men and women standing around the edge of the little clearing. He had not heard them approach. Their feet were shod in snowshoes so they could walk silently and quickly, even in the thick layer of soft snow blanketing the ground.

"This game cannot be considered yours," the individual who had addressed him finally spoke again.

"I doubt that you can question its ownership," Elric replied. A merry sparkle shined in his eyes.

He jumped up and glanced over the clan, some of whom were starting to load the slings that they used for hunting and combat. Long knives with flint blades were held in fiber crop belts around their waists. They were wearing turned out hides that were so pale they must have been almost invisible in the snowy landscape. All of them looked threatening as they leered at him. All of them were ready to raise their slings and stone him. He counted seventeen figures, including seven women whose faces were no more pleasant than the hunters'.

"The first one who arms his sling or touches his knife will lose more than his life," he warned, putting his hand on Stormbringer's hilt. But he drew the blade out only an inch. The starving sword immediately started singing a sweet, giddy song, subtle but loud enough to be heard by everyone around him.

The little man with slanted eyes, who seemed to be the hunting clan's leader, could not help grinning in terror. He motioned to his companions not to move. "You have a famous blade there, lord, but there are fifteen of us and you're alone."

"You could be twice as many but it wouldn't change your fate," Elric answered. He pointed and said, "My sword will drink your blood first."

The hunter's eyes narrowed at his adversary. He knew right away that only a small number of his companions would get out alive from a direct confrontation with such an enemy. At least he was not stupid enough not to evaluate the precariousness of the situation. And as his words proved, he was even clever enough to insinuate something that would likely make his opponent think twice.

"It would be easy for us to fool you. We could pretend to leave you the game and then wait for sleep to overcome you before murdering you without the slightest risk."

"Except that now I'm forewarned," Elric snickered. "So now you know that I won't wait for the night to bring my sword against you. And you can be sure that there will be so few of you left that all hope of taking me down me will vanish…"

"Lord," the little hunter said, "I'll tell you that all the lands that lie between the great steppe of Lormyr, the frozen sea of the North and the mountains that border the taiga of the East and West have been the hunting grounds of our horde for a long time. If we face each other, all it will take is the fastest of my hunters to run from the fight and in a few hours, a day or two at most your death will be unavoidable."

"And who among you is the fastest?" Elric asked, his ironic eye examining the little group.

"That doesn't matter. But the slowest woman would be up to accomplishing the mission." The hunter seemed to be searching for new arguments. Finally he said, "We'd be better off negotiating."

"Aye? Negotiate what? The laws of the hunt are in my favor."

"No law can withstand force, lord."

Elric did not react to the insult. The conversation amused him. "I killed this animal, so the spoils belong to me."

"What you say… We were tracking this great elk for three days when its path crossed yours. The credit for the capture belongs to us as much as you. Why not share the catch?"

"If you let me take all the meat I can carry, something can be arranged."

"Lord, there are many of us and we are hungry. We also have to think of the children and elders who are waiting for us in our camp. You have to be reasonable. It seems to me that one leg of this animal would provide you with a week's worth of food…"

"One leg!" Elric roared with laughter. "How about a hoof while you're at it!"

"Let me finish, would you? So, we give you a leg and the woman you see over there in exchange for the rest of the carcass—and your promise that you won't follow us."

Elric unconsciously scratched his chin, which was bristling with white fuzz, and considered the young woman who had been pointed out. A girl with auburn hair, even lighter skin and less slanted eyes than the natives of the land. She was the only one among the clan who was not carrying a knife or a sling. Obviously a captive reduced to slavery by the horde of hunters. Another woman, a fat, crude blonde, also a foreigner, held the end of the rope that was knotted around the girl's waist. She, too, carried no sling, but a huge knife was stuck in her belt. The chief's offer did not seem to please her: her mouth was twisted into a scornful grin. She spit disdainfully in Elric's direction. Apparently his intrusion was a damper on her plans.

"I need something more," the albino ended up saying. "Let's say…" he let a moment of silence drift over them, "… a flint blade for the woman you're offering me and for me a pair of those shoes you're wearing that seem to work quite well in this cursed snow that is shrouding this cursed land."

The chief took his time to answer. "That seems reasonable," he concluded.

He turned around to his partners and waited for their approval. Most of them nodded their heads. The chief went up to the copper-haired captive and reeled off a speech in a strange dialect of which Elric could not understand a single word. The only response from the party concerned was to lower her head in submission. The hunter untied the rope that bound her to the other woman. They gave her a knife and a pair of snowshoes, in addition to the ones she was wearing, while the hunter, encouraged by Elric's silent approval, took it upon himself to quickly cut off one of the elk's legs. The animal was really gigantic. Its leg was big enough to feed Elric and his companion for at least five days.

More than enough, he thought.

A few minutes later the albino put on the snowshoes and was on his way again, followed by the young woman who was in charge of transporting their store of food. Elric had no intention of breaking his word to the clan. He would not attack them—at least not right away. He turned around less and less often and only to make sure that no hunter was on his trail. As for the tiger, it seemed to have vanished. For the first time since he had wandered into this land of cold and death, Elric forgot about the melancholy that weighed on his mind. He found himself hoping that the snow would fall more heavily to hide their tracks from any would-be pursuers.

His wishes were answered before sundown, even though it was very early in the season. An extra blessing: the storm that arose in the evening was less violent than the blizzards he had recently faced. Without even gritting her teeth, the red-headed woman built a shelter from the snow in a ditch, covering it with branches while her companion took care of the hearty slices of meat for their evening meal. When he found her in the shelter, she had lit a tiny fire and split the trunk of a big, fallen larch tree.

263

"What are you doing there?" the warrior asked ironically. "Do you plan to build a cabin and stay here? I should tell you that we're back on the road at dawn—unless the gods of cold say otherwise."

The captive just answered by shrugging her shoulders. Having partially hollowed out one half of the trunk, she put inside it all the embers from the little fire she had lit and then motioned to the man to help her put the upper half back in place.

"The wind gods can howl to their heart's content," she said without looking at Elric. "We will not be cold this night."

"So, you talk? I thought I'd inherited a mute."

"My name is Lilah," she said. "And you, barbarian? Do you have a name?"

"Elric of Melniboné. And if there are any barbarians around here, I am not one of them, as far as I know."

A smile crossed Lilah's lips. "Very good. Now I feel better... Do you want to give me some of that meat or do you prefer to eat yours raw?"

"I prefer it cooked."

The woman gave Elric a baffling look. "That, too, makes me feel better. Do you have a little salt to make the meat less bland?"

"I do. That's clever the way you made the fire," he pointed at the split trunk in which the embers glowed, slowly spreading over the wood fiber and gently heating the shelter.

"As I told you, it's how the people of this country never get cold. They're the ones who taught me how to heat and cook like this. Lift up the top of the trunk again and I'll cook our meal."

She had wrapped the two steaks in moist wood shavings to keep the meat from touching the embers directly. Then she put them on the fire and had him close the cover of the make-shift pot.

"The larch wood will give its aroma to the meat. You're going to like it."

"My mouth is already watering," Elric let out a short laugh.

They ate in silence, sitting across from each other. Grilled just right and scented from the wood, the meat was, in fact, delicious. When they finished eating, Elric cleared off the aurochs' fur, which he had laid out on the ground for them to use as a carpet. The temperature inside the shelter was more than mild. He was even starting to sweat a little.

The woman looked curiously at his clothes and simply said, "It's true you don't look like a barbarian. A warrior, but not a savage like those hunters I spent the last year with."

"You were their slave?"

"I can't hide anything from you!" Lilah mocked with a bitter smile. "If you want to know everything, I was even the personal property of their high priestess for a year."

"That woman who was part of the group you were with? The fat blonde?" Elric suggested.

Lilah shrugged. "No. My mistress is dead. The blonde was only their cook—and their part-time whore."

"Ah!" the warrior laughed. "And you served them in the same way?!"

The interrogation of Lilah was not gratuitous. Elric was thinking that it was of vital necessity to be as informed as pos-sible on the customs and practices of the nomad hunters who haunted the region. It was not by chance that the last of the Melnibonéans was wandering in the heart of winter through the vast taiga of the north. He was tracking an individual there who, like himself, came from another world, lying low in the Limbo of time. The country where the stranger came from had fallen prey to decadence. Chaos and Law were blurred there more than in the worst nightmare. A handful of powerful men had supplanted the gods and reduced all other human beings to slavery. In this time of depravation and tyranny, men got drunk on poisons, which floated in the very air they breathed.

The human whom Elric was tracking—but did he really deserve to be called human? They told such dreadful things about his ways—this filth with the face of a man, who was called Jerry Cornelius, dreamed of imposing his hideous model of society on all planes of reality. His plans would be the ruin of it. Elric would end his dreams of hegemony at the same time as his life. Stormbringer would certainly take particular pleasure in devouring such a dark soul.

As he was thinking of his sword, he who read the future in the bowels of black sorcerers and other false prophets suddenly heard a faint hum coming from the scabbard, but he must have been the only one to hear. Had the sword followed his train of thought or was it dreaming on its own of sumptuous feasts of flesh and souls, of splendid slaughters where the predator is changed into the prey? Where, finally, on the ravaged battlefield, among the fighters and civilians killed right down to the very last one, the weapon would remain alone triumphant? A daydream showed him the vision of a vitrified land, forever ravaged, over which slowly dissipated the venomous clouds and firestorms caused by a black sword forged in poisoned metal. The death of death… Pure despair. Such was the threat hovering over the destiny of the Earth from the one called Jerry Cornelius, prince of assassins in a world suffering the full force of assassins' terror. In this poisoned, overpopulated world, humanity was like a flock of lemmings: it was running straight for the cliff.

Coming back to reality, the warrior remembered the question he had asked Lilah and that the young woman had not answered. "When you say nothing, that means yes, doesn't it?" he insisted. "So, you did other things for them besides cook meals…"

"No. As I told you, I belonged to the high priestess. Such a rank had its own advantages. A thin smile stole across the captive's lips.

"And why were you chained to the old wench?"

"My mistress died. A stranger came and killed her." She raised her closed fist, not so much in hatred but to show the arrogance, the vile sycophancy of the character she was talking about. "He dared to claim he was greater than every divinity. He took over the horde. He, too, had a strange weapon," she said, glancing furtively at Elric's scabbard.

"A weapon?" he echoed.

"A device that shot out metal needles and killed from afar."

"Bah!" Elric spit scornfully.

"Do you think you will keep me for a long time?" Lilah suddenly started asking the questions.

It was Elric's turn to shrug. "No more than necessary."

Lilah's wonderfully green eyes stared into his. "You are the master," she said dryly.

"And so it will be until I find someone to sell you to," Elric finished. "Unless we both die of hunger before meeting anyone…" A long moment of silence and then, "Or maybe I'll give you your freedom, who knows?"

The slave's eyes were blazing. "You're joking?"

"Not necessarily."

"And what would you ask in exchange for my freedom?"

"Nothing, certainly. Besides, what do you have to offer?"

"To you? Nothing."

He laughed, truly amused by her behavior. His intuition, however, was whispering that she was holding something back. And that piqued his curiosity. "There's no doubt that you would bring a pretty sum at the slave markets in the southern towns. They love women with hair and skin like yours. The only problem is the color of your eyes. People in the south are superstitious. They think that green is the color of the evil eye. Maybe I should pluck them out?"

Elric stared hard into Lilah's eyes, judging her reaction. He saw her sneer.

"How absurd! Who would want a slave with no eyes?"

"Some evil sorcerer, I imagine. I know one like that. They call him Mörnor or simply Yellow Eye. He uses his blind slaves to keep several conversations going at the same time. He burns their eyes out and then brands them with Xs.

It was Lilah's turn to laugh. "They must be really ugly." She obviously did not believe a word of what he was saying to her.

"If you lie, why should I tell you the truth?" Elric retorted.

The young woman's face darkened all of a sudden. "I'm a virgin, that's my secret. Doesn't that increase my value on the market?"

"You spent a year among those barbarians and you claim to be a virgin! Who would believe such a lie?"

"As I told you, I belonged to the high priestess. She was as jealous as a tigress and kept me all to herself. If you know a rich city woman who loves to be pampered and fussed over by a young woman, ask her to give me a try. She will offer you a better price than the black sorcerer who disfigures his slaves."

"He doesn't disfigure them. He just shaves their head before branding them. The top of the Xs cross on their forehead and the bottoms are engraved a little above and behind the ears."

"Very esthetic. But I really don't feel cut out to be a monk," Lilah grumbled weakly.

Elric's eyes shined brightly. She had just given him a hook that he counted on hanging onto. "By the way, I've been told that the priestesses worshipping the Red Goddess, Protectress of the Hunt, the highest divinity of the hordes of the great taiga, shave their heads. It's that true?"

"You've been misinformed. The women who serve the Mother of Tigers take great care of their hair, which they dye red."

"Ah! Would you be one of them?"

"No. I come from the Western Lands where my hair color is not rare. And anyway…" Lilah paused… "the horde has abandoned worshipping the Goddess of the Hunt to devote themselves exclusively to this Jerry Cornelius, the so-called Brother of Hyenas!" She turned her head and spit in disgust. She was clearly not much of a supporter of the Englishman.

"What else can you tell me about the customs of the horde?" Elric asked, his eyes wide with curiosity.

"Their tribal goddess was vanquished by the newcomer who walks in the ways of Chaos. Her ancient worshippers are devoted to cannibalism now." A shiver of fright ran down the young woman's spine. "They eat you raw when you're still alive."

"I have tough skin," Elric joked.

The girl's eyes were burning as she tried to outdo him. "They carve you up and give your hide to the hyenas. They've made a pact with them. The snow hyenas flush out the prey. You should know all about that, right?" Elric's eyes narrowed and flashed. "The group I was with was raging mad when they saw the carnage you wreaked. They had sent them to scout out game."

"I should have massacred them all," Elric stated, unperturbed.

"If it weren't for the elk, you would have been their game. And me too, no doubt. Unless they decided on the blonde!" she laughed. "They've been fattening her up for it for two years. Even with the elk, I don't think she'll live long. They might even eat her on the road before the clan rejoins the winter camp where the horde gathers. During the last blizzard she owed her survival to the chief's indulgence toward her, since she could warm him up while his companions' teeth were shattering." Lilah shrugged. "I'll stop, if my story is making you sick."

"I've known so-called civilized people whose customs were no better than these savages. Tell me again about the stranger who took over the horde."

"I hate him," Lilah grumbled.

"Because he killed your mistress? Did you love her?"

"Don't exaggerate. We'd made a pact. She kept me from constantly putting on weight, which made me less... appetizing to the hunters. And thereby prolonged my life."

"And why did the stranger kill her?"

"I told you, he claimed to be more powerful than the gods! Of course, the high priestess did not share his opinion. To prove his superiority, he forced her into a hand-to-hand duel, with his right hand tied behind his back. The priestess did not fear this kind of confrontation. To get and stay where she was, she had already had to do that and kill one of the horde's powerful warriors with her own hands, as well as a few women who were jealous of her position. As for the stranger, he could kill two birds with one stone: get rid of his most dangerous rival and fulfill the rite of admission to the horde, which obliged a newcomer to devour alive the one whose place he desired.

Elric snickered. "Logical. Hyenas have the customs of hyenas. And what happened in the battle?"

"Although the priestess had been careful to keep me thin, she had not done the same for herself. Her fat made her slow and gave her little stamina whereas her enemy was quick as a sword and never out of breath. He danced around her for a long time, dodging all her attacks and wearing her down with his prancing. When he saw that she could barely stand up anymore, he was even more cunning, letting her hit him and then pretending to lose consciousness. Thinking her victory was cinched, she ran at him to crush him under her weight. It was exactly what the stranger was expecting. They must have described to him her previous battles, which all ended in the same way, with her strangling her enemies between her legs." Lilah shook her head like she was trying to clear it of a bad memory.

"Hurry up and finish, we're not going to spend all night like this," Elric mumbled.

"The stranger was expecting this, that she would get close enough for him to bite," Lilah resumed. "He had coated his teeth with curare. His first bite paralyzed his enemy. Afterward he had no problem wriggling out of her grasp. He bit into her belly, deeper and deeper, until his head was halfway inside her. 'My new birth!' he mocked, bursting with laughter and showing everyone his bloodstained face. My mistress was still alive and then he…"

"Okay, I understand," he cut her off from her atrocious story. "Do you think the horde is still after us?"

Lilah put her left hand on her forehead and stared at her knees. "Yes. But we have nothing to fear for the moment. They don't like to split up their hunting clans. Their weapons aren't strong enough for them to attack big game in small groups. They constantly dream of capturing an ice whale, one of those huge animals, those mountains of flesh that once lived on the ice floes. At the start of last winter, they found a carcass. It was frozen into an iceberg. They felt a little frustrated because they prefer flesh that is still warm and twitching, but the whale saved our lives, me and my people."

"Were you alone when they captured you?" Elric asked softly, aware of the importance of the question.

Lilah took her time to answer. She kept looking at her knees. The clan's chief might have blackmailed her: her life and the lives of her dear ones for that of the warrior to whom the barbarian had "spontaneously" decided to give her. "What does it matter," she ended up saying. "I'm alone now."

"Don't forget me!" Elric was ironic.

The slave looked up, shook her copper mane and stared into his eyes. "They'll come back. The hunters. In eight or ten days, maybe fifteen if you're careful to stay as far as possible from their winter camp, which is located around seven days walk toward the northeast."

"Northeast, hmm. That's the very direction I was thinking of going."

"You're crazy. The stranger who rules them now has gathered ten or twelve clans in the camp. He was waiting for ten more when we left. You'll have to face at least a hundred and fifty warriors and as many women who are no less ferocious. It would be suicide."

"Suicide is my destiny. As far as the barbarians, I don't care if there are three hundred or three thousand. The black sword will sacrifice them all—the same way it has already

271

exterminated entire armies. In this world, there is no power greater than Stormbringer. Not a single hunter of the taiga will escape it."

"That's what you want? To kill yourself? You can count on Jerry Cornelius. He will help you. Crime is the way that he has chosen."

"Stormbringer will make him swallow his conceit. The black sword thirsts for blood and souls. If I don't satisfy it, it will make its final assault against me."

Lilah shifted from one leg to the other. A soft glow smoldered in her eyes. The story of her old mistress' battle with the stranger had excited her, making her feel those obscene desires for quivering flesh and spilled blood. Her captivity had made her a wild cat. She pretended to stretch, giving him a good look at her round breasts with hard nipples. "Couldn't you give up the war for a while, Lord Elric?"

He pretended to consider such a possibility. But he knew that his destiny was indissolubly linked to that of the singing sword, which existed only to kill. Without it, he would become weaker than a baby bird. Of course, he could not confide this secret to anyone. Not even to Lilah. *Especially not* to Lilah. She would not miss such an opportunity to go by herself to destroy the barbarians who were holding her mother and father and brothers and sisters captive. When that was done, and only then would she notice that in its rage, Stormbringer had also drank the souls of those she wanted to save. Then Lilah would have no more family or friends. She would belong body and soul to the black sword—and would have no other choice but to die or kill, to slaughter again and again, constantly, like Elric had been forced to do since he had met up with Stormbringer.

The night wore on. The storm howled over their shelter, carpeting it with snow, which kept it warmer and safer and invisible to hostile eyes. The comfort of the shelter encouraged its occupants to surrender to sweet lethargy, which changed any troubling promiscuity into pleasant intimacy.

Lilah put her hand over her mouth to stifle a yawn. Her eyes reflected the red glow of the fire as she stared at her companion. "Should we sleep?" she proposed.

"You don't look tired," he murmured across from her.

"Anyway I want to take off my clothes and lie down for a moment. Can I lie on your fur coat?"

"Certainly. Make yourself comfortable."

"Thank you."

The young woman smiled and immediately started taking off her fur-lined clothes. Elric intuitively understood the obvious: Lilah was only here to trap him. She was just waiting for the right time. Maybe She had told all those stories about the horde, mentioned her relationship with the priestess and recounted the hideous details of her battle with Cornelius just to arouse his wild, animal instincts. Elric knew that the most refined civilizations only managed to slap a deceptive varnish on the sick desires that lie dormant in every individual, even in the most cultured and gentlest of humans. No matter how deep its sleep might be, the Beast never asked anything but to be awakened in a dream, aroused by words that might be sugary or obscene, coaxed by the promises of some poisonous preacher or caressed by the warm, parted lips of a concubine, if not a beloved.

Retreating into despair Elric had lost interest in Lilah for a while. The touch of her bare foot against his thigh jolted him back into reality. He looked at her. She was lying on her back, with nothing on, her knees bent and parted. She was devouring him with her eyes. Her spread legs gave him a view of her round, pale buttocks: the oldest trap in the world!

"Why don't you take off your clothes? You have nothing to fear. The hunters won't come tonight."

Elric casually pushed away the foot that was trying to slip between his legs. Lilah propped herself up on her elbows, pushing out her chest and erect nipples. She bit her lip and stared at him with eyes sparkling with voluptuous promises.

"Come…" she invited.

The captive opened her legs, letting the warm glow of the fire shine on the thin, red fringe that was like a jewel case at the top of her vulva, glistening and swollen with desire. She smiled softly and watched him from between her half-closed eyelids.

"You want?" she whispered again.

"Are you about to offer me your precious hymen?"

"Take it!" she murmured, gazing longingly at him.

All of a sudden an intense heat spread through Elric's body. A sweeter, more pleasurable heat than what he felt when Stormbringer gave him the energy of its victims' souls. It had been a long time since he had had such a feeling… too long. He unfastened his tunic, stripped off his clothes, slipped off the scabbard in which Stormbringer slept and lay down to do what he had to do. He felt Lilah's soft, wet palm grab his and guide it to the edge of her vulva. He made sure to arouse her longer so that her first time not seem like rape. She ended up groaning impatiently and swaying under him, luring him into her. He felt a little resistance and then a silken tear. The contact with the blood pouring out gave Elric the same feeling as the heat of a soul stolen and sent by Stormbringer to empower him.

He dreamed of a woman whose hymen would grow back every morning so that he could have it every night and thus restore his vigor. Yes, he thought. Such a mate could maybe make me forget the taste of blood and war and quench this thirst for black souls for which Stormbringer is only the instrument.

Crazy fantasy. Elric guessed what was awaiting him.

He woke up with a start—and immediately understood what had happened. While he was sleeping, Lilah had stolen his sword. It was bound to end like this. Elric had known it forever.

"How can I be so crazy to fall for such a crude trap?" he grumbled.

A mortal weakness washed over his body. He felt punier than a newborn baby. In front of him stood the traitor, sword in hand. Stormbringer sang a crystal clear song at the end of her outstretched arm. Its black blade shone like pure diamond. It seemed to be delighted with the prospect of finally doing away with its master. But Lilah held the sword back. Her panting voice resounded in the clear morning.

"The horde... Their chief offered me a deal: Safety for me and my family if I manage to take the black sword."

"I understand," Elric whispered, fascinated by the radiance of his blade ready to put him to death. "Do it quickly!" he said.

He looked away from Lilah so as not to see her naked belly, her still swollen genitals—an open wound bespattered with thin bloody streaks where it had burst in ecstasy—and was lost forever.

"Strike!" he groaned, suddenly lifting his head to offer his throat to the rune-carved sword.

"They promised me..." the young woman said to justify herself.

Then she looked down at Elric's belly. A revolting weakness held him there, panting and powerless, motionless at her feet. His beautiful virility of the night before had vanished. He had only the hardened sack between his legs and Stormbringer's scabbard, just as empty, lying at his side.

"But I don't believe them" Lilah continued as if she were talking to herself. "They love human flesh too much to keep their word, even if they wanted to. They might already have eaten my parents."

"The black sword will take the cannibal souls with pleasure," Elric murmured, sickened by his own weakness, but unable to stand in the way of the fatal destiny awaiting him. "With Stormbringer you can avenge them."

"Without a doubt." She lifted the weapon, tip down, like a murderer brandishing a knife to finish off a victim in the throes of death. Gathering his remaining strength, the warrior managed to kneel before her, offering his chest. "May the Queen of Tigers receive you in Her domain," Lilah whispered.

Stormbringer shrilled sharply. There was a flat, dull sound when the blade pierced the offered flesh. Elric's eyes flickered and looked a last time at his one-night love.

Lilah was kneeling in front of him, staring hard at him. Her hands clutched the handle of the sword that was buried up to its hilt in her flesh, as if she were afraid that the weapon might suddenly tear away from her. But Stormbringer had no intention of leaving the cozy sheath where it nestled. It just wiggled gently in Lilah's hands, stirring the wound to make the blood seethe, singing its quenched pleasure in a pure, crystalline voice, like a spring torrent.

Lilah howled—just like she had screamed during the night. An orgasmic cry expressing the pure pleasure that she felt. Her fists pushed harder on the sword, thereby opening the wound even more.

"Excuse me for lying to you, Lord Elric. The Mother of Tigers inhabits me. It demanded a living sacrifice for her power to be restored."

Once again the flesh ripped open under the pressure of the black sword, which growled like a wild cat.

"In my country the custom is to burn the dead. Do that for me. Don't leave my corpse to the horde," Lilah whispered. Wide-eyed, staring gruesomely, she started to pull out the blade, but then buried it deeper, so violently that the hilt disappeared between the lips of the open wound under her belly button. One yank and she offered the black sword to Elric. "Take… what… belongs to you… and use it."

Her pain-foundered eyes sought the warrior's. Stormbringer shrilled exquisitely when the soul of its voluntary victim melted into its own substance. Elric put his hands on hers, still clenching the sword handle. A torrential force flowed into every fiber of his body. Once before, Stormbringer had killed a god—and flooded Elric with its vital energy. A creature of fire whose heat had almost consumed him. But the fire was nothing compared to the deluge of power that flowed into him at that time. It was like a tidal wave that lifted him up and made him howl like a wild tiger.

He stood up and yanked the soul-devouring sword out of Lilah's belly, leaving her corpse sheltered in the snow. A huge tigress stood there, baring its fangs. She only had to pounce to slaughter the man, but she did nothing. She just growled and then sat in the snow.

Three hours later, when Elric was sure that the fire would not go out before consuming all of the dead goddess, he got back on the road. After two days he found the clan loaded with the elk carcass. He surprised the hunters in the middle of a feast: unable to resist their cannibalistic hunger, they had just sacrificed the fat blonde captive. Their souls and blood fed the black sword. The quickest among them did not run fast enough to escape death. For him it incarnated in the form of a tigress that caught him in her claws and ripped off his head with her fangs.

Three days later Elric of Melniboné drew the runic sword out of its scabbard again. He raised it over his head and wheeled it around. The naked blade glittered in the twilight and the sword sang more harmoniously than usual. Fifty tigers growled in answer. One by one they leaped onto the warrior's trail. Now they were at his side. They roared in unison with the black sword's song.

One hundred feet ahead of the eldritch army commanded by Elric, the horde's winter camp was pitched. The flesh-eaters and their foreign chief were all gathered together for one last orgy of blood—ready to suffer the implacable vengeance of the goddess whom they had once worshipped and then scorned in favor of a demon.

After the death cry of the last hunter rang out, after Stormbringer swallowed the foreign demon, silence fell over the camp where six hundred corpses lay. Elric and his allies parted. Each went its way, leaving the rotting carcasses to the hyenas.

Daniel Walther published his first genre story in the magazine Fiction *in 1965. Since then, he has penned more than two hundred stories, as well as nearly forty novels, in virtually all literary genres. Daniel won the Grand Prize of French SF in 1975 for his New Wave anthology* Les Soleils Noirs d'Arcadie, *and in 1979 for his novel* L'Epouvante. *He was also the editor of the* Galaxie-Bis *and* Club du Livre d'Anticipation *imprints of Editions OPTA. His post-apocalypse novel* Le Livre de Swa *(1982) was translated by C.J. Cherryh as* The Book of Shai *(1984), and* Le Destin de Swa *(1983) as* Shai's Destiny *(1985), for DAW books; however-er, a third volume,* La Légende de Swa *(1983), remains un-translated.*

Daniel Walther: *Heart of Ice*

Some say the world will end in fire,
Some say in ice.
From what I've tasted of desire
I hold with those who favor fire.
But if it had to perish twice,
I think I know enough of hate
To say that for destruction ice
Is also great
And would suffice.
Robert Frost, *Fire and Ice*

1. The Frost Desert

The desert was freezing. And the moon beamed among the frozen stars. It was a desert of seracs, far from inhabited land, very far from the cities. No one ventured there unless they really had to. Elric had no choice but to chance these cold lands where bones cracked like the masts of ships in distress.

Elric armed with Stormbringer, the rune-carved sword that drank souls.

The albino prince let his hair fly in the west wind and felt the ice grating between his teeth. His sorrowful eyes kept closed against the onslaught of frost.

His companions rode behind him, on the watch, half-dead from the cold. They had been traveling for two days in the polar night, wearing bone goggles to protect their eyes. And they felt like the cold was loosening their teeth, about to knock them out of their gummy cells. A toothless warrior is like a muzzled wolf: easy prey for the demons and midnight ernes.

They were riding toward the White Dome, toward the Green Pole.

Moonglum had lost his enthusiasm while the mind of the Melnibonéan heir wandered in barren dreams, stripped of color and dimensions. A muffled world where corvids cawed unseen, but as persistent as they were starving.

He felt the black sword quiver.

He felt Stormbringer in the spectral cold. But he had no desire to give up an inch of land. Nor to obey the promptings of the treacherous sword that weighed on his destiny like a hunk of molten metal.

One would have thought the Gods of Chaos were riding on the heels of this small band of horsemen.

Elric, Moonglum ,and chitin knights. Followed by a braying mule laden with supplies for the men and oats for the animals…

All of them dressed and shod in shiny dark, except for Moonglum, who was wearing light-colored suede and red wool.

Studded, black leather doublets, black metal helmets, black scabbards for swords and daggers, even the quiver and arrows of Hurankon, the oldest of the chitin knights, was dark. Hurankon was as skillful as the Red Archer. And maybe craftier.

The chitin knights had been accompanying them since Trisalgon, the frozen fortress with towers of frost and meandering tunnels where rivers of ice floes ran. Moonglum had almost lost his life in one of the Trisalgon ice caves. He had been saved at the last minute by Hurankon the Old, who had just turned 67, the age when the chitin knights, also called the hornet knights, gave up their sword and sometimes their ghost. By his saving act, Hurankon had been authorized by Ichalmar, the Living Master of Trisalgon, to battle for another three years and he received the name Hurankon Immoshabteth, Hurankon the not-yet-old.

And now they were riding toward the Green Pole, the final oasis, the territory bathed by a sun buried on the edge of the frost maze.

Elric with Stormbringer at his side.

Moonglum, the survivor of the Trisalgon tunnels.

Hurankon Immoshabteth.

And the three other knights, wrapped in black, armed with dark metal.

"Elric," Moonglum said, "my bones are so stiff they must be cracked from one end to the other. What good was it for me to survive the torments of Trisalgon if it's only to freeze in this desert?"

He smiled, belying the effect of his words.

Because that was how he was.

But Elric, the prince of Melniboné, had withdrawn into his disenchantment while the soul-eater writhed in its scabbard like a serpent's tongue.

He knew by intuition that the Green Pole and the White Dome were still rather far away and that there were still countless opportunities for them to die before reaching their destination. The Gods of Chaos had allied with the Wind Spirits to gather freezing tornadoes in the white night, in preparation for a long barrage.

Moonglum sang a song that flowed with images of firebrands in a family hearth and the dragon knights shouted fiery refrains, but the night remained as cold as a frozen blade.

Elric had a heavy heart and in his soul the cold felt as intense as a burn.

2. Ghânia

Ghânia lived with her numerous kin in the quasi-ruins of Whorsk in the exact center of the Green Pole, only a few leagues from the White Dome and the Frozen Library. Everything was phantasmagoria in the everyday life of Whorsk the Forsaken Fortress. And the ravages of iron and frost, of axe and fire, had not yet escaped the memory of Ghanîa's *Sippe*. Millions of books and scrolls, at one time counted and catalogued by Es-Borgh, were still available for consultation in the White Dome, the ancient intellectual center of the dominion of Tlon Uqbar in Orbis Tertius. Later, there would be Alexandria, but Alexandria, destined to fire, would be just a little thing compared with the Dome Library, diverted by the frost, a library containing the science and knowledge of the gods and the genies who once served them.

Ghânia was a woman, twenty-four years old but still a virgin because legend said that two moons before her twenty-fifth birthday she would be the High Vestal of Tlon Uqbar, the Virgin propitiatory of the books.

Tlon Uqbar was older than memory, older than the Kingdom of Melniboné. And Orbis Tertius was a metal structure in the shape of a huge globe of metal and ice. Metal in ice, ice in metal.

Ghânia woke up this morning after a weird dream: knights in a desert that was vaster than Ibog, a frozen expanse tormented by the wind.

She saw all the men and the wind recited their names: Elric the fallen prince, Moonglum the storyteller, Hurankon the Redeemed, and the knights Norg, Süden and Esuador. All silent. The image focused on the knight with white hair, an albino's face, drawn and sad in the eyes. She felt a great desire to belong to this man, to lie with him, and let him ravish her virginity. But the wind blew in the trees of the Oasis and a black moon crossed the sky, like a meteor.

Ghânia sighed. And quietly prepared her devotions.

She had heard of the Gods of Chaos, but her family worshipped the Sacred Chronicles. Especially her father, the Archon Iosefos. And Ghânia worshipped her father like a god. The Sacred Chronicles, the voice of the Gods of the Line, opposed to those of Chaos. But the Lords of Chaos were powerful, maybe more than the White Entities of the Line. They killed and then devoured the souls.

But did not a prophecy in the Dome say:

When the white man
With hair of frost
Comes,
He will stand on the right hand
Of the God of Wind
With his wyvern-sword
Burning and cold
Devourer of souls.

The God of Wind was far away, swirling over the white mountains of Bôr. But Ghânia was sure now that the man with white hair would restore the ancient gods to their power and their worshippers to their privileges.

It burned her crotch to think of the stranger's embrace: as he pierced her through and through, begetting rubies between her thighs. Then she would not become priestess but woman. She told herself that she would certainly be better off for the change.

3. The Ice Hydras

It was Moonglum who saw them first: a cloud of sparkling frost coming from the north. "What's that?" he cried.

Elric looked up at the black sky: the thing was coming at them… very fast. A squadron of birds of prey, sparkling like a variegation of winged jewels. The flying "beings" were white, but it was as if they reflected the prism of a swallowed sun or of a moon on fire.

"By the gods," Süden shouted, "it's the flying hydras, the ice hydras. More violent than the harpies of Üxmül with their razor-sharp claws of horn."

Elric pulled Stormbringer out of its scabbard and the magic sword with the black blade quivered in his hands. He was seized by a thrill of joy: he drew wild energy from the runic hilt twitching in his numb fingers.

He saw the first hydra dragging behind it a frayed tail like countless pearls of ice and hail. The creature was half-woman, half-beast. Both at the same time and neither one in reality. But subtle and slaughterous, already opening its windy, frosty mouth. Baring its long, cold teeth that even a Tânarkh axe could not break with a single blow.

Like missiles of ice, the other hydras followed the first, swooping down upon the little caravan. One of the icy vampires sunk its teeth into Norg's chest, leaving a bloody hole in the chitin knight's armor. An arrow flew from Hurankon's bow and stuck in the wishbone of the vampire hydra. The thing spread its oversized wings and opened its wintry mouth to howl, like a death rattle, in the cold night.

"Very good," Elric shouted. "I think that one's done for."

Hurankon notched another arrow.

But the wounded hydra did not die right away; it arched its back, twisted around and tried to plant its white fangs in Norg's boot.

As for Süden, he was thrusting and slicing at another winged monster.

Stormbringer cut off the icy pseudopods of two hydras with uncontrollable fury—did these creatures possess a kind of soul?—and Elric soon found himself alone while his companions kept struggling amidst the claws and jaws of the flying monsters.

Hurankon could no longer bend his bow; his left arm hung down along his chitin breeches, bloody, shredded by the claws and fangs.

Someone had sent these creatures, like a hymenoptera queen sends her emissaries with poisonous stingers.

For the universe is swarming
with viscous hornets
and the sky
crumples up
like a bloody tissue
wriggling with the glow-worms
of death
Because fate...

The prince of Melniboné's thoughts were heavy, heavy thoughts, saturated with a cursed salt.

The hydras were repelled, but Esuador was dying, his throat slashed, already harrowed with scarlet ice cubes.

The demigod Morph was dozing in the arms of his malachite and orichalcum throne. He was entirely nude and his majestic penis lay between his marble thighs. White felines purred at his feet like outlandish cats.

Morph was a devotee of the Gods of Chaos and the son of a heavy-breasted divinity and a Titan of Kashghôr.

He had received orders to kill the albino prince and his retinue. He was told to deliver the black sword, Stormbringer, the soul-drinker, to the feet of the gods. Therefore, he had commanded the hydras to attack Elric and his retinue.

He was sleeping lightly and dreaming the same: he had ripped open Elric's skinny chest and was about to tear out his heart: a heart twitching with the last breath of life.

"Die," he said, "because *you're nothing and nobody.*"

And his onyx-tipped fingers grabbed the heart of Elric of Melniboné.

In a few short years he would pluck not the heart but the virginity from the temple servant, the beautiful Ghânia.

What did a few miniscule years mean to a quasi-immortal, an infinitesimal splinter of time?

He opened his eyes before he had the chance to tear out the heart of his appointed enemy. The hunt for the intruder—

his frost mirrors had showed him that the fallen prince and his henchmen were getting closer to the Oasis and the Dome, battling the desert winds—was about to begin.

Only half-asleep, his penis had straightened out and was standing up, a red monster, in the glow of the oily torches of the palace of Garmish. A gusty wind was blowing outside, obeying the orders of the Storm Gods.

A female slave rushed in, already naked, to calm Morph's fervor. While she was riding him, he had a hard time resisting the temptation to rip off her breasts and tear out her heart. But he still felt a guilty kindness toward these mortals who satisfied him sexually. When they seemed used up by his *semi-divine* member, he offered them to his henchmen, who often had fewer scruples than he and subjected them to despicable, inhuman treatments.

Morph ejaculated copiously and said to the girl, "If I have inseminated you, you will be rich."

A promise that the girl was glad to hear because she was just then in the fertile part of her cycle. Morph had flooded her with his semen. And maybe…

She ran off, draped in a see-through sheet.

Morph finished his dream by devouring the heart of the fallen prince. He sheathed the black, rune-carved sword and felt it quiver in his hands like a great, lava penis.

4. The Ghosts of the Dome

Ghânia was scared for her white prince.

She had seen him struggling against the predatory monsters from the arctic sky. She was afraid that he would die bleeding between their icy fangs. Like in the poem of the bard Aïn-Dolor:

And the sharp teeth
of harpies—the ogresses
tear apart
the flesh.
Greedy,

they drink the veins dry
these vampires
born of the hateful moon.
But these words rang hollow.
The world also.

Everything was hollowed out, like by a billhook. Digging out the marrow of life.

Ghânia was scared for her albino prince. Even if the black sword was his mistress and gave him its strength and violence.

She hurried to the White Dome, eager to read the verses in the Book of Prophecies about the coming of the White Man. She was wearing her linen dress wrapped around her body and nothing else. She had access to the Dome of Books, unlike the other women who were subject to a lover or husband. Because she was a virgin and supposed to be deflowered by Morph, the white wolf pizzle. But she wanted to save herself for Elric the Fallen from Melniboné in order to fulfill the prophecy.

In front of the Dome she contemplated her reflection in the water of the Winged Bull Fountain and she saw Prince Elric and his companions slice through the ice with their blades and bury the body of the chitin knight named Esuador. There were only five of them: Elric, Moonglum, Hurankon the Redeemed, Norg and Süden.

She sighed and entered the huge dome whose sapphire lamps turned it blue inside.

Daktocris, the secretary, greeted her, "Hello, my daughter. Enter and do as you please."

"Father," Ghânia said, "allow me to consult the Prophetic Book of Anrith."

"I'll fetch it for you, my daughter."

The old man went off, limping, and passing gas because he had had problems with his digestion for ages. He came back dragging his heels with a big ptix that he put down in front of Ghânia. The young woman's heart beat faster: a treasure.

She sat in a corner of the room and unrolled the thick scroll. It was a little hard for her to fathom the mysteries of the Old Tongue, but she kept at it until she found the verse she was looking for:

When the white man comes...

Nobody could come between her and the white man with silver hair, not even Morph the deflowerer.

There would be a clash between the white prince and the sexed demigod. But it would be a futile battle with no possible victory and Morph would leave the Melnibonéan to take Ghânia's virginity. For even demigods cannot oppose what is written in the Book of Destiny.

And while she was buried in her study, the young woman heard the pale wind blowing through the library and she saw the guardian huddle up in his red chair. The wind brought with it a wash of images, bloodless, drifting, it seemed, from the shores of the Hargos River, the current of lost souls.

5. The Cursed Knights

They had finished paying homage to the chitin knight killed by the hydras. The ice was piled up in asymmetrical fragments over the shredded body of Esuador.

"We must set off again," Elric said, his white hair blown by the glacial wind. "We haven't reached our destination yet."

They got in their saddles and back on their way, arduously, the wind redoubling its fury and whistling shrill melodies that bored into their brains.

Elric felt Stormbringer's nervousness, heralding the next appearance of new perils.

Crystals formed in the fallen prince's hair, catching the rays of the moon.

Then they saw the tall, pale mountains of Nôdh. It looked like their summits were stabbed by the white moon, making them bleed nettle-scented sap.

"We have to make up time," Elric said.

Moonglum hummed, "At your orders. We'll do our best, but even the gods aren't bound to the impossible."

"The Gods of Chaos can do the impossible, even if they aren't bound to it."

They spurred their horses, but the horses balked, their hooves buried deep in the snow, even though it was like sheet metal. As Moonglum's horse pushed on, soon followed by Hurankon's, Elric called a halt.

Hide tents were pitched on the double, one for Elric and Moonglum, the other for Hurankon and the two surviving knights.

They ate cold beans and a few strips of dried meat and drank juniper alcohol. Then they spent most of the night not sleeping, while the horses swallowed their ration of oats. The mule brayed so loudly that Moonglum went to see if it was not dying, but the animal was just upset.

When Elric finally managed to fall asleep, he had a troubling dream: a room lit by blue torches, big, shiny stones like sapphires, and a very attractive yellow woman who was slowly unrolling a ptix. He knew that her name was Ghânia and that she was in the legendary library of Es-Borgh under the Dome made famous by poets and bards. A kind of syrupy song dragged on in the glinting blue room. Elric approached the woman. And she stood up to welcome him.

"I am Elric of Melniboné," he said.

"And I am Ghânia… of Whorsk, in the Green Pole."

Then the walls crumbled and shadowy forms invaded the room, chasing away the blue lights. The girl screamed and disappeared in the black mist dotted with dying sparks. Elric jumped into this uncertainty and was immediately swallowed up by the semi-darkness.

"Wake up," Moonglum said, shaking him hard, "It's daytime. We have to get back on the road since the wind has died down. It's almost a beautiful day."

Indeed, a veiled sun was pouring its fluid light over the pseudo-icefield.

The mountains looked closer in that atmosphere and blue-tinted clouds appeared in the sky where the remains of the moon were fighting against the shafts of dawn.

The cold was as sharp as a white and indigo hedgehog.

The chitin knights mulled over their memories and their thoughts lingered on their dead companion.

Moonglum sang a melancholic verse, a refrain of love and nostalgia.

They traveled for another day before entering the temperate, miraculous zone of the Green Pole.

She held out to me
her white hand
and said: tomorrow,
but of course
tomorrow did not exist...

sang Moonglum. And the words grinded through his teeth like shards of frozen poetry.

Hurankon the Redeemed killed an ice bird that was circling in the sky like a vulture and they roasted the prey on a fire of resin carried by the mule since there was nothing to use as fuel on that treeless, shrubless landscape.

By the time the pale sun was hiding behind the Ypplashes Mountains, they saw lichens, then brooms and just before nightfall a tiny forest of atrophied shrubs—they looked like wild bonsai—and they knew that they were approaching their goal.

When his companions had wrapped themselves in their blankets, Elric climbed an icy peak to gaze into the distance. He could make out, vaguely, the Dome and the greenness of the Pole.

He remembered his dream, his pale loves, his hazy quests, the strength unleashed by Stormbringer and the way it soaked its blade in tortured souls. He shuddered and wondered what premonition and prophecy his dreams contained.

The highest visible summit of the Ypplashes was Mount Slumber with its 7890 feet of altitude. It had, they said, a network of caves and grottoes with blue lakes and seas of liquid silver where indescribable species had survived. No one could say why it was so named.

Elric drew Stormbringer out of its scabbard and held it up to the moon; the rune-carved onyx blade flashed like the corselet of a sphex; the sword danced in his hands, crying out for blood to drink and souls to consume.

The Lords of Chaos were watching him. They were behind the silver moon and their eyes glistened like winter wolves.

And he heard the winter wolves howl before the silver moon.

The Lords of Chaos sneered, their faces full of bile and hate.

Once again his soul was a prisoner of confused thoughts, of the melancholy of a vanquished, fallen prince.

The sword's vibrations were becoming unbearable, more and more violent. They were numbing his hands, making the nerves in his forearms tremble.

With teary eyes the albino prince went back down the side of the mountain, his body frozen, his heart gripped by the frost. The wind blew sticky hail into his mouth and nostrils and under his eyelids. In the last few hours he had acquired a mask of ice…

Moonglum was drinking eau-de-vie in front of the hide tent. He had not fallen asleep.

"The wolves…. Do you hear them?"

If they heard them…

Their racket was tracking the phantoms of the night.

The winter wolves came out of gashes in the ice. They were hungry and thirsty for blood. They were full of the fury of the lord gods of Chaos. And their hearts were petrified by the emanations from the sovereign Disorder. Sometimes Elric thought he felt their hateful breath on his skin.

It took them a long time to arrive safe and sound.

In the forest of the Green Pole, Elric would finally find the Book of Origins, the text of Anrith, maybe a start on the road to reconquer his Kingdom, which had fallen into the claws of the Masters of Chaos. Maybe. But was it not necessary to grab the slightest chance?

Every chance was good enough to grab.

Was one of the doors to the Redemption of Melniboné to be found between Ghânia's legs? Now Elric knew the name of the virgin who had appeared to him in his dream. A young virgin—still—who had so far known only solitary pleasure, promised as she was to the bed of Morph, the stupid demigod with a leathery penis, veined like an oak tree root.

When they were only a dozen leagues from their goal, a terrible blizzard rose up and whirled the ice like blue-white arrows that splintered the hazy light of day: arrows swifter and sharper than the ones fired by Hurankon the Redeemer.

6. The Green Pole

An old song told the adventure of a knight lost in a snowstorm. He went around in circles looking for the house of his love and when he was found dead, with his hands frozen to the leather reins, his corpse and that of his horse were only a few feet from the house of safety.

In that glacial fury, Elric felt his already shaken confidence wither away. He was crazy to have come on this quest and dragged his companions along with him.

They were going to die, blinded, choked by the flying ice being thrown by the wind. Their clothes gave them practically no protection against the biting white and they felt naked, eyes sewn shut by the frost, hands dead on the reins, like in the song.

He forced himself to picture the delights he was going to experience with Ghânia—if he reached the end of his voyage alive!—to drive away the cold and the breath of the Grim Reaper, but nothing helped. His thoughts kept coming back to the barrage of stinging ice.

Moonglum had no more stories or songs. His mouth was sealed by a white bar and frozen tears furrowed his cheeks.

Elric went up to his companion and offered him words of encouragement: they must be close because he had seen the foothills of the Green Pole and the White Dome from the mountainside.

As if to prove him right, they heard faint sounds in the smothering whiteness. Like a brass fanfare.

They spurred on their horses, which neighed dismally and blew jets of steam out of their nostrils.

Then the curtain of snowy fog parted and they saw the greenery of the oasis stuck in a fortress of ice. They might very well have been in an old caldera volcano because a very slight line of rock made a border between the white ice and the green trees, which were mostly prickly but a few had leaves and, it seemed, there were fruit trees, but without fruit since it was not the season for fruits.

It was like the garden of the tutelary Gods before they had passed away under the assaults of the chaotic divinities.

Elric remembered the legend of the Isle of Greenland—the green country—lost in the lands abandoned to the frost where happy people lived before the coming of the Great Cold. The world, one might believe, had no choice except between Fire and Ice.

Two men armed with fauchards hurried up to them. "Away with you, strangers, go back to the white Hell."

"I am Elric, the unfortunate ruler of Melniboné."

"You could be the emperor of Atlantis, it wouldn't make any difference," said the watchdog with wider shoulders than the other, dressed entirely in iron scales with a moth-eaten leather apron. He had the face of a snow tiger, but in these lands there were no snow tigers.

"Watch yourself," Moonglum threatened, "we didn't come all this way to be tongue-lashed by cretins like you."

The fauchard started shaking, but Stormbringer jumped out of its scabbard and obsidian sparks leaped from the fallen prince's hands.

The black blade slipped under the chin piece of the helmet and twisted violently. The guard's head dangled from the spine attached only by a few strips of organ.

The other guard dropped to his knees and begged Elric for mercy.

"You won't die today. But you're going to run to the palace of Morph to announce our arrival and ask your sovereign to send us an escort. We will wait right here."

The guard threw down his weapon to run faster.

He disappeared behind the first houses of the City of Morphas.

Dogs barked, but there was nobody there.

In spite of the late hour.

Then they saw the blind facades and figured that this part of Morphas was uninhabited on purpose, no doubt because it was too close to the white land.

They did not wait for long.

Brass sounded and a half dozen knights riding black hippogriffs made their appearance.

Straightaway, the chitin knights drew their swords.

Except for Hurankon, who notched an arrow.

The head of the detachment, a thin, pale woman, her breast sheathed in a cuirass of plaited malachite, came forward. "I am Captain Ilde. I am supposed to escort you to the palace of Titan Morph."

Captain Ilde gave a signal by brandishing her battle-axe and the knights in green cuirasses spread out to form flank guards to bring them into the center of Morphas.

It was a rather small city—no more than 10,000 people—but sprinkled with grandiose constructions, some of which were built of a transparent substance, a kind of resin the color of topaz. It had a nice effect, but a little menacing.

Morph was waiting for them, lying on his bedding, his belly jutting out and his eyes cloudy. He was already full of wine and blinking ostentatiously. "Welcome, Prince Elric. And welcome also to your companions whose bravery is proverbial. Is that Stormbringer I see hanging at your side?"

"That it is."

"They say it drinks souls."

"If they say so…"

Morph clapped softly and some slaves brought them boiling hot drinks: wine from a distant land, liquors and eau-de-vie.

Not trusting the semi-divine sovereign of the Green Pole, the newcomers drank with moderation. Moonglum was less cautious than his companions, but he could hold his liquor better.

Elric asked for authorization to go the library in the Dome in order to consult certain ancient works.

The authorization was promptly granted.

Captain Ilde was watching Elric and Moonglum. She seemed tense, on guard, her knuckles were white on the handle of her axe: a formidable polearm that she must have handled with consummate warrior skill.

In spite of her cold, blonde beauty and the diamond sparkle in her eyes, she was nothing but hostility and this hostility made her unpleasant. Then Elric asked the sovereign for a little information about the countless volumes contained in the collections of Es-Borgh, but the Titan could not care less about his wealth of books and he belched noisily, as if he was about to throw up.

Then the same slaves brought out plates of fish and fowl, fruits and yellow citrons embedded in red and green sorbets.

Ilde did not eat, but drilled her eyes into the neck of the Melnibonéan prince.

Later they took a rest in a tiled bedroom whose luxury was made for relaxing, but they took turns keeping watch, still not convinced of Morph's good intentions.

If Elric had known the import of some of the pudgy Titan's dreams, he would have slept even less calmly.

Ghânia caressed herself gently, on the border of sleep and awakening. The words of the prophecies moved through her head while her fingers moved between the lips of her vagina. She shivered from head to toe. Falling in fits and starts into the abyss of pleasure. A pleasure that she had known how to give herself for years, restrained within the bounds of celibacy and chastity by the declarations of the prophetesses... Then she saw, clearly distinguishable in the darkness, the face of the prince to whom she was now promised and whom she was eager to seduce. Who will seduce whom? I am an inexperienced girl, but I will know how to do what I must.

During her visits to the library, she had consulted secret works: *The Mysteries of the Pistil and the Stamen*, for example. She had read between the lines about the gestures and positions to study. She was convinced that she would be ready, when the time came. Provided that it did not take too long to come.

While Ghânia was moaning from the work of her fingers, Elric was drowsing in the palace of Morph, his mind disposed to portentous dreams. In a few hours he would have access to the collections of Es-Borgh. And maybe he would find out what to do in his present distress. Captain Ilde slipped into his dreams, still wearing her plaited green cuirass but naked underneath, her crotch exposed, as if she were offering herself and yet the aggressive radiance from her pupils contradicted this attitude. Captain Ilde was on the hunt and her nudity was an offering to the gods of carnage and not to men.

She slid, like a deadly ballerina, toward Elric's bed and her two hands held the battle-axe. The long handle allowed the iron to quiver like a deadly tuning fork: it was as if the blade was about to start singing. Elric figured that the weapon, in some way, resembled Stormbringer. The iron dropped and was planted in the Melnibonéan prince's chest. He awoke with a start, his heart squeezed in a vise.

In fact, a few minutes later the captain asked to speak with him.

She had no weapons except for a dagger with a richly ornamented handle hanging from her wide belt whose buckle was in the shape of a white wolf's mouth.

She inquired after the desires and projects of the guests, seeing that she was responsible for their comfort and safety.

A beautiful woman, Moonglum told himself, being present at the meeting, but terribly cold and distant. Ilde was unconsciously playing with her dagger and her fingers fiddling with the handle had something vaguely obscene about it, like a secret provocation. But Moonglum told himself that this woman had eyes only for the albino prince. She drowned the squire of the gentleman (or the man she took for such) under waves of indifference.

She tried to seduce Elric in a way that was both feminine and manly, a kind of duality that might have been fascinating but that triggered almost no feelings in the body or mind of the stranger. She realized this bitterly and after a few more attempts lost any real conviction...

7. What Was Not In The Book

Elric spent little time in the palace of Morph—Ilde's approaches had stupefied him. Under other circumstances he might have been flattered by the captain's homage, but his thoughts were confused, preoccupied by reveries in which Ghânia's face kept coming back.

Soon he called for Moonglum and asked him to go with him to the White Dome. As if she had intercepted a mental communication, Captain Ilde showed up, still dressed like an Amazon, armed with her battle-axe. Elric explained to her that he was eager to get to the Great Library to consult a few prophetic writings.

They found their horses, well fed, groomed and rested and guided by Ilde they got on the road that led to the Dome.

While they were trotting toward the higher ground, the captain made repeated overtures to Elric, then turned back into the female warrior who did not like to see her attempts being rebuffed like that.

Elric only had thoughts for the woman of his dreams, this Ghânia who was promised to the bed of Morph the Rude.

He had the feeling that the demigod sovereign was hatching plans to get rid of him.

They crossed through a bustling city, noisy squares, framed by gleaming buildings. Trees encircled the fountains: the ice was kept at a distance by an atmospheric miracle that was hard to explain. But they had told Elric that the mild temperature came not from the sky but from the earth, that waves of heat traveled through the ground like fumes from an underground inferno.

Sometimes the vibrations rose up through the horses' hooves all the way to the riders' thighs. These vibrations might have presaged future convulsions of the earth, eruptions of fire buried under the ice, but for the moment they sent into the riders' bellies only tremors that soon became unbearable. This whole part of the world was as unstable as that far-off island in the gray sea that the Ancients called Eisland, a wild island molded in fire and frost. Beaten by a foaming, barbarous sea.

Then they came upon the Dome with its azurite and lapis lazuli brilliance. It was huge and Moonglum was dazzled; his eyes burned like they were sprayed with salt.

Elric and the captain entered the place of erudition while Moonglum waited outside to watch the horses. Ilde had hung her battle-axe from her hip, head downward, in a blood red sheath.

Before he had completely entered the library Elric saw the young woman, the future vestal, and he went to her, boldly. She saw him coming toward her, smiling, all white, like in her dreams, with his silvery hair.

Right away the excitement arose and she felt all wet, open to a desire that was stronger than any other sensation.

Elric felt two gazes bear down on him: that of this woman and that of Captain Ilde. The latter was right behind him and he could feel her eyes gleaming with hate. Then he heard a voice echoing in his head: *I have come here every day knowing that you would come. Sooner or later.*

Now that he was in sight of his—double—goal, Elric had a violent vision: Ilde threw herself at the vestal and stuck her battle-axe between her breasts. The metal triangle cut deep into the virgin's chest and a fountain of blood splattered the murderess, as well as the prince of Melniboné.

"You have found me," he said. "I am Elric and I am a fallen prince in search of his destiny."

"I am Ghânia and my destiny is yours, Prince Elric."

He took her hand and led her into the maze of dark rays that was poorly lit by the light from the torches and lamps.

The captain was furious but dared not follow them.

Ghânia showed Elric a fat scroll, the prophetic book, and they used both their hands to unroll it, their fingers touching and mingling greedily.

Then the hands of Ghânia and Elric were buried in each other's clothes and they touched their nervous, tingling flesh. Tangled together, they fell into the half-light, devouring each other.

Ghânia's hymen broke completely in the first assault and she bled painlessly against the belly of the mysterious traveler.

They looked at each other, their eyes enraptured, not yet sated...

In his palace Morph was in a rage and his teeth grinded like wild millstones.

He knew that the vestal virgin who had been promised to him had just been deflowered by the albino intruder. But Ilde was going to destroy him and split open his chest with her axe to bring back the intruder's bloody heart. To show his superiority he would devour the ripped out muscle before torturing the bitch to death. With a few sexual variations for his divine relaxation. She would die slowly, realizing her failure and she would have time to beg him, to make amends with her screams. The whore...

And this son of a bitch, this pale prince, as brittle as glass—May the Gods of Chaos throw him into hell!

8. Souls for Stormbringer

They read the messages in the prophetic Book of Origins, but Elric had the feeling that once again Destiny and its pernicious cynicism were playing tricks on him. He could use some of the pythoness' information but for the most part the Message seemed out of place. The fallen prince had the feeling that the secret of the victory was very far away.

He cried in anger while Ghânia tried to comfort him by holding him close to her.

Again they dropped to the ground and embraced while down below in the palace of Morph, Hurankon, Norg and Süden battled with the demigod's warriors. Cutting and thrusting. Flesh bled, muscles tore, screams rang out.

Süden slipped in a puddle of blood and was laid out flat when a javelin pierced his chest. He yelled out one final cry of defiance and fell back dead.

Hurankon and Norg fought furiously, but there were too many of the others and the outcome of the battle seemed clear. But they battled ferociously, like the wolves of Cyberia who have silver, metal claws and tourmaline eyes. The corpses piled up around them, bloody and maimed.

Then both of them got struck by fauchards and lost blood and their eyes clouded over with red tears.

It was then that a hue and cry broke out and the One from Melniboné and his partner Moonglum showed up, weapons drawn. Stormbringer whirled furiously and hissed through the whirlwind of frightened souls.

All the more so as the albino prince had a death to revenge: Ghânia's, whose virginal blood had soaked his penis.

A few minutes earlier he was lying with her in the hidden aisles of the library, their bodies united in a frenzy of love that unrolled like a great, burning wave. Then there was a movement behind them and Ghânia's eyes reflected fear. Slowly turning his head Elric saw the captain lifting her axe above her head. By reflex he rolled over, trying to take the young woman

299

with him as he rolled. But the iron had torn through the half-light and stuck hard in Ghânia's chest, splitting her left breast in two and making a fountain of blood gush out.

The young woman's screams and those of the albino prince were in harmony, but Ghânia died almost right away, a scarlet stream running out between the left corner of her lips, which were parted, revealing her glistening teeth.

He jumped up and grabbed Stormbringer, which was leaning against the face of a bookshelf. The runic blade buried itself in the captain's throat with a kind of mad hiss.

A fierce gurgling told Elric that Ilde was on the road of no return. Her eyes rolled up in unspeakable hatred.

Now Stormbringer was wildly dancing the dance of death.

Morph's men fell one after another. Their heads flew off like graceful birds and Hurankon and Norg only had to kill when the runic sword gave them the chance.

Soon the last warriors of the crazy demigod retreated.

"Death to Morph!" Elric howled, his vengeance still incomplete.

The priapic demigod was lying on his bed when the door of his room broke into splinters and the four surviving strangers burst into the holy of holies. The cup that Morph was holding in his hand fell onto the tiles, spilling its contents.

"Cursed bastard of Chaos," Elric said in a voice twisted by anger. And he took a step toward Morph.

Stormbringer split the still air and hacked off Morph's penis like a scalpel performing a delicate surgery. The monster's crotch was soaked in black blood.

Because Morph was immortal but not invulnerable.

He clutched his groin and screamed piteously.

"You won't die of this," Elric said, "but with your virile power gone and your immortal soul, you will live forever in misery between your insatiable desires and your hatred."

Morph cursed all the powers of the earth and the lower countries.

He passed out blaspheming.

An hour later the four knights left the Green Pole, carrying a few books and ruminating on confused thoughts.

Uncertain.

The quest of the fallen prince was not fulfilled.

And his suffering battered his mind like waves beating against the shore of a world without any possible repose.

Soon they were in the heart of ice again and Elric's tears froze like pearls of glass.

A short story collection about the Multiverse would not be complete without at least one tale featuring Duke Dorian Hawkmoon of Köln, wielder of the Runestaff, the hero of what is perhaps my favorite of all the Moorcock creations. John Davey returns with a moving epilog to the saga of this remarkable hero...

John Davey: *Death of a Dark Ship*

Then the Earth grew old, its landscapes mellowing and showing signs of age, its ways becoming whimsical and strange in the manner of a man in his last years...

The High History of the Runestaff

Hawkmoon began to stride forward along the shining roadway, eager to begin the journey back to Castle Brass, where the children would meet their noble old grandfather.

"We'll purchase horses at Karlye," he said. "We have credit there." He turned to his son. "Tell me, Manfred, what do you remember of your adventures?" He tried to disguise a certain anxiety for his son. "Do you remember a great deal?"

"No, Father," said Manfred kindly, "I remember very little." And he ran forward, and, taking his father's hand, led him towards the distant shore...

The Chronicles of Castle Brass

Prologue: On Leaving Tanelorn

They had left Tanelorn. Or, rather, they had been transported from there. Five of the six great heroes of Kamarg. Duke Dorian Hawkmoon von Köln and his wife, Yisselda of Brass. Oladahn of the Bulgar Mountains, foppish Huillam D'Averc and the kindly philosopher-poet Bowgentle. Traveling with them also were Hawkmoon and Yisselda's young children, Manfred and Yarmilla.

Many adventures—on many worlds, across many lives—had led them to Tanelorn, where the Eternal Champion—in multiple incarnations (of which Hawkmoon was but one)—undertook his final quest, the Champion's last great deed on behalf of humanity.

Mighty goals are never achieved without sacrifice, and many had perished in pursuit of this one. Some, of course, would not be remembered; they had gone to their graves, seldom if ever to be named in the annals which record such momentous events.

In Tanelorn, Hawkmoon had parted company with Erekosë, who was perhaps the first Champion Eternal, perhaps the last. Perhaps both. Even, perhaps, them all; and Erekosë had found rest (of a sort), finally, from lifetimes full of trials; redemption from cosmic punishment for his great crime.

Hawkmoon had parted, too, from Jhary-a-Conel, self-styled Companion to Heroes. He said farewell to Brut of Lashmar, John ap-Rhyss and Emshon of Ariso, and to the mysterious Orkneyman, Orland Fank, all of whom opted to stay on in Tanelorn. Then, together with his family and friends, Hawkmoon had allowed Fank to put them all back on their original paths.

This is how they found themselves standing once more on the great Silver Bridge spanning thirty miles of sea between France and the island of Granbretan.

They had left Tanelorn—that elusive, mysterious city of peace, appearing on all planes of existence, a refuge, neutral in any conflict and offering solace to those who can find it—and now they were heading home.

Five heroes. The sixth, Count Brass, waited in the castle at Aigues-Mortes in Kamarg for the return of his daughter and son-in-law, Yisselda and Hawkmoon. They had left Castle Brass seeking their missing children, and were now on their way back, not only with children in hand but also with old allies restored. Friends they had believed dead or irrevocably

303

lost.

The Silver Bridge was both broad and bustling, filled with people, with beasts, with transportation of every kind, shape and size, moving in both directions along the great roadway, some hurrying, keen to reach their destinations, others dawdling, all too willing to stop and stare in awe at the engineering wonder, fully restored now after the conflicts that had ravaged Europe, culminating in the Battle of Londra where Hawkmoon and his comrades had defeated the terrible Dark Empire of Granbretan.

It was here on the bridge that Huillam D'Averc now left them, as he headed in the opposite direction towards Londra, there to be reunited with Queen Flana who loved him and mourned him.

"Come," said Hawkmoon as their friend disappeared into the crowd of travelers. "We'll purchase horses at Karlye."

Hand in hand—Manfred's in Hawkmoon's, Hawkmoon's in Yisselda's, Yisselda's in Yarmilla's, and with Bowgentle and Oladahn chatting animatedly just behind—they strode for home.

I. To the Crystal City

In the port town of Karlye they found rooms in a quiet backstreet where, although recognized, they were left to their own devices. Each room contained two small but comfortable beds. Hawkmoon and Yisselda squeezed into one, giving the other to Yarmilla whilst Manfred slept on a pile made from everybody's outer garments. In the other room stayed Bowgentle and Oladahn.

It was sometime in the middle of the night when Hawkmoon awoke and sat up suddenly, disturbed by dreams which over recent months had plagued him more and more, but which he hoped would subside after the recent events in Tanelorn.

Yisselda, immediately alert at her husband's side, looked worriedly into his eyes. "Dorian?"

"Dreams," he said. "Nothing more. Still those same dreams, in which I seem to be other people—so *many* other people—living different lives, sometimes even on worlds that are not our own."

"Something to do with this Eternal Champion? I barely understand what that means."

"Neither do I, my love. Although my grasp on the concept is perhaps clearer to me now than ever before. I expect we'll never fully comprehend it, but it seems that there is something called the 'multiverse,' a multi*tude* of alternative realities, infinite variations of our own universe and experience. On all of these worlds, Law and Chaos are constantly in conflict, each battling to gain ascendency over the Cosmic Balance, a rather nebulous force attempting to maintain equilibrium between the two. And this Eternal Champion, it seems, is forever fighting for one side or the other, in various incarnations throughout the multiverse."

"But did we not rid ourselves of all that, in Tanelorn?"

"I thought so. But then why do these dreams persist?"

"I don't know. But you believe yourself to be one of this legendary being's incarnations?"

"So I'm told. And much of what I've experienced of late seems to bear that theory out."

"Hard to credit, nonetheless."

"Impossible, almost, and still retain one's sanity. I've thought myself mad in the past. Others, too, have found me so. I believed I had lost all that I have ever loved. And now all I love is restored to me. I've tried for so long to avoid the supernatural, and anything purporting to be or to represent destiny. Fate. Or whatever. If all of this is true, must I now embrace such notions?"

"You have embraced them before, Dorian. The Runestaff. The Sword of the Dawn. The Red Amulet. What are these things, if not proof of something beyond the natural?"

"Was I wrong, then, to resist them… to question their power?"

"You had to act as you felt was best."

"But did that resistance cause more suffering, prolong the strife, bring about avoidable or needless death and destruction?"

"So many questions. So few solid answers. You and I cannot begin to take in the implications of all this new information. Go back to sleep, if you can, my love. Things will seem simpler, if not necessarily clearer, in the morning."

Hawkmoon nodded. "You're right, of course. But first I must speak with Oladahn and Bowgentle. You go back to sleep, Yisselda. I promise I'll re-join you soon." He smiled reassuringly.

"Is anything wrong?"

"No. Just something I must discuss with them before we travel on. That's all."

Bowgentle was sleeping soundly as Hawkmoon entered the second bedroom, but Oladahn woke instantly, his hand gripped around the hilt of his sword.

Hawkmoon raised his own hand, hushing his friend's fears. "*Shhh*... It's me. I'm sorry to disturb your sleep."

"What is it? What's happened?"

"Nothing. Just a feeling."

"A feeling?"

"I need you to promise me something, Oladahn."

"Anything."

"If something happens. If we get separated again…"

"What! What do you know?"

"I *know* nothing. As I said, it's no more than a feeling. But—*if* we get separated again—please promise me that you and Bowgentle will see that Yisselda, Manfred and Yarmilla make it safely home to Castle Brass."

"Of course. But I'd rather know what threatens?"

"Trust me. There's nothing specific. I just need to know that, if something happens, my family will be safe."

"Know that they will be."

"Thank you, my friend."

Next day—after the remainder of the previous night passed without incident—Hawkmoon's party set off early for Parye, the Crystal City.

They arrived as the sun was setting, which was a good thing, for to come to Parye in the height of the day was to be dazzled—blinded, almost—by rainbow colors bouncing and rebounding from building to building, all constructed from quartz of every hue, flashing and scintillating from countless glass ornaments adorning each surface, nook and cranny.

The beast-masked warlords of the Dark Empire, having razed the whole of Europe to the ground, had felt compelled to leave the Crystal City standing all but unviolated. Even at the destructive, nihilistic peak of its power, Granbretan had recognized something sacrosanct in Parye's breathtaking splendor.

Now, as the sun set, every architectural facet glowed blood-red.

As in Karlye, discreet lodgings were located and rooms secured, overlooking the wide, bright river which wound its way between the city's broad boulevards.

Hawkmoon, his family and his friends ate together, and ate well. Any fears from the previous night were soon forgotten or subdued, and they all chatted amiably about reaching Aigues-Mortes in a few days' time, anticipating the look on Count Brass's ruddy, rugged old face as he witnessed the travelers' return.

They retired late, tired but content.

This time, when Hawkmoon woke again in the middle of the night, the first thing that struck him was the silence.

He could hear his own breathing, and that of his sleeping wife and children, but there was not another sound in the world.

Parye, a bustling city at any time of day or night, was as quiet as a grave; deathly quiet, unnaturally quiet.

Through the windows came a deep, hazy red light. In his tiredness, it took a while for Hawkmoon to realize that this could no longer be as a result of the earlier sunset.

Getting up, he moved to the windows but found it hard to see far beyond them. A dense mist had risen, impenetrably thick, and it was this fog which glowed and was no doubt responsible for deadening any noise from without.

Hawkmoon stood for a while longer, transfixed by the all-encompassing, ruby hue, trying to recall why it seemed familiar. The answer refused to rise to the surface of his mind until, in and for only a fraction of a second, it was momentarily revealed.

There on the river—impossibly there on the river, for it sat between two low, stone bridges under which it could never have sailed—was the ship which had carried Hawkmoon and his comrades to Tanelorn. Some of them it had carried away again. The Dark Ship, which sailed between the worlds, borne on the seas of fate.

Hawkmoon had later been told by the ship's blind captain and his steersman brother that their craft had been lost. Yet here it was on the river which ran through Parye. He had time to recognize the red star which forever followed the Dark Ship's passage, proving beyond doubt his fleeting revelation, before the glowing fog enshrouded everything again.

Whilst he had no reason to fear the ship's appearance, neither did he welcome it. Before heading out to investigate further, he would awaken Oladahn and Bowgentle to accompany him. Their rooms here had a connecting door, and Hawkmoon knocked gently before entering. Both men still slept. He moved over to Oladahn's bed and shook him by the shoulder. No response.

"Oladahn?"

Nothing.

"Bowgentle?"

Nothing. "Oladahn!" Not a movement. Not a murmur. Not a breath. The two men did not appear to be dead, but their slumber was anything but natural. Neither stirred. Had they been drugged, or was their incapacity at this crucial time of a more mysterious, even sorcerous origin?

Dashing back into his own room, Hawkmoon found

Yisselda awake and alert, a troubled look sparking in her eyes. "What's wrong, Dorian?"

"I'm not sure." He told her of the Dark Ship's manifestation.

"What can it mean?"

"I don't know, yet. But I do know that Bowgentle and Oladahn appear to be in a stupor. I cannot waken them. It's my intention to visit the ship and find out its reasons for being here. I meant to leave you in the hands of the others, but now…"

"*No!*"

Yisselda's sudden vehemence startled Hawkmoon. "My love?"

"No, Dorian. We have already been parted from each other before—parted from our children also—and have suffered both mentally and physically before being reunited. I will *not* allow us to be separated again. None of us. If you go to the ship, then so do we. All of us, together."

"Yisselda, I can't. *We* can't. It's too dangerous."

"Nothing is dangerous yet. There's no proven threat. Just a mystery. We'll investigate it together, or not at all."

"Yisselda…"

"I will *not* be persuaded, Dorian."

"I would still leave you and the children, or just the children, with Oladahn and Bowgentle. When they awake, they can take you all to safety."

"*If* they awake. No—" she was already moving over to rouse their little ones—"we all go."

Hawkmoon sighed, realizing that there was no turning his wife from her resolve. He knew that leaving them with the slumbering pair in the other room made no proper sense, but who knew what dangers may await them—into what fresh peril he might be placing them—if they all went now to the Dark Ship to discover its purpose?

Manfred and Yarmilla were grumbling blearily as they shuffled through the misty streets, hand in hand with their parents. No one else was abroad. Whatever had put their friends into a near-coma had seemingly entranced the whole of the Crystal City.

They reached the river's bank and looked up at the craft, visible in greater detail now that the fog was thinner, although still glowing that steady, rosy pink.

It was a tall ship with high fore- and aft-castles, each deck bearing a large steering wheel. Between these was a sturdy central mast at which was furled a black canvas sail. Every inch of the ship's wood- and metalwork—every rail, the mast and the figurehead, from curving prow to rudder-bearing sternpost—all were carved, deeply and intricately, with bizarre designs, some geometrical or abstract, others depicting scenes, people and creatures, few of them familiar.

The whole thing gave off an aura of great, latent power, of hidden strengths in reserve. Devoid of conspicuous *matériel*, it nevertheless seemed ready for any turn of events. All was as silent on board as it was in the city; there were no signs of any crew, but Hawkmoon's limited experience of this craft alleviated any alarm he might otherwise have felt.

The Dark Ship floated closer to the riverside than should have been possible. Its keel must surely preclude such proximity to Hawkmoon and his family, as they stood now at the foot of an already lowered rope ladder.

"Dorian?" Yisselda looked to him for confirmation that they should ascend.

He nodded, pulling the ladder taut and placing his foot on the bottom to hold it as steady as possible.

Yisselda climbed onto the first rung, and then the second; the third, increasing in confidence as she went. Manfred followed, then Yarmilla, both children seemingly fearless and enjoying the swaying adventure of it all. Once all three were safely over the rail, Hawkmoon clambered up and soon joined them. His wife was ill at ease, trying to distract their inquisitive children away from closer examination of some of the more graphic carvings.

No one greeted them, and Hawkmoon saw no reason at

that moment to seek anybody out. It was still the middle of the night.

"Come," he said. "I was told that there are bunks somewhere below. Who knows what might be about to take place? Let us get some extra sleep while we can."

II. Aboard the Dark Ship

It was the smell of cooking that next awoke them. Hawkmoon and Yisselda sat up in their individual seamen's cots. The children, in theirs, slumbered on.

Yisselda got up and moved across the large cabin, in which there were bunks enough for many, towards the door. Gradually she opened it, peering out cautiously before bending to retrieve a heavy wooden tray laden with hot food and drinks.

"There's no sign of our mysterious benefactor," she said, returning to her bed and placing on it the attractively pungent victuals, "but for these I'm very grateful." She paused. "Is it safe to sample this fare, though, Dorian, do you think?"

"Perfectly, I'm certain. The two-man 'crew' of this ship has no reason to harm us, and if they did then I'm sure it would not have to be anything as subtle as poisoning."

He joined Yisselda as she picked up and took a bite from a delicious-looking pastry. "Should we wake the children?"

"No. Let them sleep on." Hawkmoon recognized the liquid in a silver jug on the tray. He poured two cups of it, handing one to his wife. "I know this only as the Captain's wine, but try some. It will offer you a remarkable degree of well-being, even a sharpening of the senses."

They drank. They ate. They talked.

It was agreed that Hawkmoon should track down and speak with the blind captain as soon as their fast was fully broken. Yisselda had been reluctant, at first. But the four of them could not remain inseparable for ever. With her husband's assurances that they were in no immediate danger here on the Dark Ship, she assented.

The Captain's cabin, Hawkmoon knew, was to be found under the high forward deck. As he headed there he noticed that the craft was in motion, its speed considerable, the sail full despite the absence of any obvious wind. He also saw the steersman at one of the ship's great wheels, standing stock-still and staring only forwards. The man did not acknowledge Hawkmoon's brief salute.

Large lanterns now shone at each end of the Dark Ship, but they did little to penetrate the fog through which it travelled, any more than did the light from the strange red star permanently above.

The Captain's door was made of a peculiar metallic substance which seemed to shimmer almost organically as Hawkmoon approached it. "Enter, Hawkmoon," came a voice from within the cabin, just as he raised his hand to knock, and the door swung open before him. A much brighter red light shone from within the room as he entered, and it took a while for his eyes to adjust.

The well-heated quarters smelled slightly sweet, and were richly decorated. Next to the highly polished, gold-railed desk stood the tall man, his features refined, his reddish blond hair held back from his face by a blue jade circlet, his slanting, almond-shaped eyes milky white and sightless. "Greetings, Hawkmoon," he said. "I trust your breakfast was adequate?"

"More than adequate, thank you, sir, and very much appreciated."

"Food is not something we often have to provide on this ship. Our passengers are rarely on board long enough to require any. But when we saw that you were accompanied, we rallied as best we could."

"You did not expect, then, Yisselda and our children to be with me?"

"We did not."

"My other comrades, Bowgentle and Oladahn, were placed under some kind of sorcerous trance. Was that nothing to do with you?"

"Not directly. But when this ship docks in natural waters,

which it does only to drop off or pick up passengers, it has a tendency to slow time to such a degree that potential witnesses are rendered incapable of movement or memory. Only those that are required can see the ship and join it."

"Then why, sir, are my wife and children here?"

"I do not know. Perhaps they have some part to play in all this…"

"All this *what*?" Hawkmoon felt anger and impatience rising. "I had thought my tasks completed. I have served the Runestaff, often against my will, for longer than I care to remember, and it has served me both well and ill in near-equal measures. What does it demand of me now, and what has my family to do with any of this?"

"Time will tell. Here. You will have some more wine?"

"No. Thank you, but no. I want only answers. When we last met in Tanelorn you told me that…"

"*Wait*! I beg you, Duke Dorian, say no more."

"Why not?"

"You talk of our having spoken together in Tanelorn. For you, evidently, that episode is in the past. Yet for me it has still to take place."

"I don't understand."

"I last saw you on the shore of Agak and Gagak's island. You stayed. But Elric of Melniboné and Prince Corum rejoined the ship. As did Otto Blendker. Our paths have not crossed again, since."

"But in Tanelorn…"

"I assure you that, at this point in time, we have not met in Tanelorn. I caution you to silence, my friend, because anything you might tell me, however inadvertently, of what the future holds, could both affect and alter that very future. Trust me in this, please."

Hawkmoon nodded sullenly, more confused than ever. As, of course, he had been before when hoping for the Captain's enlightenment.

"If you, Duke Dorian, are to become a fully fledged player in the Game of Time…"

"These are not *games*!"

"Indeed they are not…"

"Then tell me, Sir Captain, for where…" Hawkmoon's voice trailed off. The look in the blind captain's eyes had of course not changed, but his whole demeanor was now oddly alert, nervous, all too aware of something being amiss. "What is it?"

The Captain's voice was barely a whisper, yet holding an unmistakable note of deepest fear. "The ship has stopped."

As the pair left the cabin together, they were joined on deck by the steersman, equally perplexed.

"This is unusual?" asked Hawkmoon.

"Not unusual," the Captain replied. "Impossible!"

"How so?"

"The ship is capable of being stationary only when in natural waters. On these seas of fate, it must always be in motion. To stop is to perish."

"Then how has this happened? Why?"

"I have no idea. It is unprecedented."

As they stood there, the sail ceased its customary billowing and hung limp on the mast. Then the surrounding mist dwindled slowly away, revealing nothing above, below or around the Dark Ship but a void of total, unblemished blackness.

"Is this what is normally beyond the fog?" Hawkmoon asked in a hushed tone.

Neither crewman replied.

Suddenly a nearby hatch cover to the ship's hold began to rattle furiously, and muffled shouting from within was heard by all. The words (if words they were) could not be discerned, but their fury was doubtless. Fists and feet pounded at the wooden barrier, which held.

The three men walked towards the source of this commotion, the blind captain to one side, his brother to the other, Hawkmoon in the middle with his sword drawn.

At a nod from the armed man, the steersman pulled back the bolt securing the hatch. It must have coincided with the irate captive hurling himself full pelt at its cover, for as this was swept aside a small man tumbled out at their feet, cursing loudly and most inventively. A moment later he had flipped over onto his back, and as quickly Hawkmoon's boot planted itself on the man's chest, the sword's point at his throat.

"Do you mind!" said the man indignantly. "This material crumples all too easily." He pushed at Hawkmoon's foot, but desisted as soon as the duke's weapon dented his flesh.

The Captain spoke up: "I recognize that voice. Is that you, Master Timeras?"

"It is, Sir Captain. Or was. Or will be? You know how uncertain I can be at these times."

Hawkmoon thought that the man spoke nonsense, but also felt that there was more than a passing resemblance, both physical and verbal, to the Champion's companion, Jhary-a-Conel. As he pondered this, Yisselda came up on deck, no doubt summoned by the noisy disturbance. The children were behind her legs, shielded and held back by her outstretched arms.

"You know this man?" Hawkmoon asked of the Captain.

"I do. In many guises."

"An Eternal Champion, then?"

Timeras continued to squirm on the deck. "No, merely a pawn," he said. "Sometimes a knight, admittedly. But seldom. And never more than that. But—" he looked up into Hawkmoon's face, into his eyes—"I know you, Duke Dorian."

"You do?"

"I do—" his glance moved to Hawkmoon's forehead— "although I thought you had a black jewel in place, where now you bear that very distinctive scar."

"So I did, once. Yet I have no recollection of having met you."

"Perhaps you haven't? What do you know of the Dark Empire's Baron Bous-Junge of Osfoud?

"The name is not familiar."

"He is commander of the Order of the Snake, Granbretan's chief scientist."

"You mean Baron Kalan, surely. And the Dark Empire is…"

"*Hawkmoon!*" snapped the blind captain, making everybody jump. "Remember what I told you."

The Duke of Köln scowled, choosing merely to restate, "I know of no Bous-Junge."

"*Hmmm…*" mused Timeras. "Perhaps a different Hawkmoon."

"A different incarnation of the Eternal Champion, you mean?"

"Not at all. I mean an alternative Hawkmoon. *Um*, d'you mind…"

"*Agh*," groaned Hawkmoon, removing his boot from the man's chest and allowing him to stand. "This I cannot bear! I've only just begun to get used to the idea of there being a multitude of worlds and dimensions, let alone many so-called Champions and the fact that I'm supposed to be one, and now you tell me that there are multiple Hawkmoons! How can this be?"

"Now is not the time for such speculation," said the Captain urgently. "Master Timeras, how did you get here, and for what reason?"

"As usual, sir, I have very little idea of either. I was in Hawkmoon's… in *a* Hawkmoon's world, trying to find where I had been told you… to find where *he* would be hiding, in a cave system." As he spoke, Timeras rearranged his disheveled clothing to something approaching his satisfaction, while at the same time kissing Yisselda's hand, shaking Manfred's, and bowing deeply in the direction of Yarmilla. All three seemed flattered by his impromptu courtesies. "After a number of frustratingly vague leads proved fruitless, I entered what I thought was the correct cavern and, walking to the back of it, found my way barred by that hatch cover there. As to why I am here, I haven't a clue. But there's always a reason, is there not? I say, shouldn't this craft be in motion?"

"Indeed it should," the blind captain replied. "This, as you know, must never happen. I had hoped you might be able to explain the phenomenon."

CAW!

The raucous cry came from above. All those gathered on deck looked up. There, clinging to the rail of the crow's nest, was an enormous jet-black bird like a great crow. Somehow its color (or lack of one) was darker even than the surrounding void. The beak alone had any kind of hue, a blood-red that made it look as if it had just lifted its head from a prey's gored wound. The creature's eyes were blackest of all, at least to begin with, although they shifted through various blues and browns as it glared unblinking at the people below, and the pupils showed occasional sudden flashes of gold, sparks of malevolent intelligence.

"CAW…" said the bird. Then, "SWORD…"

"I am not," said Timeras, "over-prone to belief in omens. But does anyone here share my presentiment that we might at this moment be better off below deck?"

No one answered, but they all moved rapidly for the nearest doorway leading down to the sleeping quarters. The moment they entered them, the whole ship shuddered viciously and began to plummet down through the void. Everybody in the cabin was thrown into the air as the craft fell from under their feet and spun in a tight spiral as if being sucked relentlessly by an oceanic maelstrom. As he struck a bulkhead and felt the breath knocked from him, Hawkmoon looked dazedly around and saw that somehow Yisselda still clung to their two children, protecting them from the worst risks of injury with her own body as they tumbled. The Captain and his brother also held desperately on to each other, flying across the cabin and smashing into the wall below a bank of portholes through which he glimpsed the gigantic bird flying outside, also in circles but counter to the spin of the Dark Ship. Of Timeras there was no sign. A scream took Hawkmoon's attention straight back to his wife; she had lost her grip on Manfred who was sliding across the floor towards the open door, just outside of which was a near-vertical stairway. Nobody could survive a fall to the deck below. Manfred cried out for his parents, nei-

317

ther of whom could reach him in time. Just as the boy was about to disappear from view, an arm shot out from under a table and arrested his imminent descent. It was Timeras. The boy was safely in his arms now, and the ship's own descent was beginning gradually to slow. Everyone was now back on the floor of the cabin, yelling wordlessly, crawling painfully towards each other and the security of the bolted-down furniture. Although even now, decelerating as they were, it was unlikely that they or the ship would survive anything with which they collided. The great, crow-like bird was still squawking around outside, keeping pace with the Dark Ship as it plunged down into who knew what. Suddenly with a parting *CAW* it shot off at right angles, and all that the passengers and crew could do was brace themselves for what was likely to be a bone-shattering impact. Up until this point it was as if they had been falling through the silence of a vacuum, but now they heard the rush of bruised air tearing at the outside of the craft, and dense brown clouds buffeted the hull which seemed fit to burst asunder before they had even crash-landed. There was a whistling sound which became louder and more shrill until their own panicked screams could not be heard above it. Hawkmoon was wedged under one table with Manfred now wrapped in his arms. Yarmilla was being clutched equally tightly by Yisselda, opposite Hawkmoon, and the couple stared nowhere but into each other's eyes, letting love overwhelm terror.

Then the Dark Ship hit the ground.

III. On the Ice

Or rather, it hit the water.

Had it not been for the ship's deep, slenderly tapering keel plunging into the sea first and lessening the impact fractionally, they would have been killed in an instant. Certainly none of them expected to live.

But there was no way that they could all escape without injury, and yells of pain mingled with the crunching sound of timbers splintering and shattering around them.

These noises of collapse took a while to subside, and it was not until complete silence returned that anyone attempted to speak. First to do so was the blind captain: "Are we all still here?" It seemed an odd thing to ask, or at least an odd way to ask it. The dim light through the portholes was barely adequate for them to see each other, but Hawkmoon could tell that the Captain held his unconscious brother's wrist, seeking a pulse. In time the man nodded to himself, satisfied at having found one.

"I'm alive," said Hawkmoon. "Manfred?" he enquired.

"My leg hurts, Father. My ankle, I think."

Yisselda looked to her daughter. "Darling?"

"I'm okay, Mother."

"Whilst I *am* alive," repeated Hawkmoon, checking thoroughly on their son's injuries, "I'm not sure how. Bruises alone, thankfully, and no shortage of them."

"I, too, appear unhurt," said Yisselda. "*Ow!* Well, perhaps not entirely unhurt, but nothing serious."

From under a nearby table, Timeras's voice was strained. "I, sadly, appear to have broken my arm." There was a sharp, wincing intake of breath. "Badly."

The Dark Ship's steersman was coming to. "Are we able to stand?" asked the blind captain, clambering to his feet and helping his brother to rise.

Hawkmoon stood painfully, slowly, realizing that a sharp twinge in his side might suggest a cracked rib or two. His wife got up with Yarmilla still in her arms. Manfred, at his side, began hobbling gingerly around, trying to walk off what could be a slight sprain. Yisselda put her uninjured daughter down and walked over to help Timeras up. He was crawling delicately out from under the table, and grimaced as he turned to take the woman's proffered hand with his good one. The broken arm hung limply at his side, showing a compound fracture with a sliver of shattered bone puncturing the skin. Blood trickled from the open wound, and Yisselda took him quickly to one side, away from the children; she began to look around for anything she could use to staunch the flow and hopefully attend in some temporary manner to the break.

The Captain said, "We should leave here, find out where we are, assess damage to the ship and see if we can perhaps find medical help for the injured."

There was a sudden loud ripping sound, but it was just Yisselda tearing at the hem of her green gown in an attempt to fashion a makeshift sling for Timeras, who nodded at the others that he would be able to go with them.

A few minutes later they were all staring over the side of the Dark Ship, looking down to see where it had crashed-landed.

In every direction was ice, except for immediately where the craft had splashed down into a murky, languorous patch of sea, barely larger than the ship itself. There was no way in which it could have smashed through the ice without being destroyed in the process, and the likelihood of having found the only open water in the vicinity, without the sorcerous aid of someone or something, simply defied belief.

It took longer than anticipated to get everybody over the side of the Dark Ship and down onto the ice. The hull appeared more or less undamaged; a few planks had burst their seams, but none, as far as they could tell, below the waterline. The mast had not fared so well, and neither had the ruined aftcastle onto which it had toppled.

The ends of the rope ladder down which they had scrambled, some rather more easily than others, lay on a narrow, crystalline beach of sorts, surrounding the watery opening, and they had had to crunch their way carefully across this in order to gain the firmer, icy ground.

Looking up now, at the damaged ship, they saw above it a dark, brooding sky in which hung the barest glimmer of a sun—small, red, ancient—which was hidden frequently by low brown clouds. It was not a sun that was likely to sustain much in the way of life, they felt, thus decreasing their chances of finding help here. This place was clearly dying, perhaps dead. A twilight world.

There was an almost overwhelming smell of salt in the air. The patch of sea seemed clogged with it, so that the water no longer acted as it should. This was sluggish, thickly viscous stuff, grey run through with black. There were deep saline deposits all over the black crystals of the 'shore.'

"What now?" asked Hawkmoon.

"I'd suggest we seek civilization," Timeras said doubtfully, "if any such exists here."

"But in which direction?"

"Does it matter?"

"It might."

"Then I would also suggest, Duke Dorian, in the absence of any best guess, that a random one will have to suffice…" and with that he set off, away from the Dark Ship, and the others followed. Hawkmoon carried Manfred. Yisselda and their daughter walked hand in hand, careful not to slip on the ice, while the steersman led the blind captain by the arm.

They saw nothing whatsoever, to break the monotonous ground over which they trod, especially once the mastless ship had disappeared from view behind them.

After yet more trekking, their eyes were all rimed with salt, so when finally there was something to see, it took them a while to spot it. Timeras, still leading the group, held up his good hand, signaling that they should both stop and be silent.

In the near distance stood an ornately decorated chariot-cum-sled of bronze and silver, which had been drawn to a halt on the ice by four great beasts resembling enormous polar bears. Dismounting were a man and a woman. He was heavily bearded, armored in lacquered hide, ornamented metal and thick sheepskin; at his hip was a huge black broadsword. She had skin with a distinct silvery sheen; her eyes were very large and very black (even at a distance) and her hair white; she wore a red dress which looked in no way warm enough for the wintry climate, and she was beautiful.

Timeras whispered, and was barely heard by the others as a strange breeze blew up out of nowhere: "That is Count Urlik Skarsol, Lord of the Frozen Keep. And that, unless I'm mistaken, must be the Lady of the Chalice."

Hawkmoon thought that he recognized the bearded man; he had no idea from where. He knew for certain, too, that he had seen the woman before, perhaps recently, but again the circumstances of their meeting would not come to him. Was something clouding his judgment and memory deliberately?

The woman raised her arms and shouted something at the livid sky, but her words were carried away from the watching group—remaining unseen by the pair—on the increasing wind.

The man withdrew his black sword and held it with its point pressed into the ice. Then the woman knelt with her back to him, and slowly she lowered herself down until she lay at his feet. The sword was lifted high in the air and before the onlookers knew what was happening he had buried it in the woman's back. Hawkmoon swore, dropping his son to the ground, and made to run forward but he was restrained with some difficulty by Timeras's good arm.

"Hold, Duke Dorian, hold! This is not our world. We cannot interfere."

"*Murderer!*" yelled Hawkmoon, appalled by what they were witnessing, but the man wielding the sword did not hear him. He struggled to free himself of Timeras's grip, whilst Yisselda shielded their children from the scene.

The dying woman screamed. The wind screamed. Even the sword screamed. But all were drowned out by a new sound, a terrible wailing accompanied by a fierce, blinding light.

The group was dazzled, with all bar the Captain throwing arms across their eyes to shield them.

When they could see again, it seemed to them all as if the dying sun had somehow brightened. Their shadows were thrown for the first time upon the ice.

The bearded man no longer held his sword. He tugged its scabbard from his belt, letting it slip from his fingers and fall to the ground. With a weary slump to his shoulders, he walked slowly back to the chariot, climbed on board and took up the reins, goading the bears into motion.

Hawkmoon freed himself from Timeras and began to run after the fleeing man, crying out for him to stop and face justice, but he was forced to give up as soon as he realized that he was losing ground on the departing sled.

He stood near the fallen woman as the blind captain and his brother came up, followed by Timeras. Yisselda and the children kept their distance.

There were tears in Hawkmoon's eyes. "Why?" he wanted to know. "Why?"

None of them could answer him.

"Look," said Timeras, pointing. Close to the slain body was the unmistakable shadow of the black broadsword, but the weapon itself was nowhere to be seen. Then they noticed that the corpse was dressed differently from when they had first seen the woman. Gone was the red dress. In its place was a gown of gold, gloves of the same shade, and a golden veil covered her face. It was as if the color had drained out of her clothing as the blood drained out of her body, staining the ice.

Suddenly the place where she lay was bathed in a bright, golden light, and the gathered men watched in awe as the woman's body seemed to become absorbed by the ground. As she sank into it, the ice re-formed solidly over her, and they also saw at the same time that where previously there was just the shadow of a sword, now there lay the weapon itself.

Timeras gasped. "The Black Sword!"

Hawkmoon, too, recognized the blade. He recognized the mysterious runes covering every inch of it. He had last seen it borne by Elric of Melniboné. He feared the Black Sword, and said as much.

"So you should," replied the Captain. "So you should." He paused, then added, "We will take it with us, my brother and I. For it is needed, that blade, at a certain time, in a certain place."

Hawkmoon knew that place, and he knew that time, because for him it had already occurred; he had been there when the pair brought the Black Sword to Tanelorn and returned it to the Eternal Champion. At last he began to appreciate the importance—the enormity—of a need for discretion in these great, multiversal struggles... in this Game of Time.

Now the Dark Ship's steersman walked forward and lifted the blade carefully into his arms.

Together, they all moved back to where Yisselda stood with the children.

CAW!

Everyone stared immediately upwards. Circling them, high in the newly brightened air, was the great, jet-black bird. It turned suddenly in the sky and hurtled down towards the gathering on the ice. The group scattered as the beast landed in its midst. But when they turned again to face the creature, it was no longer a bird. Standing there in its stead was a human-like figure, but that was where any resemblance to a man ended. It was every bit as jet-black as the bird had been, but whether it was naked and with shining flesh, or whether it was clothed thus, it was hard to tell, except that there appeared to be something akin to a high collar shielding the thing's face from them. It was a featureless face, until the eyes and mouth opened. A ferocious loathing burned in those eyes, and the long, jagged teeth were swathed in bright red flame. In fact it seemed as if the whole body was awash with black fire.

The creature spoke: "Sword," it said. "Me." Then, "Elric."

"I know you," said Hawkmoon.

"You have seen this thing before?" Timeras asked.

But it was the blind captain who answered: "It is the essence of the Black Sword. Or one manifestation of it. It seeks to re-inhabit the blade."

The black figure stared intently at Hawkmoon, opening its mouth again: "Elric?"

This creature had pursued Hawkmoon all the way to Tanelorn. That it did not recognize him now was another indication of peculiar shifts in the time streams.

"I am not Elric."

"Not Elric. Urlik—" a glance around—"Arflane..."

"I am none of those men."

"You are all of those men. Corum. Hawkmoon. Erekosë…"

"Neither am I Erekosë." He drew his sword.

"All are Erekosë. He who slew the human race—the *whole* of the human race—and for what? For the lust of a wanton alien bitch…"

"Keep your foul lies to yourself!" snapped the Captain.

Timeras, nearby, merely whispered, "For love."

"Love," the figure snarled. "Love." Its flaming aura wavered. Looking at Hawkmoon, it half-said, half-sighed, "*Aahh…*" as if seeing something in him for the first time. It stepped towards the Duke of Köln, who seemed unable to resist. The creature's arm shot forward and the tip of one finger pressed into the scar at the centre of Hawkmoon's forehead. The man screamed, as he had in the past when the Black Jewel sat there trying to destroy his brain, and he fell back onto the ice. He did not move.

Yisselda yelled his name.

The black figure laughed.

Fire sparked and writhed around its feet.

It roared: "The Black Sword. What stands before me now? A dead man. An injured man. A woman and two children… tasty morsels. A blind man. And the one who holds the Black Sword. *Nothing* stands between me and the Black Sword."

Timeras tried to draw his own weapon, but his sword-arm was the broken one. The creature advanced on him menacingly. It raised its own arm.

"*Stop!*"

It stopped. It turned. It spoke. "Woman?"

Yisselda had taken Hawkmoon's sword from the ground, and was pointing it at the black figure. "Stop," she repeated.

The creature almost crooned, "Oh, I will *devour* you, woman. Then I will eat your children. I will absorb their very souls."

"You will *not!*"

The figure walked purposefully towards them, opening its flaming mouth unnaturally wide.

Yisselda stood her ground. "*No one* threatens my children!"

She looked at the creature, searching for any weak spot. Its skin (if skin it was) seemed all but impenetrable. Its chest, she knew, could not contain a heart. Were there any vulnerable organs? In desperation she lowered the weapon slightly, until its point was aimed between the thing's legs. Then Yisselda pressed the blade inexorably forward, into and through its groin. Ragged flesh erupted around it. No blood flowed. She closed her eyes, but somehow still saw as the rent widened further and turned to semi-liquid, beginning to spiral, faster and faster. Spinning outwards from this central wound, the figure lost all shape, first changing rapidly— beast-like, bird-like, human-like, sword-like—trying to find a form in which it could escape torment, then growing in size, but not in mass, as it was dispersed in front of them all. Some features remained—eyes, mouth, one elongated, imploring hand—and all protested, though they tossed and jumbled around in this near-gaseous tempest. Then, as if black water pulled towards a drain, the great vortex was sucked into the tip of Hawkmoon's sword in Yisselda's unwavering hand, until nothing was left but a mouth. All else had dissipated and disappeared. "*Me*," it said, as it vanished.

Yisselda dropped the sword, turning as she heard a groan from the ice. "Dorian!" She knelt at Hawkmoon's side, lifting his head, helping him to stand.

He looked dazedly around. "Where is it?"

"Gone," said Timeras.

"Dead?"

The blind captain spoke: "No. That thing cannot be destroyed so easily, and this sword of yours will not contain it for long."

Timeras described what had happened, and Hawkmoon for the first time found himself wondering how the Captain seemed to know so much of events that he could not possibly have seen.

"So what happens now?" asked Yisselda.

The blind man said, "I suggest we leave Duke Dorian's sword precisely where it has fallen. Nobody touch it. It seems fairly certain that civilization does not lie ahead of us. But my brother and I have been seeking the Black Sword for some time. It was no coincidence that we were brought here at this time. We may as well go back to the ship, and from there in the opposite direction, to see if anyone or anything can be found to help us leave this place. The ship will need repairing before it can travel again."

They departed.

The trek was long, and no one talked until: "It's power, isn't it?" said Yisselda suddenly. "Or desire. Or need." She was uncertain where these thoughts were coming from, or if they were even her own. "The need to control what one cannot destroy, or to destroy what one cannot control…"

Heads down against the warming wind, nobody answered her. Perhaps they had not heard her.

For a while, they kept expecting to see the ship appear before them. It was some time longer before they began to fear that it would not do so. Had they gone astray?

But no.

They reached, eventually, the opening in the ice, at the very moment that the uppermost rails of the Dark Ship's high forward deck disappeared into the glutinous, salt-heavy sea.

Hawkmoon, Yisselda, their children and Timeras stood discreetly to one side as the Captain and his brother wept for the loss of their precious, *sui generis* craft.

"I thought the ship was more or less seaworthy," whispered Hawkmoon. "What caused this?"

"Perhaps it was holed below the waterline after all," Timeras answered. "Or maybe its long course, sailing between the worlds, is finally run."

"So what happens now?" Yisselda asked for the second time.

"My brother and I," said the blind captain re-joining

327

them, "will continue on our way. If, as appears to be the case, we are on the South Ice, then the Scarlet Fjord should be in that direction." He pointed. "There we might find the means of leaving here with the Black Sword."

"But what about the rest of us?"

"That, I think," said Timeras, "is where I come in. I do not have the means to transport us *all* from here, but I think I might know a way of getting the duke and his family home."

"How?" asked Hawkmoon.

"Well, I'm not entirely sure you'll like it."

A little while later, they watched the Dark Ship's captain and steersman disappear into the distance.

The Captain, as they parted company, had said, "It seems, Duke Dorian, as if we will meet you again," before adding, with more than the suggestion of a smile, "although whether or not you will ever meet us again remains to be seen."

Somewhat more unnerved than amused by the blind captain's irony, Hawkmoon had opted not to reply.

Now the remaining members of their party stood on the black, crystalline beach, at the edge of the water.

"You're sure this will work, Timeras?" queried Yisselda uncertainly. "It hardly seems likely…"

"Without a doubt, my lady. Now hold hands, everybody. Remember, there will come a time en route that I will have to separate from you. But you must all stay close together, if you are to arrive at the destination I will aim you towards. Ready?"

"No," said Hawkmoon, "not really. You ask us to accept an awful lot, with very little if anything by way of assurance."

"I've offered you all that I have," said Timeras earnestly. "The rest, I suppose, is just a matter of faith."

With which all five of them jumped into the water.

Or, rather, they jumped onto it.

The patch of sea into which the Dark Ship had sunk seemed to have the consistency of porridge, and Hawkmoon realized as they all rocked unsteadily on its surface that their survival, when the ship had crash-landed in this unforgiving stuff, was all the more miraculous.

Slowly, they too began to sink, as if into quicksand, although they had to drag the children down with them as they proved too light to break the water's surface tension.

It was only as their faces began to be submerged that Hawkmoon found himself questioning what they were doing, what they had trusted Timeras to persuade them of.

That, for the moment at least, was his last conscious thought.

Epilogue: Returning

Gasping, choking, they erupted into fresh air. The water in which they floated with ease was as natural as any they had ever known. It was cold, and very wet indeed.

They were in what appeared to be some sort of lagoon, its banks edged with tall reeds over which they could not see.

But they heard the sounds of profuse wildlife, indicating that, if nothing else, they had left behind them the twilight world of ice.

They had no recollection of the journey itself, nor of when, during it, Timeras had left them.

Duke Dorian Hawkmoon von Köln, his wife Yisselda of Brass, and their young children Manfred and Yarmilla, all swam towards the closest shore, using the reeds to help pull themselves up onto dry land.

As they walked through the long grass, away from the lagoon, a dark shape swooped overhead and they felt the swish of a great bird's flight.

It was a giant scarlet flamingo, as could only be found in the French marshland province of Kamarg.

"Dorian, we're back!"

Ahead of them, they heard animated voices. Cautiously, urging his family to stay still, Hawkmoon sidled forward, peering through the reeds.

Two men were approaching, heard but still not seen.

Hawkmoon reached for his sword, forgetting that he no

longer had it.

But then he knew that he no longer needed it, for riding into view came Oladahn of the Bulgar Mountains and the kindly philosopher-poet Bowgentle. Each rode a horned horse.

Hawkmoon stepped clear of the reeds, seeing with amusement the looks of astonishment on the mounted men's faces.

Bowgentle, recovering himself, remarked insouciantly, "My dear duke, you seem a little damp."

Hawkmoon's family emerged from the long grass now, running forward to greet their friends.

"How," asked Oladahn, "has this wonderful coincidence come about? When the two of us awoke in Parye and found the four of you gone, we feared the worst."

"I'll explain all in due course," laughed Hawkmoon. "Where are we in Kamarg, exactly?"

"Why, nearing Aigues-Mortes, my friend. Approaching the northern watchtowers."

Bowgentle and Oladahn dismounted, offering one saddle to Yisselda and the other to be shared by the children.

They all moved on in the two horsemen's original direction, and soon reached the first tower, on top of which stood an armored guardian, keeping watch over the land. Not recognizing the oncoming group, he raised his baroque flame lance and demanded their names.

More astonishment followed.

"But please," urged Hawkmoon, "do not signal the other towers or Castle Brass. We wish our arrival to be a surprise."

"That it will doubtless be, my lord. Count Brass has been awaiting your return with some impatience, to say the least. And that was just for yourself and m'lady. Not for such an esteemed and unexpected gathering as stands before me now."

"Then most certainly we should not disappoint him." Hawkmoon looked lovingly at his wife, his children, his friends. "Come," he said. "Let us go home."

Tony White is the author of the critically-acclaimed novel Foxy-T *(2003). His latest novel,* The Fountain in the Forest, *will be published in 2017. His* Shackleton's Man Goes South *was published by the Science Museum as their Atmosphere Commission 2013—the first novel the Museum has ever published. Tony has been writer in residence at the Science Museum, Leverhulme Trust writer in residence at the UCL School of Slavonic and East European Studies (SSEES), and creative entrepreneur in residence and visiting research fellow in the French Department at King's College London, funded by Creativeworks London. He is also editor and publisher of Piece of Paper Press, and chairs the board of directors of London's award-winning arts radio station, Resonance 104.4fm.* Stormbringer *was commissioned by Bruce Gilchrist and Jo Joelson for the* Syzygy *project, written in situ on Sanda Island, Scotland, July 1999, and was first published in* Syzygy/Polaria *by Black Dog Publishing/London Fieldworks in 2002. A radio version, with live musical accompaniment by Peter Lanceley, was recorded live in Lochaber, Scotland, and broadcast in August 2014 as part of Remote Performances by London Fieldworks and Resonance 104.4fm.*

Tony White: *Stormbringer*

Imagine you're flying over the sea, yeah. Skimming over the wave tops like that gannet over there. Lost in the constant now of flight and making lightning-fast compensations for wave height and windspeed with the unthinking ease of a man like me stepping over this large pebble.

Wow.

Or, more likely, you're kicking a thirty-footer around from the sheltered waters of the loch and into the sudden weight of the Atlantic current, and you feel the boat slipping out from under you, feel waves which come from nowhere slamming into your hull, and you're steering into the current

to make good your course and fight the swell which has travelled four thousand miles across open ocean only to be fun-
neled through a channel that is just ten miles wide. And
through the spray you can see the headlands ranging off to
your starboard side, blue mountains lightening in the mist.
And as you leave Ailsa Craig behind and come around full
against the Atlantic on-rush, you're riding up the faces of
waves which began their journey to this point somewhere near
the Equator, and every now and then, a gannet will spear into
the water, or a pair of cormorants will fly low across your
bows on their way to the island which has now broken away
from the mainland, separated itself off from the line of peninsula which it seemed only minutes ago to be a part of. And if
you had the time to stop, you'd see that this island is itself
surrounded by rocks, some hundreds of feet high. Some almost islands in their own right, man.

But you continue out into the Irish Channel, and the island slips past a couple of miles off your port side, and you
don't have time to look more closely at its treeless and rocky
slopes, or that simple stone house which stands above a jetty
set in a treacherous looking bay, skirted by rocks which pull
the current into vicious eddies and mad sub-currents. You
might have seen all that if you weren't pulling out into the
Channel on your way to whatever it is that makes you foolhardy, or desperate, enough to bring a boat out on to these
waters.

You might have seen all of that, but you wouldn't have
seen me.

Not unless, like that gannet, the one that's streaking past
you now, you could just catch the sou' westerly and ride it up
the face of the cliff to wheel back and across the top of the
island to regain the fishing grounds on its leeward side.

But even then I doubt you'd see me.

The only thing, from that height, to differentiate me from
the sheep would be that I'm moving in a straight line, not scat-
tering in fright at every screaming oyster catcher, or the sud-

den appearance of a man who's walking up this track between the marshes and the bracken, like they are now.

But if you had the time to look, if you weren't caught up in the frantic economy of catching enough fish to sustain the massive expenditure of energy that catching fish exacts, if you could bank and turn in pursuit of something other than staying alive, you'd see that I am a man walking alone across this island.

Closer still and you'd see the cloak which billows out behind me, and which on days more brutal than this I should have gathered up about me to save myself from being carried off by the wind. You might also see the Moon-staff which lends my walk a purposeful air, and which is adorned with the socketless skull of a narwhal that I found washed up on the rocks next to the jetty and took for an omen, the meaning of which I have yet to fully fathom.

And if, yeah, if you weren't just a little distracted, yeah, by how fucking awesome this place is, you might notice this.

The rhythm.

Listen, man, once every four steps I swing my staff forwards and connect it to the earth; sometimes striking stone with a sudden rattle which abrades the ridges of my palm; sometimes striking the dry ground between the twisted heather roots, raising a small cloud of dust. Other times it sinks through the soft grass and into the carpet of delicate white roots beneath, and as I move forward my Moon-staff tears through the microfilaments, the sound traveling up through the desiccated interior which once drew water from deep in the Earth but which now carries just the give and crackle of tearing roots, amplified by this bony gourd. And this sound ghosts the older, louder shock; the concatenation of tearing cellulose and the sudden sharp crack which saw this staff torn clean off by wind and thrown in to the sea on some other coast than this, to drift and eventually to be pushed up between the great slabs of granite where the gulls nest on my southern coast, then flung by the winter storms onto the soft grass at the cusp of a Moon-shaped erosion next to the sheep path between the granite and the marshes where it was dried and bleached by wind, sun and salt, and where on my first circumnavigation of the island I found it and took it for a portent, and immediately held it aloft, accustoming my hand to its chalky pumice texture and finding its balance. Not firewood this, my straight and bone-white Moon-staff which I carried home hung loose and spear-like in crook'd fingers, and whose capillaries now sing the songs of the Earth.

Listen, man.

Allow me to introduce myself, yeah.

I'm the Laird, the John Logie Baird.

I'm the keeper of the key.

The one who seizes from the sea.

I'm the owner of the *feus*,[7] yeah, the Baron of Blues.

The Fief of four-four.

Warrior chieftain of the bass.

I stop walking and turn my face to the south west.

I will call on Baron Samedi, Loa of the wind, who rode the trades from the west coast of Africa to the Caribbean and brought the sugar bound for Liverpool from the plantations of Jamaica, Cuba, Guyana and funky Nassau.

I will call on Legba, the Loa of the crossroads, because I'm the Laird of the Rings, man, and no man shall enter the Kingdom but shall pass through me.

And as I lay down my Moon-staff and kneel in the brittle heather to smear warm spore-rich dung on my face, I call on the minstrel shepherd Pan.

Pleased to meet you, man.

Clapton calls me God, but right now, yeah, right now— as I stand up and clasp the Moon-staff in my hand once again. Right now—as I break off the track and follow a sheep trail through the bracken and up the side of the long ridge. Right now—as I look down at the lighthouse far below me. Right now I'm Elric of Melniboné, the Eternal Champion, yeah, and

---

[7] A term in Scottish law referring both to a piece of land, title, duties or rights in that land, and the costs of said rights.

master of the soul-eating bane sword whose runic lines sing a deep song of death, and which is called Stormbringer.

Wow.

Follow the ancient trails, carved by centuries of ovine necessity. Crouch low to approximate the ruminant imperative. Past the dense symbiotic pads of heather and moss, past clover flowers and tiny white and purple orchids growing time-lapse fungus-quick. Every available space colonized, pollen-utilized, in the need to persist, except, yeah, these narrow tracks cut through the wind-dried root twists by cloven-hoofed kamikaze baah-baahs, yeah, to whom no part of this island is inaccessible.

Dung trails.

Listen, man. What soil there is here, thinly spread across the granite, is the result of a near-geological precipitation of shit. Put your ear to the quartz-shot rock, man, and tune down to the slow, low wavelength of continual spoor-rain, now increase the frequency until it approximates the loud crackle of a Geiger counter.

I've been walking for years, man.

Dragon watcher.

Rising slowly.

Stop.

Sit down in a sheltered circle, pick wool like cotton from the sharper seed heads. Ear whistle stops as the wind gets lost in the infinite labyrinth-scape of frond and stem. Slide up the sea faders. Distant sound of snorting seal and cormorant cough. Spear staff in to the granite cleft, so skull stands man-high, then turn it to catch the ossified amplified dustbowl vibe of the plantation wind with its cargo of white trash blue grass southern negro soul, yeah. Funnel that old sound down through the artificial root until the granite sings the rum-rich songs of tobacco, cane and cotton. Now count the times the SS *Whisky Galore* has foundered on these rocks, all hands down, all cargo lost. Hereford, hemp, Havanas: the Liberty Ship loaded with Jack Daniels still broke-backed in the bay, cargo

335

vanished overnight, lighthouse keepers didn't see a thing. Black bags thrown overboard when botched IRA drug deals go wrong wind up on my western shore with rusting filigree ironwork, dead gannets, mummified sheep, orange nylon rope, kelp.

No excise here, just occasional tithes taken from a laughing Welsh pirate, yeah, who barters, bribes and bluffs his way along the old Phoenician trade routes of the Med, tricking the Shia and the Hezbollah into desperate cut-price clearance sales before swinging out of Tyre and down to Morocco, trading up to double zero then out the Straits of Gib, yeah, round Biscay and up to Mallin Head, picking up *The Archers* on the World Service and planning his drops according to the shipping forecast.

I'm the unofficial pint of entry, man. The last shipping hazard.

Time for a smoke then, eh, my Lord Elric?
Aye my friend, 'tis time.

Rising slowly, man. Moderate to good.

From my stout blue britches I pull a leather pouch of fine Ralegh ready-rubbed, papers and some of Blackbeard's *kif*. Draw leaf and bud along the crease, to writhe and tangle in front of my eyes. What Sandoz-sorcery is this, man? There's no snakes here, despite the sun-warmed bracken. This particular crystal set, yeah, was tuned to Patrick's spell, yeah, and the whole sodding lot of them wriggled off the edge of the world.

I roll, lick, light and pull deep on the smoke of Virginia, Beirut and Marrakech.

In a moment I shall take up my staff, unplug the feed, and be on my way. I must find the trail which leads to the long ridge, then scramble down between the giant's teeth, and on to the saddle at the center of the island, which gods must once have used to ride this great beast before it turned to stone, but which for a man like me is the quickest route to the top of Dragon Hill. With my Moon-staff before me I shall march through the bracken and the marsh grass, and perhaps I shall sing a song of my own to frighten the sheep; a merry shanty, or one of my grandmother's Hoxton Howlers. But for now I'm content to watch the brightling waters, and the lighthouse, and those foxgloves waving pink against the bracken below me next to the helipad.

The sun is hot, man. I loosen my cloak, then stand and silence the sea.

I have placed skulls at the four compass points of the island. Wedged the half-bleached heads into nooks and crannies in the granite cliffs.

I'm on top of Dragon Hill, and beneath here, yeah, right under my feet, yeah, is where the dragon sleeps. There's a cave. I've seen it man. I was sitting in the bay watching the seals, and all the birds disappeared, man. Like they knew something was going to happen.

Then I felt this shadow crossing the island like wind-blown clouds, and I looked up, yeah, and there it was; just playing in the air, rolling and twisting, Sun catching silvery on its scales. And before it turned and flew away I could feel the wind from its ragged, flapping wings.

When I looked back down there was just this, like, totally mad reflection on the water.

Wow.

I can see it all from here, man.

Look.

Place the Moon-staff against the stone obelisk at the top of Dragon Hill. Plant it in the dry earth around the marker, facing the wind.

High southwesterly, one or two, twenty-two miles, very good.

I look to the points of the compass, yeah, and summon the minstrel shepherd Pan to intercede. Down in the water below me to the east is a postcard of the wounded mammoth in the La Brea Tar Museum, flailing and trumpeting, cormorants and seagulls pecking at its eyes. Beneath the cliffs to the west, beyond the rotting rocket station, is where we built a fire when Denny came over with Paul and Linda in the chopper,

337

yeah, and we just sat around all night listening to the wind and playing the box-car, bone-yard blues. Far down the bracken slopes to the south, is my castle, man, and atop its flying buttresses and crenellated spires, yeah, the flags of the Eternal Champions are blowing keenly in the breeze.

Call on Baron Samedi, Loa of the wind.

Call on Papa Legba, Loa of the crossroads.

Call on the spirit of Robert Johnson, rising out of the wet Mississippi Delta clay.

Kneel and take off my cloak, my britches and my stout leather boots. Smear dung onto chest, stomach, legs and arms. Lie down on the sharp grass and feel the dragon sleeping beneath a thousand feet of granite. Rubbing warm dung on my cock I call on Ezuli, Loa of love and desire.

Feel the wind picking up, circling the island. Westerly to nor' westerly, swinging back around into southerly squalls, overlaid with a steady easterly, then stillness, sea-bird panic still noisy but abating. Dragon breath rumbling up through the granite, sparking from quartz node to quartz node, backing up against the spring flow.

Sudden rush of sun-warmth against my skin. Dark fingers run down my chest and draw a circle in the drying dung. Something biting at my skin, grazing teeth across my face, whispering Yoruba obscenities in my year. Thick thighs straddle my chest as I lap at sharp hair, bury my muzzle. Lightly tug with lips and teeth and taste the bitterness of salt-drenched wood, of tar, iron and tobacco. She laugh-licks at salt-sun-wind-bleached bone then turns, eyes half-closed and lifts her leg to mount me. Her skin tastes of milk, sugar and cassava, yeah. Of wind through grass, and dry west African clay. Grinding down in tune with the fast-twitch peristaltic rumble. Feel the sudden spasm-shudder ripple across wet skin.

Then, yeah, just as suddenly as she appeared, yeah, she vanishes and my come spray twists guano-useless in the air, then falls on rock and grass. Imperceptible sea-splash as it hits the water far below me.

Now they will come.

338

I take up my cloak and roll-scramble down the hill.

I have piled the Marshall stacks on the rocks at the head of the bay, and pulled the generator down from the lighthouse outhouse through nettle, moss and sea-gorse, past the lichen-spattered rocks. I have hefted the motor in to life and run leads across the heather.

The sky darkens over a rotting wooden plantation villa in Belize as Baron Samedi kicks up a low front in the Gulf of Mexico. He rises quickly up to the jet-streams, sucking out the pressure above the Mississippi Delta as he forces the moist air into multiple convection systems along the coast and hits the Everglades with microbursts of hail, snow and rain, before riding the sou' westerly out and across the Virgin Islands and Bermuda and on to the Atlantic.

High, south westerly, three or four. Fifteen. Moderate to fair. Falling quickly.

I fly along the horse-shoe road which skirts the long ridge, and gun the bike past helipad and rusting Massey-Ferguson, Stormbringer sheathed and strapped to my back. Wheels slip against the rough mix of damp grass, gravel, stone and instantly-anciented tarmac. Thistles flail above the bracken, unable to absorb the wind which rushes around Mallin Head and screams in across the water. I drop the speed, man, dismount breathless, leave the bike by the whitewashed wall and pick my way over the rocks to find the pre-amp. Pull Stormbringer from its leather sheath, check for red lights, check the feeds; run low along the lines of Malaysian rubber and Venezuelan copper. Find Stormbringer's jack, urgent fingers unable to locate the socket. Crackles of static shock the air as I fumble the steel pin like a Saturday night drunk with a door key.

Hurried glance to sea and sky. All weathers visible from this point: cirrus, stratus, lenticular and cumulus clouds orbit the island, creating multi-level microsystems of unclassifiable speed and inconsistency. Except to the south west, where a thin ribbon-ripple of mist comes skudding low across the sea from horizon to horizon, hitting the western cliffs and rising up on to Wood Hill, travelling at grass seed height, then spilling down around either side of the long ridge. The Antrim coast obscured by a dark grey wall. Pressure drops off the bottom of the scale as the narrow channel forces it up to supersaturation levels in a Brownian rush of evaporation and condensation.

Precipitation visible nine miles, man.

Five miles.

Two.

Sea all but vanishes as the front breaches the strait.

Plug in. Switch on. Strings hum with electric potential, strummed by the breeze which rushes in to fill the oncoming pressure void.

They have come. And now I shall make my sword sing.

As I pluck the fat steel strings the storm hits. Wolf-howl blues all but silenced by the wind despite the valves. I lean in to it as best I can, yeah, and switch to a kind of funky twelve bar, and as I make the first change the skies open.

But Samedi and Legba have not answered my call with rain.

Some other cargo has been brought up the old Atlantic trade routes.

This is precipitation pay-back.

It starts raining bones.

Ehrich Weiss was born in 1988 and is, as his nom-de-plume indicates, a magician by trade. The Sundered Worlds, *a.k.a.* The Blood Red Game, *published in 1965, was the first "Multiverse" novel, and it is fitting to see it revisited here.*

Ehrich Weiss: *Renark's Dream*

Love is eternal.

It belongs to our past, our present, and our future.

This is the story of Count Renark von Bek, he who was once called the Eternal Champion, who loved what few Men dare to love. And, as it goes with love stories, it is also a sad story...

I. Living in the Sundered Worlds

Before there was the Eternal Champion, there was the Man. Renark von Bek. The Man, the Dreamer, the Champion.

Von Bek was taken away from his family unit when he was nine.

They were freefarmers, subsisting from permanent contracts with the Dark Empire. They had suffered from a severe Nightmare Plague because of the boy. In the end, they had called Volospion. And Volospion had answered...

Slow men, in light blue uniforms, high on psychotropics, had come to take the child away. Oh, the mothers had protested, wept, but, after all, they could not raise a dreamer among them, could they? It was all for his good, wasn't it?

They had taken him to Volospion's clinic, where he was trained. Trained to seek, to feel, to project.

Trained to dream.

And to dream he had learned. For eleven years, they trained him...

He grew up there, with the other dreamers. And, one day, Volospion thought he was ready.

His Graduation Day was not memorable. He had dreamed of a sad hulking giant, obsessed with darker emotions, his style in clothing and dwelling depressing and gloomy... He did not know how many people were psilinked with him, judging his dream. Perhaps, there were none.

That day, he graduated with merit from Volospion's clinic and was sent to the Sundered Worlds.

II. Loving in the Sundered Worlds

On the Sundered Worlds, he met his love.

But I am anticipating.

His first impression of the Sundered Worlds was astonishment. His birthworld was a farm planet, with a very small population of growers. All in all, not many people and plenty of free space. The Sundered Worlds were overpopulated, rich beyond calculation. The wealth of entire systems was bought and sold during the Blood Red Game. Space fleets were armed there and their shadow darkened the skies; corps that owned planets were controlled from its towers.

Renark was to dream in one of the Psipalace owned by Volospion. And so he did. Till he met his love.

She came, one night, her silver hair floating freely behind her. She came, and her billowing black cloak made an aura of darkness around her. She came, her eyes, pools of space within her moonlighted face. She came, and went away.

But before, she had stopped at the Psipalace where Renark dreamed.

Some said she had come to stop at the Palace where he dreamed, and who can say they were wrong?

She came, and went away.

But behind her, she left the Eternal Champion.

She psilinked with Renark. And love it was.

That night, he dreamed as he had never dreamed before. Instead of sending his patterns to the dreamee through the psilink, they shared. Love it was.

He brought the power, and she brought the visions. Love it was.

Visions of darkness and despair. Planets being plundered. Visions of tyranny and cruelty. Unfettered Chaos crushing countless lives. Visions of hatred and genocides. The slow murders of primitive races. Visions of the Multiverse. Tragedies. Love it was.

"Stay" he said, imploring her. "Stay with me. I love you!"

"Help them, and you will find me," she answered. And she went away, her dark cloak swirling, leaving behind her the Eternal Champion.

He dreamed. He dreamed her love of them, and people came.

He dreamed his love of her, and people came.

And things started to happen:

He dreamed: Dorian Hawkmoon rode to Londra.

He dreamed: Oswald Bastable began to fight for the oppressed.

He dreamed: Elric of Melniboné grasped Roland's Horn.

He dreamed: Prince Corum offered Kwll his hand back.

He dreamed...

And, one day, they came for him. But he had already left.

III. Dying in the Sundered Worlds

He had been the Eternal Champion. Now, he was only the Hunted.

They tried to kill him in the heavenly residences. They tried to kill him in the sordid slums. They tried to kill him everywhere. But he always turned up alive and, for the love of her, dreamed his dreams of despair and revolt.

And, in the end, they got him.

The tale of his death in the Blood Red Game is known, and it has been sung all over the Multiverse. How he died does not matter. What matters is that, when he died, he had a smile on his lips and love in his eyes, for he had finally found her. His dark beauty, his dark dream, Death.

The Jet-Set Girls *was first published in* Retro Retro, London: Serpent's Tail *in 2000. It also appeared in* Butterfly *magazine Issue 4, 2000.*

Tony White: *The Jet Set Girls*

Chipperfield Road
Bovingdon, Herts.

21 Jan 1999

Dear Tony:

Thank you very much for your letter which arrived shortly before Christmas. Tom tells me that your writing is interesting; "good stuff, good bloke" were his words.

I'm really very flattered by your obvious knowledge of my "work" (as you put it). You mentioned the New English Library edition of *The Jet-Set Girls*—I had forgotten all about my brief incarnation as "Penny Douglas." Most of "her" titles were in fact written by Jim Moffat (as you probably know), but that one was definitely mine.

Now, to your question. How I got started in the business—the attached should answer this. Probably the same way that lots of people do—I was in the right place at the right time. My advice to any young writer trying to be published (not to yourself of course) would be this: try and find a way in through the back door.

If any of the enclosed is useful to you, then you are welcome to it. Chop and change as you wish.

As for your second request—if you think that the Literary Quarterly would be interested in an interview, I'd be happy to do that with you. Just give me a ring and we'll arrange a time.

Best wishes,

Hughie

Editor's note: *The following episode is presented largely in the form in which Hugh Johnson submitted it to me shortly before his death. I have made only one or two very minor corrections in the interests of clarity. In his day, Hugh was well known for his ability to write a novel "in one go;" he was reputed never to correct or redraft one of his manuscripts. So it is in that spirit that I introduce what we had come to hope might form a chapter of his autobiography—sadly this will never now be completed. I am grateful to Mr. Tom Aitchison and the Literary Estate of Hugh Johnson for allowing us to go ahead and print this story. We all felt that to publish this episode now would be a fitting (if modest) memorial to one of the most successful, though least recognized, British writers of popular fiction. The following story is dedicated to the memory of its author: "Hughie" Johnson, 1940-2000.*

I suppose I was shooting my mouth off. It was another night in the West End's lesser establishments. Off the radar as usual. I imagine things have changed a bit now, but back then, if you wanted to be out of reach of the police, the gangsters, the whole *demi-monde*, you had to drink with them. Anyone else was considered fair game.

Well, maybe I was wrong, on reflection, but that's how it seemed to me.

It must have been morning by the time I got to the Spotlight. It was a bit of a haunt in those days. Used to pop in and have a whisky with the touts; it was on their route from the gambling clubs to a half-hour kip over bacon and eggs in that little Greek café opposite Foyles. With Linda, I think her name was. She was there for years; certainly until Raymond put the rent up and she moved out. Sweet girl. She was then. Pretty little thing. Hard as nails. That was usually enough for me; back home to sleep it off until the next night. To be frank, I didn't have the where-with-all to carry on. More a lack of "the old LSD" (pounds, shillings and pence) than a lack of stamina. But those chaps never seemed to sleep. I don't know how they did it. By half-past nine they'd be back out on their pitches. It was as if they drew some sort of energy from their trade, in lieu of ever actually resting themselves. Part of the transaction, so to speak.

Anyway, the Spotlight. Weird place. You wouldn't know it was there unless you knew it was there. If you know what I mean. Just a door down some steps in that alley next to Denmark Street. No bar or anything. Couple of tables and chairs and some bottles of pale ale in the corner. Something stronger if you wanted. Little Cypriot called Tony used to run it. Poof, obviously. No one paid cash. Well, I did, but all the bigger boys just "ran up tabs," not so much a slate as a retainer. So much a month just to keep him open.

I'd always fancied myself as a writer. Hadn't actually done it though. Had anything published, I mean. I suppose I just enjoyed that certain "low life" thrill of doing what I imagined it was that writers did. Penguin book in the jacket pocket, you know. Reading cheap translations of the French stuff over halves in the French. Even wore a polo neck: I shudder to think of it. I normally kept my ambitions to myself though, in that kind of company. So I must have been half-cut. Still I wasn't the only one. There were one or two other people there who fancied themselves as something they weren't.

They were all at the Spotlight that night. Tony was mincing around with a grubby tea towel over his shoulder as usual. Una Pearson was there. That was part of the attraction of the place. Bit of a fading beauty by then, of course. Still called herself an 'actress' though. She could drink me under the table any night of the week. A couple of the Bazalgette brothers were lording it at the corner table. On one side was Mo. "Shaky" Mo people called him; something to do with his temper. No one said it to his face of course. Next to him was Charles, the eldest. Big chap but very softly spoken. The Bishop. That was his nickname, because if he was thinking about something he'd always get out this rosary and mull things over while he ran the beads through his fingers, counting them—and your options—off; very slowly. Never saw him drink. His one vice, if you could call it that, was an incredibly sweet tooth. Spanish Phil, the king of the touts, once told me that Charles was diabetic, but I never had any inclination to try and verify this.

I was bragging to Una about what I used to call "the great British novel"—moaning about Greene and Amis and Waugh, telling her what was wrong with them, and why my first novel was going to be better, even, than the likes of Orwell. Of course it was no such thing. And Una, bless her, was too far gone to care.

Even though I drank there several times a week, I'd never spoken to any of the Bazalgette family. So, when Mo sent a boy over to ask if I would like to join him and Charles for a drink, I suppose I was too flattered to do anything other than accept. I excused myself from the conversation with Una and followed him over. I shook The Bishop's hand, nodded a silent greeting, then sat down on the chair which Mo had pushed out from under the table with his foot.

"Charles wanted a quiet word, Hugh. Between ourselves."

The Bishop didn't say anything for a while. He was thinking. Pushing his beads around, occasionally looking up at me, or at what was going on in the club behind me. Then he put the beads down and took a Mars Bar out of his pocket. Tearing the wrapper, he took a bite, then looked at Mo and nodded.

"You can write, Hugh, can't you, eh?" asked Mo.

I looked from one to the other. Charles had his mouth full of Mars, but was staring straight at me.

"Charlie and me... We heard you was a bit of a writer," Mo persisted.

I said that, yes, I was writing a novel.

"Lovely. Thought so, didn't we."

The Bishop looked at me for a while without saying anything, then nodded before taking another bite.

"Thing is," Mo continued, "we're looking for a writer at the moment. Tell him, Charlie."

Charles Bazalgette swallowed his last bit of Mars, then spoke for the first time.

"We're looking at a new game, Hugh. Maurice thought you might be interested. Excuse me."

Perhaps the nervousness showed on my face. I didn't want to know about any of their games; old or new. People had a tendency to wind up dead in the kind of games that the Bazalgette brothers played. Ignorance is bliss, as the saying goes. He threw the empty wrapper on the floor, then pocketed his rosary and stood up, whispering something in Mo's ear before leaving the table. Mo turned and caught the eye of one of the younger lads, this real "hardnut" as we used to say then, called Davey, who immediately nudged his mate. They put down their bottles and opened the door for The Bishop. Davey went out first, then came back in and nodded. The other two followed him out.

"Publishing," said Mo, as the door shut behind them. "We've been looking into it, and we figure there's a fucking mint to be made. Cost fuck-all to print, if you do enough of 'em. Couple of bob a piece at the fucking most. Sell a few thousand copies at twelve and six each. You can work it out for yourself, Hugh."

I didn't hide my surprise. This was the last thing I'd expected to hear. I said that I supposed there was quite a lot of money in it, but that depended whether the book was well received, how the critics responded. A great work of literature, I ventured, could probably earn its publisher and its writer a good deal of money.

Mo laughed at this.

"What do your mob get paid then?"

His question took me by surprise. "Nothing" would have been the most truthful answer I could have given, and frankly, until I heard the question phrased in Mo's inimitable style, this wasn't something I'd even considered. Until that moment I had been firmly of the conviction that one wrote for the love of literature. I decided to take a stab in the dark. It varied, I said. Depending on the fame of the author. But at a rough guess, I would say that advances on royalties could probably be anything from twenty quid to a thousand guineas.

"How does a hundred and fifty nicker sound?" he asked. "Up front of course."

I could only agree. Yes, I should imagine that any writer worth his salt would be pleased with a sum of that kind. After all, I added, let's not forget that a novel can take anything up to several years to write.

Mo nearly choked on his pale ale.

"Years?" he exploded. "Several fucking years? You taking the piss, Hughie old son? We was thinking of a week!"

A week? I was astounded and told him so. I had been working away on my own manuscript for nigh-on a couple of years, and I was nowhere near to finishing it.

"So you ain't interested? Shame. Find some other cunt then, I suppose."

"Well, no, I didn't say I wasn't interested, Mo," I back-pedaled, quickly realizing that he hadn't been talking generally, but actually making me an offer. "But it takes a while to set up as a publishing house, you need editors for one thing, a reputation, before people will take you—"

"We've got a fucking reputation, Hugh. What you trying to say?"

"No, I mean a reputation in the literary world, Mo."

"Who the fuck said anything about literature? Forget that shit. That ain't gonna bring in the LSD, mate. Here."

He picked a briefcase up from the floor, opened it, and took out a number of luridly covered paperbacked volumes. Put them on the table in front of me. They had titles like *Schoolgirls Who Do*, *The Desire to Dominate* or *Lesbian Love*; all were published by imprints I'd never heard of: Luxor, Hanbury, Ship, Tallis.

"Go on then, have a fucking flick through."

I did as he suggested. The quality of the writing was fairly perfunctory; decidedly unerotic even. Some had photographic inserts to pad them out.

"And this is the quality end of the market," he said, pushing a copy of de Sade's *120 Days of Sodom*, and an Olympia edition of something called *The Story of O* across the table. "Now, this stuff fucking shifts. If you can copy it, not too fucking obviously of course, we might be getting somewhere."

I looked up at him quizzically, pointing at first one, then the other title. Mo pointed at *The Story of O*.

"Listen," he said, "Charlie's done a bit of asking around on the blower, and it looks like this mob are only gonna be doing *O*. What do you say?"

I couldn't believe my ears. A hundred and fifty was a few months' wages. I was sobering up fast. Mo looked over my shoulder.

"Oi, Tone. Come on, son."

Tony appeared with two glasses and a bottle of Maltese brandy.

"Leave 'em, Tone, eh."

"Let me get this straight. If I write one of these *books*, you and your brother will give me a hundred and fifty quid?"

"That's right, Hughie old son. If you want to. More than one, though. We're gonna need a few." He nodded at the assembled drinkers. "The lads say you're trustworthy. Just bring it here same time next week and I'll pay you for the next one. Think you can manage that?"

He began to pour two glasses of brandy.

He was offering more money than I'd ever earned before, to write a book. Suddenly the failings of the modern British novel began to seem less and less important. I felt myself nodding enthusiastically, heard myself speaking: "Thanks, Mo. Course I can."

He grinned and we shook hands.

"Keep the books, Hughie, use them for research. Money's in the bag."

"But how are you going to get them into the bookshops, Mo?"

"Leave that to us, son," he said, pushing the glass towards me. "We *own* the fucking bookshops. Hang on though," he pulled some pin-up magazines out of the briefcase, flicked through to the classifieds. "You might want to see this. Look."

His grubby finger was pointing at an advertisement.

The Story of A, it said, beneath a half-tone dolly bird, by Anonymous. 12/6 ea. + 6d post and packing. Kali Books, with a private box address in Wardour Street.

"Kali?" I asked, surprised at the brothers' knowledge of the Hindu pantheon. "After the goddess of—"

"No, it's personal, Hugh. Family thing."

"Wait a minute, Mo. You've already got one title already, then? Do you want me to start with 'B' or what?"

Mo laughed as he drained his glass.

"Don't be daft." He jabbed the ad with his finger. "That's your first book, son. Orders are good and all, so don't go letting your readers down, will you, eh?"

I drained my brandy. Mo poured another for both of us.

There was a commotion at the doorway. I turned around and saw Davey coming back into the club; he had blood streaming down his face. Tony yelped, then rushed over, sat him down, and dabbed at the wound with his tea towel, chattering away in Greek or whatever it was. Charles Bazalgette walked over and rejoined us at the table. He raised his eyebrows in my direction. Mo nodded.

The Bishop smiled briefly and put his hand out, I shook it. Then he looked at his brother. Mo picked up the briefcase and stuffed the books and magazines back inside before pushing it across the table towards me.

"Come on then, son, best be off, eh? You've got work to do."

I was woken the next afternoon by a knock on the door of my room. I staggered out of bed, tripping over Mo's briefcase as I did so, and quickly put on a dressing gown to make myself half-decent. When I opened the door I was surprised to see Una Pearson standing in the hallway outside. She was carrying a shopping basket in which I could clearly see a bottle of wine.

"Morning, darling," she said. "Thought you might like some breakfast before you start work."

"Una, how did you… Excuse me, I was just getting up. Come in."

Before I start work.

"Mo told you, did he?"

"It was me that suggested you, sweetie. Looked as if you needed the money." Una placed her hand briefly against my cheek as she squeezed past me. I was suddenly aware of how stuffy my room was, and immediately went across to my desk. Reaching over the typewriter, I opened the curtains and struggled with the sash, lifting it a couple of inches; enough to allow in a thin blast of cool air.

While I was doing this, Una had put down her handbag and her shopping basket and was busily rinsing a couple of glasses which she set down beside the sink. She began looking through the cutlery drawer.

"It's on the table," I said, clearing my clothes from the chairs.

She pulled the cork and poured, then handed me a glass whilst looking around at the room.

"At least it's cheap."

"I should hope so too, darling."

She took a new pack of Embassy from her handbag, opened it and offered me one.

A couple of glasses later I was beginning to feel a little more human.

"It was very sweet of you to come and wake me."

Una said nothing, just smiled and then got up from her chair, walked the few steps to where I was sitting and took the cigarette from between my lips. Stubbing it out in the ashtray, she leaned over to my ear. 'I had my reasons, darling.'

I could feel her breath on my cheek. Smell her perfume. I turned and kissed her. I might have been a bit green, but I wasn't stupid. I knew what this was about.

Straightening, Una began to unbutton her twin-set. She placed the cardigan on the back of her chair. Reaching behind her waist served to push her ample bosom toward me, and I could see the outline of her dark nipples through her slip. To be honest, I felt like a kid at Christmas! How many men had rehearsed this moment in their minds? She unzipped her skirt, pushed it down, stepped out of it. Then she slowly lifted the slip above her head. She was wearing a pink, one-piece girdle, which emphasized her voluptuous, hour-glass figure, and—I was surprised to see—nothing else, save her stockings. Her pubic hair was dark and thick.

"Like what you see, darling?"

"Very much," I rather superfluously replied, for Una was already tugging at my dressing gown cord to reveal the confirmation of my words. She kissed me once again, and I slipped my hands into her brassiere, pushed the straps off her shoulders. Standing suddenly, Una walked over to where her handbag was left, beside her chair. She reached in and took out a lipstick. Without taking her eyes from mine, she applied it to her lips, smacking them in the way that all women do. Then to my surprise she delicately outlined her nipples with similarly deft strokes. My desire was now more aroused than ever, and Una knelt quickly between my legs and set to polishing my glans with her tongue (the image of her licking and biting at my swollen, ripening fruit has sustained me for years). She Frenched me then, and I gasped as she took my entire length in her mouth. When she was satisfied with my resolve, Una gave my prick one last lingering kiss before clambering swiftly up on to my lap. Grasping her *derrière* in both hands I helped her to guide herself on to my proud manhood, which slipped easily and suddenly into the tight warmth of her silken sanctuary. While she caressed and teased me, with all the guile and art of the courtesan, I busied myself with the joys that I found before my face, taking first one, then the other tit into my mouth, lapping and sucking at her paps and completely mindless of the lipstick which must surely have been smearing my face.

There can be little more beautiful in this world than the delicate exclamations of joy which a woman in the throes of passion can emit. Soft as the petal-like skin of their inner thighs, these wordless imprecations can lead a man to the very brink of destruction. But nothing could have prepared me for the stream of expletives which Una, grinding ever harder on to my lap, began to scream. "Fuck me harder, you bastard!" She was pulling at my hair and biting at my shoulders. "Fuck me like a whore! I want to feel you come in my cunt!"

For a second or two I was taken aback, but then quickly redoubled my efforts, driving myself deeper and deeper until I seemed to be entering the very heart of her being. Our outlines dissolved, then. Somewhere, far away, I could hear a cry of ecstasy, but I was aware only of a beautiful unfolding, as of a rose-bud, and I felt myself to be somewhere deep in the heart of that sudden flowering; a part of it, almost. I could hold my resolve no longer, and with a final thrust I emptied myself within her.

We spent several days and nights lost in the joys that each other's bodies offered. In her day, Una must surely have been one of the most beautiful women of her generation, and even now, all these years later, I still love watching *Passport to Pimlico* and the other Ealing Studio comedies, just to catch a glimpse of her in her prime. The age difference between us seemed to me to be of little importance when we could pleasure each other with such urgency. Each time we made love I felt that she was teaching me not only about sex—though she certainly was—but about life itself. We steered clear of the Spotlight Club, venturing out only as far as the public houses and clubs in my neighborhood of Westbourne Grove, and occasionally cabbing it down to a restaurant in Mayfair for a quiet supper. The money was burning a hole in my pocket I suppose, and we lived a high old life for a few days.

I was surprised then, as we sat over our early evening drinks in the Grapes. To hear a familiar voice call my name.

I looked up and saw that Mo was carrying a try of drinks over to our table. He was followed by a man of striking appearance. Dressed in the kind of restrainedly flamboyant

Saville Row finery that only the richest among us could afford in those austerity days, Mo's companion had an arrestingly pale complexion, topped by a shock of white hair, which was cut in the Italian style, fashionably long across the ear. He was a young man, so his tow-headed appearance was all the more striking.

"Hugh," said Mo, "I want you to meet Mr. Cornelius, an associate of Kali Books."

I half-stood and shook the cold, slender hand that was offered.

They both sat down, and I followed suit.

"Mr. Cornelius was wondering how your book was coming along, weren't you, Jerry."

Cornelius nodded.

"Nearly finished now," I lied. "Only a couple of chapters left to write. I'll see you on Friday as we arranged."

"He's been working very hard," Una added. "I thought he needed a break, bless him."

Mo moved quickly, reaching over and making to slap her across the face with the back of his hand, but Una saw it coming and grabbed his wrist in mid-swing, held it there, then spat, "Don't even think about it, you stupid little fucker."

"Yeah, steady on, Mo." I put my arm around her, but she shrugged it off, then snorted derisively and threw Mo's hand down.

"The thing is," Cornelius spoke now, diffusing the tension with his quiet, even voice. "We've just been to your place, Hugh, and there wasn't much sign of activity there. You've only got a couple of days to finish it, and from what we saw you haven't even started yet."

"I…"

Mo put his brandy down, and sighed. I noticed that his hand was trembling very slightly.

"What you're gonna do now, Hugh, if you don't mind my saying," he interjected, "is go home and write this fucking book. I know you've been spending money like water, old son, so there's no chance of you paying us back, is there? Well, is there?"

I shook my head.

"So Jerry here is gonna take you home and you ain't gonna fucking leave your place until it's fucking finished, son. Understand?"

I nodded. There was clearly no point in protesting.

"And you," he turned to Una, "are gonna leave the boy alone until he's finished. Fucking disgraceful it is. You'd drop him if he couldn't afford to keep you in gin. You're old enough to be his bleeding mother!"

If Una's glass had been full, I had the feeling that she'd have flung it at Mo. As it was, she stood up. "You can fuck off, the lot of you," she spat, then stormed out. I made to follow her but Cornelius grabbed my arm in a vice grip that was surprisingly powerful for a fellow of his build. I had no choice but to stay put, but not for long; a few minutes later I found myself being hustled unceremoniously out of the pub.

"G'night, Mrs. H," Mo offered the landlady as we left.

"Ta-ta, Mo," she said, as if things like this happened every day, then, more deferentially, "*Mr.* Cornelius."

"How much have you got left," Cornelius asked when we were back in my room.

I shrugged and pointed at my jacket which was flung over the chair where Una and I had first made love a few days before. He reached into my breast pocket and took out my wallet. Opening it, he removed the two fivers that remained, along with a couple of ten bob notes.

"Don't worry about her," he said. "She'll have forgotten all about that in the morning. She'll be back, I know she will. She likes you. Mo thinks she was leading you astray. He has high hopes for you."

He folded the notes and put them in his waistcoat.

"Keys?"

I took the fob from my trouser pocket and tossed it to him, then busied myself with feeding a sheet of foolscap into the Remington.

"Just going out for a couple of things," he said, "since we're going to be here for a day or two." Then, almost as an afterthought, he turned and added, "This could be good for you, if you don't fuck it up. You know that, don't you."

I heard him lock the door from the outside, took a deep breath, and began typing.

This humorous series of vignettes was written by Mike in 2013 for the special 10th anniversary edition of Tales of the Shadowmen. *In it are some pithy observations, as well as some moving reflections, about the current course of events on Planet Earth...*

Michael Moorcock: *The Icon Crackdown*
A Jerry Cornelius Story

1.

After discovering he had less money than he needed at the checkout, Jeremiah placed the jar of spaghetti sauce on the supermarket counter and left. The packer murmured something to the assistant. He wasn't sure if the woman's expression was one of pity or contempt. He didn't care. Though humiliation had become familiar to him, he still found it hard not to blush. He left Safeway and walked slowly up Santa Monica Boulevard towards Barney's Beanery. How was he going to get back to Paris?

West Hollywood, gentrified, new-fashioned, gay, was no longer the funky neighborhood he remembered. He didn't belong here now, any more than he belonged in London. The funk had gone. Only Paris offered sanctuary. Shockingly, the Tropicana Motel and Duke's diner were replaced by anonymous cinderblock boutiques and offices. The last time he'd lived there both places had been cheap. There was nothing cheap in this neighborhood anymore. Still trying to piece together what had happened to him, he turned left and headed up the hill flanked by poplars, cedars and low hedges towards Sunset. White miniature haciendas decorated both sides of the street. He heard the roar and screech of a lawnmower occasionally hitting the sidewalk.

When the noise stopped, he momentarily enjoyed the tranquility of the afternoon with its buzz of far-away traffic.

Police and ambulance klaxons sounded as if from another plane. He looked for his old address on San Juan. Everything was so neat and clean now. That was where he and Judex had last met. His dark green Lagonda was still parked outside. Someone had taken the trouble to wash and wax his car. Los Angelinos loved automobiles the way the French loved movies. Taking the keys from his pocket, he unlocked the door, climbed in and started the engine, easing off the hand brake and turning the Lagonda into the street. At the window of his old duplex a curtain fell back into place.

Surely she didn't still live there? She might not have cleaned the car, but it was like her to pay someone to do it.

Their ghosts were everywhere. All a question of speed.

Soon he was climbing up into Beverley Hills, the palms casting long, blue shadows in the late afternoon light.

Time wasn't what it had been.

2.

Rally on TV. Texas had, at last, seceded from the Union. Resigning Gov. Ron was proud to announce the first Libertarian State in history. He would now be Cit One. In order to maintain the freedom of her citizens, Texas had granted the right of all Latinos to leave their camps for new homes and jobs in Mexico. Formal war between the two nations was rescinded when someone pointed out that the Texan army had been 94% Mexican now that Africanos had been repatriated to Mugabiland as part of the aid deal. Cit Ron had blushed when he told the second Libertarian Congress that Texas had taken the Christian option and was going to show those Catholics (by which he meant non-Baptists) the other cheek and forgive them for their high-handed demands.

Mexico was likely to have a very wealthy partner in her renewed ambitions to repatriate the South and West from Louisiana to California and get on an equal footing with the reduced US. He sat back and rolled himself a medicinal spliff. It was years since he'd had so much fun. The cards were still in the air. Mo was making a book on the first to fall.

In the motel room, Jerry thought through the psych factors. French hero-villains emerged, drenched in blood, from a Catholic culture. Torment and guilt. They who do not feel guilt are envied. Those who struggle within themselves are identified with Protestant Anglo-Saxons, like Sherlock Holmes or Sexton Blake: self-righteous, even smug, but admired.

Jerry was backing the Ace of Spades. All roads led to France. He trusted gravity far more than the human condition. He heard loud honking outside. A familiar noise. Mo had got hold of a massive old Nash from somewhere. He had dressed it up with Duisenberg fittings. The big engine was good as new and pumping.

Reluctantly, he left the TV running and stepped out of the motel into the burning Arizona heat. He wondered if he was still on the best road for New Orleans. And would Fantômas be there? His power could still be felt.

The Libertarian militias were taking a road tax every twenty five miles. On the other hand, the routes through Oklahoma and surrounding states were blocked solid. The toll roads were hardly any better.

Doc Didi Dee would be waiting near the border. She was supposed to flying her old Stokowski 10-2 modified gunship. Air was still free over Texas. And would be until the 13th Libertarian Congress met next year. The skies over all major cities were thick with competing aircraft. Last week, two massive zep cruise ships had collided by the main Austin mast at Port Sab' a few miles from Smithville. Kids were still trading shrapnel, seared human bones, bits of red, white and black silk. Tourists offered millions for skulls still in flying helmets and the region was doing a heavy trade in fakes which joined the jackalope and lamp-bleached long-horns on the shelves of the Sukey's and Shell convenience stores. Texas's income thrived on myth and legend almost as much as L.A.'s. Kennedy Plots alone brought millions to Dallas every year. Other cities had nothing like the same pulling power, but conspiracy theorists proliferated all over a country sensing the collapse of familiar currencies.

"So." Mo swung the great golden car on to Route 66. He could outrun any cop still around. Besides, local cities had long ago seen no profit to be made from a potholed two-lane blacktop going nowhere but Indian territory. On certain days you couldn't help loving reactionary feudalism.

"Ah, Utopia!" He let the wind get to his hair. "There's something about the past that always goes wrong." He took a deep breath and sighed. For a moment he enjoyed a frisson of melancholy. "We should be in Bordeaux by Tuesday. Of course, I can't say which Tuesday."

Then he was back on the road, driving into an impossible future.

3.

Holborn Viaduct, so far not greatly changed and the main route out of Brookgate to Tilbury and Le Havre, was bleak under the driving rain. Major Nye, lifting his collar against the wet, tipped his bowler hat, sending a stream of water down his neck. This civilian uniform identified him as an old-fashioned military man. An old colonial hand. Crossing above Farringdon Street, he heard the heavy thump of lorry tires below. Glancing over the railings, he saw a convoy moving steadily towards Blackfriars Bridge. They appeared to be civilian vehicles but he was unconvinced. He plodded on through the rain towards St Paul's. Not so long ago he had stood on firewatch with his Zeiss binoculars on his chest, listening for the approach of enemy bombers.

Jerry met him on the far side of the viaduct. Together they began to descend the filthy grey steps to Farringdon Street. Jerry handed Nye a thin file.

"That's all we have on the Parisian Opus Dei." Pausing at the first landing, he drew a silver cigarette case from the inside pocket of his black car coat. "Almost wholly after

Collyn's control, of course." He offered Major Nye a tipped Sherman's. "Sorry. They're the best I could get. Rationing."

The major refused. "I still favor the old pipe, you know." He glanced through the damp red file. "So you found nothing on Tigris?"

"Not what you're looking for." Jerry waited for the wind to drop temporarily, then quickly lit his cigarette with an old silver Dunhill. "His main drugs of choice these days appear to be memory cakes and licorice allsorts. Both taste of nothing but sugar."

"Needs the energy, I suppose. Fat as he is."

"Oh, he's lost a pound or two since he retired."

"Dear me, is he unwell?"

A figure appeared in the grey light of the arch below. Even in silhouette, her slender skirt and form-fitting jacket identified her. Shaking her umbrella, Miss Brunner tapped up the stone stairs in her Jimmy Choos. "I knew I should have worn a mac."

"Your idea to meet here," Jerry reminded her.

"It's the only place we all *knew*, Mr. Cornelius." She directed a glare into his eyes which would have blinded anyone else. "It's all about geography, isn't it?"

"Or class," said Jerry.

"Pathetic. Little oik!"

"I say," murmured the major blushing.

Miss Brunner pursed her carmine lips and glanced back at the rain almost as if she expected it to be following her.

4.

In the middle of the rutted field smattered with heaps of muddy snow lay an injured ewe. The crows had pecked out her eyes and she bleated softly.

"Innocence under siege," said Miss Brunner sweetly. She licked her lips.

"Poor bugger." Loosening his Browning in its holster, Mo Collier started across the field.

Unseen in the distance, the West Oxfordshire bayed in pursuit of a rotten corpse dragged behind a Land Rover.

At the wheel of the Smartwagon, Major Nye did his best to keep the tiny engine running. He frowned over the map. "I think we should have turned off just before Doncaster. There's a ferry to France, but it involves a lot of Time. Apples and oranges," he murmured to himself. "Apples and oranges."

A moment later, he was lost in an hallucination of rising waters, of the fields outside Cheese Cottage swiftly flooding. He put the truck into reverse. This could not be an attack from the Left. Could it? He did not know what to make of this impossible illusion. He prayed he had misinterpreted the images.

Miss Brunner reached out from behind him and gave his shoulder a habitual shake. "Wake up, major. You were telling me about *In Which We Serve*. Shouldn't we be in Versailles by now?"

"Is everything all right?" Mo came back, reholstering the Browning. "I used to love Noel Coward."

Major Nye opened his eyes. "What happened to those anglers? What's the point in fishing water you can set fire to? What would you catch?"

"Precooked fish and chips?" suggested Mo.

Jerry shrugged. They were attacking the structure of Time itself. Was there still any point of warning them? Yet what could they do? There was no escape. Why was France locked off?

Miss Brunner continued to show disgust. "Martyrdom is no more than an elaborate form of human sacrifice. It's not so long ago that Anglo-Saxons were shocked to find Cornish Christians practicing those rites. Few of us are more than a step away from our primitive roots. We sent our young men to Iraq as a blood offering to our gods. Didn't we?"

Mo wasn't following her.

5.

Jerry sniffed the rich fauna of the Portobello Road. Summer. Slow moving Thursday afternoon. He leaned against Mrs. Bones's bookstall watching plump middle-aged women leaf through the latest batch of second-hand men's magazines. *Slave Blondes for De Gaulle's legionnaires! Nazi Brides wake up firing! Hell-hounds of the Waffen SS! French Vampires in Govt. Tell All.* Too warm for him. He loosened the stud of his stiff white collar. He lifted his head, whistling softly. Why on earth would they disguise themselves so thoroughly? Everyone knew they were dying to catch hold of him. The last hero of Kiev. He stroked the steel of his Khartron Tommy gun. Not the only good idea Kharkov got from the racketeers.

Was it really just about the narratives? What about the ideas the narrative carried? In the opposite gutter the two villains rolled about in the tricolor he had caught them in. Mrs. Bones pretended she couldn't see them. She continued to sort out her paperbacks, putting them into categories and then into alphabetical order. Her customers also showed no curiosity about Jerry's prisoners. On early closing day, there was almost no one about. They clearly did not want to get mixed up in anything unusual.

The spies cried out to him in harsh, accusatory sentences. Were they still talking about Dunkirk? Surely they didn't expect him to apologize?

The dark green Rolls Phantom was still parked across the narrow street. Major Nye woke up at the wheel. "Anything I can do, old boy?"

"You could let me have my car back. If you wouldn't mind, major?"

"That's the spirit. Off to France again, are we?" Major Nye picked up a bunch of red campions from the seat beside him. "Are these any good?"

Now, thought Jerry, there isn't time to go home. This was probably the best he could do. He opened his paper bag and lifted out the contents. He bit squarely into 170 g of

Fortnum and Mason's pork pie. Not the best in London now that a second rate Melton Mowbray knock-off could be bought in any supermarket and Marks and Spencer's did a passable imitation of the best. But you couldn't get choosy these days. He'd been lucky to find his brother's stash. Not a sign of Branston, though.

His sister Cathy turned the corner from Blenheim Crescent and began running towards him.

6.

Back in Djemaa El Fnaa as the sun set, Jerry sipped another glass of Mecca Cola and wondered at the glory of the third millennium. The great square was crowded with the usual Moroccan water-sellers, food stalls, entertainers, almost drowning the sound of the last muezzin.

At the next table, a small boy begged his father to let him play in the ruins of a nearby mosque. He widened his large brown eyes appealingly. His father said: "Don't be ridiculous. The cuter you are, the quicker you die. Don't you remember your brother? Has Hollywood taught you nothing? Why do you think there is no music on the radio now?"

What was it about North African baguettes? They were almost as bad as the Spanish. He sighed. Imperialism didn't always improve the food. There was more to cooking than making things look the same. Another triumph of image over taste. The French understood that, surely?

Jerry left a few coins on the table and cut quickly across the square which had once been so peaceful. Now, despite the bustling crowd, the square began to live up to its name again. The architecture was over-familiar: Los Angeles, via Mexico, via Spain, via Marrakech. That's what he liked about the South. The crows chattered and quarreled in the remains of the Roman church some monks had tried to build in the wake of an unhappy victory. This time there had been no El Glaoui to maintain the balance of power. He heard a familiar puffing.

Out of breath as usual, Professor Hira, the Brahmin physicist, fell in beside him.

"What a very extraordinary mind God must have." He turned his bright brown face to the sky as if to the deity. "To outlaw himself. How long can these wars of superstition continue, Mr. Cornelius? Another bloody century?"

Jerry raised an enquiring eyebrow.

"Of course, it's silly of me." Hira was suddenly embarrassed. "I know God isn't a person. But then they said the same about Fantômas."

"But do they know that? This is the century of the wars of superstition." Jerry caught his friend's arm. "Quickly. We need to duck into the Old Quarter. *N'est-ce-pas*?"

7.

Sometimes the ruins looked as if they had eroded naturally in a matter of hours. The great grey ragged landscape stretched to the horizon.

"Why should they be so sure of me?" Major Nye stroked his small, white-flecked military moustache. Was he crying? "Why did they tell me this was France when evidently—?"

"Because they trust you. Or, at least, they trust your class. They expect you to share their views."

The major puzzled over this. "Nice to know," he said vaguely, dragging from his pocket a map and a copy of *Film Fun*. On the front page, in beautiful black and white, Laurel and Hardy pursued a cartoon Adolf Hitler through English streets. For his capture in the final panel the pair were rewarded with a mighty plate of sausage and mash. "So what's the job?"

"Old school," said Jerry. "You'll love it. We're still looking for France."

Major Nye turned his wrinkled neck and regarded his old friend through elderly eyes. "It's a bit close to home."

"Isn't everything, these days?"

Miss Brunner considered this. "In an effort to accelerate the progress of history, Hitler's bombers had ultimately stopped Time altogether. But not in Alsatia. That's the situation in which we find ourselves now. Eh?"

The others regarded her with amiable concern.

8.

"Know what I mean?" Mo tipped back his pint and finished it. "Like the smell of a fresh girl the morning after you've pulled her." He replaced his glass in the hamper and sorted through the remains of their picnic, looking for some cheese.

"When was the last time you pulled a fresh girl?" Reminiscently 'Flash' Gordon played with the buttons of his long greasy mackintosh.

They sat as far from Flash as they could in the confines of the Rolls. "Ask me that question when you're sober and I'll punch you on the nose." Mo had the haunted look of a man who has left his Kalashnikov at home and only come out with a Walther PPK. He always avoided a fight when he couldn't calculate the odds. He was beginning to wish he had joined Karen von Krupp and the others on the Pathé Tour. His sense of nostalgia was almost unbearable. Everywhere he looked in Nice he saw signs of his Surrey childhood in the Spanish-style architecture, the tall poplars and cypresses. He clutched at his roiling stomach. If he was going to get this confused, he would rather be on moving water.

"I'm not sure what we should trust least." Miss Brunner fastidiously sipped her G&T. "Chinese caution or American recklessness?"

That was the last straw for Jerry. With an angry jerk he sent the Phantom V onto the motorway and pushed down on the accelerator, weaving erratically between the abandoned Porsches and BMWs. Sometimes there was nothing left to say.

"I say, is that the sea?" Major Nye was excited.

"Are we there yet?" Flash opened bleared eyes.

9

The Madeleine they had given him as part of the Set Tea smelled strongly of almond flavoring. Cautiously he replaced it in his pocket. Jerry was miserable. There was no doubt about it. Memory was eroding. The last time he had been here, London had been enjoying the last of her quiet summer afternoons. Now, dark grey smoke snaked through the streets below. Who had called this meeting? Ever since it had been transported stone by stone to the top of Bon Marché, Derry and Tom's Famous Roof Garden was beginning to show signs of wear. Parts of the brick wall in the Tudor Garden had collapsed and there was a green slime glowing on the flamingo pond. Was this the end of the end?

"I forget when my memory started to go." Major Nye narrowed his grey-blue eyes and pinched the bridge of his nose before replacing his spectacles. He washed down his own horrible little cake with the remains of his Darjeeling. "I'm a stereotype, these days, of course, but I can't rely on that." He sniffed. "Where was it I met my wife? In some Salon de Thé or other? You?"

Sexton Blake pulled down the peak of his oddly-shaped stalking cap. His job in Paris was almost over. All main transferences and exchanges were complete. He longed for the smell of heather and deer spoor in the breaking dawn. "Tell me about it," he said. "Even my stereotype is a stereotype. How does it feel? I wish I could say." His voice echoed self-consciously around the tall walls of the roof garden. "Oh, mugger!" He clenched his teeth tighter around the stem of his Meerschaum.

"Even though you don't love him, you still can't stop wanting to please him." Awkwardly, Catherine hefted her Purdy.

Una gave her friend a sideways glance. "Yes," she said.
"What?"
"Yes?"

"You know what it's like, don't you?" Jerry's sister heard an uncomfortable note in her friend's voice. "Oh, good heavens!" Why was she developing such a strong dislike of intimacy?

Blake tapped her shoulder. He had decided to leave. Business in Marseilles. He was still on the trail of Fantômas, Monsieur Zenith and A.J. Raffles, their new collaborator. His face was full of gentle concern. "I'll check the dry cleaners first. For evening dress."

"Come on, Missy. Here's your chance." He pressed the little Glock into her delicate hand.

10.

M. Pardon met Jerry by the statue of La Grisette at the point where Canal St Martin went underground and was roofed over by a long strip of leafy park in which drunks congregated for their early games of *boules*, their ragged figures staggering amiably back and forth from the abandoned bandstand, their dormitory.

"How was Giverny?" Jerry sat down carefully on a bench from which he could watch the proceedings. "Pretty?"

"You know it? You know Monet?" M. Pardon stared gloomily at his slender fingers. "I had a manicure in Faubourg du Temple while I was waiting. I didn't expect them to paint my nails."

"But it's very patriotic," Jerry murmured. "*N'est-ce-pas?*"

M. Pardon glared at him. "And how was Damascus?" he asked spitefully.

Jerry removed a card from his wallet and handed it to his unhappy colleague. "Does that tell you anything?"

M. Pardon appeared to grow still smaller.

"Best steel in the world," said Jerry.

11.

Jean-Claude Malpurgo saw that he couldn't impress Miss Brunner with his wall-to-wall displays of *The Thriller, Union Jack, Je Sais Tout* and *Harry Dickson*. "Rarer than rubies," he told her, running his skeletal hand over the clear plastic. "A kind of black museum, I suppose. All the cultural evidence is here. Virtually irreplaceable, most of them."

Miss Brunner raised a small handkerchief to her nose. "But who on earth would possibly *want* to replace them?"

Malpurgo was irritated. "Perhaps you would rather see my roses?"

"What? Do you have a garden up here in Pigalle?"

"A garden? Mademoiselle, we have a farm. Of course, much of it is underground, these days. But happily we have excellent drainage."

"Where do you find the labor?"

"My dear lady, this is Paris! The catacombs, naturally." Gently, his fingers encircled her wrist. "Do you waltz?"

She laughed spontaneously. "Naturally."

12.

The next time Jerry met M. Pardon was in Nice in the season of 19--. They were both playing 'blacks' and doing well.

"My luck doesn't usually run this long," said M. Pardon when they had cashed in their chips and stood on the casino's terrace smoking their Upmanns. Jerry was unusually comfortable in his evening dress, but M. Pardon seemed particularly ill-at-ease. He gave the impression of a butler impersonating his master.

They walked through near-deserted streets towards the harbor.

Pardon, edgy, perhaps a little shifty, was now one of the wealthiest publishers in the South and had recently bought *The Teddy Bear* from the estate of the infamous Arsène Lupin. The steam yacht had been in dry dock for a year, but was now thoroughly refurbished. She sat at her moorings, even more elegant than when she had served the mysterious gentleman-thief. Jerry knew her intimately. She had been part of his father's estate.

Pardon paused by the gangplank. "I suppose you don't want to look over the old girl again? We're off to Casa in the morning."

Jerry declined. He didn't much care where the yacht was going or what happened to her. She was a symbol of too much that he despised. He had his eye on an aerial schooner being built in the Zeppelin yards near Le Havre as part of France's war reparations. The future, he felt, was in the air.

Una Persson, in a wealth of Liberty silk, saw them on the quayside and came ashore. She held out a cigarette in a jade holder to be lit. M. Pardon obliged. "You had all the luck tonight," she said. "Sadly, I was roundly beaten."

Jerry wondered why she was making a play for the Frenchman. He bowed and stepped to the edge. The water was surprisingly clear. "Full moon tonight, by the look of it."

Saying goodnight to the pair, he left them beside the yacht and strolled back to the casino's smoking lounge. It was late. Only Major Nye occupied the room. Stiffly at ease, he was seated in a high-backed armchair placed near the open French window. He raised his snifter of Hine into the light by way of greeting.

"Hope I'm not disturbing you, major." Jerry signed to a waiter to bring him another cognac.

"Not at all, old boy. I thought I'd take a break and lick my wounds before I turned in. Didn't lose too much. A couple of colonies and a dominion. Yourself?"

"Absolutely ace, thanks, major."

"Top hole, thanks for asking! But between ourselves the games these days are a little warm for my taste. Should have taken my leave in Kent with the memsahib, what?"

Jerry knew Major Nye well and didn't suspect suicide. He was too honorable to put his wife and daughters at risk. "Care for another?"

"Thanks all the same, old boy." He peered suddenly into the night. There were now a number of figures standing on the terrace in the thick, velvet night. He frowned. "Mrs. Persson! Mr. Collier! Tremendous night, what?"

"Tremendous." Mrs. P stepped into the light.

Jerry heard music faint against the surf.

"I think that's coming off *The Panda*," he said.

"Is that what the bugger's calling the old *Teddy Bear*, these days?" Before he could offer further offence Major Nye lost interest in the subject.

Mrs. Persson winked.

Jerry began to cheer up at last.

13.

In the thick of the shadows of Notre-Dame, Jacques Collin checked his heat. Why was Paris growing so cold? Maybe it was time for another change?

14.

The Luxor restored to her former sensational magnificence, though dwarfed by the overhead railway, stood splendid amongst the dowdy Haussmannesque apartments of Boulevard Magenta. *Les Enfants du Paradis* was playing on the late night classics season. Jerry could remember a time when it was much easier to hear the Wurlitzer. The Paris Luxor was swaggering Egyptianate, with all the confidence of that Depression era that didn't know it was depressed.

Jerry stepped out of his Duisenberg, shedding his panda skin coat. What had possessed him to revisit that appalling period of his life? Hadn't he realized what high heels did for your calves? With a certain reluctance, he walked into the cinema foyer where his mum was now in charge of tickets. "Two for tonight, please, mum. I'll owe you, all right?"

"All right, if yer like. Bleedin' littel pikey."

"Not me, mum. I was never the Egyptian's baby."

"Nar, I remember." She cackled over his tickets. "Yore the kikey's."

Jerry advanced through the doors into a cooling present. It was a relief just to have a few minutes here. The albino was already there. Jerry returned his bow. A quick shadow told them Fantômas had met Judex. Most of the Vampires were already seated. Jerry drew a deep breath. Sometimes danger was oddly comforting. "What's the time?" He checked his wrists. "My watch has stopped." He turned up the collar of his black car coat. Catherine was late as usual.

Elegant in her long, downtown dress, she hurried up to him giving her Vpad the once-over. "You were going dead!" She kissed him with restrained passion. "Seen mum? She all right? I was in New Orleans. You get better reception from the cemetery. Isn't it supposed to be dangerous? Like Stalingrad?"

"Only if you don't know what you're doing. I had to come to Paris. The movie's better here. There's a sober respect for the past."

She gave her spent pad a final flip. "Oh, fuck. Now we're sunk."

"Would you rather be dead?"

She thought that one over.

About the Translator

In his mundane Multiverse Michael Shreve has worked as an archivist, private bookseller, printer, locksmith, warehouseman, delivery driver, taxi driver, croupier and assistant mortician. He has also taught Classical Civilization, Greek, Latin, French, Spanish and English in the US, Canada, Mexico, Malaysia, Lebanon, Iceland and France.

He has translated dozens of books for Black Coat Press as well as short stories for contemporary authors such as Jacques Barbéri, Pierre Pelot and Catherine Dufour. In addition he translates non-fiction, such as Jean Meslier (with Michel Onfray) and Volatire (with S.T. Joshi).

He currently lives in Paris, France.

FRENCH SF & FANTASY

Adolphe Alhaiza. *Cybele.* Alphonse Allais. *The Adventures of Captain Cap.* Henri Allorge. *The Great Cataclysm.* Guy d'Armen. *Doc Ardan: The City of Gold and Lepers; The Troglodytes of Mount Everest/The Giants of Black Lake; The Abominable Snowman.* G.-J. Arnaud. *The Ice Company.* André Arnyvelde. *The Ark; The Mutilated Bacchus.* Charles Asselineau. *The Double Life.* Henri Austruy. *The Eupantophone; The Olotelepan; The Petitpaon Era*

Barillet-Lagargousse. *The Final War.* Cyprien Bérard. *The Vampire Lord Ruthwen.* S. Henry Berthoud. *Martyrs of Science; The Angel Asrael.* Aloysius Bertrand. *Gaspard de la Nuit.* Richard Bessière. *The Gardens of the Apocalypse; The Masters of Silence.* Chevalier de Béthune. *The World of Mercury.* Albert Bleunard. *Ever Smaller.* Félix Bodin. *The Novel of the Future.* Pierre Boitard. *Journey to the Sun.* Louis Boussenard. *Monsieur Synthesis.* Alphonse Brown. *City of Glass; The Conquest of the Air*

Émile Calvet. *In a Thousand Years.* André Caroff. *The Terror of Madame Atomos; Miss Atomos; The Return of Madame Atomos; The Mistake of Madame Atomos; The Monsters of Madame Atomos; The Revenge of Madame Atomos; The Resurrection of Madame Atomos; The Mark of Madame Atomos; The Spheres of Madame Atomos; The Wrath of Madame Atomos* (w/M. & Sylvie Stéphan). Félicien Champsaur. *Homo-Deus; The Human Arrow; Nora, The Ape-Woman; Ouha, King of the Apes; Pharaoh's Wife.* Didier de Chousy. *Ignis.* Jules Clarétie. *Obsession.* Jacques Collin de Plancy. *Voyage to the Center of the Earth.* Michel Corday. *The Eternal Flame; The Lynx* (w/André Couvreur). André Couvreur. *Caresco, Superman; The Exploits of Professor Tornada* (3 vols.); *The Necessary Evil*

Gaston Danville. *The Perfume of Lust.* Camille Debans. *The Misfortunes of John Bull.* Captain Danrit. *Undersea Odyssey.* C. I. Defontenay. *Star (Psi Cassiopeia).* Charles Derennes. *The People of the Pole.* Georges Dodds (anthologist). *The Missing Link.* Charles Dodeman. *The Silent Bomb.* Harry Dickson. *The Heir of Dracula; Harry Dickson vs. The Spider.* Jules Dornay. *Lord Ruthven Begins.* Alfred Driou. *The Adventures of a Parisian Aeronaut.* Odette Dulac. *The War of the Sexes.* Alexandre Dumas. *The Return of Lord Ruth-*

ven; The Man who Married a Mermaid (w/P. Lacroix). Renée Dunan. *Baal; The Ultimate Pleasure.* J.-C. Dunyach. *The Night Orchid; The Thieves of Silence.* Henri Duvernois. *The Man Who Found Himself*

Achille Eyraud. *Voyage to Venus*

Henri Falk. *The Age of Lead.* Paul Féval. *Anne of the Isles; Knightshade; Revenants; Vampire City; The Vampire Countess; The Wandering Jew's Daughter.* Paul Féval, *fils. Felifax, the Tiger-Man.* Charles de Fieux. *Lamékis.* Fernand Fleuret. *Jim Click.* Charles-Marie Flor O'Squarr. *Phantoms.* Louis Forest. *Someone is Stealing Children in Paris*

Arnould Galopin. *Doctor Omega; Doctor Omega and the Shadowmen* (anthology). Judith Gautier. *Isoline and the Serpent-Flower.* H. Gayar. *The Marvelous Adventures of Serge Myrandhal on Mars.* Louis Geoffroy. *The Apocryphal Napoleon.* Raoul Gineste. *The Second Life of Doctor Albin.* Delphine de Girardin. *Balzac's Cane.* Léon Gozlan. *The Vampire of the Val-de-Grâce.* Jules Gros. *The Fossil Man .* Jimmy Guieu. *The Polarian-Denebian War* (2 vols.)

Edmond Haraucourt. *Daah, the First Human; Illusions of Immortality.* Nathalie Henneberg. *The Green Gods.* Eugène Hennebert. *The Enchanted City.* Jules Hoche. *The Maker of Men and His Formula.* V. Hugo, P. Foucher & P. Meurice. *The Hunchback of Notre-Dame.* Romain d'Huissier. *Hexagon: Dark Matter*

Jules Janin. *The Magnetized Corpse.*

Gustave Kahn. *The Tale of Gold and Silence.* Gérard Klein. *The Mote in Time's Eye.* Fernand Kolney. *Love in 5000 Years*

Paul Lacroix. *Danse Macabre; The Man who Married a Mermaid* (w/Alexandre Dumas). Louis-Guillaume de La Follie. *The Unpretentious Philosopher.* Jean de La Hire. *The Fiery Wheel; Enter the Nyctalope; The Nyctalope on Mars; The Nyctalope vs. Lucifer; The Nyctalope Steps In; Night of the Nyctalope; Return of the Nyctalope.* Etienne-Léon de Lamothe-Langon. *The Virgin Vampire.* André Laurie. *Spiridon.* Gabriel de Lautrec. *The Vengeance of the Oval Portrait.* Alain le Drimeur. *The Future City.* Georges Le Faure & Henri de Graffigny. *The Extraordinary Adventures of a Russian Scientist*

Across the Solar System (2 vols.). Gustave Le Rouge. *The Dominion of the World* (w/Gustave Guitton) (4 vols.); *The Mysterious Doctor Cornelius* (3 vols.); *The Vampires of Mars.* Jules Lermina. *The Battle of Strasbourg; Mysteryville; Panic in Paris; The Secret of Zippelius; To-Ho and the Gold Destroyers.* Maurice Level. *The Gates of Hell.* André Lichtenberger. *The Centaurs; The Children of the Crab.* Maurice Limat. *Mephista.* Listonai. *The Philosophical Voyager.* Jean-Marc & Randy Lofficier. *Edgar Allan Poe on Mars; The Katrina Protocol; Pacifica 1, 2; Robonocchio; Return of the Nyctalope;* (anthologists) *Tales of the Shadowmen 1-13; The Vampire Almanac* (2 vols.). Ch. Lomon & P.-B. Gheuzi. *The Last Days of Atlantis.*

Camille Mauclair. *The Virgin Orient.* Xavier Mauméjean. *The League of Heroes.* Joseph Méry. *The Tower of Destiny.* Hippolyte Mettais. *Paris Before the Deluge; The Year 5865.* Louise Michel. *The Human Microbes; The New World.* Tony Moilin. *Paris in the Year 2000.* José Moselli. *Illa's End*

John-Antoine Nau. *Enemy Force.* Marie Nizet. *Captain Vampire.* Charles Nodier. *Trilby and The Crumb Fairy.* C. Nodier, A. Beraud & Toussaint-Merle. *Frankenstein*

Henri de Parville. *An Inhabitant of the Planet Mars.* Gaston de Pawlowski. *Journey to the Land of the 4th Dimension.* Georges Pellerin. *The World in 2000 Years.* Ernest Pérochon. *The Frenetic People.* Pierre Pelot. *The Child Who Walked on the Sky.* Jean Petithuguenin. *An International Mission to the Moon.* P.-A. Ponson du Terrail. *The Immortal Woman; The Vampire and the Devil's Son; The Police Agent.* Georges Price. *The Missing Men of the* Sirius. René Pujol. *The Chimerical Quest*

Edgar Quinet. *Ahasuerus; The Enchanter Merlin*

Henri de Régnier. *A Surfeit of Mirrors.* Maurice Renard. *The Blue Peril; Doctor Lerne; The Doctored Man; A Man Among the Microbes; The Master of Light.* Restif de la Bretonne. *The Discovery of the Austral Continent by a Flying Man; Posthumous Correspondence* (3 vols.); *The Fay Ouroucoucou* (2 vols.). Jean Richepin. *The Crazy Corner; The Wing.* Albert Robida. *The Adventures of Saturnin Farandoul; Chalet in the Sky; The Clock of the Centuries; The Electric Life; The Engineer Von Satanas.* J.-H. Rosny Aîné. *Helgvor of the Blue River; The Givreuse Enigma; The Mysterious Force; The Navigators of Space; Vamireh; The World of the Variants; The Young Vampire.* Marcel Rouff. *Journey to the Inverted World.* Marie-Anne de Roumier-Robert. *The Voyage of Lord Seaton to the Seven Planets.* Léonie Rouzade. *The World Turned Upside Down.* Han Ryner. *The Human Ant; The Superhumans*

Louis-Claude de Saint-Martin. *The Crocodile.* Pierre de Selenes: *An Unknown World.* Norbert Sevestre. *Sâr Dubnotal: Vs. Jack the Ripper; The Astral Trail.* Angelo de Sorr. *The Vampires of London.* Brian Stableford (anthologist) *News from the Moon; The Germans on Venus; The Supreme Progress; The World Above the World; Nemoville; Investigations of the Future; The Conqueror of Death; The Revolt of the Machines; The Man With the Blue Face; The Aerial Valley; The New Moon; The Nickel Man; On the Brink of the World's End; The Mirror of Present Events; The Humanisphere.* Jacques Spitz. *The Eye of Purgatory.* Kurt Steiner. *Ortog*

Eugène Thébault. *Radio-Terror.* C.-F. Tiphaigne de La Roche. *Amilec.* Simon Tyssot de Patot. *The Strange Voyages of Jacques Massé and Pierre de Mésange*

Louis Ulbach. *Prince Bonifacio*

Théo Varlet. *The Castaways of Eros; The Golden Rock.; The Martian Epic* (w/Octave Joncquel); *Timeslip Troopers* (w/André Blandin); *The Xenobiotic Invasion.* Pierre Véron. *The Merchants of Health.* Paul Vibert. *The Mysterious Fluid.* Villiers de l'Isle-Adam. *The Scaffold; The Vampire Soul*

Gaston de Wailly. *The Murderer of the World.* Philippe Ward. *Artahe; Manhattan Ghost* (w/Mickael Laguerre); *The Song of Montségur* (w/Sylvie Miller)